Empire

Hostile Nation

Hot Spot

Neutral Nation

Unified States

Entente Alliance

Imperial Norden
(Disputed Territory)

Federation

Imperial Ostland
(Potentially Disputed Territory)

Commonweath

Empire

Imperial Dacia

Grand Duchy

Republic

Waldstätte Confederacy

Kingdom of Ildoa

Republican Colonies

Unredeemed Ildoa
(Potentially Disputed Territory)

Abyssus
Abyssum invocat

THE
SAGA OF TANYA
THE EVIL

"You must be joking!
I'm an officer!"
"With all due respect, ma'am, it's the rules! ...Legally, minors are strictly prohibited from entering at night!"
Nein
Nein
Nein

THE SAGA OF TANYA THE EVIL

Abyssus Abyssum Invocat

[5]

Carlo Zen

Illustration by Shinobu Shinotsuki

YEN ON

New York

The Saga of Tanya the Evil, Vol. 5

Carlo Zen

Translation by Emily Balistrieri
Cover art by Shinobu Shinotsuki

This book is a work of fiction. Names, characters, places, and incidents are the product of the author's imagination or are used fictitiously. Any resemblance to actual events, locales, or persons, living or dead, is coincidental.

YOJO SENKI Vol. 5 Abyssus Abyssum Invocat
©Carlo Zen 2016
First published in Japan in 2016 by KADOKAWA CORPORATION, Tokyo.
English translation rights arranged with KADOKAWA CORPORATION, Tokyo, through TUTTLE-MORI AGENCY, INC., Tokyo.

English translation © 2019 by Yen Press, LLC

Yen On
1290 Avenue of the Americas
New York, NY 10104

Visit us at yenpress.com
facebook.com/yenpress
twitter.com/yenpress
yenpress.tumblr.com
instagram.com/yenpress

First Yen On Edition: March 2019

Yen On is an imprint of Yen Press, LLC.
The Yen On name and logo are trademarks of Yen Press, LLC.

The publisher is not responsible for websites (or their content) that are not owned by the publisher.

Library of Congress Cataloging-in-Publication Data
Names: Zen, Carlo, author. | Shinotsuki, Shinobu, illustrator. | Balistrieri, Emily, translator. | Steinbach, Kevin, translator.
Title: Saga of Tanya the evil / Carlo Zen ; illustration by Shinobu Shinotsuki ; translation by Emily Balistrieri, Kevin Steinbach
Other titles: Yōjo Senki. English
Description: First Yen On edition. | New York : Yen ON, 2017–
Identifiers: LCCN 2017044721 | ISBN 9780316512442 (v. 1 : pbk.) | ISBN 9780316512466 (v. 2 : pbk.) | ISBN 9780316512480 (v. 3 : pbk.) | ISBN 9780316560627 (v. 4 : pbk.) | ISBN 9780316560696 (v. 5 : pbk.)
Classification: LCC PL878.E6 Y6513 2017 | DDC 895.63/6—dc23
LC record available at https://lccn.loc.gov/2017044721

ISBNs: 978-0-316-56069-6 (paperback)
978-0-316-56070-2 (ebook)

2 4 6 8 10 9 7 5 3 1

LSC-C

Printed in the United States of America

THE
SAGA OF TANYA
THE EVIL

Abyssus Abyssum Invocat

contents

| chapter |

○

A Letter Home

Dear Mother and Grandmother,

How are you doing? I hope you are both well.
  Summer has ended, so it must be nearly time for the chilly autumn wind to start blowing. Please take care not to catch a cold.
  I'm doing fine.
  But please forgive me for not being able to write any details…not even the current date or location.
  I've told you before, but…it's regulation.
  Don't be alarmed, but the list of things we can't put in letters was updated again just the other day!
  We can't say what type of bread we ate!
  We can't say what type of meat (beef, pork, chicken, mutton) we ate!
  We can't say the exact date we received your letters!
  There are so many restrictions, it's hard to keep them all straight.
  I can say that I miss your apple pie, Grandma, but if I say whether or not I've eaten apple pie here, it would be deemed "leaking military secrets" or something.
  I'm trying to be careful as I write, but it's possible that part of it will be blacked out by the censors.
  Still, nothing major has happened here, so please don't worry about me. Honestly, it's frustrating to not be able to say what I'd like to.
  Right now, my unit is training and getting reorganized. That much my superior officer (who informed me I'm not allowed to share their name) said I could write, so no worries.
  We don't know where we'll be deployed next.
  So I don't have much to say.

With love from a base in a location I can't disclose,
  Mary Sue

On the whole, the situation in the east is good.

Imperial Army General Staff,
monthly report

From the southern continent to a long-range reconnaissance mission in Federation territory. At the conclusion of that journey, there was a direct attack on Moskva, and right when I thought I would get to head to the rear, I was transferred to participate in an air battle west of the Rhine front. The moment I figured things would settle down a bit, I was ordered to form a Kampfgruppe.

After following orders that yanked me all over the place—south, east, west—I ended up joining the battle in the east.

We were given the supporting role of escorting the main forces on their advance, but as we were gradually pushed farther east into Federation territory, my Kampfgruppe received yet another new order.

"...So we're being reassigned?"

"That's right, Colonel von Degurechaff. It's a shame we have to lose you and your Salamander Kampfgruppe, but we can't keep you when you belong to the General Staff."

A high-ranking officer in the Eastern Army Group informed me with a resigned *them's-the-breaks* smile that we were suddenly being sent elsewhere. Well, reassignment orders are almost always "sudden" to the people on the ground.

But Tanya sensed something slightly strange.

"Sorry you have to keep moving around like this, but do your best."

The comments she got from the Eastern Army Group staffers with a pat on the back were decisive.

They were heartfelt words of consolation about Tanya and her unit's transfer. Frankly, that's not the kind of thing said by staff officers who have just had troops *suddenly* pulled from their lines.

A Kampfgruppe reporting directly to the General Staff getting pulled out is simply the result of a properly functioning Imperial Army. No one can object to it. Moving its own unit from the A lines to the B lines is the General Staff's prerogative.

But if you think about it this way, everything makes sense.

It's simple to understand if you imagine us as a skilled anesthesiologist. The General Staff is a university hospital that dispatched their anesthesiologist upon the request of a private hospital, which would be the Eastern Army Group. If the university announced to the impoverished, understaffed regional hospital that it was pulling out its anesthesiologist...it would be weird not to encounter some protest, right?

And yet the officers here were calmly passing on the orders without any fuss? That had to mean they had known about this for quite some time.

The only one who didn't realize was me. It's probably correct to suspect that I was being informed at the last possible minute.

I was rushed through the handoff (yes, there was time for a handoff, so there was definitely some advance consideration that went into this plan), and before I knew it, I was rocking along on some train.

The efficiency of all the arrangements makes Tanya sick. These reassignment orders came down without any delays or other trouble, no missed messages.

But despite all the preparations (it should probably be said), the reality of it being a reassignment from the front lines can't be ignored. *For example*, thinks Tanya with a sigh as she looks around the first-class train car.

The train ticket certainly says "first class," but this is a passenger car of an armored train on a military-use line for delivering supplies and personnel to the front. "First class" means you're lucky enough to have a seat.

Considering the supply line situation, it could be considered surprising the higher-ups even allowed for a first-class train car. Granted, the facilities available for travelers on board are scanty. It's something else entirely from a first-class car back home. At the end of August, with summer ending and autumn about to begin, the temperature in the Federation is cool enough that the lack of air-conditioning is tolerable.

Still, though they call this a sleeping car, the only furnishings included in the sparse compartment are a wooden bench to lie down on and a sturdy desk. And the bench is so small that if you weren't short like me, it would be quite a tight fit.

"If I were home in the Reich, I would have sworn at them. 'Do you think you're transporting cattle?'"

Really, it's hard to deny the possibility that some planners may very well have requisitioned an actual livestock transport car. In any case, calling it first class is absurd. At the same time, even with all those faults, there is a truth that mustn't be overlooked: One of our trains is up and running incredibly close to the front lines. Our forces must have performed quick maintenance on the rails in occupied enemy territory—evidence that both the Service Corps and the Railroad Department are doing their best. You could say it's possible to catch a glimpse of the supply situation on this trip.

Though it might not be related...a good example of this is how the food tastes relatively good.

When a sandwich on bread that wasn't stale and coffee were served for lunch, Tanya was elated to an embarrassing degree.

And surprisingly, a newspaper was provided after the meal. When Tanya looks at the date—don't be alarmed—it reads August 28; in other words, it's today's paper.

It may be afternoon now, but it's possible to have the morning's paper delivered to the forward-most positions.

That in itself speaks volumes to the determination of the Imperial Service Corps in fighting the logistics battle.

On the other hand, Tanya has a mind to complain as she grumbles to herself.

"I get that this is wartime coverage, but what garbage..."

Saving paper and keeping military secrets are important, but the newspapers in the rear are a bit too far removed from the real world. What appears to be reader reactions to the ridiculously titled column "Life of the Brave Soldiers on the Front Lines" in particular makes Tanya crack up.

"As usual, it's too censored and too full of propaganda. I can't help but think it would be better to tell the home front what it's actually like on the front lines."

This drivel they call patriotic sentiments in the form of letters from schoolchildren. The fact that they have so many writing in... Well, it's probably not a bad way to boost fighting spirit. But apparently, schoolchildren these days know all the abbreviations and slang the troops use on the front lines.

Their knowledge is comprehensive enough that I want to burst out laughing as I read.

"You're going to post reactions to this fake news? Okay, then."

The more I read, the more suspect it seems. It's like they're not even trying to hide the fact that only one person wrote them all—it's obvious when a bunch of boys and girls use the exact same phrasing. The most telling part, though, is that the openings have long since been written according to a template. This is an awfully careless way to fight an information war.

"...The Federation and Commonwealth are probably better at this sort of thing."

Well, I guess there's no good way to beat liars at their own game. Tanya sips coffee from the military-use pseudo mug and sighs. It's good that the Imperial Army is aware of how important information warfare is.

But if the method they choose lacks sophistication, it'll only backfire.

"Sheesh, having time on your hands is poison for someone who lives to work."

It's not strange that Tanya's complaining.

Seeing other people's sloppy work is bizarrely irritating. Looking out the window with nothing to do, she sees a vast wasteland.

It's currently the tail end of August. The sun is shining gently, leaving the weather too comfortable to associate the east with mud.

But Tanya doesn't attempt to hide her annoyance with the massive expanse of land that seems to go on forever, even when viewed through her binoculars.

For crying out loud. If we try to take this huge swath of land, the army will be spent. Despite massing the majority of our forces on this front, we don't have the manpower to cover it all.

This is like dashing into a tunnel without knowing if there is an exit or not... Having thought that far, Lieutenant Colonel Tanya von Degurechaff smiles wryly, though it's out of character for her.

I guess the view out a train window invites people to think in an unusual, meandering way.

Still, Tanya ends up pondering a certain point anyway.

There's been a thought smoldering inside her for a while now.

In the history books of Earth that I know, the German army was fated to melt away on the eastern front. The reason was simple: They took too many losses at each position along their overstretched lines.

That war of attrition was fatal. In this world, the Empire's human resources haven't dried up yet. But the phrase *haven't dried up yet* applies only to the present. It's not a guarantee for the future.

Still, that's assuming events here match what happened during World War II. In the First World War that I remember, Germany won in the east, managing to push the lines forward.

To be frank, the Empire is winning in the west at the moment. That doesn't mean we have to lose in the east, though. Same as before, it's not obvious which way this battle will go.

Objectively speaking, we still have a definitive chance at victory. Of course, we could lose as well.

"...I suppose I have to admit that I don't know."

True, we can say, *Well, that's how war is* and leave it at that, but I really don't like this uncertain outlook. *Fog of war* is an apt turn of phrase.

The wise men who came before me must have really cursed this fog.

Still, it'd be nice if I could see through it.

It's only natural to want to know what lies ahead on the path you're walking, right? What's at the end of the dark tunnel?

Apparently, a funny tale they tell in this Communist country says that beyond the darkness lie hopes and dreams.

Tanya can only answer with a sigh. Sadly, here in the east, the answer is always the same. Believing in hopes and dreams, you go through the tunnel and just find *snow country*. If this were some atmospheric work of literature, it would surely be a delightful discovery.

But reality isn't as beautiful. Works of art often smooth over imperfections. In real life, there is no fantastic scenery to behold. Only *muddy snow country*.

That's the morass the Imperial Army unconsciously dives into.

It's an unpleasant sight. If we knew the way forward, we wouldn't have to suffer so much. We're so in the dark that it's hard to know what to expect. How dreadful.

"Hmm? Oh, I guess we're almost at a stop. Surprising that they built one in the middle of the massive eastern front. The Railroad Department is doing quite a thorough job."

Marveling at the sound marking their deceleration and the high-pitched whistle, Tanya picks up the newspaper and starts reading again. Perhaps due to the current war, the quality of the paper seems awfully low, but it's still not as bad as the content.

Setting aside politics and society, Tanya notices that even the culture section of the paper is focused on raising morale via a feature on charity concerts. Having the people come together and sing patriotic songs probably isn't a bad way to increase their sense of belonging to the group, but…I'd like to see actual concerts continue, too.

This is why foreign media bitingly covers "concerts in the Empire" and reports that they're "patriot conventions" rather than places to appreciate music.

"I'm not in a position to comment on cultural policy, but… Hmm?"

Right before Tanya sinks back into her thoughts, a precise knock sounds on the door.

"First Lieutenant Serebryakov, requesting permission to enter, ma'am."

"That's fine. Come in."

"Excuse me, Colonel. We've received word from the home country via the station."

Lieutenant Serebryakov pops into the cabin with brisk movements. In her hand is one of the thick envelopes the General Staff tends to use for sealed mail.

"From the home country?"

"Yes, Colonel. It's from the General Staff. And…someone who has just boarded the train is here to see you."

"Someone here? To see me?"

"That's no way to greet an old classmate, Colonel von Degurechaff."

Tanya is about to open the envelope when the familiar voice makes its way inside; realizing whose it is, Tanya leaps to her feet.

How nice to see an old face. The man stands in the entrance to the compartment with a smile to hide how utterly exhausted he is.

"I've come to bug you. You'll have to forgive me entering a lady's sleeping compartment."

"What a surprise. I never expected my esteemed colleague Lieutenant

Colonel Uger to barge in on me. Don't you know there's an etiquette when visiting a woman's room? If your wife knew you had such bad manners, she would surely be disappointed."

"Oh dear, to think I would upset even my beloved wife and child. What a pesky business military duties are. But orders must be followed—I'll just have to curse my misfortune."

We exchange friendly quips as we salute each other.

But he was supposed to laugh boldy. Unfortunately, Colonel Uger doesn't seem to be equipped with a proper sense of humor. Perhaps he didn't serve enough time on the front lines.

Colonel Uger isn't the type to banter or make jokes naturally, and it seems he missed out on the opportunity to cultivate better comedic sensibilities on the battlefield.

"Ha-ha-ha. I hope this will be enough compensation to have you pretend this never happened."

Then Tanya realizes something strange and freezes.

...Has someone who was never the type to make jokes picked up a sense of humor? Even if it's a lousy one? That's not a good sign at all.

Both Colonel Uger and I are straitlaced types. Even if I don't know him well enough to make declarations about his character, I'm confident that he's not the type to make jokes. The officers selected for war college are either idiosyncratic or sincere, like me.

Both Uger and I are on the serious, hardworking side. I deviated from—or I guess you could say acquired a sense of sarcasm from—my environment; a major factor was my harsh experiences on the forwardmost line. War can't be fought with a straight face, so I had to cultivate a sense of humor up there. But Colonel Uger shouldn't have had the same need.

This is...extremely uncharacteristic of him. Why is he trying to joke around anyway? His eyes seem to be smiling, but they're not.

"...What's this?"

"Arabica coffee I received from an officer stationed down south. I figured it's hard to get any on the front lines, so I stuffed two kilos' worth in my staff pack. By the way, I roasted a hundred grams, and the rest I sealed up well in some bottles."

"Well, well. You have my thanks."

Colonel Uger laughs as if it's nothing and hands the pack to Lieutenant Serebryakov, then he takes the seat opposite Tanya.

...So he's even being considerate of conditions soldiers face on the front lines. That's ideal for a General Staff officer serving in the rear, but to be honest, Uger isn't the type to be comfortable mixing business and personal errands like this.

In other words, he's here to talk about something so bad that his conscience made an exception? I can't show it, but my mental state can be compared to how a bomb disposal technician feels when sent to the site of a huge explosive about to go off at any second.

"I thought I would come visit my classmate for the first time in quite a while on the pretext of observing the front lines. When you're doing desk work for the General Staff, you start to pine for chances to get some air."

"Well, commanding a Kampfgruppe is a pretty fun job that affords lots of discretion."

"I'm jealous. Seems like I'll be the only one whining about my personal problems."

Lieutenant Colonel Uger, one of the few serious classmates I had among the monsters in the General Staff. Yet he wants this to look like a private conversation?

That has to mean he has something to discuss that he can't let other people hear. An unofficial message. That's a warning sign if there ever was one.

Holy hell.

He's going to bring up something massive. The higher-ups who are always trying to shove extra work off on those out in the field can rot.

"Heh, there's nothing I can do about that. I get to be out and about and do as I please. I'll have to lend you an ear, then! Oh, Lieutenant Serebryakov, go grind some beans and make us coffee. Do a thorough job and *take your time.*"

"Understood. I think it will take a little while—yes, probably a half hour or so—but I'll prepare two cups of coffee."

I don't think I put too much emphasis on that last bit. It's excellent that my adjutant picked up on that subtle cue. She performs a beautiful salute and politely takes her leave.

I see her out and lock the compartment door.

"Okay, then...," says Tanya, returning to Colonel Uger. "What are we actually going to talk about?"

"Oh, nothing good... I never thought I'd have to say something like this to our own troops. It makes me sick. If you were old enough, I would have brought us a stiff drink."

This straitlaced military man wants to drink on duty?

"Hmm?" Though the surprise she can't voice reverberates in her head, Tanya feigns calm and limits her reaction to merely cocking her head.

"Colonel. General von Zettour is concerned that this offensive is sprawling too much. He's especially opposed to expanding the combat front any farther."

"That makes sense, doesn't it?"

Tanya nods without thinking.

Lieutenant General von Zettour's idea is actually a staunchly safe plan. If we're going to focus not on expansion but on reorganizing our forces, we can focus on the work without tripping through the mud and snow.

In order to operate in the swamp of the east—not to mention the fearsome cold—without getting stuck, preparation is essential. I can't say his comment is anything but logical.

"The problem is General von Rudersdorf's view."

"...You mean the opinion of the Operations Division?"

When he answers yes, Tanya stiffens. It's fine for the guys in charge of actually planning operations to have their own ideas. But someone who prefers a flexible style of operation, like General von Rudersdorf, could become the seed for trouble, opposing a safe plan.

"...And what is the general's view?"

"The guys in Operations are prioritizing *time*."

"Colonel Uger, you mean they don't want to give our enemy any more breathing room?"

"Exactly. They're anxious about giving the enemy time to reorganize."

Colonel Uger lays out the logic of the Imperial Army General Staff's Operations staffers. It's problematic, to be sure, but when I listen, it's as *correct* as Zettour's view.

On lines of this scale, reorganizing units and tidying up positions is practically unavoidable. After all, a disorderly army scattered about the field loses much of its effective fighting power.

On the other hand, a force that's reorganizing can't attack.

The pressure we can rain down on the enemy would drop dramatically. In other words, if we stop to reorganize our lines, the Federation Army will also get a grace period. Yes, if nothing else, time would be granted to all in equal measure.

If that happens, our enemies will definitely reorganize as well. Essentially, it's a never-ending dilemma.

"Apparently, the guys in Operations and General von Rudersdorf want to surround and annihilate the Federation's field army even if this offensive seems impossible. That means...," he says, looking out the window, and Tanya understands what the higher-ups are after, even if she doesn't want to. "...They want to resolve things as soon as possible."

"...You mean because winter is coming?"

It's still August. But it's the end of August. Even if we're prepared for September, it's highly improbable that we'll still have weather suitable for military operations by the end of October.

"Our time is limited, but it's not entirely hopeless. The higher-ups want to push for a massive envelopment using our army's mobility."

The fact that Tanya doesn't scowl the moment she hears this, that alone is a feat of self-control.

One month can be guaranteed but not two. It's absurd—a massive gamble. It's far too great a risk to attempt a major operation now of all times. If only she could criticize such a criticism; it would be like a huge weight lifted.

But whether in the market economy or out on the battlefield, there's no chance of victory without taking a risk.

"And what does the General Staff think we should do?"

"Opinions are split."

It would probably be rude to nod and say of course they are.

But it'd be good for Tanya to smile vaguely. People wouldn't be surprised to see her accurately forecast the General Staff's mood as sunny with a chance of explosions.

"The guys in Operations are aggressively optimistic. They're saying they still have time to engage in a battle to encircle and annihilate the enemy. They say they'll get it done if they have two months. But it's those two months that we're not sure about..." He continues, "On the other hand, the Service Corps guys we're closer to are angry. Their general demeanor seems to be 'You really want to put our already fragile supply lines in danger?' As long as it isn't guaranteed that we'll have two months to conduct operations, the Service Corps seems to want to use the remaining time to prepare for winter before snow makes that difficult."

"You make it all sound so arbitrary, Colonel Uger."

Uger responds with a "Hmm," perhaps because he's aware of that. Tanya doubles down on the discussion.

"Another thing to consider is that if we give the enemy time to reorganize, we may end up having to support the front in a prolonged fight with weakened supply lines. The Service Corps's plan entails risk, too."

"Theoretically, yes. But vexing as it is, the logic on both sides of the debate is sound."

He's right about that.

That's what the root of the issue is, Tanya considers internally. Truthfully speaking, there are all too many occasions where people are required to pick the better of two lousy options. Maybe if we had perfect information, it would be different, but we can't know everything. We have to use what's on hand to reason out the best option.

"Considering how slow-moving our enemy is, the aggressive plan's chance of succeeding might be higher."

If taken one thought at a time, Colonel Uger's gripes are logical.

"*If* the enemy *can't* use their time effectively…and *if* our side *can* use our time effectively…then there's a benefit to us reorganizing and building a stronger foundation."

If, if—it's a parade of conditionals. Sheesh, there are too many unknowns.

"Colonel Uger, may I say something?"

He nods. "Of course." Not that she's particularly happy to see it before she hits him with something that has been bugging her.

"All I've heard is that our upcoming mission will be escorting the main army. I'd appreciate it if you could tell me how this debate in the General Staff affects us…"

It's impossible to think of getting transferred away from the front and receiving a visit from her old classmate as sheer coincidence.

Reading too much into events will only lure me into concocting a ridiculous conspiracy theory. But it would be a lie to say there is nothing deliberate going on here.

"The generals' opinions clash. But for better or worse, they're both pragmatists. They both detest empty theory."

"I agree. They're both soldiers who place importance on what's occurring on the actual battlefield."

"Which is why, I guess you can say…Colonel von Degurechaff, I really feel for you. They don't want a clash of theories but to have their ideas verified on the battlefield."

Tanya almost tilts her head quizzically at the word *verified. No, hold on. Verifying things on the battlefield would mean…* Right as that thought comes, Colonel Uger continues, rapidly delivering the conclusion.

"To put it in extreme terms, they'll make their decision after reconnoitering the enemy army."

"And we should lodge a formal protest about how awfully leisurely they'll be about it. Where are we going to get the time for that?"

"Unfortunately for you, whether we attack or defend, it will take time to prepare the troops…meaning there is time for a survey."

Argh. Her bad feeling about this begins ringing the alarm bells, but it's too late.

"Their conclusion is simple. While supplies are being stockpiled, your Kampfgruppe will go check out the enemy."

"Recon-in-force?"

"Not quite. It's a mission to defend a salient."

Tanya knows it's bad manners to glare at people.

Still…

Colonel Uger just told her that command wants to put her in a dangerous area, giving her plenty of reason for her gaze to bore into his eyes.

"There is one area where we've deliberately given the enemy time to regroup. We want you to engage them and get a feel for how powerful a force they have. In a nutshell, it's a probe. We want you to perform an experiment on a strategically unimportant piece of land that we've left for them on purpose."

The brass wants us to be coal-mine canaries that let them gauge the danger by seeing when we sing and when we can't anymore!

We're even lower than guinea pigs!

"This is a terribly rude question, but…are you saying my unit has been ordered to go and die to ascertain which of the two generals is correct?"

"That's a harsh way to put it, but…yes. The General Staff's problems are the General Staff's problems. In other words, we General Staff officers have to solve them among ourselves."

As far as Tanya knows, I suppose it should be said…

General Staff officers, including Colonel Uger, have a sense of duty for their office that is, for better or worse, too strong.

Noblesse oblige is the nice way to put it.

Obligations of the elite is haughtier but also honest.

But a guy like Colonel Uger isn't the type to share that kind of thought out loud. That's what an elite should be like. A representative like Uger conveys his nobility though actions not words.

Yet, he's talking about it…in terms of General Staff officers? I can only assume that there's a huge land mine afoot.

"I beg your pardon, Colonel Uger, but the way you're talking, it sounds like perhaps something happened?"

"…Yeah. It's classified, but…I'm the one getting you involved in this, so…I would say it's my moral responsibility to inform you."

He looks up at the ceiling of the train compartment and doesn't even try to conceal his sigh; he must be in quite a state. Looking closely, I can see that the fatigue hasn't completely left his eyes. Most noticeable is his utterly exhausted tone.

There was at least some life in that voice until just a minute ago, but it suddenly turned weary.

"Supreme High Command has been in an uproar for some time now. The government, the General Staff Office, and the court have all been a barrel of fun lately."

He certainly doesn't sound like things over there have been very enjoyable. More like he's stopped caring.

"On top of that, we can't ignore public opinion. We're getting a storm of complaints from around the Empire. Everyone says we should 'get it over with.' It's no wonder there's a gigantic hurricane blowing through the General Staff Office." He groans and quietly adds, "The voices calling for a swift resolution have grown to the point where we are feeling the pressure. And I can't say this publicly, but this argument between General von Zettour and General von Rudersdorf is an extension of domestic politics. Their positions and duties are simply too different."

Mumbling that he's said too much, he turns to the window and clams up. Tanya understands how he feels, of course.

I see, public opinion.

I was just reading that wartime newspaper full of rows upon rows of garbage stories with nothing else in it... The national mood is a monster, and it appears to be growing more insistent by the second.

I don't know who planted the seeds, but since they weren't harvested, this is the obvious result.

It would seem that the more decent a person is, the harder their life is. Well, it has to be better than the front lines. I want to work in the rear like Colonel Uger.

At the same time, I realize it's not easy. For example, General von Zettour is in charge of the Service Corps. Put in extreme terms, the person in charge of acquiring resources for the war domestically is compelled to face a never-ending stream of problems.

From the perspective of private demand, the Empire is pouring its limited resources into the bottomless pit known as the eastern front—and at a horrifying rate that is probably difficult to comprehend for people outside the military. The way things are currently, the discontent of all the civilian sectors that are getting the short end of the stick must be incredible.

No, it's impossible to even imagine.

Reading just one of these ridiculous newspaper articles makes it plain to see.

It's too dangerous to have the person writing news articles so out of sync with the actual situation on the battlefield. Being intentionally vague to protect military secrets is sensible. But if the people disseminating information simply don't know anything to begin with, we have some serious work to do when it comes to following best practices in communication and conveying intel.

We're just like an underperforming corporation. We're one step away from that classic, vicious cycle of savagery and emotionally fueled blunders.

"...Colonel Uger. I've received the orders, and my unit will follow them. We will head to our new location and conduct combat missions."

"All right. Well, saying, 'Sorry to cause you trouble,' would be insensitive even coming from me. Colonel, I can't guarantee any additional supplies, but as your former classmate, I can say this much: I'll do everything in my power to maintain the supply lines for you."

The person bowing, openly relying on Tanya, is a mid-level General Staff officer in charge of handling supplies. Normally, he would be able to make anything happen if it was necessary for the war effort.

Yet the most he can promise is to keep the lines open?!

"Have things really gotten that bad?"

"They really have. I'm sorry."

I want to groan at the ceiling. The situation is dire.

A lieutenant colonel in the General Staff working directly with railroads and logistics can't secure extra supplies for the Salamander Kampfgruppe, a single unit that's deploying on orders straight from the General Staff?

He can promise only the existence of some supplies?

This isn't a brigade or an army but a Kampfgruppe pulled together from a hodgepodge of forces! The protest rising up in Tanya's throat is not incorrect.

But the suffering in Colonel Uger's grimace! Nothing else could more accurately convey the true feelings of those stationed in the rear.

This must be why General von Zettour is vehemently opposed to the expansion of the front no matter what. More importantly, he can't possibly divert any more national resources for military use. Tanya empathizes with his struggle so much she feels sick.

It's also extremely frustrating that, paradoxically, she can understand why General von Rudersdorf and his men propose a swift resolution. The commanders aren't wrong when they say the campaign on the eastern front, where vast quantities of resources are being exhausted, needs to wrap up as soon as possible.

Even if you don't want to be conscious of your relationship with Supreme High Command and its demand for quick victories, if you work in Operations, you have to be. *Resources are finite.* That's why *we must stop using them.* But *the necessary resources have dried up.*

Both generals are right, which is why it's such a frustrating issue.

"…What a morass," I mumble in spite of myself. I'm seized by the urge to cradle my head and scream.

And Colonel Uger, who left with a wordless nod, must have understood how I felt: *How did this happen?*

▶▶▶ AUGUST 30, UNIFIED YEAR 1926, THE SALIENT ON THE EASTERN FRONT ◀◀◀

And so…

If we're going to tell this story in a somewhat logical order…

The Salamander Kampfgruppe under the command of Lieutenant Colonel Tanya von Degurechaff has safely deployed to a little salient no one but historians will ever take any interest in.

The unit has nonstandard combat capabilities for its size. But it should probably be clearly stated…though it boasts armored vehicles, self-propelled artillery, and an outstanding aerial mage unit, it's still a Kampfgruppe by nature, a force that was thrown together on short notice.

When it comes to securing a bulge indefinitely, this Kampfgruppe with its limited infantry strength is destined to fail.

"…It's the same dilemma."

Though they're defending a base, Tanya is compelled by necessity to opt for an aggressive mobile battle. They don't have enough men to only play defense.

Not that they have any extra hands for attacking and securing strategic locations.

"If we leave some troops each time we seize a new position, we'll end up completely spread out. Splitting up is out of the question when the front is already so massive. We can't let our already slim forces get picked off unit by unit."

The Imperial Army's experience on the eastern front is perfectly represented in miniature right here.

Our experiment might as well be called Operation Canary. Of course, officially, it's Research into the Usage of Kampfgruppen for Base Defense Tactics in Combat—a plausible excuse.

It's so unproductive, but apparently the General Staff must run an experiment on holding a massive front with a limited number of troops.

And that's why we're still out here killing one another. In the history books, the lull on the main lines will be depicted as a stationary period, but that has nothing to do with us. And certainly, if neither the Empire nor the Federation is carrying out corps-size operations, then it's correct in a big-picture way to say that it's all quiet on the eastern front.

But that's not quite right, she mentally adds with a sigh.

Just because a battle wasn't worth covering in a textbook didn't mean it was all nice and clean.

"Start the mop-up and make sure to get the rest of them! Be careful!"

The commanders barking orders all have their guns at the ready, vigilantly searching.

They're not out enjoying the autumn season but stabbing freshly harvested bales of hay with their bayonets and checking houses for hiding enemy soldiers. Will this moment make it into the history books?

"Here's one! Don't let him get away!"

"Grab him! We'll make him give up the names of everyone he was working with!"

After a few shouts back and forth as well as some curses, I hear several gunshots and then silence. Sounds like they didn't manage to take him alive.

I told them to capture enemies because we want to gather intelligence, but…I guess for the troops of my Kampfgruppe, taking an opponent alive in a life-and-death battle is a pretty tall order…

…Or perhaps the first issue to complain about is how our enemies aren't people we can take prisoner?

Most of the enemies we encounter are irregular militia, which I'm so familiar with that I'm sick of them. Since they aren't officially soldiers, they have no right to be taken prisoner. According to the laws governing war, these bands of rabble who don't make their alliance clear don't have the right of belligerence.

Of course, I wonder how effectively enforced the law of war is. Still, having a good chance of being killed and definitely being killed are two different things.

If your opponent knows death is certain, that makes their counter-attacks even more desperate. There's something wrong with the status quo of kill or be killed…but the fact that we can't do anything about it makes it worse.

"It's sad, but it's only one part of this war of attrition. At this rate…our troops really will melt away." Tanya grumbles as she glances around like a vigilant commander should…

And off in front of her, she witnesses her men swinging shovels down on the body of an enemy soldier to make sure he's dead.

Even the ones who hesitated when they first arrived on the eastern front are now merciless servants of efficiency and certainty. When Tanya forced them through the experience of gruesome irregular warfare… they adapted in no time.

It's been only two days since we were stationed on the salient.

The troops are more comfortable now with the shift from tidy battles fought between regular military forces to the muck of unconventional warfare. Or perhaps we should get philosophical and say they were forced to change?

Because we have to is a phrase that causes abrupt transformations in humans.

I mean, not a day goes by that we don't get attacked. Federation commando units started becoming very active right as we took up our positions. The prospects for this cleanup operation are awfully gloomy.

The Salamander Kampfgruppe was originally formed to fight mobile battles. We're not at all suited to this sort of counterinsurgency mission.

To speak in extremes, it's like sending cavalry to take on a fortress.

"Colonel, we've finished eliminating them!"

"Were there any enemy mages?"

"Not that we saw. I think it was mainly a guerrilla force made up of militia."

Tanya nods to convey her understanding. Inside she feels like things are not going well.

If it were regular forces against regular forces, they would be ready anytime. At least, her Salamander Kampfgruppe can kick the ass of an equally sized Federation unit with no problem.

But Tanya's frustration lies elsewhere. Really, all that her unit should be used for is kicking ass. They don't have the manpower to secure an area by combing it for resistance fighters and plucking each partisan out.

There isn't enough infantry. Failure is virtually inescapable.

"We have to avoid this swamp at all costs…"

But how? Even the General Staff is still looking for the answer! This is what you call answering your own question.

Tanya—no, even the other staff officers are aware of the issue. Everyone understands where the problem is, but figuring out what to prescribe for it is proving difficult.

Taking time to organize their thoughts would be a profligate luxury.

You can't simply take your time in a guerrilla fight, because any visitors you receive will be sudden.

The transmissions that come to us never take our schedule into consideration.

"Salamander 05 to 01. A new enemy's shown up!"

First Lieutenant Grantz, who I have on guard, delivers a report that contains the word *enemy*.

Those five little letters force my brain to change gears. To protect my peace-loving self's personal safety, I have to be fully prepared to face the enemy threatening it.

"Unverified hostile mage unit approaching from the northeast. There are…four of them. And I guess…they're flying NOE?"

"Salamander 01, copy. 05, nice work. Those must be their hotshots. I'll head over, so if you're racking up points, I hope you'll leave me my share."

My Kampfgruppe is spread out, sweeping for any remaining enemies.

They must have been aiming for this. They waited until my troops committed their attention to the ground battle to send aerial mages on a hit-and-run strike out of the sky.

It's a textbook approach, rigidly faithful to theory. That's how I know it's their main objective. For better or worse, it's easy to understand.

"Oh," Tanya continues as if she had forgotten to mention something. "I wanted to warn you, 05. Make sure your reports are accurate. Are they flying NOE or not?"

"05 to 01. Apologies. But it's less like they're flying and more like they're trying to imitate ducks in the air…"

"01 to 05. Now you're talking. Ducks?"

Hmm. I wonder what he might mean as I fly. Increasing my altitude, I take out my binoculars and begin scanning the direction Lieutenant Grantz said the enemy is coming from.

"Yes, ducks! It would be easiest for you to just see them yourself... But the way they're moving is not so much contour flight as it is level flight. We can aim at them from our position right now. How should I explain this...? It's like they have their hands full simply flying so they forgot to keep an eye out for threats above them."

"Ah, I spotted them... Fine, do it."

When I finally see it for myself...I understand that Lieutenant Grantz's description is apt.

Through my binoculars, I see unsteady Federation mages struggling to maintain their erratic path through the air. I'd be hard-pressed to call them aerial mages if that's the state they're in. They aren't flying through the sky as much as drowning in it.

"...I never thought we'd encounter an enemy who can barely stay in the air."

Back on the Rhine front, I would have thought any mages seeming so preoccupied by basic flight were a ruse. I might have shouted back at Grantz, *Take a closer look!* At least, I never would have imagined that these four mages were the enemy's main attacking force.

I would have thought it was a harassment attack to dull our edge before a major offensive or possibly a simple feint. Both the Rhine front and the eastern front feature cheap trick after cheap trick, so the fog of war is thick as ever.

But on the eastern front, the rules are a bit different.

The enemy is waiting for the Imperial Army to exhaust itself and collapse.

I mean, come on, Tanya thinks while looking up at the company flying above her. Being on guard against enemy approaches and maintaining company-strength forces in the air as cover twenty-four hours a day is tiring.

And after all that effort, our opponents are...four enemy mages who can barely fly.

"The defending side can't know when or from where the enemy will appear, but there's not anything we can do about that... This'll be rough."

"Without a doubt. But our respective attrition rates are very different. We've done a great job so far, so I'm sure we'll be able to keep it up."

Tanya breaks into a smile at Major Weiss's comments.

Then, as if to back up that confident declaration, the troops who had gone out to attack unleashed a company's worth of disciplined fire.

Lieutenant Grantz was in command.

"Now, let's see how skilled they are."

Tanya wonders what would happen if they missed...but she doesn't consider it a necessary worry. She's been with these men since the Rhine.

I'm not so thickheaded that I'm oblivious to the improvement of my subordinates. Even Grantz, who used to always make me worry, has made progress.

War is a lousy experience. But...live combat does make a person grow. The men and officers under me who have gained experience, endured trials, and put their abilities on display are true assets.

I invested in Grantz's human capital and trained him. Now his skill is worthy of being praised as professional.

He discovered this pseudo-NOE flying platoon at what was something approaching ultra–long range, then shot them down from a considerable distance.

"Marvelous. All threats are confirmed down."

New recruits who I initially find to not be of much use rapidly gain experience in the field, and their abilities blossom.

...Even if it's difficult to call the skills involved in waging war "productive," I have to hand it to them for their earnest attitude toward getting better at their jobs.

"That's four joint scores. At this rate, nothing will remain of the current Named system by the end of the fighting on the eastern front. I mean, the way we're going, we'll be mass-producing Nameds."

"Ha-ha-ha! But that said, I doubt the alias White Silver will ever be overshadowed!"

"Hmm, I wonder."

I can't say this to Weiss, but his comments assume that the Empire wins the war. From his perspective, perhaps that's accurate.

But Tanya has to wince at her own position. Maybe other people can believe in the Empire's victory, holding faith like an innocent maiden in love, but she's different.

Tanya gazes into the clear blue sky and sighs. A hundred or a thousand years ago, or a hundred or a thousand years from now, the sky probably has and always will be the same.

A universal constant of nature. Staying as it is.

I'm so envious of the sky.

Though it's uncertain whether the Empire will be around for a thousand years or not, the sky will abide at its leisure. *Will the Empire still exist after the fighting on the eastern front ends?* That is where Tanya's true worries lie, so of course she is apt to look up in envy.

I don't want to pity myself, but what a miserable situation I'm in.

Still, I should prioritize the work in front of me over my existential woes.

"Salamander 01 to all units. It seems like the fighting has cooled down. Begin recovering our injured and searching for enemies to take prisoner."

The army's work isn't done just because it repelled the enemy attack. It's more like a party, in that cleaning up afterward is the hardest part.

If you can't feel lucky for having to worry about cleaning up, you can't keep going. Regrets and reflections are privileges of the living. If you die, there's no nothing.

"Second Company, stand by for rapid response. Third and Fourth Companies, keep patrolling the warning line. I'm putting 02 in command of the warning line."

"02, roger. Leave it to me."

"Great."

Now then, even after entrusting some of the necessary tasks to Weiss, there are still way too many approvals and various decisions to make.

If one of my troops dies, I have to send a letter of condolence to the rear. Naturally, it's stipulated that we have to write to the bereaved family in a considerate way. If it's too perfunctory, Personnel will complain in a way that affects our performance evaluations, so we can't just phone it in. They even recommend that we send notes about injuries.

When your human capital decreases and your workload increases, you start to really abhor the deaths of your subordinates, whether in battle or of illness, and even their injuries.

Purely in terms of market principle, there can't be many occupations more peace loving than that of the soldier.

Ahhh, damn it, Tanya curses mentally. But the job has to be done. Therefore, in order to fulfill her duties, Lieutenant Colonel Tanya von Degurechaff faces her pen and ink and boldly begins to tackle the hopeless amount of work she has to do.

I should place faith in my work ethic and the coffee beans I received.

That said, given the fact that my consumption is increasing exponentially and our supply of coffee beans is unstable, my worries about the overall supply situation are headache inducing.

Having our supplies cut off would be horrible.

No, thinks Tanya, stopping her pen. She reconfirms their connection to the rear.

Colonel Uger promised that even if we can't expect any extra supplies, he would maintain the existing supply lines. It's probably safe to look forward to a periodic delivery of coffee beans.

"Ah, caffeine. No one has ever claimed victory after their supply of it was cut off... So I guess that means if the Empire can provide such luxury goods to the front lines, it still has some fight left in it?"

If you look at the history of coffee, it's clearly a luxury item.

Cultivated by human hands as a commercial crop, according to humanity's tastes, it's delivered to places far from its origin. At the foundation of this system is an extraordinary logistic network that allows for stable distribution.

I suppose that's significant...

The fact that Uger says he can maintain distribution proves the system's greatness. If the organization is still holding together, then the Empire has a chance at victory.

While she was applying herself to her work, thinking those things, the sun set.

"Sheesh, management is a pain. It may be discretionary labor, but I don't really..."

Tanya intended to finish her sentence with *get much discretion*, but her grumble is interrupted by the awfully familiar sound of gunfire followed by multiple explosions.

...Honestly, it makes me want to complain.

The Federation Army is truly violent toward the silent veil of night.

"The first report is in! Several shots and explosions echoing from a nearby settlement! The patrol discovered the Federation's regularly scheduled attackers and has engaged! All units are currently repelling the attack!"

Upon receiving the report from Lieutenant Serebryakov, who is on duty, Tanya gets up with visible aggravation. These guys don't know how to properly enjoy an autumn evening.

"Geez, these guys work too hard. Do they have no concept of labor laws?"

"It doesn't seem like it, Colonel. We might end up getting used to all this."

"Absolutely. We should lament our misfortune of acclimating to this nastiness."

Once something is familiar, it's not as hard to handle. But that comes with the caveat that it's difficult to be genuinely happy about getting used to it. Poking my head into the command post, I see that the enemies are moving in the same manner as usual.

It's not too difficult to put together the gunshots and the reports from each unit to get a grasp on the situation.

For better or worse, habituation to the enemy's simple patterns can invite carelessness, but...as long as you're not screwing up in how you deal with them, it's not too bad.

"From the field, Colonel."

Taking the telegram, I listen to the reports and finds that it's what I expected.

"HQ, this is Infantry Third Company. We fought off a minor attack. It was a night raid conducted by a small number of armed commandos. We're currently cleaning up the battlefield."

After all, it can be said...

The attacks we're experiencing are classic harassment attacks—the insensitive kind that aim to disrupt our sleep—but if we're discussing each individual strike, they're relatively straightforward to handle.

Defend, repulse, and recover—that's it.

"What's the damage?"

"Since the patrol spotted them early, there are no major losses aside from one burned-out building."

That's good. The fewer letters of condolence I have to write, the better.

"That's some nice work. Who was on patrol?"

"It was Corporal Kurtz and his men."

"Got it. Give them a gift from me later. And send me the details of the incident when they're available. Have your unit stay sharp."

Keeping damage to a minimum is good, but on the other hand, it's proof that trouble is still constantly following us around here. We may have repulsed the attack with negligible damages, but the more times this happens, the more likely it is for a mistake to occur.

And mistakes eventually lead to catastrophes.

The commander's reply to Tanya is a reliable "We'll be careful."

Tanya smiles wryly, since he could have left that unsaid, and urges him to continue with his report.

"The commanders at each level are tabulating the details now, but casualties appear to be extremely low. This time we discovered the enemy early and reacted swiftly. I don't think you'll have to wait long for the detailed report. The only thing is that we had to wake up napping troops. Please bear in mind that we're running on very little sleep."

"Not much we can do about that." Tanya groaned, sharing his understanding.

Cornering us so that we can't relax while they do their best to disrupt our sleep—the enemy's guerrilla units are really having their way with us.

Considering the enemy efficiency and lack of hesitation, they must have green-lit a scorched-earth campaign—destroying all infrastructure within reach, basically.

"I have to admit that regardless of how well it can build things, Communism sure can tear them down."

"That's for sure. But we'll at least resist by being efficient at fixing things. We'll show those demolitionists."

The commander and I exchange banter that hardly qualifies as small talk, or joking for that matter. It may seem stupid, but it's clear that if we can still afford to screw around like this, things are all right.

No one is as fragile as a soldier on the front lines or in the trenches who has lost the ability to smile.

While taking things seriously may be a virtue, being humorless when you're in a tight spot renders people helpless—to the point that they would contribute more to society by being shot.

On that point, lack of sleep is bad for mental health as well as morale. Infantry Third Company, whose beds were burned up, won't be able to get a good rest until the firefighting and restoration are done. Since it's fall, it's still just barely possible to camp...but if at all doable, infantry should sleep with a roof over their heads.

"Do your best. I'll send some refreshments over soon."

The minute she puts down the receiver, Tanya follows through on her promise. It's times like this that it's most important to be considerate. Encouraging subordinates and appreciating their work a little can make a big difference in the field. The most basic rule of personnel management is to make sure that subordinates know the high-ranking people can see their hard work.

When there isn't enough effort put into the essential principle of rewards and punishments, nothing but utter collapse awaits. Principles are principles for a reason and must be respected.

"Oh, Lieutenant Serebryakov. I need to give something to Corporal Kurtz and his men from Third Company. Send one of the bottles you have stored in the battalion treasury."

"Y-yes, ma'am!"

After making her expectations plain, Tanya sets about reorganizing her thoughts. She switches gears from personnel manager back to her role as commander.

The situation is clear.

The building Third Company was garrisoned in has been burned down in the night by a guerrilla raid. Something like this happens every night, so the troops are used to it, but...the question is whether there will be another attack tonight or not.

If the raids are likely to continue, Tanya needs to tell the units on patrol to raise the alert level. But if the enemy doesn't come, that would mean cutting into their precious sleep time for no reason.

Should I leave the alert level as it is and let my men get some rest? Or should I raise it and be prepared for a raid? The choices are in direct conflict. Either way, it's a tough decision.

"Okay...what should I do?"

Her uncertainty probably stems from the fact that she hasn't been getting enough sleep, either.

In an attempt to open her eyes, Tanya reaches for the coffee that had materialized at some point, and the moment she smells it, she smiles ironically—probably because they're the beans she received from Colonel Uger the other day.

Her nose is so used to the frontline-issue ersatz coffee that she learned not to breathe in the smell. But for the first time in a while, she sniffs at her drink in pursuit of the pleasant scent.

That simple fact is enough to put her at ease about the supply lines. The smell of the unusually fragrant coffee sinks into her tired body.

Colonel Uger has excellent taste.

Taste? At that thought, Tanya recalls something. Her current situation is not at all to her liking. In fact, it's downright disagreeable. If she acted according to textbook, she would alert all units that one of theirs had been attacked and shift everyone into a state of readiness.

The problem is that standard doctrine doesn't really cover the combat environment in the east.

Strictly speaking, the forward-most line and the main lines are no-man's-land, so handling things according to textbook would be fine. But salients consisting of freshly occupied or abandoned villages and forested areas are hotbeds of partisan[1] activity, so the theories don't hold up.

"...Even a plan that plays it safe, in the long run, would be..."

It's important to be on their guard.

But she should also avoid keeping her soldiers sleep-deprived night after night.

It's absurd, but these two choices are inescapable. Which means that Tanya, as commander, is stuck picking one or the other.

---

[1] **partisan**　In this context, it means combatants who are not regular enlisted soldiers but members of an irregular militia. Whether they should be referred to as a resistance, terrorists, or freedom fighters is an extremely sensitive issue, so I won't deal with it here.

"Major Weiss, I'm not sure whether we should put a warning out. There's no warning from the forward patrol, right?"

"No warnings. The periodic reports have all been normal, as well."

"...Then I suppose I should..."

...*let the Kampfgruppe sleep.* Tanya nearly says it, but then she thinks again. You can hate sleep deprivation only if you're alive.

Staying alive is my style. So I should be true to myself.

"Wake up some of the troops. Combat readiness three. Get them on alert."

"Are you sure?"

"We don't know if the enemy will stop at one raid. The fact that we're so used to their nightly attacks might be dangerous. I'd rather risk the resentment of the troops once they've gotten home than end up regretting exposing them to the enemy in a careless moment."

To be honest, it pains me to make other people go along with my preferences.

But ordering someone to do what I say in order to keep them alive must be...within the realm of the permissible, as a soldier. It's like an extension of their tasks or duties. I'm sure even the Labor Standards Bureau would forgive me.

"If that's what you prefer, then who am I to disagree?"

"Colonel Uger taught me the value of good taste."

"Oh, is he the one who gave you that coffee?"

"It's my secret stash. I have to check later to make sure Lieutenant Serebryakov isn't using too much of it. Now then," Tanya continues with some pep in her voice. "Shift to combat readiness three. Begin giving the notice."

"Understood," Weiss says before leaving to relay her instructions. It's certain that everyone will understand the need for security as their beds call to them. They'll only get up with some reluctance.

That said, if some rise, others can stay asleep. Combat readiness three uses shifts, so some people are free. Of course, that includes the officers at HQ as well.

"Oh, Lieutenant Serebryakov. You should rest, too."

I need my adjutant to have decent judgment. I'd rather have her well rested and levelheaded than sleep-deprived and fuzzy brained.

The decrease in cognitive ability humans experience when sleep-deprived must be a biological response.

When we require sleep as a given, neglecting it is truly inept. Any capable person should ensure they get the minimum required amount of rest without fail. If I don't want to consider myself incompetent, I have to give my subordinates as much rest as possible.

"But I don't want to leave you and Major Weiss…"

"It's not a suggestion. Get some rest. That's part of your duty as a soldier. You heard the order, right, Lieutenant?"

Getting proper rest and sleep could be called a part of an assistant's duties.

It's impossible to maintain performance at 100 percent with willpower and guts alone.

"Yes, ma'am, understood."

Her bow as she excuses herself is ever so conscientious. Perhaps it's conceited to say that I made Serebryakov into what she is now, but it makes me so happy to see what a great officer she has become during our short time together.

I'm incredibly proud to have contributed so much to the growth of human capital on our team. Of utmost importance, however, is a plan to utilize that human capital properly. On that point, Tanya does think waking up soldiers to put them on readiness, even if only level three, might be a bit too cautious.

It's important to be appropriately wary of risks. Fearing them too much invites its own problems. In the end, it's important to have common sense and balance.

Easier said than done.

Why have there been so many of these either-or choices lately…? Tanya smiles wryly at the thought.

"Hmm, if I wake them up for no reason, they won't like me very much, will they?"

"…What about just leaving the lookouts and canceling the combat-readiness order? We could let the unit get a little sleep…"

If we do that… Tanya does the numbers in her head. They would be able to scrape together some time for the troops to rest in bed, even if only for a few hours.

It's not a bad suggestion.

But... The thought also crosses her mind that it's too soon for that.

"Not bad, but let's take a look at our situation. It's almost dawn. Late at night or early in the morning are the times to strike. During this time of day, we need to be careful."

"Understood. Shall I wake up Lieutenant Grantz?"

"Grantz is on backup and scramble duty. Let him sleep. A sleep-deprived scrambler will only cause an accident."

She's really happy that his unit has become a real fighting force. She's incredibly proud to have trained up First Lieutenant Grantz.

Cultivating people is an important job within an organization.

In my work in personnel, I never cultivated anyone... "Hmm," Tanya murmurs as she breaks into a smile. "Maybe I actually have an aptitude for teaching people."

"I'd like to ask the two first lieutenants you put through the mill how they feel."

I may have been a strict teacher, but I got results. Not that I'm arrogant enough to say they could thank me and I wouldn't be surprised.

Setting aside how he may have interpreted her silent gaze, he's probably thirsty if he's cooped up in the command post. Before she knows it, he's holding up his cup and asking, "May I have another cup of coffee?"

She glances at him and sees his eyes hungry for brewed arabica beans.

"Hmph, I should have told you to sleep."

"If you wish..."

"I guess I have no choice. You're being responsible and following orders."

With a bit of a smirk, she pours him a cup as an apology for making him go along with her selfishness. Friend of the night, bosom buddy of overtime—coffee is a fine companion. She regrets sharing her private stock a little. It's also maddening that the supply situation is poor enough to warrant regretting something so minor.

Not long after serving Weiss, Tanya nonchalantly looks up at the hands of the clock and grumbles. "Hmm, it doesn't seem like there will be a dawn attack. I guess my intuition has dulled."

If there was going to be an assault, it would be happening right around

now. Preparing for an attack meant moving into position before sunrise…
but the enemy won't make it in time anymore.

If there's no sign of them now, all this readiness was for nothing. Morning will come, and all I'll have accomplished is letting my vice commander drink up my stash of good coffee. I guess I should just be happy the enemy didn't come.

Tanya is nearly dozing off as she muses, but all of it gets blown away with a jolt.

"C-C-Colonel, we've got an emergency!"

"Give me a sitrep."

"It's two battalions! Federation forces have penetrated our territory with battalion-strength units! The patrol made the discovery, and the rapid response unit has engaged them!"

Conducting a night raid with battalions?

There's no time to think how bold a move that is. This is more than provocation. It's a clash of two professional armies.

"Wake everyone up! They're here!"

Did they aim for the moment we'd gotten used to their harassment attacks?

Or does this happen to be right when they received reinforcements? No, neither of those things matters right now.

We can investigate their motive later.

Right now, we have to crush the enemies standing in front of us.

"But why would they time their dawn attack for right now…? Wait a sec."

Two battalions in a dawn attack.

The surprise factor is tremendous, but it's even more bizarre that the Federation doesn't second-guess whether two battalions might have trouble defeating an entire Kampfgruppe. The Salamander Kampfgruppe is an ad hoc combat force made up of armor, self-propelled artillery, infantry, and aerial mages, and they've been skirmishing with us for a while now.

"I'll go to intercept!"

"Wait, Major Weiss! The 203rd is a reserve unit."

"Yes, ma'am, b-but…"

If it was a sudden encounter, I could understand. If the enemy commander decided to have them rush in, he could be forgiven.

But would an enemy who already has a good idea of our combat strength through multiple skirmishes conduct an attack this clumsy?

The answer is...

No way.

"It doesn't make sense to try to force their way in with only two battalions."

For anyone who wants to avoid risky situations, the regret of excessive caution is preferable to the satisfaction of assuming you've seen through the enemy's plan. Well, perhaps in an offensive battle, people wouldn't like the idea of being cautious.

But this is a defensive mission where the goal is to keep attrition to a minimum.

"Tell the armored unit to assume these are enemy reserves. The mage unit will be held back for putting out fires. But scramble the backup company. I don't expect them to participate proactively in the fighting. Tell them to be our eyes on the battlefield."

"Yes, ma'am!"

Weiss performs a perfectly textbook salute and rushes back to his unit. Watching him go, Tanya smiles wryly. *I'm sure he'll work hard enough to earn the coffee he drank.*

I say "the coffee he drank" for the sake of cost consciousness.

Being aware of costs is proof that I've regained a healthy sense of market principle. Even on the front, where you're liable to lose your humanity, I seem to be maintaining both my mental and physical health.

There is nothing more pleasant for me as a modern, free individual.

Sheesh, the freedom to bask in contentment would be nice. But no, the battlefield doesn't allow for even such a simple joy.

"C-Command! It's the enemy! The enemy is—!"

"Enemy attack! Intercept them!"

I knew it. I anticipated it. But really? They're attacking headquarters?

If we were in trenches, this would never have happened. The partisans must have spotted us during the day.

It takes more than a few days to map out the geography of a village we're garrisoning.

Even with a patrol out, an unexpected defeat is still possible. But reality is harsher than I imagined. The area we have to defend is larger than we thought, and we don't have enough manpower to properly cover all the ground.

Insufficient personnel led to holes in the warning line, so naturally we've allowed this totally unforeseen attack to happen.

"They're coming directly for headquarters?! Shit, they're too good!" The troops curse as they grab their rifles.

But even if the Kampfgruppe's rear personnel put up their best fight, it's only the few staffers attached to headquarters. They're soldiers, so of course they can shoot a gun, but...whether they can land any shots or not is another story.

The ones we should rely on at times like this are the conscripts who guard HQ. But we were already short on soldiers. After drawing from the guard unit to bolster the front lines, our extreme numerical disadvantage is inescapable.

"Shit, I knew it... Fighting on the eastern front is totally different from trench battles!"

Unlike on the western front, there are no trenches in the east. The supremely simple, clear reason for this is that the battle lines are too long. We don't have enough troops to build trench works and man the whole front.

That means there's no way to tell the first and second lines apart.

Even the soldiers in the rear may have to fight. In a lax moment, idiot soldiers can be turned into idiot corpses by knives, bayonets, or shovels.

I was right to require the bare minimum of training for the staff working at the command post.

"C-Colonel! We're completely surrounded!"

"Calm down! Take a closer look! We're just following our original plan of holing up at this position and defending! The enemy isn't even sure how to attack us!" As she roars directions at the rear personnel, Tanya smiles.

Just because the enemy is clever doesn't mean you have to go along with their plan. If you want to really scatter them...all you have to do is blow them up from their core.

"Now's about time! Their main forces must all be here. We can assume they're attacking with almost their full strength. Major Weiss, scatter them!"

"Understood! Battalion, move out! We need to intercept them immediately! Don't mistake friendlies for the enemy!"

I'm sending out the pet reserve unit in my pocket, the unit I wanted to keep on hand even if I had to decrease the number of guards at the headquarters—the 203rd Aerial Mage Battalion.

Having gained experience in Dacia, Norden, and the Rhine, it continues to function as a perfect apparatus for violence in the vast lands of the east. I suppose you could say it works wonders.

The Federation infantry battalions probably intended to surround and grind us down, but we treat them to a volley of head-on explosion formulas, occupy the sky above them as they panic, then advise them to surrender.

Before long, things are shaping up to end in the Empire's favor. A single mage battalion held in reserve can be quite a wildcard. Whether it's a defense or counterattack, no one can casually settle into a leisurely shootout with a mage battalion coming out of the sky unless your position is honeycombed with anti–air guns.

There's no way the infiltrators are hauling anti–air machine guns. After regrouping, the Imperial Army infantry conducts maneuvers to drive our point home, causing the attacking Federation forces to meekly start lowering their guns.

Honestly, I was worried they would resist to the very end, so surrender is good news for me.

"Phew, I'm glad this ended without having to fight them down to the last man."

Oh. That's when it occurs to Tanya that these enemies are wearing proper uniforms.

I'm not partial to their tendency to use even dawn attacks to distract us, but I truly appreciate that the whole organization surrenders in an orderly fashion.

That means... Ever scrupulous, Tanya repeats aloud the words that popped into a corner of her mind. "Make sure the prisoners are accommodated appropriately according to regulations. I sure hope I don't have any subordinates dumb enough to be violent with captives."

"Understood, Colonel. We can handle it, of course."

The infantry officers nod, so they must understand how I do things. Since I was repeating myself, they may have felt the insistence.

Still, it's critical for those in command to constantly reinforce policy. That's why I have to say it even though I know they get it.

"It's not as if I'm worried about you guys. What I want is for you to fill in everyone beneath you. I want even the privates at the bottom to understand what those at the top understand and what we're focusing on."

"Ngh! Yes, ma'am!" With the abrupt realization showing on their faces, the infantry officers all straighten up.

This was probably the first time they considered the possibility that their subordinates could cause trouble. The troops are used to mopping up irregulars, but if they thoughtlessly tormented uniformed soldiers, that could be a huge problem. Now would be the time to rein in the grunts where they need to be reined in.

I can't say whether this is to be expected or what. The officers of the Salamander Kampfgruppe have excellent qualifications, but most of them still lack experience. They weren't so green that they would conduct themselves improperly during the heat of battle, but expecting them to know how to appropriately settle things after the fighting was over was optimistic.

That said, they have good heads on their shoulders. They won't make the same mistake twice. Tanya stood at attention with a click of her boots, then let the commanders know there was nothing to worry about and that she was counting on them.

"All right, we have a lot of work to do."

The village we're garrisoned in is a bit of a mess.

Most of it emerged unscathed from the fighting. In the ten days since we've been deployed here, I've been working my subordinates hard to set up warning and defensive lines, but maybe it would be better to have them focus on base maintenance so they can get some sleep.

But when Tanya thinks about how few hands she has, she can't help but frown.

One option would be to put the prisoners to work. But without a proper camp, it would be impossible to supervise their labor.

The infantry of the Salamander Kampfgruppe is mostly combat units, and we have only the minimum complement of military police.

They're for enforcing regulations within the Kampfgruppe, but maybe they could supervise the prisoners temporarily... Still, in a crisis, even the MPs are manpower. I don't want to tie down any personnel to prisoner duty like that.

"Man, I don't know what to do. There's too much I want to have the MPs do. We're totally understaffed."

"If you like, we could have some infantry personnel handle it."

"I appreciate the offer, but I don't want to tire out our combat troops. Have those units mop up and secure the battlefield on the double."

As the infantry unit COs acknowledge with a salute and leave the room, Tanya watches them go while thinking about how young they look. For some reason, she suddenly realizes, everyone is in their twenties.

...They may be outstanding, but I can't believe such young officers ended up in my unit. Well, if we're going to have that kind of talk, Visha is only in her teens, and that's before getting into the issues posed by Tanya herself.

Rapid expansion, attrition on the Rhine, lack of key personnel, increasing use of the younger demographics.

The logistics network is still functioning. We get replacement troops. *But how much longer will the Empire's strength hold out?*

"...There's no point in thinking about it."

The Empire is chipping away at its people, its human resources and capital.

And in such an unbelievably primitive conflict.

Even in the trenches on the Rhine, we were engaging at close quarters fairly often.

But over there, the times both sides would commit to hard hand-to-hand combat were mainly when operations were being launched; it wasn't a daily occurrence. Certainly, it's a different ordeal when compared to the depressingly gruesome skirmishes out in no-man's-land between patrols and commandos.

Still, on the Rhine front, close-quarters combat indicated the battle was in its final phase. To speak to extremes, I'd say it's what happened when charging trenches. In the east, even though we're sleeping indoors, it's become routine for the soldiers to get woken up by an attack and then fight for their lives.

If this is the barbarization of warfare, then…what a pity. Violence at close quarters on a regular basis. It's an awful thing.

"Sheesh…this time was pretty bad."

Tanya grumbles in disbelief about the attack on headquarters. I understand how great it feels to mount an attack on an enemy HQ, but I have zero interest in being on the receiving end.

"I get that we're in enemy territory, but we really haven't been able to rest at all. At this rate, we'll collapse in exhaustion."

On the eastern front, we've long since entered Federation soil, so everything around us is enemy territory. Whether we like it or not, we should be aware of this. I'd really like to invite the illustrious law experts who came up with the words *noncombat zone* and *rear area* to this charming locale.

Fatigue may not appear clearly in our reports or stats, but it still chips away at the troops' ability to continue fighting.

A tired army is fragile. No, not just armies. Any organization made up of exhausted people will inevitably make mistakes. And in an exhausted organization, there isn't any leeway to cover for the errors of individuals.

Once you reach that point, all that awaits is doom.

"Get back to resting as soon as possible. Everyone who isn't on duty should hop to it."

That's why Tanya is especially passionate about urging her troops to take a break.

Humans aren't machines. They require a proper amount of rest. She's convinced that if the troops' well-being isn't taken care of, catastrophe will be unavoidable.

"But, Colonel, shouldn't we post extra lookouts?"

"I've made sure we can respond quickly. Adding any more guards will just wear our people out."

"It's only been a few days…"

"Gentlemen, please be aware that even if it's only been a few days, we're still fighting a battle of attrition."

Currently, the Kampfgruppe's human attrition is minor, but according to several texts I've read, the research on war and mental health says that over three months of frontline service is bad news. Was it an American study? I forget. My knowledge of psychology doesn't go very deep, but... who knows how things will turn out if this battle gets prolonged?

It's because Tanya has this sense of crisis that she firmly reiterates her orders. "Taking a break is part of your job. Remember your pay grade and rest up."

"Understood, Colonel."

"Good answer." She looks out across the troops in the area and makes sure the officers understand that their men should rest, too. Taking a break is part of a soldier's job.

That being said...

Commanders—officers—are different. Of course, the minimum amount of rest is essential. A sleep-deprived officer making a careless mistake and sending a unit out to their deaths doesn't make for a very amusing story.

But the luxury of sound sleep...is reserved for people whose work is done. After repelling an attack, officers have a mountain of reports to make.

Thus, the officers who drove off the enemy have gathered at HQ and are sorting out the situation despite the haggard looks on their faces.

A small room, a cramped table, and meager lighting.

Still, what's important to a career soldier isn't a comfortable war room. If it's serviceable, then it's fine.

Upon gathering up the concise reports from all the commanders from Major Weiss on down, Tanya makes a conclusion.

It was sloppy.

"This was a dawn attack conducted by a single regiment. As the crowning touch of their counterattack after thoroughly harassing us... it's pretty weak."

According to everyone's reports, the enemy intended to mount a serious counterattack...but they weren't very cohesive.

"The enemy forces seemed to have a hard time coordinating. I would speculate that it was a hastily assembled unit." Tanya's vice commander nods as he voices his agreement, and he's probably right.

The lack of the proper coordination that's vital for conducting an effective attack at dawn indirectly speaks to how underprepared the Federation Army is.

Normally that would be good news.

But Tanya can't help but point something out in her youthful voice.

"It's aggravating that we're being tired out by these guys. They're like crops raised out of season. We need to get some good sleep and soon. If this one salient is such a handful, we won't be able to be too confident about what comes next."

Major Weiss's earlier observation may be correct, but…the enemy probably engineered that apparent weakness in coordination to trick us.

Using an impromptu force composed of two battalions to mount a distraction and sending the rest of their soldiers to attack our headquarters is a rather sketchy plan. To be frank, it's the type of operation you can probably expect some results from without needing to fine-tune the details.

The enemy commander, who seems adept at considering what he can do with the limited resources he's got on hand, accepted this imperfection from the planning stages and secured some redundancy.

I'd be lying if I said I couldn't feel the Federation-style, coolheaded realism of the returns that can be won from targeting high-value enemies with low-value soldiers.

"We experienced this on the Rhine front as well, but we really need to come up with a fix for the unit's fatigue."

"Major Weiss, how often would we need to rotate out to get unit exhaustion under control?"

"If we can limit frontline stints to three months, I think we can maintain a minimum baseline of combat strength."

"Makes sense." Tanya nods, although in her head she's anxious. "We have to add the caveat that it depends on whether we can secure replacements. Man, at this rate, the unit will only get weaker and weaker."

It's purely based on her experience…but while Tanya feels she can rely on the veterans who have spent a long time on front lines, as a unit, they could abruptly weaken.

Managing personnel on the battlefield is different from HR strategy in a corporation in many ways. Training up some experts and then keeping their unit on the front lines for too long will lead to a buildup of fatigue, leaving them at risk for serious injury.

Which is why we need replacement troops...

"...Gentlemen. To be honest, our prospects for receiving any rein-forcements or replacements are poor. But we're soldiers. If the home country hands us orders, we don't get to have an opinion."

If we don't even have enough troops, then getting replacements is a dream within a dream.

If we have to operate under the extremely harsh premise that man-power is scarce, then I can understand why some of the General Staff are scrambling to reach a quick resolution.

Apparently back at the General Staff Office, the Operations folks are planning a major offensive to bring the war to an end, but...if we can't guarantee the safety of the rear area, it will be hard to avoid this turning into a stalemate.

The most a single Kampfgruppe can do—even the Salamander Kampf-gruppe that can respond at the drop of a hat—is hold a point.

As long as we can't resolve this dilemma, we'll be stuck.

Plus, the decision to throw us onto the front line for this convenient proof of concept can only be rooted in panic. For those of us forced to go along with it, it's pure misfortune, but Tanya understands that it's neces-sary and shakes her head to clear her mind.

"If we slightly overwork ourselves, it's not impossible to control an area. But I guess it's ultimately still a fool's errand to wear down the unit simply to secure this patch of wasteland."

If we split up the unit, it would probably be possible to hold a sizable area. But in exchange, we'd lose our mobility, quick response time, and the ability to hold forces in reserve. It's not worth it at all.

But that said...

At this rate, the Empire won't be able to avoid bleeding to death.

It's fine that we dealt the enemy a heavy blow in the early battles and knocked them down. But that's all it was. It was rumored that the Fed-eration Army was collapsing, but they continue to mount counterattacks that, despite their reliance on numbers and repetitive in tactics, are still fierce.

Frankly, you could say that Federation forces are resisting with no regard for casualties. Unfortunately, that feat is impossible for the Empire. We're already at general mobilization, but we're putting in enormous effort to only just manage to make up for the fact that we're hurting for more human resources.

Draining our limited manpower pool will eventually lead to the extinction of the Imperial Army. At the rate we're going, it's only a matter of time.

We need a plan to fix it.

"It's true, but where am I going to find something like that?" Tanya grumbles quietly, but her voice lingers obnoxiously in her ears. *I've got to find an answer, no matter what it takes. We're doomed if I don't.*

Thus, Tanya struggles to find a way out of this mess. She won't stop grasping for a solution until she exhausts both her intellect and the wisdom of all humanity.

>>> **SEPTEMBER 12, UNIFIED YEAR 1926, A SALIENT ON THE EASTERN** <<<
FRONT, THE SALAMANDER KAMPFGRUPPE

Despite mulling it over and over, Tanya still hasn't found a way out.

All she has found over these past days is an inexhaustible supply of enemies. She has to keep facing the obnoxious Federation forces day after day; it's a kind of torture.

That explains my current demeanor, I suppose?

Tanya is incredibly eager in her search for an escape or a change to the current status quo.

She's willing to do anything. But despite comprehensive efforts to acquire the necessary information, she still has no idea what to do.

Technically her unit has prisoners. And quite a few of them, at that.

Capturing enemy soldiers means holding people who know the inside details of the enemy forces. Tanya was anticipating that they would be able to get some idea of the enemy's situation.

Of course, any single soldier will have only a tiny amount of intelligence. But she figured if she gave a number of them to the Feldgendarmerie, they would come up with something.

That was her naive fantasy.

The results were utterly atrocious.

The prisoners answered the officers' questions all the same; the interrogators couldn't get anything out of them besides the cookie-cutter responses of hard-core Communist sympathizers. Thanks to that, apparently now they're looking to see if there is some sort of propaganda that would break down their will to fight and allow us to draw some intel out of them.

But I've received a report that even with this much effort going into the interrogation, the short-term results we can expect to see are limited. The Feldgendarmerie is awfully pessimistic about getting intel out of the prisoners.

In fact...

Given the way the Federation soldiers unflinchingly attack in our daily battles, I can understand why the MPs want to throw in the towel—because what can the Feldgendarmerie even do to them?

"But it's strange."

Right after the unit repels another clockwork attack from an enemy commando unit, Tanya turns to Major Weiss to ask him, "What is?"

It sounds like he's going to start a lengthy conversation, and she's sure her vice commander is a soldier who knows the time and place for it. Tanya has him continue and listens closely because she can tell it won't be pointless griping.

"I was wondering...why do you suppose these soldiers go along with these reckless offensives?"

"I guess I'd say the Communists are merely hard to understand. It's not impossible to reason out their line of thought. But anything beyond that is tricky for us normal people. I have no idea why they think that way." It's when she murmurs, sounding fed up, "I really wonder what's on their minds," that it happens.

"Er, Colonel?" The one speaking is Lieutenant Serebryakov, who is standing by next to Tanya. She nervously makes a suggestion. "If...you have a question, then what if you tried asking them directly?"

In a way, it's a supremely reasonable idea. It's rare to have access to an intelligence source as useful as a prisoner.

But Tanya is forced to consider the nuisance of the language barrier.

And even if she could theoretically overcome it, the Federation is a multiethnic state... The prisoners' "official Federation language" is often heavily accented. Maybe to a native speaker it seems like just another dialect, but interpreting it is practically impossible with only basic language education.

Language really is an obnoxious issue… is what Tanya's thinking when suddenly, she recalls Lieutenant Serebryakov's background. Since her family entered the Empire as refugees, she must speak native Federation language.

But Tanya still turns her down for now. She may not have asked herself, but the Imperial Army had questioned prisoners along the same lines before.

The Feldgendarmerie hasn't been slacking on that count.

"I'm grateful for the suggestion, but they're already doing that. The Feldgendarmerie is surveying them."

"So what are they fighting for?"

"Good question, Lieutenant Serebryakov. I read the reports because I was wondering the same thing, but…it turns out we have no idea."

"A report from the Feldgendarmerie? I beg your pardon, Colonel, but may I see it?"

"Sure, I don't mind." Tanya hands over the document, and after scanning it, Serebryakov silently looks up at the ceiling.

She's so smooth, she even gives a little sigh.

"…Lieutenant Serebryakov?"

"Here you go, Colonel."

"Hmm." Tanya takes what she discovers is a handwritten note. It looks like the sort of simple note she would get from the MPs after an interrogation…

"It's the outcome of briefly questioning some prisoners the Kampf-gruppe captured just a bit ago."

"Hmm? Oh, you did some quick questioning before handing them over to the MPs…? Huh?" Tanya does more than a double take, rubs her eyes. "That's strange…," she murmurs. She could really use some eye drops.

The soldiers were talking in their normal, natural voices.

To be frank, Tanya has never read anything like this before.

She's looked over mountains of MP reports, but she doesn't remember ever seeing a single one featuring "normal soldiers."

…It was a mistake to unconsciously assume it was because they were interrogating Communists. I had made up my mind that they were all committed to their ideology, but the notes from Serebryakov indicate the exact opposite.

What Tanya sees in the notes are normal soldiers answering the questions they are asked in a matter-of-fact way. There are no "Communists" to be found.

Just people.

Just raw soldiers.

In a nutshell, individuals.

In the reports Tanya has read up until now, the answers were standardized as if they had received resistance to interrogation training. What's going on when they talk to Serebryakov?!

...It's like they transformed from robots into humans.

"Wait a minute, Lieutenant Serebryakov. It's not that I doubt you, but you're saying you questioned these prisoners yourself?"

"Yes, we asked a few people, mainly noncommissioned officers, about their ranks and units. Some of them kept silent, but overall you can expect them to be fairly cooperative. You can even acquire intelligence through small talk during the interrogation."

How wonderfully proactive and inventive. This is what an officer should be like. Nodding in satisfaction, Tanya continues, "So then. You're saying that apart from the political commissars, they all put some distance between themselves and the 'Communists'?"

"Strictly speaking, they don't support the current party."

"Sure, I don't care about definitions. In any case, the guys who are supposed to be resisting as fanatical Communists actually detest the party? Was it a penal battalion or something?"

Given the unit the rebellious men were in, Tanya guesses they must be an old regime faction.

But her adjutant's reply catches her off guard.

"Judging from their badges, they were regular army, and not only that but a unit mentioned in the Eastern Army Group's intelligence documents."

"You're sure of that?"

"Yes." The reply is resolute and contains the pride of an expert who is confident in their words.

...What the hell? Tanya pinpoints something unsettling inside her.

She has overlooked something.

"Gather the documents right away and make arrangements for an officers' meeting. Lieutenant Serebryakov, can I see you for a moment?" Tanya asks. "If this is true, there's no way to explain why the Federation Army isn't collapsing. If their faith in their state's framework is shaken, why do they keep resisting so stubbornly?" Tanya nearly continues with *How can this be?* but shakes her head and stands up. "A picture is worth a thousand words. Guess I have no choice but to take a look for myself."

Her subordinates absentmindedly acknowledge her.

As if to ask them, *Were you not listening to what I was saying?* Tanya sighs and breaks down her intentions for them.

"...Major Weiss, I want you to come with me. Lieutenant Serebryakov, you can interpret, right? You come, too."

And so the heads of the Kampfgruppe appeared before the captured enemy soldiers.

The attitude of the restrained noncommissioned officers was rather nervous but not exactly brimming with hostility. Maybe it was more accurate to say they were thinking about the future in the abstract.

But Tanya decides she might be able to have a fascinating conversation with them.

She is cautious, but incredibly optimistic.

Major Weiss is going to perform the interrogation, since he can make the scariest faces.

He's a decorated, mid-ranking magic officer, so he's the perfect interrogator. They hastily throw an enemy soldier into the room in one of the garrison buildings that has been designated for questioning, and the conversation unfolds as Tanya watches from the back.

"Oh, an officer? Could I trouble you for a cigarette? I ran out a long time ago..."

"Sorry. I belong to an aerial mage battalion."

"An aerial mage battalion? Surely in the Imperial Army a unit like that is well supplied."

"I can't deny that, but regulations prohibit smoking because it ruins your lungs. We're not allowed to carry cigarettes."

Shrugging his shoulders and apologizing, Weiss takes an unmarked white paper box out of his breast pocket and nonchalantly places it on the table.

Saying how sorry he is to disappoint the prisoner, he pushes the box toward him with quite the practiced motion... Soldiers at war have an incorrigible but very real love of cigarettes. I can't be critical of their personal tastes.

Nevertheless, it should probably be said... There are almost no smokers in any aerial mage battalion, much less the 203rd. The high altitudes and low oxygen concentration they encounter regularly are bad enough. Hence, Weiss's acquisition of cigarettes as a tool is praiseworthy.

"Oh, well, nothing to do about that, then. Could you at least lend me a light?"

"What? You don't even have your own lighter? Sheesh, here you go."

It's a silly exchange, but the technique shortens the distance between the questioner and the prisoner. The smoke is unpleasant, but I have to prioritize results over my personal preferences this time.

"Now then, tell me something. What are you guys—no, what are *you* fighting for? For the Federation?"

Keep observing. Tanya watches over the proceedings as Weiss asks the question and Serebryakov interprets.

"Me and the other guys all fight for ourselves. Isn't that obvious? ...We're fighting for a better future."

"A better future?"

"If we beat you guys, our society should improve somewhat."

That must be the message the enemy is sending with their propaganda. *It may not be completely new, but it's important information.* Just as Tanya is about to nod...

"...Let me rephrase the question. You think your society will improve by fighting us? Why? Do you believe in Communism?"

The moment Serebryakov translates Weiss's casual question, the atmosphere grows strange.

"...Yes, sir. About as much as you guys do!"

...Wait a second.

What did he just say?

"What a witty reply. But I understand even less now."

"What in the world is there to not understand?"

Weiss smiles wryly, as if to say *C'mon*, but asks, "Why are you fighting for Communism?"

Yes, that's the question. Where do they get the spirit to fight for an ideology they don't even believe in?

Weiss, the observer Tanya, and the attending interpreter Serebryakov all want to know the same thing.

Even if Tanya isn't personally dedicated to the Empire's history, traditions, or norms, she finds the current regime better than the alternatives, and it's her intention to support it.

Which is why this makes no sense. How can they fight for a no-good state?

"Hey, Mr. Major. You stupid or something?"

"Hmm?"

Weiss's blank-faced reaction aside, the enemy soldier's question sends a chill up Tanya's spine.

"Who doesn't have feelings about their homeland? How can you even argue this point? Am I wrong? I don't think so!"

…It's not for the party. Not for the party but for my homeland.

"Just to confirm, you're fighting for 'your homeland'?"

"I heard imperial soldiers were smart, but I guess you can't believe every rumor you hear. You're about on the level of the political commissars."

"That's a pretty dramatic way to put it."

Weiss, flustered by the sarcasm, and Serebryakov diligently interpreting no longer appear in Tanya's field of vision.

Don't make light of the word's Logos.

It has the power to change the world. When the frame, the paradigm, has its logic knocked out from under it, a shift must occur.

"Do you need a reason to fight for your hometown? Plus, if we do a good job, those annoying idiots in the party will have to listen to us at least a little bit."

"So if you defeat the Empire, your lives will get better?"

"Don't you think? I mean, the party is only so headstrong about everything right now so they can face you guys. Once we don't need to fight you anymore, things should get better."

"Hmm, very interesting. Now then, I'd like to hear a little bit about the unit you belong to…"

The conversation between Weiss, Serebryakov, and the enemy soldier continues.

But Tanya doesn't care anymore. What matters is the truth she learned.

Our enemies, the Federation soldiers, aren't Communists at all.

That one sentence.

That right there is the key.

And she hates this feeling of being shown how incorrigibly wrong she was.

After the interrogation ended and once the enemy soldier had been sent away, Tanya can only stare absentmindedly up at the room's ceiling.

"Colonel?"

Her subordinates are probably worried about her. She would understand that under normal circumstances.

But right now, it's impossible.

"...Fucking hell!"

The curse is directed at herself and her country's carelessness.

"So they've thrown their ideology away to fight a 'great patriotic war'! No wonder they're so raring to fight, then! Argh, damn it! What the hell!"

Her second-in-command looks at her blankly. If this was combat, Major Weiss would pick up on her intentions and react right away, so she's frustrated by his lack of comprehension.

Why doesn't he see how important this is?

"You don't get it?! We've been fighting nationalists this whole time as if they were Communists!" she spits.

The significance of that: a nationalist war. The more she thinks about it, the more she wants to curl up in a ball.

This was a complete mistake.

This is idiocy of the finest order, foolishness that will make it into the history books.

Weiss sinks into thought next to her and will probably figure it out eventually. She knows he has a decent head on his shoulders.

But she doesn't have time to wait around for him to think things through at his leisure.

"We, the Empire, have been fighting a completely different enemy! We're helping them, not beating them."

"Our actions were benefiting the Federation...? Could that really be true?"

"Major Weiss. The way we've been fighting so far, the more we win, the more unified the enemy grows. We thought that if we won, it would chip away at their will to fight, but we were wrong! It doesn't lead to their collapse, but the reverse! It stimulates their solidarity and makes their resistance even stronger!"

When fighting an ideology, all that's necessary to win is to attack the validity or the righteousness of that ideology. And the flaws in Communism have been proven. At least, Tanya is personally convinced. It's not difficult to show how inefficient Communism is.

But fighting with nationalism is no good.

"...What did he say? 'Who doesn't have feelings about their homeland?'"

"Yes, the prisoner did say that."

The fatherland is in crisis. We can't say that the Federation's people don't disapprove of or doubt the party or feel angry. But more than that, the citizens have been roused by their fatherland's desperation. We were convinced we were fighting Communists, but they have the fire of nationalism burning in their hearts.

Nationalism isn't logical. It's emotional, passionate.

Attacking Communism is like fueling the fire of their nationalism. Once that happens, even if the nationalists hate the Communist Party, they will still unite against the Empire, their common enemy.

Yes, we truly have been helping them.

"What a huge mistake. I should have realized sooner."

Apparently, Serebryakov has a much higher language ability than the guys in the Feldgendarmerie. She picks up the minute implications that might be lost in a literal translation and delivers suitable interpretations of the meaning.

A proper interpreter, a proper translator is a must, especially to grasp the core essence of the message. They say the devil is in the details, and I think that holds true for conversations as well.

The Federation soldier wasn't hiding anything; he said it straight out.

"We're fighting for our homeland."

"This makes my head hurt. Why didn't anyone realize this?"

This must be what it feels like to whine without even meaning to.

What kind of mistake did the Feldgendarmerie MPs need to make to interpret this as "They're fighting for their ideology"? It could be because they didn't dig into the prisoners' responses that they were fighting to protect the Federation. It might also be that they aren't as good at interpreting as Serebryakov.

Ohhh, crap. Tanya makes one correction.

"The MPs are always chasing after Communists. They have experience with them at home, so it's no wonder they were convinced from the start."

Year in and year out, MP units are conducting counterinsurgency against cells of domestic Communists back home. In the MPs' minds, Communism and the Federation had become one and the same without them even realizing it.

"So the Feldgendarmerie has been conditioned to uncritically connect anything with the Federation's fingerprints on it to Communism?"

"Conditioned, ma'am?"

"In other words, it's like assuming that just because a bell rings, it's time to eat."

Our guard dogs have developed an awfully peculiar habit. It's really quite a pain in the neck. Thanks to them, we're stuck in this difficult spot.

"They associate Communism with the very word *Federation*. Does that mean...the work they usually do misled them?"

"That's what I think, Major Weiss."

If she wasn't in front of her subordinates, Tanya would cradle her head and sigh. But she let them see a glimpse of her anger already. As an officer and commander, she can't conduct herself so disgracefully.

Swallowing many of the things she wants to say, Tanya instead declares they'll look into it. "Lieutenant Serebryakov, sorry, but I'd like you and Lieutenant Grantz to reinterrogate the prisoners. I want to do a thorough analysis of the enemy psyche," she continues with a bitter smile. "I'd like to ask them myself. But I only have a smattering of Federation language ability from the short accelerated course at the academy. I can't flatter myself and say I'm capable of picking up subtle emotions."

The Feldgendarmerie must have been conceited.

Those types do exist. There's no doubt because I know idiots who make a mess of things due to the difference between studying a language and actually speaking it. Even though I worked in HR, I had to struggle with the same issue. We had to be able to speak English or we couldn't do our jobs. There are so many people who brag they're good at languages even though they couldn't score that many points. And the parade of idiots who then fail to communicate in the language they're supposedly good at is never-ending. It was so sad I always wanted to scream, *Know your limits!*

"In that sense, it's really great that we have Visha."

Tanya nods emphatically in response to Weiss's remark and responds with "Indeed."

Near-native ability in a language might seem vague and difficult to grasp from a pure data perspective, but when someone can comprehend an essential point, you can really tell the difference.

I never thought I'd be tormented by language issues during a war. Geez, the people who thought to build the Tower of Babel and the god who destroyed it can all eat shit. Anyone driving up communication costs is an enemy of society.

A question from Serebryakov, however, sends Tanya's righteous indignation out the window. "But, Colonel, may I ask why you want Lieutenant Grantz to do the interrogation?"

"What?"

"The subtleties of emotion appear in more than just words. I realize you're busy, Colonel, but if we could capture those subtleties, wouldn't it be better to have you with me?"

Lieutenant Serebryakov suggests that in order to grasp the emotions the prisoners reveal, it would be better for me to interrogate them personally. Certainly, under normal circumstances that might be the case.

The Federation soldiers' will to fight is a serious problem.

The Federation Army is putting up a repetitive, crude, yet fierce resistance along the entire front. If we could get a handle on their combat psychology, we might even be able to crack their mental defenses. I'm sure the General Staff would be terribly interested in that.

The Imperial Army is desperate for accurate intelligence.

But Tanya spits, "Listen, Lieutenant Serebryakov. Look at me."

"Huh?"

Her subordinates look puzzled.

"Look at me, guys."

As she is about to say, *You don't get it?* she realizes this is a waste of time. Apparently, not a single one of them has any idea what she's getting at. She inadvertently sighs at their lack of understanding.

Of course, she collected the members of the 203rd Aerial Mage Battalion based on their fanaticism for war, not for their empathy or thoughtfulness... If she chose them for their combat abilities, she can't very well be upset at them for *their ignorance of emotional subtlety.*

Although it is annoying.

"Guys, I look like a kid!"

"...Mm."

Grantz apparently has no clue what I'm talking about, and Sere-bryakov looks confused. *If both the lieutenants are no good...* She turns to her vice commander but immediately thinks to herself, *Tch, he's worthless, too?*

She's explained this to some extent before, but apparently they all forgot. Maybe they shoved it into a corner of their minds because it didn't have anything to do with combat. This is the problem with war freaks.

"Major Weiss, I'm a child. They may not take me seriously based on my appearance. I'd really like for you to realize such things before I have to say them..."

"Huh? Oh! V-very sorry, Colonel."

>>>> THE SAME DAY, THE SALAMANDER KAMPFGRUPPE'S GARRISON, THE <<<<
COMMANDER'S ROOM

And so, Tanya holes up in the space she's been allotted for her personal use to think. Coffee is on hand.

The smell, out of place on a battlefield, hangs lightly in the Kampf-gruppe commander's room. The mellow fragrance of the arabica beans from Colonel Uger, the brew's unadulterated flavor. Normally, she keeps the beans refrigerated and drinks in tiny sips to make it last; this coffee is a rarity from her personal stash. But just for today, she's gulping it down like standard-issue muck water; she can't even taste it.

What she's staring at with a pale face are the transcripts of the prisoner interrogations First Lieutenants Serebryakov and Grantz did. Tanya was somewhat prepared. She had guessed the report's conclusion to some extent at the time she ordered the survey.

Still, she can't help but grit her teeth. Subjectively, we've been fighting Communists. Which is why we've been fighting to break the Communists' spirit. And why we're doing that even now.

But the Federation soldiers are fighting for their homeland in the name of ethnic nationalism.

"I'm such a fool."

It's impossible for Tanya to ridicule herself even if she wants to. She's that huge of an idiot. Who is? Me. I am.

Overlooking the fact that we were failing to fight what we should have been? A fool who understood neither the enemy nor myself? Yes, me of all people.

At that moment, Tanya von Degurechaff screams in her room.

"Those bastards got us!"

We've been tricked.

"Damn Communists, of all things—of *all* things—you took our cause away!"

Usually, Communists endlessly criticize nationalism. They crow that the truth of the world is not represented properly in ethnic nationalism, when it's actually a class war, as viewed from the perspective of scientific history. How careless of me to assume they followed such a creed! Embarrassment is only the beginning for something like this. I'm so angry I want to shoot my past self.

"Why didn't I realize something so obvious?! How did I miss it?!"

I'm aware that I'm not controlling my emotions very well.

But...there are times when you just want to pound the table and scream. I'm so disappointed in my rawness and my contemptible carelessness. This is the definition of an untenable position.

What a stupid situation.

I should have known how easy it is for Communists to cast off their policies! I keep asking myself how I could have forgotten—it's that grave of a mistake.

Unconsciously, or perhaps she has merely closed her eyes...

"This is the worst."

…Tanya von Degurechaff weakly curses her failure.

They got me.

Now I can't scoff at people who get tricked by Commie propaganda. They really had me going, meaning I'm no different from those schmucks.

No, I know how the Communist Party works, so my error is incomparably worse… I'm simply incompetent. This is the fruit of indefensible stupidity. No matter what I say to excuse myself, I can't trick my own heart.

I shouldn't have been going on about analyzing the situation in enemy territory with such a worldly-wise look on my face.

I have to oppose the mobile offensive.

It's not even an issue of winter anymore.

Penetrating farther into enemy territory will only unite the enemy further.

"Annihilating their field army? Impossible."

I need an alternative to suggest instead. And quickly—as soon as possible.

"Let's take a historical view. There are extremely few instances where a relatively small regular army was able to get guerrillas under control… And even the examples of success that we have are only *limited* victories."

In Vietnam, even the American empire's overwhelming matériel resources couldn't solve the issue. In Afghanistan, the Soviet and American armies proved how difficult it is to maintain control over mountainous regions. It was only an option to burn down whole resisting cities like the Mongols during eras when the law of war didn't exist yet.

Nowadays, our hands are tied.

If you look for an example of counterinsurgency that ended in victory, you have the British Army in their colonies in Malaya, but those were colonies, so…*hmm?*

"Colonies? Yes, colonies. Where the suzerain state is the minority. You can rule with small numbers through military, but…"

Ohhh, thinks Tanya, forced to realize that her brain is depressingly rusty.

It's simple, isn't it?

To be perfectly honest, there's no need to take them all on.

"We'll divide and conquer."

"Hoo-hoo-hoo." Tanya laughs because she has it completely figured out. But in one respect, it's also the plain truth. If you succeed in dividing the enemy, the number you have to fight is smaller. If we do it right, we might even be able to use some of them as allies.

And for better or worse, the Federation is a multiethnic state.

If, beneath the pretty words *ideal Communism*, the party is suppressing the self-determination movements of different ethnic groups...it might be possible to forge an alliance. If we're merely speaking about the possibilities, any of the ethnic minorities within the Federation could potentially become imperial allies.

"After all, we're not asking for their land. Frankly, the Empire is like a big hikikomori. Its interests don't come into conflict with ethnic groups within Federation territory that want independence."

That's how we solve it.

"I found the answer! I found the way out!"

All I can do is race forward.

A state has no eternal allies and no perpetual enemies.
Only its interests are eternal and perpetual.

Saying borrowed from
3rd Viscount Palmerston

The moment Colonel Tanya von Degurechaff enters the General Staff Office, she heads straight for the office of Lieutenant General von Zettour, with whom she has an appointment.

Even describing them generously, her steps can't be called light. Of course, the flight over the long distance from the east to the capital is tiring. But even the physical fatigue of transferring between transport planes and flying herself for part of the trip is nothing compared to her worn-down mental state.

Out the window, the sky is overcast.

If Being X is maliciously pulling strings, then he has an appallingly good understanding of our situation.

I really hate when the sky is like this. It expresses my mental state too accurately.

But if the sky represents my current feelings, then will it clear up?

Will that day come eventually?

No, I have to get past these gripes.

Colonel Tanya von Degurechaff must admit her mistake as the deeply shameful truth that it is. It's humiliating and a complete blunder, but she would hesitate to hide it.

Only people who are truly incompetent hide their mistakes.

A hopeless fool. Oversize garbage. Execution by firing squad wouldn't be enough punishment. No matter what words I use, they don't cut it.

Accidents happen when small mistakes are repeatedly covered up. An organization that hides small mistakes will eventually be done in by a mishap too huge to conceal.

Humans are creatures who make mistakes.

If you don't admit your mistake, that mistake will crush you.

Which is why, or more like, "therefore…" The only way to deal with imbeciles who hide their mistakes is to shoot them. I'd really *like* to shoot inept workers, but imbeciles who hide mistakes *must* be shot.

That's a self-evident truth.

Rather than a saying or axiom, it's more something proven by humans through the experience society has acquired.

Though it may not be perfect, I have a modern intellect. Rather than be the bungler who hides her mistake, I am forced to be the bungler who reports it.

Thus, even if Lieutenant Colonel Tanya von Degurechaff is ashamed, she has to redeem her failure.

"I'll be frank, General. We killed too many. But luckily…it's not so late in the game that we have to give up on changing policy."

"I thought total war was decided by the weight of the enemy corpse pile."

He's right.

General von Zettour's understanding of total war is *completely correct.* There's no better strategy than to pile up enemy corpses.

But if the premises change, then the correct answer also changes. That's why she has to report the mistake she discovered.

"As you say, sir. But I think decreasing the number of our enemies with words is cheaper than using bullets."

If someone is an enemy, there's nothing to do but kill them. But that's only if they're really an enemy.

For better or worse, Tanya is partial to streamlining. If there is a lower-cost option, that's the correct one.

"We need to keep the home country's resource situation and production capacity issues in mind. We need to rethink our habit of approving the indiscriminate scattering of bullets."

Words are a much lighter burden for logistics than bullets.

Divide and conquer.

The first thing in support of that great principle is words.

Words, language, names, and propaganda played a critical role in the rule of the colonies of those only-partial-to-sports-and-war tea nuts, right?

"If we don't have to send them from the home country, then that certainly is cheaper."

Considering the labor and materials that went into making a single bullet, plus the costs of transporting them to the front lines, this was the correct approach to prepare.

From the logistics perspective, Lieutenant General Hans von Zettour thinks Tanya's idea is fine.

"But, Colonel. The issue here is not only cost but also utility."

With the expectation of results as a proviso.

"Utility, General?"

"Bullets have a physical function. Ideological arguments haven't been very effective in the countryside—even with the General Staff and Supreme Command working together."

It's only natural that a decent soldier would want to drive a wedge into the hostile Federation. It'd be weirder not to.

The Imperial Army is a precise apparatus of violence.

The Empire is on the ball when it comes to waging war. As part of that, the General Staff has been working on pacification efforts from the early stages. General von Zettour himself had even ordered a study on psychological warfare and inspected the results.

But honestly, there were no results. We haven't had any successes. Which is why while admitting that he understands where she's coming from, Zettour declares, "Frankly, Logos falls silent in wartime."

"General, don't you think that unlike law, Logos *can* be heard during wartime?"

"...Maybe in theory, but you know..." His next remark is difficult to categorize as affirmative. "To be candid with you, we started in with the same anti-Communist pacification program as we use in the home country almost immediately after the war started, but...we haven't gotten any results. There's probably room to consider it research, but it's not ready to be counted as a practical option."

Logos, words, reason, logic. It's terrifying, but Zettour is shaking his head that they haven't been fruitful.

"Anti-Communist pacification efforts, sir?"

Those words speak to how, though words are a weapon, they're far from perfect. *Ahhh.* Tanya sighs as she opens her mouth.

That's a terrible misunderstanding.

The weapon known as words is complete. No, she can declare that it has even been combat proven.

Chapter II

The Imperial Army and its General Staff fail to realize that because of their intelligence. Intelligent people, due to their superior intellect, often fall prey to this fallacy. Illusions that trap you because you're reasonable are so insidious.

...I've realized that textbook knowledge is often a fantasy because some smart, reasonable person wrote it with reasonable individuals in mind. Humans are usually the virtual opposite of reasonable.

"Yes. The Feldgendarmerie is taking the lead with it. If you're interested, I can give you the verification results."

"General von Zettour, I predict that that is precisely our bias. Please toss these anti-Communist pacification efforts straight into the trash," Tanya quietly declares, although it does pain her slightly that she was also a prisoner of the anti-Communist view in the beginning.

Of course it does.

After all, she herself was so sure they were up against Communists that she believed it to be self-evident. But she should have been deeply skeptical and required proof for everything.

Yes, it's necessary to treat axioms, self-evident premises, and the like as assumptions.

We committed the folly of assuming our enemies were Communists. In reality, not a single enemy soldier has given any indication of seriously believing in Communism. It's a contradiction.

We should have observed more closely and realized. The price for letting our assumptions cloud our eyes is enormous for an already huge error.

But I've figured it out now.

So I have a duty as an intelligent being. The unproven axiom and the contradiction occurring in reality must be reconciled.

"I don't think the ideology matters one bit."

As Zettour urges her to explain, the look in his eyes is one of confusion.

"It's not reason that's important, General, but the people's emotion."

As a weapon, words work just like bullets. Shooting where there's no target is just a waste of precious resources.

An apparatus of violence must use its weapons effectively.

"Our pacification efforts shouldn't be something that chips away at their hostility toward us but something that divides them."

"You're saying it's not ideology sustaining this war?"

"Exactly. The enemy's mainstay is nationalism *masquerading as ideology*. We're missing the mark by criticizing their ideology, so it makes sense that we're not currently seeing results."

Going by what she's seen in the field, Tanya has given up on ideology-based attacks as wasted bullets. If you have a contradiction that can't be resolved, it's almost certainly an issue with your premises.

If the base upon which you're building your assumptions is wrong, you have to admit your mistake despite the shame.

Why would you expect to be able to build a decent structure atop a rotten foundation? I swear on my modern intellect and rationality that I couldn't stand to construct a condemned building to show off my ineptitude like some masochist. For a decent person like me, that would be sheer unendurable suffering.

Which is why Tanya has to accept her shame and tell her superior officer.

"Our only hope is to distinguish the Communists from the rest. We won't be able to get away with idly viewing the enemy as Communists."

"So divide and conquer, then?"

"Conquer? General, isn't that joke a bit much? Why in the world should the Empire have to take over?"

Administrative services, by their nature, are not an industry that brings about profit.

But it's true that in an occupied territory, the military government must carry out minimal maintenance of social order, application of the infrastructure, and so on.

Up until now, Tanya has just barely accepted those things as necessary costs. It irritates her to admit that it's an emergency where market functions are paralyzed, but she understands that's why maintenance is necessary.

But, she adds with conviction.

Ruling is out of the question. Management via military government is already putting an excessive burden on their organization. Conquer?! If we tried to do that, the army would disintegrate. From there, it's a straight shot to being an understaffed unethical corporation.

"General von Zettour, if we try to conquer, our military org will collapse from exhaustion before we even fight. What we need is a wonderful friend to whom we can outsource."

There's no need whatsoever for the Empire to conquer. Every man to his trade; personnel management must be optimized.

"...That's an interesting thing to say, but unfortunately the Empire doesn't have many friends."

"Then we just need to make some."

"When you get older, it's not so easy."

These pesky problems keep holding us back. It's a bit late to worry about acquiring friendly state relations with so much historical baggage making things difficult.

On the other hand, I suppose, there are frequently alternative ways to use one's given conditions. You may be convinced something is useless, but if you change your point of view, you find a way. Poison can be medicine depending on how it's used.

Even the extremely harmful drug thalidomide, which caused birth defects, was effective against some diseases. *And that's exactly why...* Tanya continues with confidence, "But if we build up trust and results, though, maybe we can meet someone. Don't you think it's possible for us to meet a new friend?"

"What?"

"Don't we have the resource of old enemies?"

There's a saying in diplomacy: *The enemy of my enemy is my friend.* That may only mean your interests overlap, but overlapping interests are reason enough for two nations to become friends.

"Given the Empire's traditional international relations, no one doubts that the Federation is an enemy. So we might be able to cultivate friendships with the antiestablishment factions within it."

"The Federation is a multiethnic state, but...are you arguing that we should try to achieve solidarity with separatists inside it?"

"Yes, General."

"I see your logic, but Colonel, the issue is whether we can apply what's written in the textbooks in the field."

Tanya nods that she understands. It's not what Zettour said, but she knows that textbooks provide only one possible answer under one set of circumstances.

You only get points for following the textbook in school.

What people want from you in the field, once you go to the front lines, is results. Any idiot whining that it's not his fault because he did it according to the textbook should be given a swift kick.

"Certainly, the Federation is our enemy. But just because someone is an enemy of our enemy doesn't automatically make them our ally."

She does have to agree—he's right. It's only logical that even if you have a common enemy, the question of whether you can achieve solidarity or not still remains.

"After all," Zettour continues with a sigh, "it doesn't even seem like the separatists distinguish between us and the Federation authorities."

True, that's an extremely important thing to note.

And in reality, the advancing Imperial Army has been ordered to avoid conflict with the locals to the extent possible, but...the troops have made a lot of mistakes. From seeing how the Feldgendarmerie was operating, Tanya can easily understand why.

"The cause of that is simple. General, we're nothing but armed outsiders. With no one who can mediate, trouble is unavoidable."

In terms of having someone who can talk to them, the Empire is at a hopeless level. A mediator, a negotiator we could trust, or at least an interpreter who could facilitate communication... We should have gone in with someone like that. But we're currently lacking in that department.

"We're completely missing the boat when it comes to language in our pacification strategy." *Of all things...* Tanya reflects bitterly on their situation.

In the Imperial Army, there is currently no one who can converse with people on the ground. We're at the stage of hurriedly pulling someone from the Foreign Office, but we'll be lucky if we get someone who has set foot on a battlefield a couple of times. As for someone who can negotiate, we're only just starting to consider where we might even look.

"Officers should be able to speak the Federation's official language, though."

"Yes, General, as you point out...we have learned a tiny bit of Federation language, but..."

Tanya knows the grave truth. To the antiestablishment factions in the Federation, the official language is the language of the enemy.

"General, we're speaking to allies in the enemy's language. It's folly."

"…You're saying we shouldn't use the official language?"

Tanya nods yes, her mood grim.

She wants translators who speak the languages of the antiestablishment factions' ethnicities, but she knows how well that is likely to go, because she had Serebryakov look into it.

Any specialists in those languages are probably professors in the Empire's universities. Minority languages are only one field that linguistics experts study. They won't be able to build a program of systematic language education overnight. In short, it will be a hopelessly long time before the army will be able to talk to these people.

"So it's a structural weakness in the Imperial Army because we didn't anticipate expeditions in foreign lands due to our foundational interior lines strategy."

"Frankly, I don't think our longtime defense strategy is a problem. The issue isn't interior lines strategy in and of itself. The root of many of these problems is that *we didn't follow through on it and instead sent troops across the border.*" Tanya points out the truth. "At least interior lines strategy will continue to prove effective."

"That's fine, Colonel von Degurechaff. So what's our plan?"

"Our task is clear. We must acquire competence in deploying soldiers abroad, whether we want to or not. And regarding occupation by military government, we should try to improve things as soon as possible and seek new friends in our occupied territories."

It's not as if Tanya isn't aware that she's asking a lot.

Whether they want to install a puppet or back a friendly power, if the key player isn't present, the plan won't even get off the ground.

"Colonel von Degurechaff. You know how few people there are willing to cooperate with the Imperial Army. Do you think you can find the right person under these conditions?"

"I believe it's possible."

Zettour urges her to explain.

Perhaps it's the product of all his hard thinking? His eyes look wise as he stares at her, unflinching.

So Tanya proceeds logically.

"General von Zettour, it's true that we've already had issues with residents of occupied areas. As a result, they're also somewhat blood-thirsty and hateful, but...they have someone to compare us to."

"Someone to compare us to?"

"The Federation government. Frankly, in a choice between the heartless Communists and the violent Imperial Army, I think the people are levelheaded enough to choose the latter."

"So you're thinking radically, then. Very well, let's suppose we're able to join forces with them. Are you saying that our method of occupation should be to make use of the local forces?"

"Yes." Tanya nods, and Zettour sinks into quiet thought as if mulling over her words before shaking his head to indicate it would be difficult.

"Frankly, I can't see the advantage. I'll give you my view as someone keeping logistics working in the rear. If we're not sure if someone is a friend or foe, in a way, it's much easier to deal with them as a foe."

To that opinion, all she can do is sigh. If a fool were uttering it out of foolishness, she would be able to laugh it off as absurd.

The reason she sighs is simple.

"You make a good point, but as for whether they're friends or foes, they're definitely friends."

General von Zettour is a strategist and the polar opposite of a fool.

He's a great man who understands the field of operations, is well versed in the affairs of logistics, and even keeps busy working on relations between the government and the military as the leading figure in the Service Corps. You can't really call him one of those guys who are biased toward the army in all respects, who are pro—any kind of force; at any rate, he's someone in Berun who can bring the arguments between military officers and civil servants to a compromise.

Even someone so competent is, with perfect composure, saying things that I am forced to declare mistaken?

Is the Imperial Army's paradigm so problematic?

"What...? Colonel von Degurechaff. I never thought the day would come that I'd have to point something out to you. There is a mountain of reports from the Feldgendarmerie on the ground. Read whichever one you like."

"You mean those guys who can't tell friend from foe?"

"Yes."

This is the kind of thing that makes people go, *Agh*.

The cause of this is simple. The mistakes are getting mixed together. General von Zettour's conclusion is helplessly warped by puzzle pieces that don't fit.

"General, I'll be straight with you. Most of the MPs in the Feldgendarmerie can't even speak the official language of the Federation. All their mistakes of assumptions, prejudices, and relying on untrustworthy interpretation have resulted in a misunderstanding that might as well be called a delusion."

"…Go on."

"We need to sort out this situation. What we need is to be able to tell the difference between friend and foe. The vast majority of the ethnic minorities inside the Federation are more hostile toward the Communist Party than us. I don't think forming an alliance would be impossible. Which is why," Tanya declares, staring right back into her superior's eyes, "rather than employing hunting dogs, even excellent ones, with faulty noses, we should hire normal, local hunters who are well informed."

After a few seconds, thinking in silence, General von Zettour furrows his brow and says, "…That makes sense, although the question is whether such convenient hunters exist… But fine. Who, then? This is you, Colonel von Degurechaff, so I'm sure you have your eye on someone."

"Sir, I think the best would be the police organizations and national councils."

"That's a novel viewpoint, Colonel."

The look she gets is a stern one.

He must really not like that idea, Tanya frets inwardly. Are ideas that are perfectly reasonable to her still considered radical by the key people at the top of the Imperial Army?

"I'm sure you're aware, but the Feldgendarmerie considers those very bodies guerrilla hotbeds, and I've been told they need to be disarmed. At least, those are the reports coming in as we mop up the partisans."

Zettour's half-grumbled words exhibit—*aha!*—the approach of a good officer who endeavors to understand the troops' situation by reading reports.

But. Tanya musters her reply. There is one factor that Imperial Army members such as General von Zettour have no way of understanding.

"General, I think we need to change our point of view. Certainly, we are imperial subjects, whether we're from the east or the south. We all belong to the Reich."

"And?"

"It's true that both the police organization and the national council have guerrillas mixed in. So in that sense, maybe it makes sense to think that the people are standing up united against the invaders. _But_," Tanya declares forcefully. The documents on which General von Zettour is basing his understanding of the situation are fundamentally incorrect, from their very premises. "General, please listen. It's all a mistake."

If your premises are wrong, you'll be mistaken no matter how sharp and prudent of a strategist you are. There's no way for you to understand the actual circumstances correctly. When planning strategy, mistaken data analysis causes fatal discrepancies.

Correct information from the ground and a correct understanding of the situation must form your base.

"I'll speak from my experience fighting guerrillas. They do exist certainly, but not everyone who takes up arms is one of them."

Soldiers don't hesitate to take up arms.

They're educated to pick up whatever weapon is within reach and fight the enemy. It makes sense, since they're armed and disciplined at a nation's expense to be ready for combat. In fact, they have to be that way.

But civilians are different.

"General, please understand. In the region in question, weapons are considered tools for self-defense. The MPs find fault with weapons for self-defense, but...I don't understand their interpretation. To speak in extremes, it's the same as arresting everyone who puts a lock on their door."

"...Self-defense? Colonel, they're _Federation military rifles and submachine guns_."

"General! That precisely is the root of the misunderstanding."

"Hmm? Go on, Colonel."

"Please consider their situation! Of course the only weapons they can get currently are Federation Army castoffs! Do you really mean to say that their circumstances allow them to import small arms with proof of purchase from a vendor in a neutral country?"

The market principle is simple. Items of which there are a surplus supply will proliferate; it's practically historical truth. The people can acquire large amounts of Federation Army weapons cheaply from the Federation Army supply when they are cast off.

It's virtually inevitable that the people should buy guns for which it's easy to procure ammunition rather than expensive automatic pistols. To employ a phrase I don't much care for, you could even say it's the *invisible hand of God*.

Even under Zettour's sharp gaze, Tanya unwaveringly makes her declaration. "Only a terrible minority is taking up the arms they've acquired against the Imperial Army. General, what's playing out now is a scenario purposefully designed by the minority."

Where there's no fire, there's no smoke, but there are often malicious arsonist types who want to turn a tiny flare-up into a giant blaze. Isn't that how the Bolshevik lineage maintains itself?! I mean, it's totally their specialty.

"It's true that there are destructive elements trying to start what barely deserves to be called a resistance movement by fanning the flames of discord and distrust on both sides. The problem is not so much the resistance but rather that we're failing to apprehend the instigators."

"So most of them are opportunists? They're stirring up Federation cells that they may or may not...actually support?" Zettour nods with a huge grimace.

Even with a mind as sharp as his, I suppose it should be repeated that when basing decisions on mistaken premises, it's impossible to reach the correct answer.

A brief silence follows.

Keeping silent, Zettour looks up at the ceiling, begins moving his mouth to say something, swallows his words, and then finally gives a small sigh. "...I see what you're getting at. In other words: We are one. But the enemy may or may not be one, right?"

Tanya is relieved to hear him say that.

As could be expected, I suppose, General von Zettour's intellect is apparently unclouded.

That he could so quickly see the truth of a minority controlling the majority through fear...is even a surprise to Tanya.

"Yes, General von Zettour. Most of the enemy soldiers we questioned on the battlefield are fighting not for the party but for their ethnic group.

Chapter **II**

To put it another way, we don't have to go along with the delusion that every Federation civilian is an enemy."

"…That's headache-worthy news. If it's true, we're fools. We've committed yet another strategic blunder that we should have avoided."

"I apologize for taking so long to get a handle on what was really going on. I leave whether I should resign or not up to you."

"No, there's no need for that. On the contrary, you did a fine job realizing all this. We figured it out before it was too late. Let's consider ourselves lucky."

I'm grateful for his consolation, but at the same time, it's a keen reminder of my incompetence. My loathing of Communists caused a serious issue.

My prejudices severely warped my observations, which should have been objective.

Even Zettour's words speak to the gravity of our failure. If we were "lucky," then that means we avoided disaster only by chance. We were saved by something as unreliable as luck?

We can't even say we were saved, then.

A mistake once made must be rectified, or it will be repeated.

Colonel von Degurechaff left with a composed salute, and after seeing her out, General von Zettour fell into silent thought for a time.

When he doubted their assumptions and considered the situation… it probably required immediate action. It wouldn't do to make the same mistake twice.

He reached for the receiver near at hand and said it was urgent. And when Colonel von Lergen appeared soon after, Zettour got straight to the point. "Colonel von Lergen, I want to change my next inspection destination."

"Yes, sir! I'll make the arrangements right away. Will that be the southern front you were anxious about? To observe General von Romel's operation?"

An excellent, ready response. It was natural that a member of the Operations Division would be thinking of the recently stagnant situation on the southern continent.

"No, the east."

"The east? Operations' inspection unit will be heading there in a few days. Are you going to go with them?"

Despite the fact that Zettour had launched straight into the business at hand, Lergen was able to offer a plan immediately. When it came to coordinating and providing assistance, Colonel von Lergen was a model staff officer.

But even he was mistaken. No, it was less that he was mistaken, more that he just had no way of knowing. If the fundamental terms in the east had changed, operation-level inspections would be meaningless. What they needed to do was revise the rules of the game.

Zettour shook his head to clear out extraneous thoughts and continued his concise explanation. "I intend to borrow you from Operations, but I don't have plans to accompany them. I'll talk to General von Rudersdorf. You just make the necessary preparations."

"Yes, sir! May I inquire as to our objective?"

Even if he has doubts, he swallows them as is appropriate. It's amazing that this mid-ranking officer can support Rudersdorf, with all his overflowing confidence. The only reason someone so irresponsible is so efficient at carrying out operations is his people. Under the circumstances, it'll be tough, but I would really like Lergen for a secret operation.

"Sure. We're going to inspect logistics administration in the rear area and also for one confidential matter… Oh, right. There's another favor I'd like to ask of you. Look for a specialist in ethnic group issues. The faster the better."

"Understood. Would the member of the National Congress we're seeking to cooperate with in Operations work?"

"I don't care, as long as we know for sure that they're not a spy. If possible, the best would be someone we can trust to maintain confidentiality."

"Do excuse me, General, but please allow me to ask a nosy question. From what you're saying, sir, it sounds like…the confidential matter has something to do with ethnic issues?"

"I won't deny it, Colonel. You can think of it as part of our pacification efforts. If possible, I'd like to consider meeting with leadership on the ground."

Chapter **II**

"Understood. We want someone who has connections in the area and can keep a secret. By when, sir?"

He's a quick one, thought General von Zettour with a smile. He was going to cause a lot of trouble for Colonel von Lergen, who was nodding that he had gotten it all through his head. But he didn't have a choice.

"The beginning of next week."

"G-General?" *But today's Friday* came through unsaid in Lergen's bewilderment. Zettour had called him up at the end of the day and ordered him to make arrangements by early Monday.

Of course he was bewildered.

But Zettour pressed the strict order on him and gave Lergen a firm look that said, *And what about it?* They were at war. In wartime, necessity trumps all else.

For an officer of the General Staff, carrying out their military duties with all due haste was their sacred duty.

"Sorry, but please get it set up. If need be, you can work the Service Corps personnel to the bone. Anyhow, we're short on time. Get going."

"Yes, sir. Right away."

>>> SOME DAY IN SEPTEMBER, UNIFIED YEAR 1926, ON THE OUTSKIRTS OF <<<
THE COMMONWEALTH CAPITAL LONDINIUM

The duties of an intelligence agency during wartime were manifold and include sharing and analyzing information with related national agencies, as well as gathering raw data.

Even just the collection of intelligence—military, economic, political, public opinion, technological, and so on—had become a subdivided world where only experts could tell the wheat from the chaff.

Chaos, chaos, and more chaos.

It wasn't easy to sift the precious stones out of a pile of rocks. Even the methods of collection were a complex mix of SIGINT and HUMINT.

Although budget restraints were being removed during the war, intelligence agencies were far from flush with cash. They would have to make do as best they could.

Even just pacifying the heads of each group, who were all convinced their own section was highest priority and deserved the most money, was a struggle in itself. Apparently, Intelligence staffers all have "strong" personalities... Finding someone cooperative was enough for him to want to thank God in spite of himself. Even a slight butting of heads between Intelligence and the Foreign Office was bound to upset his stomach.

But the leader of the Commonwealth's intelligence agency, Major General Habergram, thought he had accepted all that. So far, he had.

He earnestly believed that steady efforts to regulate things would ultimately bear fruit, and because of that, little by little, he had started to see results.

Currently, the SIGINT efforts to gather military intel were going fine. Their approaches toward enemy identification, jamming, and code breaking were getting results no one could complain about, except how they were eating excessively into the budget.

And even in terms of HUMINT, they had improved all their observation methods. Though there were as many challenges as ever in imperial territory, they had the former Republic covered.

They had a general handle on the movements of the Imperial Army units scattered all over each region.

Even the tricky business of collecting intel on the southern continent was solved when they dispatched a crack agent. He was an old man who grumbled and sent in complaints, but he was unexpectedly persistent.

He had organized multiple raids, albeit small in scale, on enemy supply lines... And the network of nomadic contacts was being built on schedule. Habergram could leave things up to him for the foreseeable future and have no problems.

Still, it had to be added. There was the inadequate budget, the internal and external arguments, the bureaucratic head-butting between sections. And to top it off, along with everything else, the plausible question of whether a mole had infiltrated their organization haunted him every night.

General Habergram had been suffering for a long time like a CEO in charge of a company about to go bankrupt.

And furthermore, aside from the mole issue—the *only* hopeless issue that had been endlessly haunting him since the war broke out— something else had mushroomed into a problem so difficult it was virtually impossible to handle.

"The budget but also just people. The intelligence agency is so under-staffed. At this rate, we're just…"

It was people. He didn't have enough people.

He wanted to puff on a cigar and gripe about the lack of capable people. And it wasn't just staff. They were also desperately short of management-level leaders and executives.

But although Intelligence had been facing a serious shortage of people since the war began…strictly speaking, they weren't understaffed in the beginning.

It was once they plunged into wartime that they became thoroughly lacking.

There were two reasons for that.

One was attrition due to war deaths.

It had been a huge mistake to dispatch task forces made up of old hands on joint operations with the Entente Alliance and Republic. They were all attacked by a special unit from the Reich identified as the 203rd Aerial Mage Battalion. The damage done by the loss of their invaluable veterans was extensive.

As they rebuilt the organization, educated personnel, and reconstructed their network, the undeniable truth was that he couldn't regret that heavy loss enough.

The Imperial Army had come out swinging with such perfect timing. Even General Habergram, though he didn't want to suspect his own subordinates…had to think there was a mole lurking in their org.

The Empire's luck had held out awfully long for it to be a coincidence.

The problem was, he hadn't yet managed to grasp the thing's tail. The moment he found this shameless mole, he intended to kill it dead.

All that was more than enough of a headache, but his suffering was compounded by the way the army and navy treated the remaining human resources.

The second issue was that all the veteran agents on loan from the army and navy had been taken back.

"Shit! I can't believe they would trip up their own allies…"

The army and navy said they were transferring all their personnel to the front lines and packed them off. Habergram would have liked to give them a piece of his mind.

"We don't have any people as trustworthy as the ones you need to work in Intelligence."

The logic made sense. But to then basically take them all away by force… The intelligence agency was in shambles.

Thanks to a double punch from both enemies and allies, there was a severe shortage of veteran agents.

As a result, almost immediately after the start of the war, Intelligence was nearly incapacitated by serious losses. Obnoxiously, the disorderly personnel changes were causing issues with the mole hunt.

As if not having anyone to trust didn't already have him at wit's end.

Though the ultra-confidential secret that they had broken the Imperial Army's code hadn't leaked, everything else had. He couldn't help but shudder.

No, with the sloppy state of their anti-espionage efforts, it wouldn't be strange for even top secret intel to leak anytime.

And even under these difficult circumstances, the requests for Intelligence kept coming in.

The Foreign Office was requesting "an urgent survey of the cooperative relationships between the Empire and other countries."

The Ministry of Supply had given strict orders to investigate "the Imperial Army's plans for commerce raids."

The Office of the Admiralty was fairly screaming at them to acquire "all manner of military intelligence on the Imperial Navy's submarines as well as the whereabouts of their fleet."

And as for the War Office, it was somehow managing to demand details from the ground on "the status of both the imperial and Federation forces in the east."

The cabinet was a cabinet, so each minister inquired after their own interests and areas of jurisdiction.

Of course, General Habergram understood that it was both an important job and a patriotic duty to do so. *And as a public servant, I respect that. But*, he was forced to lament.

Every section was convinced that their requests should be highest priority in this national crisis, and they didn't hesitate to stubbornly insist on a certain order of things.

Of course, if it were possible, he would want to cooperate. But as it was, he wanted to scream that he didn't have enough people. Even if he cried out for trustworthy personnel who had passed the screenings, there was no reply.

The strict order from the Committee of Commonwealth Defense was to do his best with what he had.

It made him want to hold his head in his hands.

No, that was all he could do.

He couldn't even send any Intelligence staff to the continent in the first place because he didn't have the bodies.

Which was why a plan was proposed to educate the replacements and transform them into a proper fighting force. Logically speaking, that was a sensible response—if you shut your eyes to the social trend of promising young newbies volunteering en masse for frontline service.

General Habergram himself was from a distinguished family.

He knew how their youth felt.

As one of their forerunners, it wasn't as if he felt no warmth at the manifestation of noblesse oblige.

When the youth left college to volunteer for their fatherland, he could only bow his head in respect of their determination and drive.

If there was a problem that he couldn't overlook, it was that the determination of the young people offering themselves up for their fatherland was too stubborn.

When all the bright students volunteered for the army to fulfill their sense of noblesse oblige, they applied for air units, mage units, service in the naval fleet, or frontline service in a ground unit and so on.

The conclusion was clear.

They had no interest in rear service. The more outstanding and patriotic, the more brimming with perseverance and intellectual capacity—precisely the traits the intelligence agency needed—the more likely it was that they wanted to stand at the head of the pack as a frontline commander or officer in the air or mage forces.

The mental fortitude to not go running for rear service was commendable. And truth be told, General Habergram thought very highly of them.

Their determination was admirable.

But he also wished from the bottom of his heart that they would throw him a bone, as the leader in Intelligence, which made its base *in the rear*.

Naturally, they couldn't put out a public call for more Intelligence personnel. And due to the system of recruiting personnel who dealt with confidential information, they couldn't openly ask for people who wanted to serve in the intelligence agency.

When they reached out to someone, they had to do it under a public-facing name and purpose. Since their identities were confidential, the recruiting calls necessarily ended up being for rear-serving officers for the War Office or the Office of the Admiralty.

Thanks to that, they were having...an awfully hard time recruiting outstanding officers. The army and navy wouldn't let the truly superior officers go.

So they had no choice but to reach out to individuals one by one... But when you invite a talented, patriotic individual with a strong sense of responsibility to bid farewell to the subordinates they've been in charge of and do desk work in the War Office or the Office of the Admiralty, you have to be thankful you're not getting a kick in the teeth.

"Apparently, someone once even asked, 'You need officers to abandon their friends on the forward-most line and go to the rear?' They're not wrong."

The problem plaguing all the recruiters was...how pure the young people were. Though they praised the youths' noble spirits, they were in a real fix.

Ultimately, they decided to focus their recruiting efforts on disabled officers who were barred from war-zone service due to their injuries. Superior talents frequently stood up again with an indefatigable spirit.

Officers who voluntarily came back after being injured in battle and still wanted to fight had become extremely capable Intelligence personnel. General Habergram was sure they were worth more than their weight in gold.

But because of the peculiarities of their appearances, he hesitated to send them into the field as spies. Not that disabled military men were rare, but in neutral or hostile countries, he wanted to avoid attracting attention.

"...Maybe we should start recruiting women as agents?"

He realized that if the military in enemy territory was fully mobilized, then women might actually stand out less. All the adult men had been conscripted and sent to the front lines. And the fact that adult women were starting to fill general labor positions in the rear was another important point.

It wasn't a bad thing to note.

"Hmm, but when it comes to having women parachute into enemy territory…"

Would the General Staff and Whitehall approve of that? Well, since it's a secret operation, I could probably proceed at my own discretion, but…

Was there any danger of them being used by the enemy in their propaganda war?

Considering the political mess that would result if one of them was captured, doing it unilaterally was a big risk. The more he thought about it, the more things it seemed there were to consider.

An expanding workload and dwindling Intelligence personnel…

"Things just don't go how you'd like."

General Habergram tapped his finger on the table in irritation.

There was a shortage of the human resources Intelligence needed. Yet the amount of work was rapidly increasing. He may have been a gentleman, but it still made him curse his situation.

But apparently, having no time to think was just part of war.

There was already a subordinate official, carrying a small mountain of paperwork, peeking his head in.

He set the documents down on the table with a thud.

Blimey. With no time to fall into despair, he reached for his pen, and that's when he realized something. His subordinate was holding out an envelope.

"Excuse me, sir. This is urgent from the Committee of Commonwealth Defense."

"From the defense committee? Oh, the summons circular?"

Thinking how rare it was to get a summons, he tore open the envelope and looked over the contents. Then he corrected his mistake.

"No, it's a request for me to attend a meeting. That doesn't happen very often."

Having a member of Intelligence attend a meeting that will have official minutes? He wanted to ask what the prime minister was thinking. Still, an order was an order.

And he had no reason or way to disobey a directive the right person gave via the proper channels.

"It says to attend the Commonwealth defense meeting tomorrow. An official request from the prime minister's office. I'm busy right now, but I guess I can't argue. Make sure there's a car ready for me."

But really, he wondered what the prime minister was going to say to him.

▶▶▶ SOME DAY IN SEPTEMBER, UNIFIED YEAR 1926, THE COMMONWEALTH ◀◀◀
CAPITAL LONDINIUM, IN THE WHITEHALL AREA

At the Commonwealth defense meeting...

One look at the high-ranking officials in attendance was enough to gauge the Commonwealth's situation.

Ashtrays crammed full of cigar butts. Point people from both the army and navy who didn't even attempt to hide their exhaustion. Rows of bureaucrats who looked vaguely ill.

Utterly spent public servants.

The only one among them with plenty of color in his face was a man like a bulldog who had learned how to sit. Whether he should be seen as arrogant or described as a trustworthy man full of fighting spirit depended on your point of view.

This was His Royal Majesty's first subject, the leader of the Commonwealth defense meeting, Prime Minister Churbull himself.

"The prime minister hopes that the fighting will move toward the eastern front."

With worn-out looks on their faces, everyone present turned to the seat of honor. *If only! Then we wouldn't have to suffer.* Everyone was screaming internally, that much was clear.

Even General Habergram sympathized with them.

"I'd form an alliance with the devil himself if need be, but what's so awful about saying what I think? I'd be glad if the two devils duked it out among themselves." Prime Minister Churbull spoke boldly but without pretension.

That was his strength.

Chapter II

Though he was a crazy war nut, he was stubbornly anti-Empire. Or he was an expansionist warmonger who proudly bore the Commonwealth's stubborn imperialist principles. He was called many things, but in any case, in the Commonwealth's political circles, Churbull was talked about in this way.

It was even common to call him a bulldog.

"So you're quite devout, then."

"Ah, finally ready to be tucked in?"

Would they be strange bedfellows, or was he a pious man yet tolerant of heresy? Apparently, even the roundabout nastiness delivered as jokes couldn't pierce his thick skin.

"You needn't praise me so much, gentlemen. And that's enough chit-chat. What we need is time and manpower to defend our homeland."

If you let unpleasantness simply pass you by, it doesn't have much effect. It's quite astonishing, this man's heart of steel.

"Very well. I'll report on our current status."

A representative from the Air Ministry seemed to endure some dizziness to stand and proceeded to read a compact overview of their combat situation.

The clashes with the attacking Imperial Air Fleet and mage units were on a larger scale than imagined.

"Several major air battles have already broken out, but the Royal Air Fleet has been successful in maintaining air superiority."

The interception battles against the enemy in the southern part of the mainland were the very definition of intense. Most of the enemies came from air bases in what used to be the Republic. *How ironic that the Republic's fall should come back around to bite us.*

Still, it was encouraging that their air screen was still functioning. Just as General Habergram was about to let that weight off his shoulders, thinking he could relax...

A man who seemed to be enduring a stomachache interrupted... It was the head of the air ministry, the inspector general of the air fleet.

"As the inspector general, allow me to add one thing. At present, we're dipping deep into our savings. Going broke is not a question of if but when."

"And more specifically?"

"We're seeing rapid increases in attrition of aircraft, fleet personnel, and the support and relief mage troops. We're rushing to fill the gaps with voluntary units of refugees and university student volunteers, but…"

The loss of veterans, their replacement with green troops—it was the exact same dilemma that General Habergram was facing in Intelligence.

The moment he realized it, he couldn't help his shock.

The air units get preferential treatment, and they're still having these issues? When he saw the graph of current losses up on the board, his eyes popped wide open.

They had maybe two thousand air troops. They had already lost over two hundred pilots. Adding in the injured, nearly half of them had left the front. In many cases, it was unclear if they would be able to return.

Still, they were putting in the effort to maintain their fighting force. The Air Ministry had managed to replenish the personnel who left the front with the young ones stolen from Habergram in Intelligence.

But…all they had was a head count. It would be impossible to expect the combat ability of pilots who completed their training before war began from the ones educated on an urgent basis.

"Excuse me, but may I? These are battles to defend the airspace over the mainland. Anyone who gets hit should be able to land and then go back up again. Doesn't this loss rate seem a bit strange?"

The response to the question was more cause for headaches.

"There are two problems."

"Explain."

"First, even if they get hit, the pilots are loath to use their parachutes."

"…Why is that?"

"The other day, a few imperial aerial mages landed. Do you remember that?"

"Right, it was a special unit that came in to rescue some prisoners or something, I believe?"

Most of the people attending the meeting weren't aware of it, but General Habergram and a few others knew that the monsters who conducted the raid were the 203rd Aerial Mage Battalion.

They were a unit that reported directly to the Imperial Army General Staff.

Why would they send such a valuable unit in on a rescue mission?

Chapter **II**

And why have such a trump card, identified as belonging to the General Staff, deployed on the western front at all, even for an aerial mage battle?

For a time, the various Commonwealth agencies debated the questions... but now they knew the answers.

"The police engaged the enemy soldiers who came down. This information was passed around and transformed into a rumor that enemy soldiers came down. Then it was reported multiple times that they were wearing our uniforms, and now mistaken attacks against our own ejected pilots won't stop."

In wartime, gossip spreads like germs.

So why didn't the rumor that civilian police were attacked by an imperial special ops unit go around?

By the time they realized, the stories had spread like wildfire and the pubs around town were full of them.

So everyone could just see it: enemy soldiers raining down from the sky.

The significance of the precedent carved into the minds of the citizens was a terrible thing, but the Commonwealth Army didn't realize it until it was too late.

"Additionally, ever since a voluntary pilot parachuted and was attacked and killed due to language issues, the pilots all say that if they get hit, they would rather die in the sky."

"...Try to fix that—urgently. It's awfully backward."

It was a tragedy that elicited sighs from everyone present.

A refugee who volunteered to fight for the Commonwealth, of all people, was attacked by a civilian in a patriotic frenzy the moment they touched down on Commonwealth soil.

Even graduates from public schools were getting beaten the moment they touched down and would have been in danger had they not provided identification. They couldn't expect an increase in pilot morale if stories like that were going around.

By the time they found the jump in pilots dying in their aircraft, it was too late. It was such a dirty move that General Habergram felt personally tricked.

"So what's the other problem?"

The prime minister pressed, and Habergram had a guess what the answer was.

"We're short on maintenance troops and other behind-the-scenes staff. Production facilities have increased along with the rapid expansion of our air units, but...there are too many types of aircrafts, and the maintenance teams haven't been expanded to keep up."

The Air Ministry representatives protested their harsh reality one after the other. The miserable difficulties the Royal Air Force was facing were incredibly severe.

"As a result, it's going to be hard to avoid lowering our rate of operation..."

"We've also received feedback from the air units. They're saying they're having too much trouble with engines lately. When they look with an impartial eye, there are maintenance problems, yes, but the primary issue is poor manufacturing."

"It can't be helped. We're bending over backward to expand the production lines. We're almost at the point where we'll have to start using mobilized workers with little experience..."

Usually, any heated debate between officials would include a vague blame game. But this grumbling with lifeless voices and borderline careless looks that said, *It isn't my division's fault?*

It could only be called a crisis of low standards.

When he glanced at the seat of honor, the prime minister was sighing.

"Let's assume our overseas colonies are our friends. Now then, we have many friends. And how about that devil we just signed the deal with? How much will they do for us?"

"I think it will be an extremely tough fight. The attaché we dispatched says that due to previous political troubles, the structure of the Federation Army is...far weaker than anticipated."

"I'm sure they can't be as bad as Dacia."

"Well, no."

The War Office representative replied that they weren't that disappointing but in quite the vague way.

Well, of course he was vague.

Habergram himself had reported to the War Office on the Federation's status. The results of the survey they'd performed on the army's request were dreadful. Even an optimistic, or perhaps "extremely optimistic," estimate said over half their officers lacked experience. The higher ranks of generals had completely collapsed due to years of purges.

Chapter **II**

Personnel was at a model loss.

The air and mage units that played such a critical role in modern combat had completely fallen apart due to a class struggle or some such.

Though they were being hastily reassembled, their gear was all terribly old.

As for land war weapons and artillery, they were keeping up to standard, but...since report after report said the ground troops were hopeless at cooperating with one another, the situation was grim.

Even if it wasn't as wretched as the Principality of Dacia, Habergram had a thorough idea of how bad things were inside the Federation Army.

"But there's no escaping a hard fight. After all, they aren't in a position to leverage their numerical superiority."

"...What a waste."

"Even so, they're taking on the brunt of the imperial forces."

It was pointed out that the eastern front was becoming the main fighting ground.

Well, the Empire was anxious about its naval forces, and the Commonwealth was anxious about its ground forces... The Federation and the Empire were connected by land, so they clashed in a huge way, while the Commonwealth and the Empire continued to have aerial battles over the strait separating them.

Frankly, the Imperial Army was putting its emphasis on the eastern front.

"If we could shore them up, perhaps we could take some of the pressure of the aerial battles off."

"How exactly?"

Prime Minister Churbull's interest was piqued, but in response to his question, the army gave a response that would cause everyone besides itself to suffer.

"What about deploying an air unit? On top of opening up the northern route the Federation is hoping for, we could establish a joint transport route defense squad."

"The navy strongly opposes the army's suggestion."

"The air force also declines. Do you not understand our mainland defense situation?"

It was no wonder; for the side receiving the advice, it must have been obnoxious.

That word *strongly* indicated they would not back down. *What attitude from the navy and air force as they glare at the army!*

"I beg your pardon, but may I ask why?"

In response to the disappointed army representative's question, they left him high and dry.

"As you in the army are no doubt aware, creating a single chain of command often leads to trouble. We don't need to go out of our way to work jointly," the higher-ups in the navy spat as if it was the idea of a joint plan that they disagreed with.

Meanwhile, the air force representative silently took out his wallet and flipped it over. His performance, as he tapped the underside, showed that not a single, measly pence would fall out.

The meanings of both their actions were clear.

"Would it really be so hard to cooperate with a Federation unit?" Prime Minister Churbull interjected, unable to simply stand by.

"Our air force doesn't have the wherewithal for such a venture."

"To comment from the navy's perspective, our doctrines and structures are too different. The officers serving there and the liaison officers say it's a better bet currently to simply maintain some degree of contact."

The air force didn't have anyone to send.

The navy might have been able to scrape together a unit, but it had no intention of doing so. And it was no wonder, given the Federation Navy wasn't even up to brown-water operations. The idea of abandoning their essential mainland defense duty for a supply mission in airspace under enemy control didn't thrill them.

"Things just won't go our way, huh?" someone murmured, and everyone took up their cigars in an attempt to ignore the awkward silence that ensued. To give the room in its purple haze a weather forecast, it was perpetually overcast like the Commonwealth sky in autumn.

They couldn't help but feel gloomy.

"And? How about our dear colonists? Are they about ready to send us something besides voluntary forces?"

"That's a definite no. Public opinion is firmly against entering the war."

More than one annoyed tongue click rang out in the meeting room. It was just as those prideful Commonwealth men were reluctantly seeking help...

If the public was raging against providing support, biting down on a cigar wasn't going to be enough to help them endure it.

"…Could the Empire be meddling in their opinion?"

"General Habergram, your response?"

At the facilitator's question, all eyes fell on him. Everyone wanted to know the answer. *So the situation is such that they're casting off their official disinterest? They must really be expecting a lot out of the colonists.*

Unfortunately, Habergram had only bad news for them.

"Honestly, the Empire's influence is…not enough to be considered significant."

That was an indirect way to put it.

Since he had no clear evidence, it was part speculation, but…there wasn't even any sign that public opinion maneuvers in the Empire had a unified policy.

Just barely, perhaps. It was only the people in the embassies, as was usual for diplomatic outposts, fighting the publicity fight in the neutral countries. And it really came down to individual skill.

He didn't get the sense that there was an organized propaganda campaign.

"Their local equivalent to the Empire's Foreign Office is active. In that sense, we can't say the Federation isn't meddling at all, but their efforts can't amount to much."

"Why? Stealth intelligence operations aren't unheard of. They're a crafty lot. Couldn't the Empire have been influencing public opinion all along?"

"Trying to 100 percent deny that would require the devil's proof. But please recall the Empire's traditional stance toward foreign parties. It isn't the sort of nation that places a terrible amount of emphasis on public opinion. The people on the ground are probably the ones making the decisions."

There was an "Ugh"—several attendees must have stiffened at the mention of how awful the Empire was at diplomacy.

The emerging military power was a product of the modern age, having made innovative advances in many realms—technological, manufacturing, economic, military, and so on.

But for some reason, or perhaps for that very reason, the Empire was incapable of grasping the subtleties of diplomacy.

"The imperial government's outlook is pure idealism. We're talking about people who believe that reason rules the world, you know! I wouldn't be surprised if they were writing off the Unified States' participation in the war because they couldn't fathom the benefits of it."

The arrogance to think *This is how the world should be*—that was why large developing nations that hadn't had a setback yet so often made a misstep.

But regardless of how authorities in the Unified States felt, it was true that public opinion was negative on intervening. In that sense, it was perhaps natural that the Empire would lower its guard. The imperial government's greatest ally, then, was the will of the people.

"So this negativity is…the will of the people?"

"Yes, Mr. Prime Minister. Unfortunately, the people of the Unified States wish to keep their distance from war."

He spoke dispassionately.

Giving bad news in an emotional way was unpleasant. Any upsetting news should be delivered as objectively as possible.

"How incredibly inconvenient. I'd really like to drag them into it…"

"I think for that, we'll need some time. The Foreign Office and Media Ministry are currently drawing up a wartime propaganda plan. We're aiming to hit the intelligentsia regardless of whether they're from the left or right."

"I hope allying ourselves with those devils has some benefits."

Had they been thinking of the pros and cons of taking the Communists as allies? Several people nodded with vague comments, which conveyed to everyone how problematic Communism was.

But how much do they really understand? General Habergram had no choice but to critically shrug. The real problem with Communists was their ability to multiply and infiltrate. They'd ooze in like infantry through some hole or another, and before you knew it, there'd be a whole nest of them.

Well—at that point, Habergram had to smile bitterly—*we can worry about all that after we win this war.*

"…At any rate, we have a lot of problems right now. We must buy time. And to add to that, I don't want to wear down our fighting force."

"Then perhaps the northern route brought up earlier is a good idea after all."

The prime minister and the facilitator brought the plan back around

Chapter **II**

to building a supply line to the Federation. Considering how efficient sea routes were for transportation, it wasn't a bad idea. But...that was with the caveat that the ground, sea, and air forces had to come up with the manpower to do it.

"Mr. Prime Minister, as we said—"

"Wait." Churbull held up a hand to quiet the navy representative and offered a proposal in a calm, informed tone. "I realize we're in the extraordinarily trying situation of being tight on ships. And that's precisely why...I want to propose adding civilian boats to the convoys."

Civilian boats? It was a proposal that had everyone cocking their heads in spite of themselves. The waters in question were clearly dangerous. Insurance companies would definitely refuse the contracts.

It was hard to imagine any ships other than the ones they had already requisitioned would head for the northern route. At least, not normally...

"Allow me to confirm one point." A member of the Foreign Office, who had until then remained silent, quietly spoke. With command of the Commonwealth specialty, triple-dealing diplomacy, his mind was the very definition of sharp. "Does that include ships from neutral countries?"

The question seemed inconspicuous, but its implications were major. If they added neutral nationality ships into the convoy...couldn't a "grave accident" take place?

Which was why everyone waited for Prime Minister Churbull's reply with bated breath. *Does he want an accident like that to happen?*

"Well, all I can say is that in the long run, it very well may. Of course, at the start, I intend to move forward with our own boats. But...it is possible that vessels will become scarce. It's just difficult for me to answer a hypothetical question."

"Ha-ha-ha. Yes, as you say, sir."

His answer was ambiguous.

He didn't deny it, but neither did he affirm it. Still, those who knew the ways of Whitehall understood what wasn't said.

Since he didn't deny it with a no, the prime minister would definitely do it if the need arose.

"Gentlemen, give me that mean laughter. This isn't a public school hall. Let's conduct this war seriously."

The prime minister with his indirect remarks must have made up his mind to pursue raison d'état to the last. Hence, no one was surprised by the next thing he said.

"Now then, let's review our policy. We'll keep the air battles in the west to interceptions only. If we do that, then that many imperial soldiers can head to the eastern front, right? Meanwhile, our main goal will be to get the colonists to join our side."

"If we take too long, the Federation may not be able to hold out."

"We'll deal with that if it comes to it. Ideally, they'll knock each other out. Of course, the worst case would be if the Empire survived. So I want to wear them both down."

The prime minister chuckled slightly; those comments had to be his real thoughts on the issue.

And yet, most of those present would probably support him unconditionally. If blood was going to be shed, better to have some other country's youth do it than their own.

Above all, for the Commonwealth, having the irritating Empire and the equally irritating Communists take each other out would be absolutely fantastic.

"I have one suggestion. As a show of friendship with the Federation, let's commit a Unified States voluntary unit and some marine mages to guard the northern route."

"…What voluntary unit do you mean?"

"They're from the Entente Alliance. I think both militarily and politically, as well as in terms of propaganda, dispatching some units would be wise."

The Foreign Office had been rather quiet up until this point, but their explanation put weight on the propaganda war. Frankly, it was a proposal that completely ignored military practicality.

"What does the navy think?"

"We're opposed."

"Opposed?"

"The aim is fine. And it's not that I don't understand the objective. To be blunt, however, we're lacking that most critical method."

This wasn't the sort of operation those in the field would happily risk their lives to carry out. With the frowns the navy representatives were wearing, it was impressive that they accepted the aim as valid at all.

"You're saying we can't send troops to guard the route?"

"We're already noticeably short on escort vessels. If we're asked to draw off any more, our maritime escort efforts are liable to fail."

"What?"

Even subjected to Prime Minister Churbull's stern gaze and tone, the navy's answer didn't change.

There was no way it could change.

"Mr. Prime Minister, I'm sure you recall how it was during your days as First Lord of the Admiralty."

"…If that's what you're talking about, then I remember it being possible to poach enough destroyers."

"The fleet's answer is that it's not. The total number of destroyers is already having a hard time standing up to an increased rate of attrition, and if the main fleet is missing escorts, then…"

"Exactly. It could hinder the fleet or anti-sub combat."

"There's one thing I'd like to ask. The imperial submarines are having their way out there, but what are ours doing, taking a nap?"

"…With all due respect, there's a difference between the Empire, a continental state, and us, a maritime state! Please take into account the fact that we depend on maritime trading routes and the Empire is already cut off from them!"

"If you understand that much, then you must know how precarious our trading routes are, right?"

The representative saw where the conversation was headed, but Prime Minister Churbull didn't give him the time to cover up his mistake.

"To protect a trading route that important, we need destroyers. Until we can mass-produce them, pull them from the fleet. Use marine mages to help with anti-sub combat."

The atmosphere was filled with the will radiating from the prime minister's entire body. For a moment, the naval officers were nearly swallowed up by it, but then they all raised their voices to retort.

"Mr. Prime Minister! Anything but that!"

"Please rethink this! The fleet's destroyers are the elite fighters in decisive fleet battles! If you go throwing them into an attrition battle, we'll never be able to annihilate the enemy fleet!"

These were the voices of men who knew the sea. But they seemed to forget that they were on a hill.

"Shut up!"

One shout.

The argument was decided all too easily the moment the prime minister barked at the men from the navy and they failed to respond.

"The Commonwealth cannot last a single day without maritime trading routes!"

That was the fate of a maritime nation. They had to cross the water to survive. Everything their existence as a state required was found in foreign lands.

If they desired something, their only choice was to carry it across the sea.

Whether they were for or against it, the Commonwealth couldn't exist apart from the sea.

"Isn't that what the navy is for? If it's not, then we might as well let our seawalls rot! Look at how strong it is! What enemy would dare challenge us? What do I care about a decisive fleet battle that may never happen?! Survive tomorrow! That's our priority!"

"…Understood."

There was no one who couldn't sympathize with the shame of the bowing Sea Lords.

Their subordinates would curse them. The northern seas were rough. Of course, no one would be happy to have their unit broken up and committed to a place like that. Their hearts would probably remain set on a decisive fleet battle.

But once a major objective had been decided, the state had to carry out its big plan without delay.

"Can we move on? Under these conditions, how much of a force can the navy send to the northern route? Be aware that we have to expect some losses."

"If we send a group of high-speed transport ships, we can limit the amount of time we spend in dangerous waters. And I think the Home Fleet can provide high-speed destroyers to escort them."

"I want those transport ships to be able to cruise at eighteen knots minimum."

"Impossible!"

"Do you know the attrition rate in our coastal waters?"

"Are you saying we should try to break through enemy-controlled waters with a sluggish convoy?!"

What they were debating was how to do it. Whether or not it was possible was no longer up for discussion.

"Isn't that why there's an escort?"

"The assumption in our coastal waters is that our fleet is nearby! If we're crossing territory where the Imperial High Seas Fleet is active, that's a different story!"

Unless the convoy was fast enough to outrun the enemy, they could be captured by a surface-level ship. Voices urging the risk was too high persisted in pointing out the problems.

"There's a risk of getting captured by aircraft or mages either way, so wouldn't a slower yet bigger convoy with more protection have a better chance of success?"

"Slow convoys are the ones supporting our country's supply needs, you know!"

"Wait, wait, wait!"

...Even if the discussion had gotten a little off topic...

The Commonwealth had decided on a policy of opening up a northern route.

In that case... General Habergram became absorbed in thought. *Certainly it's not...a bad plan. But isn't it almost too convenient for the Federation?*

At a glance, the conclusion seemed to be in pursuit of the Commonwealth's interests.

"Gentlemen, can we assume we've heard everyone's opinions now?"

Everyone nodded yes...and they were probably glad to not have any objections. Unanimity was a harbinger of unity.

It was good news that made even an attendee like General Habergram smile at how bright prospects were. He wanted to think that things were going in a good direction. Which was exactly why he couldn't quite accept it as the head of the intelligence agency, having been forced to endure such constant hardship.

"We've at least agreed that we'll send a marine mage unit escort to the northern route along with the Unified States voluntary troops. So the only sticking point is the ships. Now, then..." Prime Minister Churbull puffed his cigar in silence…and waited to continue until everyone's patience had just about run out. "I have an idea about *one boat.*"

The comment made Habergram "hmm."

An idea about where to scrounge up some ships would have been understandable. Perhaps in that case he would have talked to someone in charge of shipping schedules in advance. But…a single boat?

That said, it was the prime minister speaking. Everyone politely squelched their doubts and waited for him to continue. *Ohhh.* General Habergram revised his assessment.

The navy representatives had all gone pale in the face; they seemed to have some idea what he had in mind.

"We can pack it full of cargo, and as a bonus, it won't even need an escort. Right?" he asked the navy, and they were already panicking.

"P-p-please wait, Mr. Prime Minister!"

"Not that. Anything but that—you mustn't!"

You could say it was quite a spectacle, seeing naval officers, who usually prided themselves on being so on top of things, practically foaming at the mouth in agitation.

And their desperation only made their comical irritation funnier for some reason.

"It's the conclusion I arrived at taking the scarcity of escort vessels you complained of into consideration."

"But that one, that ship—"

"We're using the RMS *Queen of Anjou.* Make sure to relay that to Fleet Command."

Habergram remembered that name.

It was the Commonwealth's largest ocean liner.

In other words, the world's largest cargo-passenger ship. And if he remembered correctly, the fastest cargo-passenger ship. Before the war, he knew it as the fastest luxury passenger ship in service.

He had heard it was requisitioned, but *I see. Judging from how upset the navy is…it must be even handier than the rumors said.*

"But!"

"Choose your best marine mages for the escort. Don't let her sink!"

After one murmured "Oh no," the navy members felt silent and just stared reproachfully at the army members, who suddenly busied themselves with puffing on their cigars and began looking toward the ceiling where it was safe.

The air force officers seemed intent on surviving the moment with stone-faced expressions. Keen to not get mixed up in it, they plunged into an extremely specialized technical discussion of airplane engines.

The members of the Foreign Office and other government officials looked as they always did, like none of this had anything to do with them.

A danger zone like this is no place to linger. If I accidentally stay too long, the chances I get caught up in some needless trouble will spike. My best bet is to leave now... But just as General Habergram had decided to withdraw...

He noticed the voice of a young official beckoning him.

When he followed the call...he arrived before the one who had up until moments ago been locked in a furious exchange of opinions with the navy, or rather had been mocking them—Prime Minister Churbull himself.

With a big smile on his face, the prime minister gave him a familiar clap on the shoulder. Most people would consider that an honor.

Such was the bliss of ignorance.

"Excuse the delay, Mr. Habergram. I'm sorry for the sudden invitation, but I'd be happy if I could join you for tea tomorrow at three o'clock. If that's fine with you, I'd appreciate if you came to the prime minister's residence around that time..."

"It would be my pleasure, sir."

An invitation from the prime minister was a de facto order. Unless he had a tea party planned with the king, he would have to be with Prime Minister Churbull at three o'clock the next day.

"Very good. Then I'll have my butler prepare. Is something on the light side fine with you?"

"Yes, thank you, Mr. Prime Minister."

 A CERTAIN DAY, THE COMMONWEALTH CAPITAL LONDINIUM, THE PRIME MINISTER'S RESIDENCE

The next day, Major General Habergram appeared at the appointed hour at the prime minister's residence.

Along the way, he had looked at the drabness above. The meager sunlight was normal. It wasn't so unusual for the sun to not peek out in the autumn sky.

He'd been raised in that climate from birth. He couldn't complain. Sometimes he wanted to pop off to the Inner Sea and enjoy a beach vacation, but this was wartime.

Society and beaches were for after the war was over. He was practically used to the dull military-issue items and the world being dyed beige.

Surely even the institution of three o'clock tea couldn't escape the scourge of war. Near the prime minister's mansion, there were anti–air artillery positions, in light of the aerial combat, and a few dugouts; here and there, soldiers were having tea *at their stations*.

Compared to the principle of the thing, which was to take your time, relax, and chat, there was nothing sadder.

When he was led—"Right this way"—to a table in a corner of the prime minister's residence, the buckets set here and there in case of fire reminded him they were at war.

"There you are. Take a seat."

The prime minister offered him a chair, and the butler left to prepare their tea. Before the war, Habergram never would have dreamed he'd be sharing a table with Prime Minister Churbull.

Though he was honored to have such an opportunity, it brought him no joy. He felt awful because he knew it meant his fatherland was in trouble.

For example, the people around him. The service staff, with their crisp movements that practically embodied discipline, were pros, but...many of them were quite old. Even the youngest had to be over fifty.

It was no wonder, considering the army had snapped up most young men. At some point, everything they had taken for granted had become the past. Consciously noticing the passage of time always made him melancholy.

That the uniforms of the people bringing over the tea things were as impeccable as before was actually depressing.

"My apologies, but as we're at war..."

Tea was served with the implication that this was all they could manage. Habergram was about to take the comment at face value when suddenly, he couldn't believe his eyes.

Chapter **II**

A glimpse of silver polished to an unnatural beauty.

Silver tarnished so easily—was it even possible to polish it so well? Considering how scarce labor was, he wasn't sure if he should be impressed or disgusted.

So tea with porcelain and silver like the good old days? In wartime, at the prime minister's residence when he and his people are under the pressure of leading the war?

"My butler is too picky. The tea is fairly good."

"Considering the wartime distribution circumstances, I'd say it's surprisingly good."

The Assam tea he was prompted to drink wasn't bad even for peacetime standards. Considering the commerce raids they were currently facing, you could say it was unexpectedly delightful.

"I'm sure my butler's ideal is to serve only what is in its quality season. Of course, I'm not thrilled when we can't get the good stuff and are forced to make substitutions, either."

Discriminating taste, love of tradition, and that unflappable demeanor. Even if he was putting up a brave front, that he was displaying the Commonwealth's traditional attitude was truly encouraging.

"I can't deny that we in government have some serious work to do when it comes to ersatz products. The tea delay is unexpectedly severe. Can't fight a war without tea." The prime minister laughed, and General Habergram found himself smiling wryly.

Certainly, fighting a war without tea was out of the question. Anyone who encountered such horrible luck would surely find some somewhere. One good example was the intelligence officers sent to the southern continent. Despite the fact that they had been dispatched to a desert, they were apparently managing to get their tea one way or another.

Or to put it another way: They were able to find tea in a desert. Maybe they had the talent to perform even if he worked them a little harder.

"But I suppose we can't spend our time chatting. Shall we get down to business? It's just as you heard at the Committee of Commonwealth Defense meeting."

Ahhh. Habergram realized he had been getting a bit too relaxed. He straightened up and got his ears ready to listen.

He wondered what in the world the prime minister had called him for.

As the one responsible for Intelligence, he did report to the prime minister, but…this was the first time he had been invited in private for tea.

"We don't have enough of anything. From daily necessities such as tea to, on the war front, destroyers, other ships, or even trustworthy, civilized ally countries."

They really were forced to admit the Commonwealth was facing a crisis. And it was all because they hadn't been able to stop the defeat of the Republic on the continent. They were stuck paying the cost of their intervention coming too late now by facing the powerful Empire without their ally.

"That's the true state of things here in the Commonwealth. Although things have gotten a bit better than when I said in parliament that this was their best of times and our worst of times…"

"If things have gotten better and you're still this upset, sir…"

"Exactly."

Churbull offered a cigar case and said to take one. *He still loves to smoke, I see.* Habergram cracked a wry smile, but he wasn't opposed himself.

When he gratefully accepted, he saw that it was the highest quality, as usual. *So even in these troubled times, there are cigars around if you know where to look.*

But even as he was smoking, the question remained. *Why was I summoned?* He couldn't help but wonder as he enjoyed the fine cigar.

The topic jumped around, but…so much time had passed that he began to feel this was an awfully roundabout way to get down to business. That's when it happened.

"Mr. Habergram, I'll be straight with you. I don't want to regret this deal with the Communists."

"I see, sir."

His intuition responded to Prime Minister Churbull's sudden remark. *So this is about the Communists!*

He realized his throat was dry, but when he reached out for his cup and sipped the Assam tea, he couldn't taste it.

"Has there been any progress in finding the mole plaguing Intelligence?"

"My apologies, but the investigation is still under way; we haven't identified him. Since nothing seems to have been leaked recently, it's possible the mole was one of the officers on loan from the army or navy." Habergram himself was doubtful of this, but he went on. "The tricky thing is that we can't rule out that he's been converted into a sleeper. All we can do is keep managing our intelligence the best we can."

He'd done a thorough check on his subordinates. To be sure, he wasn't interested in suspecting his friends, but he knew that it was necessary, if unpleasant.

He had done all that.

He thought for sure that he would be able to identify the barefaced villain soon enough…but so far they had come up with a fat lot of nothing.

It had been suggested that perhaps the mole was one of the officers on loan, but…without evidence to back it up, that seemed like wishful thinking.

For the sleeper, not being suspected anymore would be a big win. It wouldn't do for Habergram and his men to lower their guard just like that, which made the whole ordeal especially rough.

Hence, as head of Intelligence, General Habergram made an official apology.

"In conclusion, all I can do is apologize once more. The fact is, we're still investigating."

"…About that."

"Yes, Mr. Prime Minister?"

I'll content myself with being scolded. Even if he's harsh with me, I'm in no position to argue. Habergram braced himself.

"There's a possibility it's the Federation intelligence agency."

Which was why that revelation was completely unexpected.

It was only due to his long years of self-control and discipline that he didn't immediately ask, "*What?!*" The conclusion his brain just barely managed to reach hinted at the truth—that the mole was… *Wait a minute— why does the prime minister know this?*

"…What do you mean?"

"You're familiar with their Commissariat for Internal Affairs, I'm sure? You probably know more about them than I do, but at any rate, they've come forward with a proposal to halt all espionage activity on each other."

The surprise rendered him speechless.

Should I ask, So? *Or should I wonder,* Why? Both of them seemed appropriate and yet not.

"So you really made a deal with the devil…"

"We can think of it as a signal. Anyhow! Their head of the Commissariat for Internal Affairs, Loria, said as their representative that they want to have a working-level meeting about exchanging intelligence and combating the Empire together."

I see. It made sense.

Frankly, the idea that he, from the Commonwealth, would be able to meet with people from Federation Intelligence was a revolution on a Copernican scale.

This was what it meant to be utterly astonished.

It made him keenly aware that the paradoxical adage of the intelligence world—*the only thing that is certain is that nothing is certain*—was the truth.

"Is it an official invite?"

"Of course. And it came with the pledge to void all past warrants of arrest and guilty verdicts at trials in absentia for intelligence agents!"

"That's…Wow."

Should I say that's encouraging? Will we be fools for believing a guarantee from the Communist Party's secret police? Or should we be stunned by their sincerity?

The choices were so extreme.

"Mr. Habergram, depending on how the arrangements turn out, I'd like to have you do the meeting."

"Understood. Say the word, and I'll take a man and be off immediately, sir."

Hesitation was pointless.

If he was told to go, he could only go and do his best.

"Very good. If it suits you, how about using the RMS *Queen of Anjou*? We're still settling the exact date with the Commissariat for Internal Affairs, but once things are arranged, we're planning an unofficial exchange of personnel, as well."

"It would be a lie if I said I wouldn't be ashamed to release bloody traitors, treasonous bastards, and Communists, but…," Habergram continued.

Chapter **II**

On his face was an expression different from the stiff, nearly inhuman mask he had worn up until now. Out in the world, people would no doubt describe it as relief, acceptance, or perhaps joy.

"I can't complain if we can take back our people from those Communist assassins."

His colleagues, so worthy of respect. Once they were imprisoned, there had been no news. The Commonwealth's intelligence agency had no illusions about how gentlemanly the Communists were.

The pro-Communist-leaning academics couldn't seem to get it through their heads, but...the Commissariat for Internal Affairs was incredibly harsh even on its own people. If he could get his colleagues imprisoned by that band of sadists back alive...

It was enough to make even the top of the intelligence agency, dispassionate by necessity, feel like cracking a smile. After winter came spring. If you knew the peaceful days would return after the hard times, why would you neglect preparations for making it through the winter?

"It would be even more perfect if we could offer the returnees first-class accommodations."

He had read the fate of captured intelligence agents in reports. It was what people meant when they said, "*Worse than you could ever imagine.*"

Since they were full of top secret intel, the reports couldn't be made public. But if they could be, the absurd debate about how cruel humans could be would be put to rest.

The answer? *Infinitely.*

So then, what tortures, what suffering, had they endured? Even the thought of his colleagues' fate brought tears to his eyes.

"Of course, we'll want to have plenty of champagne and wine. We may need beer by the barrel."

Banter to mask the awkwardness. Better to flash an invincible smile than tearfully whimper. That had to be why they were joking.

"Ha-ha-ha, the hospitality of stiff drinks? I'd request cigars myself, but booze is also much appreciated. Excuse the joke—I suppose first-class rooms are impossible."

Habergram was fully aware of the navy's ship shortage. He didn't even have to be told—which was why he bobbed his head and apologized for having the prime minister go along with his silliness.

"The RMS *Queen of Anjou* has been fully outfitted as a military transport ship. The luxury rooms were probably all removed to make spaces to carry cargo and soldiers."

"Well, that's got to be better than a Federation concentration camp. If it was too opulent, they'd die from shock, so that's probably just right."

Drinks from their homeland, cigars from their homeland, and their countrymen. Even a token gesture was enough.

Even if they couldn't put their feelings into words, they would mourn and grieve over their fallen friends and silently toss their glasses. Their friendship was strong enough that the gestures would convey all they needed.

Habergram tended to get sentimental about such things but decided to give himself the whip this time.

"Allow me to return to our earlier conversation. Regarding the release of the agents we're—well, technically speaking, my anti-espionage unit is—holding…"

His reason for refocusing the conversation on the task at hand was simple.

Even if it was in your hand, a victory wasn't yours until you'd grabbed it.

How much better was it to laugh off excess caution after the fact than to enjoy a short-lived happiness? To intelligence officers, especially those in the Commonwealth, who had experienced a string of errors, it was self-evident.

"Basically, I think they should all be released. We can consider hiding some. Really, I'd like to send a few back as double agents…"

Sending enemy spies back to their home country as double agents was a plan that anyone involved in espionage dreamed about.

But Habergram understood the situation as soon as he heard Prime Minister Churbull trail off in a pained tone.

"But we're strictly forbidden from causing political trouble."

"Exactly. We've got to think long-term."

It was one of the annoying things about diplomacy and politics, the issue of what was permissible with ally countries. Even if it was only a formality, as long as the Commonwealth and the Federation were on the same side, that would have to be taken into account.

The two countries may not have been friends, but they were in the same boat. They were only serving the anti-Empire cause in a delicate balance. You could venture to say that the Commonwealth and Federation actually harbored deep mistrust of each other. It wasn't a good idea to fan smoldering suspicions.

And it made sense that this would require some self-restraint. More than anything, the Federation's people were probably thinking the same thing.

There was no way they wouldn't grill their released agents upon their return.

"Understood. I'll make sure my subordinates are aware as well. There's just one problem."

For now, it was best to refrain, but there was one thing Habergram needed to confirm.

It was an extremely simple matter.

He had just been instructed not to send in double agents.

So here was the problem.

"There are some agents who have been cooperating with us for some time. What should we do about them?"

What should they do with the cooperators they had already obtained?

"I'll leave that up to you. Just keep us out of trouble."

"As usual, then. Understood, sir."

He was given a free hand to deal with them how he wished.

"Thank you for the terrifically good tea. Oh, when do you think we'll be able to board the RMS *Queen of Anjou*?"

"We're thinking after it's made two or three trips back and forth."

"Understood. Then if you'll excuse me, sir."

>>> MID-SEPTEMBER, UNIFIED YEAR 1926, MOSKVA, THE PROVISIONAL <<<
LOCATION OF THE COMMISSARIAT FOR INTERNAL AFFAIRS

In the lifeless office of the Commissariat for Internal Affairs, Commissar Loria was dispassionately approving documents. He had a lot of work to do, since they were at war.

He was undeniably busy, but...the content of the work was different from before the war started.

Stamp. The papers he was placing his seal on were documents for releases.

"Comrade Commissar, are you sure about this?"

"You mean about sharing intelligence with the Commonwealth? Or about the unofficial personnel exchange we're doing simultaneously?"

The hands of the Federation's Communist Party were nominally white ones that proudly shook the hands of the people.

It was a huge lie, but that was their official line.

Logically speaking, secret police and the like shouldn't exist in Communist states. Thus, it followed that the secret police couldn't be restraining Commonwealth agents who had infiltrated the Federation.

If there were any, they could insist it had to be some kind of "mistake." So he had been able to sound out the Commonwealth off the record. They would exchange prisoners to "resolve the issue plaguing both countries' immigration bureaus."

Basically, there was no admittance of wrongdoing, just the peaceful message that they wanted to make a deal.

The Commonwealth's reaction was quite favorable. Negotiations were proceeding smoothly, and Loria, who had planned everything, had high expectations of the outcome.

If there was any problem, it was the idiots in front of him.

"Setting aside the former, exchanging prisoners might be—"

Loria glared in contempt at the dissatisfied-seeming official and pressed his point. "Listen. All we're saying is that there were unfortunate mistakes made on both sides."

Officially, they should make it so there had never been any hostility between them.

As long as it wasn't made public, reality was to be minimized, treated as a trivial thing one could shut one's eyes against, and yet...

"B-but they're prisoners!"

"Comrade, they are not prisoners."

"*We caught them!*" *How obstinate these fools are, hung up on their achievements!*

"We didn't take any prisoners, and neither did we get any taken. Look." He put a hand on the man's shoulder and spoke in an unusually slow way to get it through his unreasonable head. "The immigration bureau made a *mistake*. Both of us are, *in good faith*, releasing people who were temporarily detained due to legal and technical factors. And in order to not make it into a whole ordeal, neither side will apologize." He stared him right in the eyes as he spoke. The man's gaze wanted to waver, but Loria pinned it down to observe his reaction and said, "So we're simply exchanging people who were given trouble. What's the problem with that?"

If the man couldn't read between the lines, it wasn't his fault. The problem was that a person incapable of picking up the subtleties that accompanied secrets and diplomacy worked in a department of secrets.

Of course, people with imprudent mouths would also need literal zippers, then.

"…Understood, Comrade Commissar. So should we also stop illegally spying on the Commonwealth?"

Luckily, the man wasn't too dense.

Good. Loria smiled.

"Yes, keep it to hiding sleepers. Tell the handlers to be cautious when making contact, too."

"Yes, sir."

If he's hanging on by the skin of his teeth like this, he must have some promise. People who can recognize a crisis for a crisis are capable of living long lives.

And they're pretty handy, too.

Now, then, Loria thought with a smile, gazing warmly at his subordinate. *What can I have this former head of espionage in the Commonwealth do?*

Frankly, Loria was no longer interested in the Commonwealth.

"I'll put it plainly. For now, I don't want us doing any illegal spying that could endanger the relationship between our two countries."

"Then should we increase our intelligence-gathering efforts through normal diplomatic means?"

"Exactly. I don't want to defeat the Commonwealth—I want to cooperate with it."

His personal view was that the Commonwealth was not a foothold to be conquered but a road to be peacefully used. A road that could be infiltrated in secret that led to everywhere else. That was what the Federation really hoped for out of the Commonwealth.

"It's not that I'm making light of the grand old country. Its power is still alive and well in the form of its huge navy. Even its unchanging culture reveals institutional design supported by its history."

"So?"

"Rather than make an enemy of them, we should make use of them as an ally."

But their fairy tales are garbage. They're like sanitized myths. It was impossible for them to arouse any desire in him.

He had to say, his interest in the country had really just faded. Having come to his senses, he saw that a war of espionage against the Commonwealth…would result only in cons.

There was nothing appealing about it as the target of illegal spying.

"Also. Comrade, we need to change our image."

"Huh?"

"I want to allow the ones devoted to the ideals of Communism to keep having their illusions. In other words, I don't want to do anything overly forceful."

Communism was an idealistic doctrine.

The official dogma said the party couldn't get its hands dirty. Everyone involved knew the reality, but constructing a facade had proven highly effective.

"…So you mean an image strategy?"

"Exactly. And I'm not just talking about with the Commonwealth. I want to focus on personality over competence for all our overseas officers. Whenever possible, choose an idealist who is loyal to the party. Someone who's incompetent but a good person is perfect."

Party members devoted to ideals frequently ended up causing trouble for the party.

One good example was the humanitarians.

Loria had had a lot of trouble from people opposed to the purges.

It was difficult to dispose of party members whom everyone agreed were pure, innocent, and devoted. People with nothing to feel guilty about were truly a pain—although during a war, there were plenty of things you could do with them.

"…C-comrade, may I ask you something? Why are you so worried about our image?"

"Understand the way democracy works. The movers and shakers in the political world of the western nations are elites like us, but they're subordinate to public opinion. There is far more merit in using legal means to get the masses on our side than breaking the law."

Not that he intended to downplay the role of scheming. He was merely changing his approach. They needed to optimize their strategy for their circumstances.

People devoted to dazzling universal philosophy, goals, and principles wouldn't be criticized. On the contrary, perhaps they would earn sympathy. Everyone admired integrity, after all.

"Idealists are perfect for dispatching. We have no use for them at home anyhow. So I'd like to have them spread a good image of our country abroad."

Good people whom anyone would label as trustworthy.

Any foreigner with a friend like that from the Federation couldn't have too horrible an impression of the country. If someone wary of Communism met an idealist as their first "real Communist" acquaintance, would they be able to maintain their hostility?

There was probably nothing harder to pull off than ordering good people of another country to hate good people from the Federation. After all, taking the long view, not hating them would be more beneficial.

It was extremely simple to build good relationships with fellow combatants in a war. Nothing brought people together more than fighting against a common enemy for a common purpose.

"Luckily, we're at war with the world's enemy, the Empire."

"Wh-what?!"

Loria nearly snapped that it was obvious but instead declared, "This fight may very well set the party's course for eternity. Failure will not be tolerated."

A common enemy.

Even if a state had no perpetual enemies, it had current enemies. And the Federation's current enemy was an isolated enemy. *We're the world's mainstream.* How could someone be too stupid to recognize the Federation's current strategic position as a welcome change from when it used to be isolated itself?! He could only consider his subordinate hopeless. *How thoughtless he is, staring blankly back at me.*

Why is it always these carefree dimwits who end up in civil-military relations?!

The Commissariat for Internal Affairs needs crafty strategists, but we're currently overrun by scum and sadists. I don't really care about their character, but their ineptitude is incorrigible.

He began to despair that perhaps he should trade them out for the people in the gulag.

"War has no meaning unless you win and end it. Everyone knows that. But almost no one knows how to win. How stupid!"

"…Y-you may be right."

"And a win, comrade, must be something we can accept. Which is why we must show the world we are good Federation citizens."

A state had no eternal allies anyway. Only interests. *But*, thought Loria, doing calculations in his mind, *why is it asking too much to be the winner's friend who gets to sink his teeth into the fruit of victory with them?*

The difference between Communism and capitalism was being passed over out of diplomatic necessity due to the Empire's arrival as their enemy.

…So we should get as much out of that situation as we can. Loria had a hard time believing how only vaguely aware of that party officials were.

"Either way, we won't be able to avoid casualties. So we should fulfill our responsibilities. How do we capitalize on the casualties we can't avoid? *That* is what we need to figure out."

For victory, the party would have to be prepared to make sacrifices. Judging by the piles of corpses on the front line, it felt like they were indifferent to human attrition.

The casualties probably needed to be incorporated into victory as a given condition. Rather than crying over the cost, they had to think how to best take advantage of it.

If the youth of their homeland were going to die, they needed to make their deaths as effective as possible.

"We'll make them owe us a favor. We'll have our nation's youth die for a great cause." Loria restated it in terms understandable even to the numbskull standing before him with a look of confusion. "We'll make them martyrs."

The nobility of an action was determined not by the result but by the thought.

Chapter **II**

How many people have praised stupidity as virtue in the context of history? Then it's simple. Appeal not to logic but emotions—and via the ultimate self-sacrifice that no one can disparage!

"We'll man the forward-most line of freedom, peace, and humanity against imperialism! ...And we'll make sure no one abroad can condemn the Federation's morality."

Whoever controls traffic over the
seas can rule the world.

Every time she goes through the gate to the General Staff Office, Tanya thinks, *The higher-ups really just do whatever they want.*

It's been mere hours since she pulled her Kampfgruppe out of the east and returned to the imperial capital. They'd been sent there on the pretext of surveying the situation, but a single sudden order called them back.

Lieutenant Colonel Tanya von Degurechaff is diligent, has a rich work ethic, and is a far cry from those slackers who hate doing their salary's worth of labor. But even she finds a bone to pick when the General Staff keeps changing her assignment.

It's no easy task to move an entire Kampfgruppe from the east back to the capital.

After all, we report directly to the General Staff. And we were deployed to a region on the eastern front under the Eastern Army Group's jurisdiction. It wasn't that we were on loan to them, but we were stationed there. Of course, with orders, we were permitted to leave, but...a rapid withdrawal couldn't possibly go smoothly.

The biggest problem was how to get back to the capital. It's not as simple as a long train ride with a smart card. There are limits to which train cars the Imperial Army can use. Even if we're told on paper that efforts will be made to make a transfer more convenient...that's not always the case in the field.

Even in the comfy plan with the big official stamp on it, the space we are guaranteed on the trains can be lost thanks to the weather, technical issues, or someone else cutting in.

About a week ago, Tanya had been rushing around arranging space for the armored unit and artillery's heavy gear and managed to get her helpful adjutant to pick up some souvenirs from the east.

Chapter **III**

A few days ago, she just barely managed to nap in the cramped first-class compartment.

Last night, she arrived at the capital.

And as she was busy with all that, she received yet another telegram from the General Staff. It was a message from Lieutenant General von Rudersdorf before she could even report in. It really makes you feel that the higher-ups think only of their own convenience.

Of course, that was her personal feeling. She couldn't very well refuse a request based on proper function and authority.

So if she was summoned, she had to go. The moment in the middle of the night that she received the telegram saying to show up at the crack of dawn, she elected to take a nap, and she was right to decide that sleeping even a few hours would give her a clearer head than none at all.

She was slightly less tired when her adjutant woke her up. Then all she had to do as a magic officer in the Imperial Army was put on her immaculately pressed uniform and pry her eyes open with some ersatz coffee, and it was time for work.

As long as she was headed to the General Staff Office, she figured she should bring the souvenirs from the east, so she packed up her officer suitcase and prepared to leave.

Flawlessly dressed according to regulations, she feigned quiet contemplation and nodded off in the car the General Staff sent around—she got her sleep where she could.

From the moment she arrived at the office, she's been willing her sleepiness away. She approaches the MP desk with a disciplined gait.

"State your name and rank."

As usual, it should probably be said? Reception at the General Staff Office, though a formality, is staffed by pros who don't slack.

I don't want to admit it, but I know that I stand out with my appearance as a little girl. These are guys stationed at the entrance to the General Staff Office; they must have superior recall.

"Magic Lieutenant Colonel Tanya von Degurechaff of the Salamander Kampfgruppe, currently assigned to the eastern front."

"Colonel von Degurechaff. One moment please."

People who don't understand tend to scoff at these procedures as a waste of time. Sadly, that means they've gotten too comfortable. Even if both parties know that omitting the administrative tasks goes against regulations, it happens fairly often between friends.

But these fellows at the General Staff Office don't forget to challenge visitors. It's a manifestation of a healthy focus on their job. This is what it means to have a favorable impression of someone and respect them. How could I object to their handling of the situation when it's based on regulations?

"We've received confirmation. You're expected. Please proceed to the Operations Division."

She leaves them with a thank-you and walks the halls she knows by heart. From what she can tell at a glance, there is none of the hustle and bustle that precedes a major operation.

None of the staffers coming and going looks very tense. *So then*, Tanya cocks her head. She was worried that she had been summoned to be sent into another big operation, but...

Was I wrong? She takes a closer look at the passing personnel's expressions, though not close enough to be impolite, but... Just then her gaze rests on a certain face.

"Oh, long time no see."

"If it isn't Colonel Uger. It's been a while."

They exchange salutes and pleasantries upon meeting each other again. When Tanya glances at her watch, she sees she still has some time until her meeting with General von Rudersdorf.

"Well, it's great to see you in one piece. Hey, are you busy today?"

"I arrived much earlier than necessary, so...I do have some time."

"Then, well, come with me for a minute."

He winks and suggests they talk as they walk, but Tanya says, "Before that...," sets down her suitcase, and takes something out. "I'm glad I ran into you. I was going to bring this by later—a thank-you for before."

She's taken out a glass jar. It's one of the many souvenirs she had First Lieutenant Serebryakov buy up in the east.

"It's honey from the region I was stationed in. You can share it with your family, if you like."

"Oh, honestly, this is great. Thank you."

Hmm? Tanya wonders about the *relief* in his words of gratitude. *It's only honey... Is it really something to be that happy about?*

"Well, you gave me coffee, so I thought it seemed right."

Chapter **III**

"Ha-ha-ha, yes, I suppose we both ended up with what we prefer."

Tanya knows Lieutenant Colonel Uger fairly well, since they went to war college together.

He's a person who can be described as tremendously serious and honest. If a mere thank-you gift of honey is enough to get a handshake of gratitude, this is pretty strange.

"…Is the food situation in the rear as bad as all that?"

"It's not a crisis, so in that sense, it's not so horrible."

So he must not be starving. None of the people walking by seemed to be going hungry, either.

Well, Tanya adds.

This is the hub of the Imperial Army, the General Staff Office. If even the staff officers were starving, it would be *no time to fight a war.*

"And actually, rationing is going more smoothly compared to the beginning of the war."

"So life on the home front is all right?"

"Yeah, it's all right. Technically, we should say it's perfectly fine *in terms of calories and nutrition.* Although we're going to get awfully sick of rutabagas this winter."

The tired tone of his voice says it all.

The ration system is working, but only so far as nutrient intake. Rutabagas are a root vegetable and a turnip with no reputation for flavor, at that.

I heard they were originally used as feed for livestock. If that sort of thing has made it onto the ration list…it's easy to gather what the actual state of affairs is like.

"To inquire bluntly, what about luxury items?"

"We probably can't expect many when we're at war. The Commonwealth's naval blockade has deprived our tables of coffee completely."

"Ahhh," she can't help but lament.

I don't *dis*like meals aiming for efficiency, but humans are humans due to their culture and creativity. From the standpoint of respecting personal liberties, it's sad that people's freedom of diet has been limited.

It's another cruel facet of war.

"That's quite serious, then, isn't it? Let's hope for retaliation from our submarines."

"Indeed. Colonel von Degurechaff. I don't know if you have time or not, but if you do, come by the Service Corps desk. I'll treat you to lunch."

"Understood. I'll be looking forward to it. Oh, but it is time, isn't it?"

A glance at a clock on the wall tells her it's nearly time for her appointment.

"Okay, if things go well, I'll see you later."

Though she's worried about the home front, her duty comes first. With a bow, she heads deeper into the General Staff Office where the Operations Division is.

Tanya braces herself, unsure what awaits her...and encounters her greatest enemy: General von Rudersdorf beaming with a plastered-on smile.

The smile of a war planner is never a good sign. If he's laughing? You'd best be turning right back around and escaping, if you can. It's like being sneak attacked by the enemy—who knows what will happen now?

"It's been a long time, Colonel von Degurechaff."

"Yes, sir, it's been a while. My Kampfgruppe arrived in the capital yesterday! We're currently located at the designated barracks."

"Yes, I've heard. I feel bad for the officers, but I thought we should give the men a few days on leave, so I've gone ahead and made those arrangements. To the extent you can, allow them to go home."

"I appreciate your consideration for my subordinates, sir."

Their conversation is based on the formulaic standard, but there is open affection. Though within the framework of superior and subordinate, their exchange seems to indicate their mutual respect.

This is strange as well.

Alarms go off in Tanya's head. *It's really weird for General von Rudersdorf to be so diplomatic.*

A military man who usually gets straight to the point is inexplicably beating around the bush today?

"All right, let's get down to business. Colonel von Degurechaff, you've done a fine job with supporting the main army on the eastern front, investigating the enemy's status, and commanding the experimental Kampfgruppe."

What warm remarks.

If she didn't know what he was usually like, she might have been touched. That's how amicable his tone and eyes are. Conversely, since she does know how he talks on a normal day, she shudders.

He tells me we're getting down to business and then praises me...? What soldier impatient to the point of rudeness would do such a thing?

"I merely did my duty, sir."

"There's no need to be modest. It's due to your peerless devotion. General von Zettour sends his admiration as well."

Now the chills are really going up her spine.

"That and please accept this without protest."

"Thank you, sir."

He offers her a small wooden box.

Wondering if she's being given a bomb, she nervously takes it and finds it to be much heavier than it looks. Now she's sure it must be a bomb, but when she opens it, she finds...a medal?

"It's the White Wings Grand Iron Cross, awarded for your intelligence gathering and test run of the Kampfgruppe. And the recommendation came from—how fancy—the General Staff Military Intelligence Division."

"That's...Wow. I'm so honored."

A "recommendation" from the General Staff Military Intelligence Division? *For a White Wings* Grand *Iron Cross?*

To express her sentiment in metaphor, being presented with a hand grenade would have made her feel more at ease.

This is the Operations Division deep inside the General Staff Office.

But. Tanya tenses up. She might as well be on the front lines. No, this place is as dangerous as no-man's-land on the intense Rhine front.

"Now then, Colonel. You've performed so splendidly, so it's hard for me to say this, but I have an order for the Kampfgruppe to be disbanded."

Tanya gasps. It's so sudden.

"I beg your pardon, General, but what did you just say?"

"I'll be frank, Colonel."

Her superior's joke is hard to grasp. *Is this what it's like to see your shocked expression reflected in General von Rudersdorf's eyes?*

"The Salamander Kampfgruppe has accomplished what it was formed to do. Now we're going to send the units back to their original stations."

"...What?!"

Send them back?

For a moment, Tanya is speechless, but then she yells at her superior.

"Please don't break up my Kampfgruppe! They've finally come together as a combat group!"

"It's the Empire's Kampfgruppe, Colonel."

"…Ngh, please excuse my outburst."

The general wears a small, wry smile and says it's fine as he hands over the sheaf of orders. But Tanya still can't accept it and raises her voice again.

"I worked so hard to train them! A commander like that can't abandon their unit!"

They're my pawns to move.

She doesn't want even a superior officer laying a hand on her men.

…Whether in a company or the military, the chain of command works the same way.

Nothing good comes of a commander's superior overruling them!

Yet now…the General Staff is stepping in on my command?

"It's unheard of to disband a unit that is prepared to be deployed at any time!"

"All your arguments are valid."

"If that's true, then—!" She's about to beg him to reconsider when…

"Colonel von Degurechaff, I'm sure you remember this, but the Kampfgruppe was formed and tested as an ad hoc task force, not as a regular unit."

"…So you're saying I shouldn't have invested in it?"

"The intention was for you to test the 'ad hoc formation' part. You built a magnificent team of elites—too magnificent. I can understand that it's a shame to disband them, but…," he continues soberly. "A single elite Kampfgruppe isn't what we need. Kampfgruppen make many types of combat possible. But the critical factor is the doctrinal knowledge on how to form them ad hoc on an organizational level, not the strength or talent of a single commander."

The logic is sound. Thinking of the entire Imperial Army, it's better to have universal standards that can be applied everywhere rather than outstanding individual feats.

When it comes to Kampfgruppen, I can see how they would want to be operating with many of them.

"I'm sure you understand. In order to create a foundation where the General Staff can form Kampfgruppen and entrust them to officers, we need to acquire the know-how."

We shouldn't go about making an irreplaceable cog. He's right that we need a few people who know about making, duplicating, and employing cogs in an organization.

And in the military, where attrition is a given, it's important to have multiple backups. Logically, it does make sense.

But even so, Tanya still argues. "Please take the situation in the east into account!"

She's practically shrieking.

She has just returned from the forward-most line on the eastern front. For someone aware of what is happening in the present tense, it's impossible to blithely follow logic.

Reasoning that works in one context isn't necessarily sound in another.

"This is only a lull! Shouldn't we acknowledge the value of having a good, able combat asset like a Kampfgruppe as a strategic reserve?"

"Of course we considered using it as a strategic reserve. But the lull is a stroke of luck. Now is the time to look ahead."

"Ahead?"

"Our rate of attrition on the eastern front is severe. If we keep losing soldiers at this rate, our army's combat capability will be worn down to nothing."

"Nrgh." Tanya is lost for words despite herself.

She can't help but nod… The Empire has been pouring vast amounts of blood and iron into the east at an unbelievable pace.

It's not as if the army will cease to exist by tomorrow.

Neither will there be any operation issues next week.

Even next month, the forces should be able to maintain their combat capability.

And with luck, they might make it through next year without collapsing.

But it would still chip away at the Empire's finite human resources. They would slip away like grains of sand in an hourglass.

…But unlike an hourglass, there's no way to flip over and start again.

"Soon we'll be forced to make use of crumbled units. That day may not be tomorrow, but it's coming. So it's essential that we, as an organization, learn Kampfgruppen doctrine so we can reorganize units on the fly, even if it's atypical."

Considering the nightmare of their decreasing human resources, I can understand why Operations would jump at Kampfgruppen operation as the knowledge for reorganizing collapsed units.

"That you pulled off the formation so quickly gave us hope, and we're grateful for that. So I'm sorry, but it's time for the General Staff to test out that know-how. Go back to commanding the 203rd Aerial Mage Battalion for now."

"...Yes, sir."

There's no room to argue. When she thinks of all the authority being taken away from her...she feels downhearted, even.

"That said, at the moment, the only one with successful experience leading a Kampfgruppe is you. In the not-too-distant future, we'd like you to lead one that we form and collect data for us."

"Understood. I'll do my best. When will I be posted to the General Staff–formed Kampfgruppe?"

"Actually, you won't have to wait very long."

"What do you mean, sir?"

"Work is already under way. It should only take another week, maybe ten days. The objective is to give young officers experience. And we don't want you to be without a Kampfgruppe for too long, either."

The idea of having her veteran team taken away from her and being given a test team selected by the General Staff makes her dizzy. I get it because I used to work in HR: It'll be a team that is convenient for HQ but which doesn't take the people on the ground into consideration.

"So what will the battalion and I do until then?"

"I would have liked to give you leave, but the Empire isn't in any position to let free units twiddle their thumbs. We've got work for you to do, Colonel."

"Yes, sir!"

Though she replies gallantly with her heels snapped together, her mind is gloomy in inverse proportion to her voice. This is what it means for your nerves to start wearing thin.

"Very good. Then let's have you play pirates. You can teach real pirates how to fight a war using live ammunition."

He sets an operation plan before her, and the paper makes a slight noise.

Surprisingly, we're being assigned to the north, not the east where the intense fighting is going on. It's a patrol mission over the autumn Northern Sea... If I'm going to do it, I'd much rather do it in the summer.

"...We're joining a maritime patrol line?"

"Yes. There aren't many mage battalions that can handle long-range searches over water. The guys up north came begging us to lend you to them."

The Northern Sea is famous for its cold temperatures. Even though it's only the beginning of fall, it's sure to be chilly already.

Of all the times of year to do long-distance flights through sea breezes... We just keep getting the short end of the stick.

"Nominally, it's an on-the-spot inspection. Well, you'll be given the details when you get there. That said, this is all very sudden—I do feel bad about it. Plan on being gone about a week."

"Understood."

I do understand.

Even if she doesn't accept it, it's an order. *So then.* She grits her teeth. She has to do as they say.

She performs a salute according to the manual, all her fingers perfectly in line.

Thus, after losing her Kampfgruppe, Magic Lieutenant Colonel Tanya von Degurechaff takes in the news that she will be flung into a literal frigid nowhere.

She had no choice. No, she wasn't even asked. She was told. It was unavoidable.

I gotta get this off my mind, she thinks and begins looking forward to the free lunch Colonel Uger promised her.

Not that she doesn't regret that.

...I must have been more sleep-deprived than I realized. What Colonel Uger said was true.

The meal was indeed free.

It was the food from the General Staff Office army dining hall—if you can call the horrifically stewed lumps "food," that is.

"Ha-ha-ha, I heard the news! General von Rudersdorf sure works his people hard."

Sitting across from her, laughing with luxury flatware in hand, is her dear old classmate.

You can't just... Tanya decides to warn him. "Are you familiar with the words *military secret*, Colonel Uger?"

"That's a very good point." He laughs. "But you don't need to worry." He averts his eyes from the not *in*edible thing the General Staff dining room served as lunch and shrugs innocently. "Disbanding the unit and reassigning you guys falls to the Service Corps. In other words..."

He brings his fork to his mouth, frowns for a moment, picks up his water, and washes down whatever it was to continue speaking. It's not good manners to have things in your mouth, so he drank the water for the conversation's sake... Of course, that's just how we dress up the chore of extracting nutrients from disgustingly flavored food.

I'm compelled to remark that the offerings of the General Staff Office's banquet hall taste as horrible as ever. It's like the food quality is sacrificed to and becomes the inverse of the plate quality.

"To give away the secret, I'm in charge. Naturally, then, arguing with you about your assignment is part of my responsibility."

"How nice to have a close friend on the case." She is grateful but also a bit wary, since it's different from usual. "I was sure it was Colonel von Lergen."

They eat as they talk. That way, they can distract themselves from the alleged "food" provided by the mess hall the General Staff is so proud of.

Speaking strictly of the flavor, the food on the forward-most line is a bit...no, quite a bit better. This is a moment she is glad to be a magic officer provided with a high-calorie diet.

The chocolate and cookies they get as extras taste pretty good. If they were the same quality as the banquet hall food, it would be difficult to avoid losing the will to fight.

"Who knows? It's probably just convenient. It's not as if we need to know. Still, a search-and-destroy mission over waters you're assigned to sure brings back memories."

His eyes are expressing something like a smile, but he's not smiling.

Oh, I see.

If he's telling me indirectly not to ask what Colonel von Lergen is up to, then...is that what this is about?

"But...it sure is a pain. As the free unit being sent in, we can't help but be puzzled. An operation premised on an on-the-spot inspection of civilian ships…?"

"Right, what if you accidentally sank them? You have a record, after all. We in the Service Corps will be concerned for the digestive health of our colleagues in legal."

I feel like I've been hit where it hurts. And Tanya can't help but wince. That was an accident, but yeah…I can see how it would be considered a "record."

"And in the Northern Sea…? Commerce raiding up there would be politically problematic."

"So we're being considerate to the people residing on some other continent or whatever?"

There is only one nationality of ship sailing the Northern Sea that would require an on-the-spot inspection. It would only be ships from the Unified States.

When you think about it, there's no reason a civilian ship would be crossing such dangerous waters.

No, there should be no reason at all, and yet strangely…retired Unified States Navy sailors are apparently finding new positions on civilian ships in the Northern Sea.

"It's ridiculous, but on the other hand, I can't say we shouldn't go through with it. Am I wrong, Colonel von Degurechaff?"

So all Tanya can do is respond with a wry smile.

"No, I think you're right. It makes sense."

The General Staff and Army Command, who want to prevent the Federation Army from getting any stronger, have pulled Navy Command into this strange relationship—where they actually have different ideas but are working together—on the pretext of letting them finally take credit for something. Then the Foreign Office must have stepped in to request some political consideration. They're right, but it's the ones in the field who have a hard time.

This is just the kind of situation when you have to hold back a sigh. Bad food, depressing conversation. And on top of that, the annoying situation in the field and political backdrop.

Sheesh. Then just as Tanya is sipping her pseudo–ersatz coffee…

"…So I'm just talking to myself, but…" Colonel Uger speaks suddenly once the waiter has left them. "The Northern Sea operation your unit is being deployed for is made possible by the joint intelligence agency of the Army and Navy Commands."

Tanya cocks her head in spite of herself.

The bad relationship between the General Staff Military Intelligence Division and the joint intelligence department of the Army and Navy Commands is legendary. They always clash on vertical hierarchy, budget allocation, and authority issues. She heard they needed to work on integration, but...

Apparently, this White Wings Grand Iron Cross is going to bring trouble, just as I thought.

"The disbanding of the Kampfgruppe had already been decided. But I heard the higher-ups wanted to put you in the instructor unit doing combat skill research."

...So an extremely reasonable and utterly peaceful life in the rear was stolen from me yet again? *Again?*

"It was a quick intervention that resulted in the change to the north. Intelligence is moving really fast on this. Well, it's no wonder. They're in a much more delicate position than the guys in the Military Intelligence Division."

...They'd messed up in the fights with the Entente Alliance, the Republic, and Dacia.

After ignoring the somewhat forceful warnings from the General Staff, the army and navy must be aiming to regain their power even if it means risking their honor.

"That's why they're so keen to bring down something big."

"And what's that?"

"...I don't know. It doesn't seem like they're planning any major operations."

If the Service Corps isn't aware of it...then they can't be moving that many troops. It would be difficult to use a big army without stockpiling supplies ahead of time with the support of the Service Corps.

"In which case...I'm just talking to myself, but...something smells like trouble."

So that's what's so fishy.

We, the 203rd Aerial Mage Battalion, are inherently fairly easy to use.

We're one of the few commands with outstanding firepower that can be deployed without putting too much stress on the logistics network.

We must be extremely convenient.

The intelligence agency must be envious.

"I'll bear that in mind, although I don't really expect Intelligence to collect accurate info."

"How could you? Those guys need help." With that comment and a wry smile, Colonel Uger's tone of voice changes. *Oh, I see, so that's the end of that conversation, then?*

"…Speaking of needing help, first up should be this dining hall, no?"

"I heartily agree, Colonel von Degurechaff. The General Staff definitely needs some superior intelligence officers and some cooks with a sense of taste."

She agrees, but she also notes that he's holding the conversation back due to the proximity of the waiter, so she arranges her knife and fork and tamely feigns ignorance.

Once their dishes are cleared and Tanya is enjoying her post-meal tea, Uger addresses her, as if he just remembered something, in a businesslike manner. "Now then, I have a present for you. I had Colonel von Lergen arrange a going-away party for your Kampfgruppe at the officers' club. So I hope you'll drink up."

"So there *was* a reason to suffer through this meal."

"Ha-ha-ha. I'm taking a page from General von Zettour's book. Every chance he gets, he treats people from outside to this food."

"The world is going to start calling you Service Corps officers out on your nasty habits."

"Oh, we risk our lives so you guys on the front know how hard we are working. All right, I'll see you again sometime."

"Yes, see you again."

>>> **SEPTEMBER 28, UNIFIED YEAR 1926, EVENING, IMPERIAL CAPITAL** <<<
BERUN, THE NEIGHBORHOOD OF THE OFFICERS' CLUB

Lieutenant Colonel Tanya von Degurechaff is a distinguished magic officer with the Silver Wings Assault Badge, a seasoned aerial mage crowned with the alias White Silver. She's a diligent officer who adheres strictly to the rules but also grasps the concepts of authority and duty well enough to exercise appropriate discretion during missions. As such, she's a good person who hews closely to the image of the Empire's ideal officer.

Thus, Colonel Tanya von Degurechaff has been extremely loyal, if only superficially, to the Imperial Army's paradigm.

Until today, at this moment.

"...Move, Corporal. Do you know whose way you're in?"

"Sorry, Colonel von Degurechaff, but I can't do that."

The one holding his ground even under Tanya's stubborn gaze is...a corporal at the officers' club. Well, if he's an imperial soldier working at the officers' club in imperial capital Berun, then I see—it makes sense that he would be chosen for both looks and ability.

He's not timid, but he also has the proper courteous attitude. Tanya isn't against calling him the best sort of honor guard.

"I'll make myself clear. I'm an active-duty aerial magic officer. If you try to obstruct the exercise of my valid rights, I don't care if you're an MP from our side or not—you won't get off so easily."

"With all due respect, ma'am, it's the rules!"

The only problem is... Tanya repeats her request and sighs internally.

Rules, rules, rules.

What a stickler.

He's like an RPG villager who only repeats his programmed lines. I really start to wonder if all he can say is *It's the rules, so you may not enter.*

So Tanya speaks up with determination. "You must be joking! I'm an officer! Can you not see these?" She points at the insignia on her collar and shoulder and even thrusts her General Staff braid at him, but he doesn't react at all.

"With all due respect, ma'am, the rules prohibit it."

"Sorry, Corporal. As far as I know, there's no rule against officers making use of the officers' club."

"That's true, Colonel, but the law prohibits minors from smoking and drinking!"

"Huh?" The question slips out of her throat in spite of herself as she scowls at him.

What did he...What did he just say?

"S-smoking and drinking?"

Colonel Tanya von Degurechaff is a high-ranking officer who adheres strictly to the rules. Naturally, she is more than well aware of the age restrictions on smoking and drinking.

She doesn't drink or smoke.

Of all the things to say...

"Should I just take that as an insult, Corporal? Who's trying to smoke or drink?! I'm just telling you to let me into the bar!"

"My sincere apologies, Colonel von Degurechaff. Your intent is not at issue! It's purely your age!"

"I'm here on military business!"

The words *age restrictions* disappear when it comes to military business. How could the younger guys fight in the night battles if they had to follow the curfew?! At that point, every last high-ranking officer would have to be dishonorably discharged for aiding and abetting public morality violations.

"It's possible I'm uninformed on the matter, but I haven't heard any ludicrous stories about officers of units fighting in no-man's-land on the Rhine front being indicted by the Ministry of the Interior for commanding minors."

"Huh? Colonel?"

"On military business, the military laws of the Imperial Army take precedence! At a military facility, military law should be applied, no?"

"My apologies, ma'am, but this isn't a military facility! It was established with private capital, so please understand that, legally, minors are strictly prohibited from entering at night!"

When Tanya asks for clarification, the corporal unflinchingly provides the basis for his assertion.

The moment she hears it—*aha!*—she understands why he has been repeating, "It's the rules. You can't enter," even if she doesn't accept it.

It's a problem of interpretation.

Apparently, because the bar is operated by civilians...this corporal doesn't view it as a military facility. *But*, Tanya smiles.

She's quite confident in her legal interpretations.

"The officers' club is funded with private capital. In other words, people who pay the monthly officers' club dues have the right to use it."

Just like mandatory insurance, the dues are deducted every month from her wages. *They force me to pay club dues!* Tanya is therefore compelled to insist on her rights.

As a free individual, she must protect her rights.

I don't care about alcohol or tobacco in particular, but I'm determined to defend my rights from being violated with everything I have. That's the duty of a free individual in modern times. I've got to get bastards like Being X and other numbskull idiots to understand the concept of sacred, inviolable rights.

"I have the right to make use of the facilities." So Tanya doesn't back down. "I'd like you to let me use them."

"I don't mean to deny your right to use the officers' club! But I can't make the call about your use of the bar inside."

So you're going to put up a fight, then? They stand in conflict, frowning at each other.

To Tanya, this futile argument is only a waste of time. She glances at her watch and sees it is nearly time to meet the others.

Of course, officers come five minutes early.

People are waiting for me…, Tanya laments in her head.

Even if it's Weiss, Visha, and Grantz from her battalion, making people wait itself is extremely irritating to someone who is punctual.

Tanya's delicate sensibilities can't endure any more time wasting.

"…This is an official warning, Corporal. Did you get an explicit order from your direct superior to not let minors in? Or are you refusing me on your own discretion?"

She asks if it's him or his superior.

If it's his own discretion, she's determined to push past him without hesitation.

From experience, Tanya knows that you should handle idiots differently from people who have to follow idiotic orders.

If the cause of the issue is a small fry, you should just get rid of him. But if the fundamental issue is higher up, Tanya knows to blame the superior officer.

"I have orders from my direct superior based on the Wartime Public Morality Control Ordinance."

"…Fine, Corporal. I respect your duties. Tell me who gave this shitty, stupid order. Then I want you to call someone who is inside for me."

"Yes, ma'am. Who shall I call?"

"Get First Lieutenant Serebryakov from the 203rd Aerial Mage Battalion. We're going to get a proper record of your statement and then go and protest to your boss."

Which is why...

Even though she knows she'll be laughed at later, she requests that her adjutant be summoned so they can change the venue of the party.

Thus, I suppose?

To mention only the outcome, though it became a small incident that gave the person involved an ulcer, what ended up going in the MP log that day was "Nothing to report."

>>> **SEPTEMBER 30, UNIFIED YEAR 1926, ON A NORDEN-BOUND TRAIN** <<<

Tanya received the sealed orders inside the train that had been arranged with bizarre efficiency.

The officer must have been instructed to politely deliver it in person. The young first lieutenant, who seemed to have come from the academy, mistook Major Weiss as the commander and had to take back the envelope he had nearly handed him, but apart from that and the necessity of making a formal complaint to Army Command, there were no issues.

But...it might be good to add that considering the trouble the day before at the bar, Tanya had every right to be irritated.

And so, though part of the 203rd Aerial Mage Battalion was abnormally tense, the unit entered Norden and finished deploying to the provisional base on the northern edge of the former Entente Alliance territory.

Judging from the collapsed houses and other buildings...the recovery effort wasn't proceeding very smoothly. But the base that had been established, apparently as an aerial foothold, was equipped with the minimum necessary facilities.

There were lodgings for personnel, control officers, and, most importantly, a canteen.

Since she had been told not to open the sealed orders until further notice, she tossed the envelope into the battalion safe and conducted air battle exercises to get her troops used to the climate and the sky.

She even had them do a scramble exercise the exact moment everyone was hung over from dousing themselves in beer after the first exercise.

Once they understood what would happen to them if they let themselves go, she relaxed the reins a bit.

Which is not to say she told them they could drink as much as they wanted. But she did arrange for the canteen to have a stock of alcoholic drinks at the official price as long as they could maintain moderation.

Of course, that put them in the red, so she had to assist with "General Staff Confidential Funds," but...Army Command was picking up the tab this time. The Inspection Division's suggestion that this was appropriation for my own personal use was a misunderstanding.

Tanya kindly replied, "An officer too childish for a messenger to give her the time of day couldn't possibly drink alcohol. It's all merely operation costs to boost morale."

Frankly, if I had a way to embezzle money, I would embezzle as much as I could and worry about it later. Isn't that what they say? To snatch up funding and authority while the snatching is good?

A few days after that, Army Command apparently took some care when sending someone over. The captain who brought documents addressed to Tanya didn't make a mistake.

Upon prying open the sealed orders, she nodded and relayed the information to Weiss.

The captain whined about keeping it confidential, so Weiss and Tanya left First Lieutenants Serebryakov and Grantz with him and went to consider their situation.

The conclusion was that it was worth it to trust the information Intelligence had given them and do a search. Not like they could have refused after being ordered by the General Staff to fulfill as many of the joint intelligence agency's requests as possible, but still.

So it was that, once the briefing had been conducted, the forty-eight members of the 203rd Aerial Mage Battalion flew, in full gear, into the sky over the Northern Sea.

Even in the northern sky, visibility is surprisingly good. No wireless noise or long-range signal hindrances. The elites at Norden Control are providing navigation support.

"Colonel, we've received a transmission. It's a wide-area broadcast from Norden Control. They're saying Case C43…"

"Case C43? So it's what we expected, then."

Tanya groans at the report from her adjutant Lieutenant Serebryakov in spite of herself. Case C43 means the sub unit has discovered the target as expected. Apparently, the Army and Navy Commands' joint intelligence agency is competent enough that they can overcome their vertical structures to support each other laterally for the sake of their mission.

…Yes, awfully competent they are.

"Mm." Tanya nods in deep admiration. "So the army and navy intelligence agency or whatever actually exists. The way they've been working, I figured they were freeloaders at best."

"Ha-ha-ha, you're right. This might be the first time Intelligence has been useful since I've been stationed under you, Colonel."

Serebryakov, laughing next to her, had been with her suffering on the Rhine front—and the reason for that suffering was the failure of command and the General Staff to acquire intel.

Did they work so hard this time to make up for that huge failure?

"I wasn't convinced when I heard they nailed down the route, but we can't ignore it when they give us such a detailed projection bursting with so much confidence."

Expected route, estimated speed, and info about its escort.

The fishy operation plan they approved said that attacking and taking out the engine would be good enough, but now that we know the subs have spotted an enemy ship, the data seems much more reliable.

"Did they break the Commonwealth's code or something?"

"Who knows? They're not about to tell us."

Information sources are protected on principle. You can even call it a rule set in stone.

You might be able to guess things, but the world of espionage is all about deception.

Even if they did tell us where the intel came from, we wouldn't be able to know how much of what they said was true. There can be any number of sources for analysis, from human intelligence assessments to legal means of intelligence collection or even SIGINT.

So it's a waste of brainpower to try to worry about it.

"That's for sure. But, Colonel, if the enemy finds out that we know what they're up to now, won't that hamper future espionage efforts?"

"Visha, we're here to execute. If the top hands us some intel and tells us to move out, worrying about where the intel came from is pointless."

There's a heavy sigh.

To think they would hear an easygoing Lieutenant Grantz come booming over the wireless... I thought he was pretty tense, but he must be an optimist deep down.

"...I'd actually like you to think a bit, though, Lieutenant Grantz."

"M-Major Weiss, that's a little..."

Weiss with his common sense probably can't stand that sort of talk. There's nothing wrong with optimism, but it depends on the context.

No. Tanya has a second thought.

Though they are flying a mission, they haven't yet encountered the enemy. *If Weiss is playing around, I'll join in, too.*

"I agree with Major Weiss. Lieutenant Grantz, if you haven't been using your head, then you're not tired at all, right? How about you use your brain to do the battalion's complicated paperwork?"

"C-can I beg for mercy?"

Grantz must be used to the battlefield enough to catch the change in tone.

"Hey now, Lieutenant Grantz. They say the commander's supposed to lead the charge, right? Are you lacking initiative? This is no good. I can't believe a company commander is revealing his lack of fighting spirit before the enemy..."

"Major, give me a break!"

"That's enough. It's important to ease the unit's tension, but I don't think anyone in my battalion is delicate enough to be nervous except for me."

"Ha-ha-ha-ha. Now you really must be joking!" Weiss laughs cheerfully.

"Don't you know what a young girl's heart is like? I guess my only friend here is Lieutenant Serebryakov."

"Excuse me, but Colonel? We're concerned that our dear Visha will vanish. Just what kind of monster are you trying to develop her into?"

"A proper magic officer, clearly. I'd appreciate it if you wouldn't make it sound like she's evil."

Chapter **III**

Just a little show of banter for our subordinates before we head into combat.

"...All right, you two, if you could leave it at that. There's signs of a ship up ahead on the route where we're projected to encounter the enemy. I've spotted it."

The one who goes so far as to warn us to quit joking around is the one we were talking about. Lieutenant Serebryakov doesn't even need to be developed—she's already a fine soldier.

Abruptly switching gears, Tanya takes her binoculars and points them in the direction her adjutant indicates.

It's a little dot, but she can see it. Actually, with that size...if she can see it at this distance, it must be pretty huge.

No doubt about it.

It's the prey they were expecting, the giant RMS *Queen of Anjou*. It would be difficult to mistake this singular ship capable of carrying large amounts of both weapons and personnel.

"It's huge, huh? It's just one transport ship, but it's still pretty overwhelming to see. Well, I guess it's not quite appropriate to call it just a transport ship. It's like twisting reality with words."

In terms of size alone, it appears to surpass even the capital ships of the High Seas Fleet. This ship, weighing tens of thousands of tons, races at incredible speeds across the water and would no doubt break through anything besides a minefield. Once you lay eyes on it, you realize how imposing it is, even if you don't want to.

"...Colonel, this is bigger than expected, I guess you'd say," Weiss murmurs in shock. When he comments on how gigantic it is, all she can do is nod.

Tanya herself should have known—it was something big enough to warrant a special mission. But even so...the spectacle before her eyes is formidable.

"...Intelligence back home is asking too much."

"I heard the terms, too, but this is..." Lieutenant Serebryakov trails off. From the way she is peering through her binoculars, the remark was probably half to herself.

"Hearing and seeing are two very different things. They say a floating castle of iron is a warship, but that's a floating *palace* of iron."

It came from my heart.

It's been a long time since there's been a fierce battle between a maritime guard and a commerce raider over the water.

About the only carefree lone ships are of neutral nationality or ships that the warring countries have agreed to allow to pass—medical boats or prisoner exchanges. Any other ship going alone in these waters would get laughed at as not a daredevil but just plain reckless.

To any unit watching sharp-eyed for prey, an unaccompanied merchant ship is a sitting duck. The Imperial Army's submarines and air units are excellent hunters.

"And it's awfully fast. I'm just eyeballing it, but it seems like they're going…over thirty knots."

"They sure are. It's weird… I thought merchant ships had a max speed of twenty. I'm sure that's what we were taught."

"There's always an exception, Major Weiss."

And this high-speed transport ship before their eyes is one of those few exceptions. It's a huge ocean liner built not for economic efficiency but out of national pride.

I'd like to laugh it off as a white elephant, but the harsh reality is that I can't.

"I can see why the imperial blockade basically wouldn't function."

Usually, the bigger a ship gets, the more speed it sacrifices. The heavier, the slower. So as a matter of course, a huge ship ends up slow no matter what you do.

Large transport ships tend to be extra slow due to the added weight of their cargo. But apparently, those rules don't apply to this ship.

"I'm altogether jealous. It must be so stable. If only we had had a ship like that for going to the southern continent, then no one would have gotten seasick."

"I agree, Major. It's hard not to be envious of a maritime state's cargo-passenger ships."

The sea is rough, but this giant ship isn't pitching at all.

No, its conspicuously elegant hull slices through the waves as it speeds along. This queen is one wild filly. She can't be going less than thirty knots.

And astonishingly, that's its *cruising speed*. And if you consider that it's

packing enough fuel for a round-trip…it'd be practically impossible to catch with a run-of-the-mill navy ship. I'd like to ask them if they even know what the word *economical* means.

"That's with a typical transport ship load, so I'm utterly amazed."

If it was simply a fast transport ship, it would still be easy to deal with. It would have been a distraction but tolerable. The problem is that it's enormous.

It was originally built before the war as a passenger ship… Full of people, it rushed across the open sea.

It was the fastest way to travel besides a plane. And if you wanted to, you could pack it with tons of people and cargo.

This is just an estimate, but I bet it could carry a division's worth of personnel at thirty knots. Or you could fill it with weapons and ammunition and send it cutting across the vast ocean with that thirty-knot speed.

It's practically a moving maritime logistics base. *Palace* was the right word.

"All right, battalion. Obviously, we can't let that thing be."

"We sure can't!"

To the Imperial Army, this is nothing but a strategic nightmare. No matter how thorough they're being with the commerce raiding operations, it'll be meaningless if the RMS *Queen of Anjou* gets through.

If the enemy laughed off the blockade mission the submarine units were making such harsh sacrifices for, where would that leave us? And that's why…we must sink the RMS *Queen of Anjou*.

"Well, that's why they picked us to give these orders to. Battalion, prepare to attack."

"Yes, ma'am. Battalion, prepare to attack!"

"If possible, stop the enemy warship, er, boat. Use explosion formulas to blow away the engine or the rudder!"

For a second, she nearly calls it a warship—it's that imposing. The order to halt Her Majesty as she calmly crosses the vast ocean is definitely another instance of getting the short end of the stick.

I'm impressed the joint intelligence agency managed to pick it up. And I can see why Operations would want to send us in. Even with an ambush, it would be pretty hard to capture it with our existing ships.

"This boat is just too much. They've shaken off our superficial efforts and existing paradigm and technology with that size and speed…"

For starters, there's no way a submarine is going to catch a ship that was a contender for the Blue Riband. I can feel myself ready to grumble at the sky.

It's not like the imperial subs are subpar.

But subs that even on the surface reach only the twenties when pushing their engines to the limit just can't compete. And they never expected to have to go up against such a giant monster of a ship.

So it surpasses the imperial subs. The only ones who can chase it are the air forces the Empire is so proud of.

But sadly…

The Empire's planes are severely limited when it comes to anti-ship attacks.

After all, it's an issue of whether the mission fits the scope of a tactical air force aiming to support ground troops and fight air battles. Have they begun outfitting themselves for maritime aerial power?

With horizontal bombing, it's hit or miss. In that respect, aerial mages—the other air force—are much more accurate.

Hitting the boat, we can do.

I've even heard that troops in the south and west have had success in operations attacking smaller ships and torpedo boats.

"Understood. But I think stopping that ship is going to be pretty tough…"

"Even just the engine is probably built to be strong."

"Right, we can't ignore the question of whether our firepower will penetrate it."

But even that is full of issues, as Tanya is forced to point out.

First, aerial mages don't have unlimited firepower. Particularly when it comes to stopping a huge ship, all we can do is hope for secondary explosions.

"Or maybe we could attack the sides and cause it to take on water or damage the propeller…"

To rob the ship of propulsion, we could probably pull off a focused attack on the stern. *But.* Tanya is at a loss in this vexing situation.

"But don't you think they'd have taken some measures against that?"

"Yes, I'm sure at that size they have buoyancy to spare. They may even have a spare rudder. I don't think we can expect results if we go into this without more info."

Tanya nods at Weiss's complaint.

"If only those guys in Intelligence could find us a map of the layout."

"Apparently, they at least know that there aren't many escorts."

"But that's a given, isn't it, Major Weiss? It's way too reckless to ask us to take on that mobile foothold with such few numbers. If they didn't have that sort of intel, we wouldn't be taking on that huge ship."

Our target is a passenger ship. To be explicit, it's a boat that carries *people*. We're fatigued from our long flight, while the enemy is brimming with the energy to come up and intercept.

We wouldn't have even considered coming near this thing if Intelligence hadn't guaranteed us that *the Commonwealth is relying on its speed and not attaching many escorts*.

"…Huh?"

Something seems slightly off.

"Abort the attack! Turn around—now!"

It's not as if I believe in the frankly suspect idea of a sixth sense, but something is weird.

The moment Tanya senses it, she doesn't hesitate.

The 203rd Aerial Mage Battalion was in assault formation, ready to swoop down and attack, but they respond to Tanya's command immediately.

"Break! Get out of attack formation! Increase altitude! Hurry!"

"Yes, ma'am!"

Her subordinates neither question nor argue, and Tanya is thankful for their understanding. Right as everyone begins climbing in prep for an attack from below…

"Mana signals! Multiple signatures from the enemy ship?!"

"Disciplined fire, incoming!"

What they shoot, without using their sights to aim, is an attack calculated to hit the entire area. The mix of regular and formula bullets is far more orderly than haphazard firing.

Even a battalion won't make it through unscathed if it flies into a hail of bullets. If we had been a few seconds later, we would have been turned into Swiss cheese.

"It's a battalion—no, a r-regiment?!"

"The mana signals are rapidly increasing! What the—?!"

I can't help the screams of my men echoing in my head.

Since we dodged quickly, the battalion hasn't taken any losses. But it's probably too soon to call it a close shave and be done with it.

As the situation continues to rapidly evolve, Tanya bites back her curses and suddenly thinks: *Our augmented battalion is being fired on by a regiment.*

If an enemy you have no intel about attacks you preemptively, it's hard not to break step. Really, we're probably blessed, considering we didn't lose anyone.

"01 to all units. Abandon the original plan! Abandon the plan! Ascend—get some distance!" She clicks her tongue in frustration as she has them get out of assault formation and climb. "This isn't what we were told! Those bastards in Intelligence are freeloaders after all!"

She means what she shouts.

We were told that due to the difficulty in mustering manpower, the ship would have only the minimum escorts…but that is clearly not the case. Intelligence has really half-assed it.

I don't know if they cocked it all up, or latched on to some bad info, or what.

But in the end, it comes down to their work being hurried. Cursory. We should have beat the General Staff's philosophy—the devil is in the details—into those administrative numbskulls' heads.

"Colonel, it's a unit of Commonwealth marine mages! A regiment and closing in fast!"

"That can't be all. Assume they have two regiments."

"Roger!"

Our premise that the giant ship had only minimal escorts…has been shattered. The ship is huge. If they wanted to, they could fit a whole division on it.

If we just got attacked with discipline fire from a regiment, there must be more where that came from.

"If we can rob it of propulsion, the submarines should be able to work for us, but…it's unclear if we'll actually be able to stop it…"

He had heard it said. Major General Habergram had warned him: "*Since we have a mole, the enemy might show up.*"

Lieutenant Colonel Drake, leading the Commonwealth's marine mages, recalled the superior officer who had guaranteed him, "*That said, with the deception and the thorough information war we've carried out, there should only be a few if they do show up.*" He heaved a sigh.

"...You dodged *that*?"

He thought it was a perfectly targeted shot. The enemy had been in formation to dive and attack when his troops had unleashed a screen of anti–air fire straight down their path.

They had even suppressed their mana signals so they wouldn't be detected beforehand.

Despite all that, the enemy mages veered away at the last possible moment. Given the distance and the timing, the only possible explanation was that their commander had suspected something immediately before the charge.

"What is it, Colonel Drake?"

"No matter how you look at it, their intuition is just too good. And I recognize some of the signatures in there. This is the Named we fought the other day—I'm sure of it!"

He just barely kept his face from tensing and looked up to see the enemy unit increasing their altitude. They were so full of fight they not only saw through the sneak attack but were even taking distance to overcome their numerical disadvantage.

Even a high-speed military transport ship boasting a cruising speed of thirty knots would be slow against opponents in flight. It would be very bad to allow them to remain hanging around.

And so, they had to approach their braced enemy.

"Apparently, General Habergram is unfamiliar with the battlefield. Didn't he say that...ambushing them with two regiments would be plenty?"

Given how important this route is, did they go all out with their guard unit?

Chapter **III**

Are we being ordered to fight this Named unit with this few people?

This was nothing like what they'd been led to expect.

…He should have expected that the unit reporting directly to the Imperial Army General Staff would show up. Not that there was anything they could do about it now.

"That said…we can't let them get away without a fight…"

The bitter memories trickled back.

He had learned from experience in their encounter on the Rhine front, so he was aware, whether he liked it or not, of how much trouble this imperial Named unit was.

They had spirit and skill, but they also had a habit of taking the initiative and doing what their opponents hated. *Surely they all have devil tails.*

"These are the warmongers who hunted the voluntary army from the Unified States. Stay on guard. Attack with all your might. This fight will take everything we've got. Get both regiments in the air. This boat isn't about to sink from the firepower of a mage unit, so let's get up there and attack!"

"Pirate 01, this is Anjou CP. An all-out interception is fine, but it'll lower our guard against subs. Even just a battalion is fine, so please leave a reserve force as direct support for the *Anjou*."

"Sorry, even giving you a single company will leave us hard up. I'll leave a voluntary mage company, but consider any more than that impossible."

"I heard it's a Named, but are they really that tough?"

Drake sighed over the wireless as his response. To him, it was so obvious it didn't need to be debated.

They're our natural enemy, a serious threat.

To put it plainly, he loathed them so much, it made him want to whine in a pathetic, ungentlemanly way.

"If there is anyone I don't want to encounter right now, it's them."

"I understand that you think highly of them, but they've flown a long way to get here, right?"

"Even if they have, and they're terribly tired, facing that battalion will still be a struggle for us. It would be easier to clash with other imperial forces with numbers equal to ours."

He meant every word of his grumbles. Marine mages were brave. Many of them were skilled veterans. That said, they had been worn down since the start of the war.

They were replenishing their losses with fresh soldiers and new recruits, so they weren't in ideal condition to engage in combat. If that was their situation, regrettable though it may be, they had to consider the possibility of a breakthrough.

"Anjou CP, a word of warning. This might be the same imperial unit that attacked them before. Please keep an eye on the voluntary troops."

"Roger, Pirate 01. Things'll be much easier if you guys can clean them up properly."

"We'll do our best, but don't expect too much."

His quiet reply was his true feeling.

With neither vanity nor condescension, he was confident they were the best marine mages. It was a conviction regarding their pride and self-assurance, or perhaps their duty.

But he was fully aware that they weren't guaranteed the glory of victory unconditionally—that's not how things worked on the battlefield. He wasn't a green newbie, unfamiliar with the fog of war. He'd seen many a defeat snatched from the jaws of victory, only a stone's throw away.

Only God knew what would happen when their greatest enemy and their greatest ally clashed. Drake wasn't arrogant enough to assume the winner. As a man in the same business, he understood the Imperial Army's ability so well it made him sick. And against Named, he knew it would be an intense fight.

But that didn't mean anything.

Pulling off a win while you were nervous was a fantasy.

"...*That* tough?"

"Yeah, that tough."

If they put in every last desperate effort, would it work?

Well, maybe. So that was enough. If they could bet on the possibility, then they could carry on through power of will. *All right, we've got to try it.*

"Pirates, it's time for war! And we've got them heavily outnumbered! They've come such a long way, so give them a nice welcome!"

As he shouted his command, warriors adapted to the sea air took off.

Though even a two-thousand gap in their altitude was painful, the enemy was already ascending to eight thousand.

Is that gap actually eight thousand?

Absurd.

If they ended up getting shot down in a one-sided attack from above, they'd end up a textbook-case laughingstock.

But we have no choice.

"Split into companies and eat into the enemy defensive fire! All units, this is a fight to punch through! Rush them!"

Each company commander encouraged his subordinates within earshot as they rose, weaving through the bullets, thermic beams, and explosion formulas that rained down.

One bad hit and they'd be shot down like that.

"Don't flinch away! We're a regiment! Our opponent's a battalion!"

"Keep pushing till we've surrounded them! Show them how to fight a war, gentlemen!"

"We're gonna show these landlubbers how we do things at sea! Let's go!"

It was just a charge to overwhelm the enemy's processing power with numbers. It was a confession of ineptitude, a stupid plan to crush the enemy under the corpses of his subordinates.

It was nothing short of a brute-force move, but he had no other choice.

"All right, you gentlemen sons of bitches! Follow me!"

 THE SAME DAY, THE 203RD AERIAL MAGE BATTALION

We're actually eight thousand above. No normal mage units would challenge us under those circumstances.

There shouldn't be... Or so I wanted to believe.

But apparently, these Commonwealth jerks take sports, war, and nothing else too damn seriously.

Suppressing a tongue click, Tanya looks down at the Commonwealth mage companies each making their own approach. Even throwing firepower at them to keep them down, they haven't lost any momentum.

I'd like to write them off as daredevils, but vexingly, their fighting spirit and skills don't seem to be inversely proportioned. They're coming at us with magnificent evasion, defense, and teamwork.

…If we really engage, their numbers will probably crush us.

"01 to all units! Prepare to withdraw!"

My abrupt decision is to avoid the encounter.

"01, if we withdraw now, they're likely to pursue!"

"I know! My company will charge to cause confusion! The rest of the units I'm leaving to you, 02. Have them perform delaying combat and support the charge!"

My unit and I will distract the enemy with an attack on the RMS *Queen of Anjou*. I leave the rest of the battalion to Major Weiss and an evacuation operation.

"05 to 01. Please let my company do it."

"Why not give your subordinates a chance to shine once in a while? I'm confident I or 05 could do it."

A proposal from First Lieutenant Grantz and an encouraging rejoinder from Weiss.

Tanya suddenly wonders something and brings it up. "So how come you don't include my adjutant?"

"Ha-ha-ha. Because we know it goes without saying."

"All right… Hmm."

She does think relatively highly of the others' abilities. They may be a bit overly war crazy, but they do know when to quit.

…*Who should I send as the distraction?* She's unsure until…she suddenly thinks…

"Then we'll all go." Her subordinates are about to acknowledge, but she beats them to the punch and says, "These are orders from your battalion commander. All units, split into companies and charge. I say again, split into companies and charge."

When you think about it, if the enemy is coming up at us…we just have to obliterate them with impulsive force. Adding the speed of our fall to our charge, we'll have the energy advantage over our climbing enemy.

"Dive! If the enemy is going to come up, we'll beat them down!"

Just because the enemy wants to see if they can saturate our processing power doesn't mean we have to go along with it. If they're split up, it means they have holes.

I'm reluctant to leave things up to probability theory.

But even in a 2-D trench battle, you can keep casualties low by running around. In the 3-D sky, as long as there aren't any proximity fuses…if all we're trying to do is break through, it shouldn't be impossible.

"Cut straight through! These guys are convinced the sky is small, so let's show them how big it really is!"

The point isn't a charge by an augmented battalion.

"Maybe they could stop an augmented battalion, but can they stop four augmented companies? Follow your commander's judgment and crush them!"

Tanya howls fiercely in the salty air. It serves both to encourage herself and to announce a charge that will probably kill some percentage of her troops.

"All units, charge!"

An augmented battalion vs. two regiments. There's no way to make up that numerical disparity. Normally, it would be suicidally bizarre for the Imperial Army to choose a charge under these circumstances.

Which was precisely why it was totally unexpected for Lieutenant Colonel Drake. He was so certain of his troops' numerical superiority that he had been thinking what the best way to chase the enemy mages would be.

No, no one on the Commonwealth side anticipated this.

"…?! Disciplined fire! Stop them!"

He shouted, but he wasn't fast enough. There was no time for interdiction fire. For the Commonwealth mages, this was a literal bolt from the blue.

"Don't bunch up! Break!" "Don't take it?!" "No, stop them! Don't let them get the boat!" "Assume there'll be damage!" "Tear through the confusion!" "We can't help you if you drop out!" "Just look straight ahead!" "Jettison your gear!" "Move!" "Speed up!" "Slice through! Forward!"

*   *   *

Chaos, shrieking, shouting, screaming. But amid the tumult, the battle cries of each level's commanders as they work to maintain discipline are reassuring. I'm glad to know that subordinates are doing their jobs.

"...No irregularities here. I guess we made it through?"

A little grin appears on Tanya's face in spite of herself.

Making it through despite the mistaken intel they received brings her no small satisfaction. Things are simple on the battlefield: The one who makes the right decision first gets lucky.

And the Goddess of Victory has smiled on the Imperial Army, who took their enemy by surprise by charging from the heavens. It was a breakthrough battle where they employed their magic blades at close quarters to cut off the heads that seemed to belong to enemy commanders. They had pounced from above. The freedom to choose their prey belonged to the 203rd Aerial Mage Battalion as they accelerated due to their fall velocity.

"We broke through the vanguard!"

"Company, break! Penetrate in squads! You can withdraw after each shot! It's practically a harassment attack, but as long as it connects, that's fine!"

This is all even the two climbing regiments amounted to, once taken by surprise.

Tanya smiles in satisfaction and savors the fruit of her determination. The enemy mages they've left behind are in utter turmoil.

True, the Commonwealth companies certainly have excellent commanders. *But...* Tanya chuckles to herself. Because they're so excellent, they're chasing two hares.

It can be said that the commanders of the few companies who are already turning to give chase are making an appropriate call in an unexpected situation.

Not letting us get to the object of their protection, the RMS *Queen of Anjou,* is correct. And their attitude, in an escort mission, of trying to defend even if they have to stick to us isn't mistaken, either.

Likewise, the other fellows' choice to try to occupy the sky is also valid. It's a textbook handling of the situation and the very definition of an appropriate tactical decision. If they can secure the position above us, then the tables will be turned and they'll be the ones one-sidedly firing down at the 203rd Aerial Mage Battalion.

There's just one problem.

They're outstanding, but the quick decisions born of that eminent ability are their misfortune. In other words, they shouldn't have chosen either of those.

"Use the Commonwealth mage units on our heels as a shield and close in on the ship!"

The ones giving chase are preventing the ones in the sky from shooting us. Several companies have been suddenly and effectively taken out of the game.

Without even fighting, the enemy force has been halved, if only momentarily.

Then, because of their superficial excellence, they make a mistake.

"Colonel! The enemy companies coming after us are splitting up! They're trying to secure a line of fire!"

"That's some armchair theorizing by someone who doesn't know how hard it is to fire through your allies during high-speed maneuvers. Adjust your angle and avoid their line of fire!"

"Yes, ma'am!"

Tanya barks and the battalion's seasoned officers respond.

"This is so nostalgic. It reminds me of the Rhine front."

"You said it, Lieutenant Serebryakov. You're exactly right. It reminds me of the trench battles! All right, troops, time to play a game from back in the day: tag!"

With the enemy in pursuit, we strike our target. It was like how we used to do company-scale night raids in the trenches, where if the enemy reinforcements caught up to us, that was it.

Our target this time is the RMS *Queen of Anjou* sailing leisurely below us. The only thing between the battalion and the ship is a tiny defense unit.

Lieutenant Colonel Tanya von Degurechaff has a sudden thought: *I think we can do this.*

*　　*　　*

Mary Sue would probably never forget that moment.

It always came out of nowhere.

…Suddenly, the alarm signaling combat rang out on deck.

"Warning, enemy approaching! We've also succeeded in identifying their wavelength! It's a Named unit!"

"What's their status?!"

"It's the one we confirmed on the Rhine front!"

"On the Rhine?! Those guys?"

Those guys.

That…

…The one who killed my father.

And my friends.

My… Our enemy.

Which is why I set off running. With my rifle and my orb tight in hand, I ran up on deck. My friends who came after me have the same thing on their minds.

Revenge.

Our anger, our friends' anger, our families' anger.

Above all, we don't want to lose anything else. To protect, we have to fight. The power to do that, my weapons, are in my hands.

"All marine mages, prepare to intercept! Get up there!"

Believing that, I told the officer in command, Colonel Drake, "We'll go, too!"

And having asked for a part to play, I was met with…a cold refusal.

"Sorry, Lieutenant Sue. You guys are on direct support for the RMS *Queen of Anjou* on the lookout for subs. Stick close here and don't let them approach the ship!"

My brain can comprehend the Commonwealth commander's firm words. We, the voluntary army…aren't without our faults.

"But…" *I tried to tell him how I felt, but there was no time.* "…Colonel Drake, we can do it. Please let us avenge our friends."

"This was our decision after considering our situation and your level of training. There's no time to debate. I'm not accepting objections."

So up they flew.

All we could do as we watched them go was hope they would win. While our friends, everyone, was fighting, we were left behind on the ship.

I know holding down the fort is an important duty.

...Still...

"...This is so frustrating. I didn't know being unable to do anything was so hard."

A teeny, tiny murmur.

What I, what we, the voluntary army, could do or not do didn't matter. It was just an infuriating situation.

Looking up at the sky, I saw my friends fighting my enemy and shedding blood. Please win.

Let everyone be safe.

With those as our only wishes, we stood there watching...and everything changed before our eyes.

"Emergency! The enemy broke through!"

"What?! Against that gap in fighting power?!"

Shock and confusion echoed over the wireless. But Mary and only Mary knew it, somewhere in her mind. *Ahhh.*

What did you expect? They're like devils.

"Direct support unit, intercept immediately! Lieutenant Sue, you're good to go up, right?!"

"Y-yes, sir!"

A chance, her enemy, came at her.

I have to defend.

I can't let them take anything else.

Harboring determination in her breast, Mary inhaled slightly and glared up at the diving enemies.

This time we can do it.

We're not letting you get away with this.

Considering how things are going, it's not impossible to complete the mission to perfection. But after thinking things all the way through, Tanya concludes they should cut their losses.

She thought it was doable and was very nearly determined to do it. But what dampened her enthusiasm were the battalion's losses. She doesn't want to say the mission was pointless, but they are in the middle of nowhere...so having their human resources needlessly expended is the worst-case scenario.

"Somebody give him a shoulder to lean on! Get him upright!"

"Lieutenant Grantz, I'm fine..."

"I'd rather get a lecture from the colonel than be the kind of first lieutenant who leaves a man behind!"

The transmissions crisscrossing internally are shrieks and screams that indicate losses. The battalion is still maintaining discipline and functioning as an organization, but she can't ignore the fact that they have casualties.

In other words, the troops are just barely holding out and not collapsing. Even my battalion of unrivaled strength is a collection of humans. I don't want to make them bend over backward any more than necessary. If you could win a war based on mind-set alone, the megalomaniacs would be the strongest force in the world.

In other words, I need to reevaluate my hand.

We've taken repeated casualties. We just barely managed to break through and approach the ship, but...the enemy is starting to react. Shockingly, we're already taking long-range fire.

These Commonwealth guys...they must have, surprisingly, resigned themselves to missing some shots, because they've begun pointing a nasty amount of long-range sniping formulas at us.

"Colonel?"

"Withdraw! We're withdrawing!"

Even my vice commander who laughs over the wireless can't be all right with sacrificing his subordinates. Even I don't welcome human attrition.

"We'll scatter the enemies up ahead as we pull out! Score one hit-and-run!"

Now, then. Tanya is determined to follow through on her original plan of one attack.

Intelligence's request to take out the RMS *Queen of Anjou*'s engine is now virtually impossible. Putting in the effort to pull off a hit-and-run on their way, out of obligation, is the most they can do.

If we carry out our minimum duty, all that's left is to RTB.

It's time to cut our losses.

Only a fool would continue pouring resources into this hopeless project.

And we can act out of obligation to HQ and Intelligence for only so long. I won't let them chip away at my finite and irreplaceable resource, the subordinates I trained, any longer.

"All units! If you're hit, prioritize withdrawing! Everyone else, we're gonna nail the ship once and get out of here! There's no reason to hang around!"

""""Roger!"""""

My troops acknowledge enthusiastically; morale is running high.

"An enemy mage company is rapidly approaching from up ahead! We should maintain combat distance and—"

"No need. Cut them down!"

Serebryakov's thought as she shouts a warning isn't bad, but Tanya cuts her off.

"Colonel?"

It's only natural Serebryakov would question directions that go against theory, but Tanya assures her. "These enemies are late in coming. They're under a different command. I'm guessing they're second-stringers meant to detain us. Our priority is to punch through. Don't use explosion formulas, since they could hit friendlies. Expect a brawl once we cut in. Mop them up with sniping and close-quarters combat—our intent is to trounce them!"

Right before engaging, Tanya instructs her troops to switch from explosion formulas to sniping formulas.

Then...perhaps they're wary of area-of-effect attacks? The enemy company splits up in orderly textbook fashion, and the 203rd Aerial Mage Battalion with its comparatively dense formation charges.

It's as good as punching out scattered enemies with a hardened fist.

"Geez."

She shrugs as they fight a simple battle to mow down the recklessly engaging enemy mages. *These guys never learn.* She chuckles to herself.

Then just as she draws her submachine gun to take out an enemy mage.

When she feels an extreme chill, she abruptly accelerates. The next moment, she gasps as she nearly gets burned by radiant heat.

A thermic beam?

She doesn't even have time to shout, *What the—?!*

"This is for my father!" The enemy mage charges as if she wants to clash blades. Her eyes spell trouble—a mix of pure hostility and hatred.

I want to yell, *What did I do?*

In fact, Tanya actually does. "What did I do?!"

"D-d-don't play games with me!"

There is no reason I should be accused of playing. I always take my job *very seriously.* I can proudly declare that to anyone.

I'm not the type to play games while fighting a war.

On the contrary. Tanya snaps, "I can't even believe I'm fighting someone so ridiculous. We're fighting a war, you know! Yet you have a personal grudge? Preposterous!"

"B-b-but you!"

On the furious enemy mage's face is a hideous grimace. If she was smiling, she'd have a face like a flower, but she twists it up with hatred to project her hostility at me.

I don't remember her face, but did we fight somewhere before?

Eh. Tanya stops thinking at that point and fires off three formulas to hold her at bay. Apparently, the enemy isn't foolish enough to strike when it's impossible. When she dodges, she's calm enough to launch a few optical formulas as she takes some distance.

"Colonel, the enemy marine mages are on our tails. We should withdraw!"

"Roger. What's the status of the enemy ship?"

"We're strafing the deck. We should also have scored a few direct hits to the engine, but..."

"Just make sure we have a photographic record. It'll be handy, I'm sure."

My battalion briskly accomplishes all the tasks that need to be done—they're wonderful. When I glance over at the ship, I see my valiant subordinates bombarding it with formulas.

But that acts as a trigger, and the enemy regiments head rapidly our way.

"Okay, any more than this is a waste of time. We're pulling out!

Withdraw!" As she's about to yell, *Let's go!* she just barely evades another attack.

The murderer who fired the optical sniping formula is the mage from before. Surprisingly, though she doesn't exhibit much skill in building the formula, it has exceptional power and speed.

Apparently, she's manifesting extra-fast by forcing more mana into it.

"You're running away?!"

"Quit your yapping! We're in a hurry."

The energy for a long-distance flight, a battle, and now a withdrawal. All considered, I don't have time to putz around with a persistent opponent.

"Colonel, hurry!"

"I know, Major! I'm coming!"

To restrain the enemy, I fire another three explosion formulas. It's an attack that prioritizes the area of effect over power, so it's obviously lacking in the latter.

The numbskull tailing me flutters away like a kite, but she's still flying, which means I didn't down her... She's amazingly tenacious for a newbie. I guess you'd have to say she's a survivor.

No, on top of that, her defensive shell was stronger than I expected... What a pain. Considering what could happen later, I'd really like to finish her off now.

"Tch! I guess it'll take more than this to get away."

I don't need Weiss to tell me I don't want to get chased around by a regiment of marine mages. I'm not into life-and-death tag. Even at times like this, I want the freedom to choose who I play with.

"...At this rate, it's going to be a struggle to get back."

We flew long-distance, then got exhausted in combat, and now we have to deal with creeps trying to follow us home?! This is the worst withdrawal leg I can think of.

I suppose I should laugh at how humiliating it is to fail to finish off a numbskull with skin only slightly thicker than a newbie's... When it rains, it pours.

"Ngh?!"

Tanya twists her body to dodge a thermic beam—shocked.

She almost shouts, *Again?!* but it's different this time.

It was a long-range optical sniping formula. I can't believe those Commonwealth marine mage bastards can aim accurately from so far away!

When she looks up, she's irritated to see that they're beginning to regain discipline.

We'll be no match for a one-sided rain of rapid fire from above. It would be target practice.

Sticking around here any longer will only be a waste of time.

Tanya accelerates to resume her withdrawal, ignoring the numbskull enemy mage dogging her. She zigzags in random evasive maneuvers and meets up with the rest of the battalion.

"05 to 01. Before we go, if I may?"

"What is it?"

"Partly to slow them down, I was thinking maybe we could use long-range formulas to set the deck of the ship on fire."

Since they're close together, the intra-unit signal comes through clearly. Hearing Grantz's suggestion, Tanya smiles. *Aha, not bad.*

When you're accelerating away, sniping most moving targets is impossible.

But a huge target like this ship is a different story.

They were sticking close to the RMS Queen of Anjou, *but now that you mention it...* To the escorts, this ship is precious. So we should give them the chance to protect what is precious to them. I'm sure they'll be thrilled.

"...Good idea! Long-range explosion formulas minus the crushing effect!"

We were ordered only to stop the ship. She's the princess. Even these obnoxious pirate knights can't very well abandon their princess.

"Put all your mana into the flames! Prepare to manifest! Fire in unison! They must be cold serving in the Northern Sea; let's warm them up!"

"Understood! Leave it to us!"

Just as she's about to shout, *Here we go!* Tanya senses an enemy rushing her headlong. *She just won't give up!*

"W-wait!"

"I'm touched that you miss me, but...?"

I need to hurry. I can't get caught up with this obstinate pseudo-stalker and lose my chance to withdraw.

"I don't have a pacifier, so suck on this!"

The trick I conjure up is one of the Imperial Army's lovingly crafted potato mashers.

Normally, they only explode an area ten meters across, but this one has a formula bullet embedded in its head.

With the formula absorbed and unbelievably condensed, Tanya casually tosses the grenade.

Yes, the object she lobbed her pursuer's way *looks* like a normal hand grenade.

"How—"

—*futile!* The moment the idiot overestimates her protective film…

…the formula bullet activates at close quarters. On top of the explosion formula, the head of the grenade scatters.

"Agh…… Gah…!"

"Ha! That's what you get!"

"One down! Brilliant!"

Just as Tanya is about to nod a *yeah*, she notices something. The mage had started to fall, but now she awkwardly stabilizes. *Could that mean…*

…she recovered?

"Mm, nope, one unconfirmed."

"It looked like you got her."

"She seemed to recover at the last second. If you're unsure about an achievement, it's best not to count it. It's better to be happy with a lower score than be laughed at for padding."

It's hard to say for sure that I got her. And if she lands on the water, there's a pile of enemy mages flying around, so rescue is likely.

Even if she fell into the frigid sea, the possibility of her survival is not low.

"Man, she was stubborn as a cockroach! And how is she so sure I killed her father? Does she just hate imperial soldiers so much that we all look the same?"

"Ha-ha-ha. It's because—you know. Remember your appearance, Colonel."

"But they say you shouldn't judge a book by its cover."

I wish they wouldn't stare at me like that, looking like they want to say something. I understand reality just fine.

"Yeah, I know, but that's not what this is about."

Besides, isn't looking like a little girl my distinguishing characteristic?

The famous line about not judging a book by its cover only means that you shouldn't speculate about what's inside. Appearance is very useful data when it comes to identification.

I don't like sticking out on the battlefield just for being small.

"I was sent away from the officers' club for being too young to smoke and drink—I get it."

"You'll have to excuse me, Colonel, but that was hilarious."

"It really was. While we were waiting for you to show up, I was seriously worried that Major Weiss was going to go bankrupt playing cards!"

Maybe they're trying to dispel the heavy atmosphere? My vice commander clowns, and my adjutant laughs and laughs. I guess I have to go along with it.

"It makes me want to hurry up and grow—even though smoking and drinking are bad for you. I at least want to take back the freedom to ruin my health as I please."

"Ha-ha-ha-ha! That's a wonderful liberty, Colonel. As the deputy commander of this battalion, I guarantee that we have no shortage of maniacs who would risk their lives to rebel if that particular freedom was going to be taken away. I hope you'll keep that in mind."

The moment she's convinced they've gotten enough distance for bullshit like this, it hits her.

…We've taken pretty heavy losses.

A mage unit is far from a big family.

A company is twelve. A battalion is thirty-six. And even the augmented 203rd Aerial Mage Battalion is only forty-eight.

You can tell just by looking how many are missing.

"I know, Major. Even I wouldn't try to keep off-duty soldiers in check… I'm sure the ones off duty in Valhalla must be drinking like fishes."

"…I bet they are."

For better or worse, it's a small world. To put it in extreme terms, we're the size of a class at school or a little bigger.

"Tch…I guess more of us went down than I expected."

That's why before they even get back to base and she has them line up, she can see that familiar faces are missing.

"Yes, ma'am. Four dead, three unable to fly, three seriously injured."

"What a horrible loss."

"Colonel, the battalion's return is complete. We've also sent the injured to the rear and made arrangements for the articles of the deceased."

People who were fine this morning are gone by dinner.

Major Weiss makes his report in an even voice, and Tanya responds calmly, "...It really is a horrible loss."

A full complement is forty-eight. We lost ten people. And not just ten people. They're the kind you would never treat as disposable, because they're difficult to replace—they're elites. They *were* elites.

They were the cream of the aerial mage crop. Setting aside their coaching ability and basing it on their skills alone, my subordinates could be employed tomorrow as aggressors in the instructor unit, they're so capable.

Objectively speaking, my subordinates have the most impressive combat experience in the Empire.

"We essentially lost a company. That's enough to say we were partially destroyed."

They may have escaped death, but the severely injured still had to be counted as out of commission. That means a company's worth of our invaluable personnel has dropped out—a company's worth of truly matchless elites.

Just the thought of reorganizing and replenishing our numbers has me at wit's end.

Replace nearly a quarter of my highly trained unit with newbies?

It's going to be hard to cooperate for a while, even if we try.

Julius Caesar hated replenishing units with new recruits and made whole new armies instead; he was right. No, I'm sure the nugget of historical knowledge that crossed my mind just now...was escapism.

"...Maybe I was arrogant. Maybe I thought...that if it was my—the battalion I trained, that if it was the 203rd Aerial Mage Battalion, that amid any enemies..."

"It's not your fault, Colonel. We...took them too lightly, too. We thought if anyone could take them, we could..."

"No, Major Weiss."

The one in charge exists to take responsibility. Of course, if it's not my fault, then...I need to find the offending son of a bitch and make them pay.

But who believed the numbskulls in Intelligence? Pretty sure that was me.

Believing those freeloaders, in other words, was my mistake. It's undeniable that I was provided faulty intel. But that's only something to take into consideration. It's not a reason to exempt me.

These putzes who flee responsibility are utterly contemptuous of the fundamental modern principle of trust...

I took action according to my own judgment. So ultimately, it's my responsibility. I'd rather be deemed inept than a despicable degenerate.

"Laugh at me. Scoff. It was my mistake."

"It was the army's orders... It wasn't your fault."

"It was a mistake to try a hit-and-run with a unit that was worn out from a long-distance flight. We had been in the air for hours, and then in that exhausted state, we plunged into combat—numerically disadvantaged, at that. I'm sure any manual would tell us to avoid all that."

I know I'll be ridiculed as a classic fool.

"It's not as if we accomplished nothing."

"Major Weiss, it's as good as nothing."

"But we carried out the minimum requirements of the mission. We slowed them down! In the photos we took before we left, you can definitely see that we hit the engine."

I'm grateful to have someone with common sense like Weiss being kind to me.

But though I appreciate how considerate he is...we need to look at things objectively not subjectively.

Did I hang in there? Did I try hard? Did I do my best? *So what?*

The actions themselves have no meaning.

Intentions don't matter.

Good faith, ill will—you can save your subjective truths for the judge in court.

It's the results.

Results: Without them...it's all for nothing.

This is an issue between my good sense and how I should be. As a modern, rational, free individual, for me, it's an issue of conscience, goodwill, and ego.

This is garbage. Steeping in self-satisfaction and then licking your wounds is proof of ineptitude.

"...And the report that our submarines did a marvelous job stopping the ship?"

The response to my query is silence.

In reply to my vice commander's sorrowful speechlessness, I slowly ask the same question again. What I want to know is the result.

"Well, Major Weiss?"

"So..." He frowns, having difficulty answering. At this point, that's plenty. I can imagine the results with unbearable ease.

Even interpreting them through wishful thinking, it's going to be bad.

"Fine. Then Lieutenant Serebryakov, Lieutenant Grantz, I'll ask you. Did you hear that we sank the ship?"

I ask just to be sure, but I'm met with their blunt silence.

They politely feign hearing issues and look away to escape the answer. There's no way it's good news.

"So that's that, then. Our actions didn't produce results."

A half-baked attempt at consolation isn't going to do anything. It's so bad Tanya wishes she could be anywhere but here.

The truth is the truth. I have to accept it.

"I don't want to...admit that it was all for nothing, but..." She speaks dispassionately—as dispassionately as she can. "Our unit has suffered serious casualties. And after all that, the results didn't follow. The submarines didn't sink the ship."

These words are necessary in order to accept the truth.

I lost veterans of the 203rd Aerial Mage Battalion. It wasn't my preference to choose war nuts. But they were essential talent for executing my duty—for waging war. They were battle-crazed golden eggs who, after passing a thorough screening, experienced all of the Empire's main lines and were forged in combat.

"I put so much into them, and now my brothers-in-arms are gone. They're gone."

They were veterans, the rarest breed during wartime.

And they, of all people...

After wearing themselves out on a lengthy flight, they were forced into combat with an enemy whose numbers far surpassed ours, and I lost nearly a company.

"I feel adrift. I keep thinking, *If there's anyone to do it with, it's them, so...* or *If they're on the job, then...*"

This is a reliable group who knows their jobs inside and out, has been well trained, and above all, understands my intentions immediately. With part of that group ripped away from me, I can't possibly stay composed.

Business is all about how efficiently you can use the number of personnel at your disposal. Any action that decreases your number of optimized, most useful people is...the worst. Whether it was deliberate or an error, it mustn't be overlooked.

"I'm going to make those bastards in Intelligence and those bastards in our enemy countries pay for this." At this moment, Lieutenant Colonel Tanya von Degurechaff is furious. With her little fists clenched and her eyes burning with rage, she quietly voices her determination. "...My men *died*!"

She looks at the battlefield cross erected in the ruins and grieves.

Even though she ordered the battalion to leave them, no one could forsake the fallen, and they carried them back. She'll have to send their personal effects and letters to the bereaved families.

"I have to write those letters...!"

She puts out her hand. And what she reaches for is the helmet set on top of the gun to form the battlefield cross. It's warped, dented, and has a hole in it. There was no repairing a bullet wound to the head.

"Sorry, troops, I guess I've been going around in circles a bit. We need to get back to our mission."

"Colonel?"

"May their souls be with us. My fellow soldiers, let us wish for the divine protection of the fatherland—but only after we're gone." She quietly hints at her grudge.

Tanya von Degurechaff doesn't believe in gods.

As long as that multifarious monster Being X is allowed to go free, a holy being can't possibly exist in this world.

To Tanya, that's practically axiomatic.

Chapter **III**

Therefore, thinking logically, trust should be placed in people. Believe in the power of people, and if everything falls apart, then you can try throwing the problem at God or whomever.

If you get saved, great. If not, you would be right, so that's better than the alternative. Either way, you lose nothing.

"Asking God for help just isn't our style!"

"Exactly, Weiss."

"So shall we sing an old song?"

"Yeah, that's a good idea." Tanya smiles. "'We Had a Comrade,' troops. Your thick, tone-deaf voices will do, so let's sing it for them."

In hoarse, trembling voices, the soldiers sing a sorrowful song.

When she feels it's time, Tanya wails along. "You went through a forest of swords and hails of bullets, comrades. Rest in peace. Forgive us, for we cannot hold your hands. You remain in our memories. Glory to you, comrades."

Pistols drawn. Blanks fired into the sky. A three-volley salute. Then Tanya loads a single live bullet and aims it at the White Wings Grand Iron Cross.

Stupid sectionalism, everyone holding one another back.

What a damn pain it is to work with Intelligence!

[chapter]

IV

Long-Range Assault Operation

It's an officer's duty to act on their own authority when necessary.

From the remarks of Magic
Lieutenant Colonel Tanya von Degurechaff

The 203rd Aerial Mage Battalion has suffered heavy losses in Norden. Teeth-grindingly heavy losses. It was an unbelievable waste of human resources and capital.

If you're like Being X, a piece of trash who can view humans only as numbers, then you would probably say, *It was only ten people.*

But to the modern, free individual, Lieutenant Colonel Tanya von Degurechaff, it goes without saying that the loss of ten elite soldiers is a huge loss for society.

So many resources and so much time were invested in their training.

"We're an army. I realize that casualties are a given, but…"

Logically, there are no irreplaceable gears in an army.

And the units with losses will be allocated replacement personnel. But textbooks and the real world don't always get along.

In actuality, there are tons of valuable gears on the market whose supply is monopolized by a single company.

And if that precious source is struggling under too much demand, even if you request a replacement gear, you have no way of knowing when it will arrive.

As soon as she leaves the companies to their commanders—First Lieutenant Serebryakov, Major Weiss, and First Lieutenant Grantz—she thinks, *Even so*, and follows standard procedure, getting through the paperwork to apply for the replacement personnel. For her new gears.

It's a solitary battle.

Pen, paper, ink, and me.

What is effective in a culture battle is the deceptive power of words.

In the real world, though, it's as if there's a fearsome wall of bureaucracy in the way. Even the Imperial Army, a precision military machine, can't escape red tape. How irritating!

"…What we should really be afraid of is bureaucracy…"

The process, complicated to the point of futility, makes me suspect that the higher-ups are determined to reject applications for replacements. But desk work requires perseverance.

"Hmph, government forms are always complicated. Well, I'll just read these administrative texts with the care of an exegete."

Having returned to their lodgings with that determined murmur, Tanya has now been chained to her desk for over twenty-four hours finishing paperwork. She processes the documents, gulping down the coffee from Lieutenant Colonel Uger, which she has requested brewed so thick it tastes like awful muddy water.

Even the Anglo-Saxon spirit during the Victorian era, famous for its perseverance, is child's play compared to the discipline of a modern corporate employee like me.

If the documents don't get approved, that's fine.

I'll just keep filing them until they do.

Thus, about two days after shifting the battlefield to her desk…

Lieutenant Colonel Tanya von Degurechaff achieves a modest victory.

On October 6 at exactly midnight, she has her adjutant Serebryakov send the paperwork and burrows into her bed to get as much sleep as she possibly can.

Then, when her eyes pop open, it's morning.

As she munches the breakfast with coffee that her adjutant prepared for her, she finally has the wherewithal to begin thinking about what comes next.

"Still, man…"

A little sigh slips out.

She can think and think, but thinking will get her only so far.

At any rate, their current situation is exceedingly vague.

According to their official orders, they're a support unit.

The 203rd Aerial Mage Battalion was sent as patrol personnel as part of the Northern Sea operation. Therefore, the failure of the operation to stop the RMS *Queen of Anjou* doesn't translate to the end of their deployment.

Theoretically, their mission is ongoing even now. On the other hand, that's all it means.

Additionally, the 203rd Aerial Mage Battalion's position as a unit directly under the General Staff deployed to the north is unique. *As a result*, I suppose?

The bureaucratic consensus within the military machine is that the General Staff lent them the unit for the mission to stop the RMS *Queen of Anjou*. For that reason, even if they wanted to divert the unit to a different mission, the theory of the organization went that they would fall off the promotion track if they broke the contract.

I guess the inertia of bureaucracy is formidable? Contrary to our official orders, we aren't even being incorporated into the patrol rotation.

Thus, in order to not waste time, Tanya takes up her pen again. She writes the letters of consolation to the bereaved families that are her duty as a commander.

But in terms of word count, letters of consolation aren't very long. Lieutenant Colonel Tanya von Degurechaff is unexpectedly running out of things to do before it's even lunchtime.

"…I get that we're experiencing some issues, but having nothing to do is actually pretty unbearable," she grumbles with a bitter grin.

I don't count myself as a workaholic, but in this sort of ill-conceived situation, my thoughts tend to wander. If I don't have something that requires an immediate judgment call, maybe it's not so bad to leisurely ponder the long term.

But the future is grim. Maybe spirited speculations on your bright future can be productive, but having to expect a dark one is no fun.

Of course, whether it's fun or not is just an emotional issue.

I have no intention of ceasing to think just because I'm upset.

If I'm going to stop thinking, I'd rather take my pistol and blow my brains out.

That said, there are some realities that…can't be changed no matter how much you think. Just as I'm running out of high-quality coffee beans, the Empire's resources must also be dwindling.

That goes for human resources, too. Tanya is compelled to frown bitterly. The 203rd Aerial Mage Battalion is short ten members.

The only people who can say it's *only ten* are the ones who have zero understanding of human capital management.

To find a parallel, it's like the massive numbskulls who fire all their veteran sales staff and replace them with low-salaried part-timers and then wonder why things aren't going well.

Ten members, rich in experience and accomplished as well, were taken from us. From a department of only forty-eight. For now, while our duties are limited, it shouldn't be a serious problem.

But…there's no telling when we'll get replenished.

"I guess we'll be able to fill our slots with…newbies who have only the bare minimum of training…"

It's a predictable situation… No one has any veterans to spare.

No, they probably just stubbornly refuse to give them up. I mean, if they asked me to pull a few, I'm sure I'd give them a flat no.

After all, veteran experience and optimized unit coordination aren't something you can achieve in a day. It's possible to turn know-how and accumulated experience into a manual, but acquiring that knowledge and mastering it through experience take time.

That's the first thing you have to remember when using human capital.

"Going by that principle…I really just have to cultivate them? It'd be better if I could simply get some mid-career hires somewhere…"

It's only natural for someone working in personnel to fret about filling vacancies. But when there's a war on, getting replacements doesn't go very well.

Although officers have a measure of discretion within the army, they don't get to choose their subordinates. You can complain when something sucks, but it's virtually impossible to simply take what you want.

…The situation is very different from the time we pulled together an augmented battalion from a mix of Eastern Army Group and Central troops.

And so, Tanya's mind is completely occupied by the word *replacements*. Unfortunately, there's no time you're less likely to have a great idea than when you really want one.

Just as she notices her thoughts going down a dead end, there's a knock on the door. She raises her head.

When she looks toward the door, it's her vice commander standing there with a message. The fact that it isn't a messenger but Weiss himself means it must be fairly important news.

"What is it, Major Weiss? If you're not in a hurry, I'd appreciate if you'd stay and have a cup of coffee."

"How kind of you. I think I will." He bobs his head and doesn't seem nervous. If he was tense, he probably would have refused a leisurely teatime.

So it must not be an emergency, she figures. As she offers him coffee, she tries to guess. *Then what could it be?*

"Colonel von Degurechaff, these are orders from home."

Ohhh. She doesn't have to think for that to make sense. *So the General Staff has gotten word of our failure? Is it a reprimand? Consolation? Or word of a new mission?*

Well, whatever it is... Tanya straightens up.

"Hmm...? Redeployment orders?"

"Yes, ma'am. As soon as our replacement unit arrives, we're to take up a position on the eastern front main lines along with the reorganized Kampfgruppe. We've also been instructed to incorporate the replacement troops we'll receive."

She takes the papers from Weiss and looks them over. *I see, so it's a proper notification.*

But there is something giving her slight pause.

"Redeployment and reorganization in parallel? And on top of that, reorganizing on the main lines in the east? With no orientation training?"

"...Yes, the General Staff says to lead the unit they've formed."

After reading the orders, Tanya sighs in spite of herself. This is almost exactly what I was griping about earlier!

"So we're stuck having our veterans replaced with newbies! That's just one step down the path to a giant failure... What the hell."

No. She shakes her head. If she pushes the shock from her mind and employs some self-control, she can understand what the higher-ups are trying to do. The General Staff probably doesn't have anywhere they can secure human resources, either.

But just because she can understand doesn't mean she can accept it. Even considering what this war situation demands, it's not enough time!

Chapter **IV**

As the commander, she's had to lodge a complaint.

Kampfgruppen are created via ad hoc formation.

These words say it all: *ad hoc formation.*

Confusion will be inevitable once the quickly scraped together band of officers and men has to carry out an operation. She can describe what she wants from them, but it will be hard to avoid a breakdown somewhere. And that's why she wants the core to be her own forces that sync perfectly with her.

But they won't even give her an orientation period?

"Any more than this is just going in circles. I guess we should be happy we're getting replacements, but the unit they're allocating doesn't look so great. They say they modeled this Kampfgruppe on the Salamanders, but as far as I can tell, it's probably best not to have very high expectations."

"…At face value, it seems to have been fortified." Weiss's observation is half-right. Just the other half is wrong.

"To some extent, I'm sure that's true. But there are too many newly established units. Even if the foundation is veterans, you know what will happen if the ratio of newbies is too high, right?"

In stories, in heroic tales, one might encounter new units that turn out to be elite. Or we could probably give up on education and at the last minute send in elite units made up purely of veterans and instructors.

Conversely, if you're fighting a war like usual, it's extremely difficult to imagine forming a new unit containing only veterans.

"I want to hope the core personnel are decent, but no one wants to give up any veterans. We probably can't expect too much."

"You're right about that. I see, so it must be made up of whatever units they had on hand back home. In that case, they'll be weaker than they look."

He must have understood. An awkward smile appears on Weiss's face. Well, that's the only possible response to this sort of reality—a vague smile.

We're not replacing our losses like we want and instead are getting units so new it's unclear if they've been tried in live combat yet.

"It makes me think of General von Romel. I remember how he always used to say he wanted units that were easy to use."

It was the catchphrase of my former superior officer. He used to grumble over and over how badly he wanted a decent unit.

Now I understand what he meant quite well. No matter how they gloss things over at home, without proper manpower, it's going to be hard to continue fighting a war. How sad that the day has come when I can sympathize with the gripes of my former superior.

"Ahhh, man," grumbles Tanya as she pours herself another cup of coffee with a sigh. *"Do the best with what you have.* They're simple words, but doesn't it feel like a last resort? Don't you kinda get the feeling they're just shoving the whole issue off onto us in the field, Major Weiss?"

"But, ma'am...all we can do is train the new recruits."

"I guess. It's going to be a struggle. Training the mage unit will be up to you. I hope you'll turn them into troops we can use."

"I'll do my best. Still, I think in this case...it's really a fight against time."

I absolutely agree. Even without Weiss pointing it out, I know that training new people is a challenge in any era.

Humans don't work the minute you install them, like programs. You can allow them to grope along and spit out errors, but it will still take a huge amount of time.

Time and effort are essential for fostering newbies no matter what.

But even if you understand that necessity, it's still one of the most difficult jobs. Normally, in the military organization, personnel will be deployed once they've completed the minimum training...but as the war continues on and intensifies, the standards have greatly shifted.

Currently, I really wonder if they'll be at a usable level.

"How much time can we take to retrain them? The orders didn't specify... So what do you think, Colonel?"

"I wouldn't expect the usual standard. Even if we're being sent to a war zone, we probably won't be in the hottest area, but... Well, they definitely won't let us have six months. We can probably expect them to tell us to train during the winter lull, since it's a test operation." She swallows the rest: *It's probably hopeless.* "I want to give you as much time as possible. I genuinely want you to train them hard."

Unfortunately, there's a limit to what gets decided based on my opinion.

"The problem is what the General Staff is aiming for with this formation. It seems like they want Kampfgruppen that can be formed in a short amount of time for special missions."

The Salamander Kampfgruppe was a great preliminary run.

Having been formed quickly, it achieved adequate successes in multiple field tests, such as proving its concept, supporting the main army's flank in the east, and getting a handle on the enemy's status.

Tanya's personal view is that she showed the brass the utility of composite units made up of troops from multiple branches of the org. And that seems to have been acknowledged as the truth.

But, she does end up thinking. As she told Weiss, she thinks the General Staff has put too much emphasis on the ability to form them quickly.

"The existing types of units, formed with specific scenarios in mind, aren't flexible. Kampfgruppen are different in that they can be formed in an optimal way on the fly."

"So they really have a lot of potential, then. I imagine they'll be especially useful for putting out fires."

"Exactly. In other words, Major Weiss, I'm thinking…that you need to be prepared for them to expect the sort of convenient unit they can send on errands. And as long as they do, it's hard to hope for a generous training period."

If the mobility and firepower to cover those vast lines can be arranged by adjusting a single unit, Kampfgruppen will be a good fit for mission-oriented orders.

To be frank, they'll be super-handy. If you're a commander, you'll be thinking, *I want a ton of those ASAP.*

People who work on logistics like Lieutenant General von Zettour and people from Operations like Lieutenant General von Rudersdorf are sure to be desperate for Kampfgruppen. The new type of unit scratches their itch.

Which is why Tanya can understand the line of thought for the General Staff.

"The guys in the General Staff must be thinking to develop the know-how to form a ton of these at the drop of a hat. We're going to be forced to go along with this major research initiative, so we should probably brace ourselves."

"…If it works out, the army will have a lot more options, huh? As a soldier, I'm honored if I can contribute to my fatherland in such a way."

She needs to finish her mug of coffee, but reality is so harsh, she can't possibly drink. It's unbearably awful, but we're going to have to work our asses off. We're going to suffer terribly.

After all, the higher-ups' objective is to locate problems through trial and error. There's no way we'll have an easy time of it in the field like that.

"It's like we're playing house and being told to sample their cooking. And though this is a presumptuous thing to say…the ones cooking aren't even going to sample it themselves."

It may be necessary to go through various processes to turn an idea into something concrete, but this just makes her want to cradle her head in her hands.

"It's no good," she says, and they both wince.

"Then should we tell them it's inedible?"

"That would be like whining that you hate it without even trying it. Unless, Major Weiss, you want to make a direct appeal?"

"Please have mercy, ma'am."

"Right." Tanya nods and gives a little sigh.

Weiss's resigned exhalation should probably also be called a sigh.

"We don't have a choice."

"Yeah, I guess not."

Awash with emotions, she laments openly. One of the bad things about the army is that your preferences become irrelevant.

The pair can only grumble: "How uninspired. We're stuck." The officers simply admit to each other that there's nothing they can do.

That said, neither of them had any work they had to rush to do. And so they have time to sigh but no time for training and reorganizing; it hits them how poorly resources are distributed.

If you give it enough thought, things can't go on like this. As Tanya is looking for a topic to chat about over their coffee, she finally realizes something.

"Actually, Lieutenant Grantz was once a replacement. What if we left training up to him?"

"…I never thought of that. But…" Weiss nods with interest. "Before, I might have argued against it. Now, though, Lieutenant Grantz has built up experience commanding a company. He's made a lot of mistakes, but he might actually make a great instructor."

"So it's worth considering?"

Weiss nods yes. "Training new recruits will probably be good experience for him."

"Undoubtedly." Tanya nods.

Teaching someone else is a learning experience for the teacher, as well. Tanya has been reminded of that numerous times since meeting Serebryakov on the Rhine front.

Once a conscript, she's now a fine magic officer, too.

Tanya is about to comment on the delights of helping with personal development when there is a polite knock on the door.

"Huh? Come in!"

Speak of the devil. Well, surely it's nothing like that.

Peeking in with a sudden briskness is Lieutenant Serebryakov, whom I was just reminiscing about training.

"Lieutenant Serebryakov, come on in!"

She salutes and walks over with a smile. She must be in a great mood. Maybe she's at that age where any little thing has you giggling?

On the other hand, the Serebryakov I know is a pragmatist. I do wonder if there's been some sort of good news.

Tanya asks with her eyes, and Serebryakov must understand, because she begins explaining.

"Colonel, we've received a report from the air fleet."

The air fleet?

Maybe it's not my place to wonder, but why is the air fleet reporting to me?

Though I'm clearly perplexed...my adjutant pays it no mind. She hands me an envelope, and her face brightens with a proud smile. "It's aerial reconnaissance photos. I won them off the air fleet playing cards."

"Are you betting military secrets? Visha, I don't mean to criticize you, but you might want to take it easy. No, this is even more serious than that. Encouraging intelligence leaks is worse than most types of gambling."

Weiss's grumbles are legitimate. But the documents Serebryakov brought made those worries seem trivial.

Inside the envelope are several aerial photographs.

I don't even have to look at the data, analysis, and other notes written on them.

"The RMS *Queen of Anjou*? It's as absurdly huge as I remember."

The giant ship is so magnificent, it makes others look small. It's the most famous ocean liner by far. We have lots of data on it, so there's no way to mistake it.

The air fleet analysts must have felt the same way. It's natural that they declared it the RMS *Queen of Anjou* in red ink.

Just then, Tanya notices something.

In the notes on the margin of the photo, there are some doubts written about the status of the ship's mooring.

"They're…performing maintenance?"

Even from the photos, the damage to the ship's deck and more is visible. But there's something drawing Tanya's attention even more: the large number of tools and workers.

"Does this mean our attack to slow them down got some results?" Weiss remarks, sounding somewhat ashamed.

Well, of course he sounds ashamed, if this is all we achieved… But then Tanya rethinks it.

Does the fact that it's not docked…mean the damage is only slight?

Really?

Now she has doubts. *Could it be?* she thinks. *Or maybe…*, she hopes. Either way, when she looks over the photos again…the answer is clear.

Just as I thought, I suppose?

"Nah, Major Weiss. Just because it isn't docked doesn't mean we have to be self-deprecating about our results. I mean, what dock can accommodate that huge ship anyhow?"

"…That's true."

Weiss stares speechlessly at the photos and starts thinking about something, but Tanya has already moved on to the next issue.

Only one thing is important.

"Lieutenant Serebryakov, the air fleet brought this to you, yes?"

She's confirming that it wasn't intel she pressed them for. If her adjutant has gone above and beyond to ask them…

…it would mean that we went to pick up *requested* information from them.

"That's right. I did tease them, but they brought it to me without going through HQ."

"Just to confirm, the air fleet *offered* this, right? They weren't responding to a *request* from you?"

"They called me and I picked it up." She declares it with conviction and doesn't seem to be hiding anything. So perhaps they really are just being friendly.

Of course, it's also possible that the air fleet is trying to show off their skills or make up in some way for their deficient performance in the attack on the ship. It's hard to tell exactly what their intention was.

But it's not as if we asked them for it. In other words, they volunteered it. Good. Tanya continues to dwell on this point.

Aerial reconnaissance and these photos... Unlike with a reconnaissance satellite, this photography required a manned aircraft to fly over enemy territory. Though it was taken from a high altitude, there was still a lot of risk involved.

If neither Tanya nor Serebryakov requested recon and this report showed up...

...Is it encouragement or reassurance, then?

This was sent by people who know about our mission related to the RMS *Queen of Anjou*. There must be some kind folks in our org somewhere.

"Lieutenant, choose whatever alcohol seems appropriate later. If we don't have enough, you can dip into the battalion treasury. Send it to them on my behalf. They did a good job, so I'd like those brave pilots to drink their fill."

"Yes, ma'am. Leave it to me, Colonel."

A good job deserves respect. I'll give the air fleet a heartfelt thanks for their fine work.

If this were a corporation, I'd be on my way to accounting to see about a special bonus.

Unlike the stuff we get from the inept joint intelligence agency of the Army and Navy Commands, this is fresh intel guaranteed by the air fleet.

And most importantly, it's highly reliable.

"I should simplify things," Tanya murmurs.

When you need to make assumptions about unclear facts, it's best to simplify them as much as possible.

There's no need to speculate about the intentions of the air fleet. They're friendly forces, at least, so it's safe to rule out the possibility that they'd feed us false intelligence. In which case, it's much more likely that this data is as it seems.

Ships move, but ports don't. So the conclusion is exceedingly elementary. It's not hard to take out an opponent that can't run.

"Let's go!"

"Ma'am?"

"Yes, ma'am!"

These officers are from the same unit, but I suppose the difference in their replies is a reflection of how long they have been with me?

Weiss looks puzzled and asks a question; Serebryakov acknowledges her understanding.

My adjutant picks up on my intentions immediately. She assists me like a wife of many years and is now comprehension incarnate.

"The air fleet has set the stage for us, so let's go along with it. Tell the submarines. Lieutenant Serebryakov, round up the troops."

"Understood." My adjutant gets right down to business without interjecting any questions; she's one of those rare great aids.

She jogs straight to the submarine unit HQ without a single complaint. Even though I've been having her do a brutal amount of paperwork since we've been back on base, her passion hasn't flagged at all.

She has a model work ethic, no two ways about it.

I've been lucky to have such a talented subordinate with me ever since the Rhine front.

Meanwhile, thinks Tanya as she accepts the questioning look on sensible Major Weiss's face.

"It'll be a long-range operation, so it'll extend beyond the bounds of our current operation area. If we apply to cross the border, will we make it in time?" His implied fear is that the enemy might escape during that time.

As my vice commander, Weiss fills the important role of devil's advocate. When we're about to go through with something, he voices quite rational hesitations. He gives great advice, even going so far as directly urging superior officers to exercise caution.

"That's a good point, Major Weiss. If we're going to perform a raid, we need to hit them during this short period before they can move."

It's true. Tanya nods. She also wants to nail the ship before it moves. No, they *must* nail the ship before it's able to move, or this will all be pointless.

It would be no joke if we went over there all ready for a raid and found an empty nest.

"So we have to follow the ancient saying that soldiers value foolish haste." She looks into his blue eyes to make him understand. *You get it, right?* "Applying to cross the border? That's out of the question. We can't waste time with roundabout administrative procedures. Considering the risk of a leak, acting on our own discretion seems like the right answer in this case."

"A-acting on our own discretion? We may report directly to the General Staff, but if we leave the operation area without permission...they may say it's purely arbitrary."

That's true. Tanya nods internally.

Still, she's compelled to point out something else.

"For commanders, or probably all officers, really, acting on their own authority is their duty."

"That brings back memories, Colonel."

Everyone, including Serebryakov, who had jogged off, had had that line beaten into them at the academy. Even if proper communication is an absolute requirement in society or any organization, on the battlefield, things are frequently different than orders or previously received intelligence indicated.

For that reason, to accomplish their missions, officers must take actions that conflict with their orders when necessary.

"We need to consider the objective of the orders we were given, right?"

"Do you think the General Staff and the Army and Navy Commands meant for us to sink it?"

"I do, indeed. Major Weiss, I don't want us to be the kind of inepts who adhere to the formality of the orders we were given under these circumstances. Even if we were sent here to stop the ship, we must infer that we are meant to work with the submarines to *sink* it!"

Grouchy[2] would say, *It's Napoleon's orders*, and continue on an absurd advance. But look at Davout[3] or Desaix.[4] They ignored the great authority of Napoleon's orders—because it was essential to *achieving the objective behind the order.*

You have to understand the objective of the orders and, if necessary, change the method of fulfilling them according to your own judgment. That's what acting on your own authority means, and it's an officer's duty.

Only fools who can't think for themselves follow orders, carry them out faithfully, and then writhe about when they fail. That's a truly inept worker. They should probably be shot.

"So, in faithfulness to our orders…let's go. I'm sure the submarines aren't such chickens that they would hole up and refuse to come out when their gambling buddy Lieutenant Serebryakov is the one pressing them."

"But, Colonel. Remember what we're talking about. We may have been given some degree of discretion, but I think leaving the 'formality' of the district is a bit of a larger issue. Isn't it dangerous to take it lightly?"

"Certainly, the issue will be the district. But conversely, if that's the only obstacle…then it would probably be more useful to figure out some way to deal with it."

---

[2] **Grouchy**   Marshal Emmanuel de Grouchy was Napoleon's last marshal! The last marshal! It has such a cool ring to it. Except for the part about how he was appointed only because there was no one else…

He was a general who had forces during the Battle of Waterloo but failed to act on his own discretion (meaning he didn't make his own call and take the optimal action).

One hundred percent adherence to orders isn't right. What's right is accomplishing the mission the orders are asking you to. He's a classic example to bring up during such discussions.

By the way, he was also one of those unlucky types who was actually surprisingly talented but got pummeled in the history books for that one failure.

[3] **Davout**   Marshal Louis-Nicolas Davout is known as probably Napoleon's best marshal.

Not only did his military prowess make Napoleon envious, he displayed prodigious talent in many fields including government and organizational management. Aside from the things that made him a bit too cutthroat of a boss—his uncommon strictness and adherence to the rules, his uncompromising separation of public and private spheres, and his excessive belief in meritocracy—he was perfect.

[4] **Desaix**   Like Grouchy, he was on an operation with a detachment, but…when he heard the cannons of the Battle of Marengo, he acted on his own discretion, and his name went down in world history.

Under Napoleon, who was on the brink of defeat, he dashingly rushed forward, shouted, "There is yet time to win another battle!" and charged into the enemy forces. He was a great general who saved Napoleon from defeat and died himself in battle.

Which is precisely why I've found a way.

"To cut to the chase, we already have our answer. Read the orders from the General Staff. They ordered us to, 'Above all else, stop that enemy transport ship.'"

"…'Above all else'?"

It was just one phrase in the document. Exegetics may be dry to most readers, but it all depends on how you use it. If you read between the lines, the amount of freedom with which you can act rapidly increases.

Though it's one step away from broad interpretation, if you can provide your reasoning, then everything's peachy.

"It's an order that says to achieve the objective, above all else. It's obvious that the objective is to send that ocean liner to the bottom of the sea, and the location of our target is clear. Now, under those circumstances, is there really any meaning in holding back out of consideration for the district?"

"No." The distinct light of understanding shines in his eyes as he nods.

We have orders that say to do it, above all else. It's…impossible to think that we should have to worry about the operation area. After all, it's the brass who gave the orders. Even if they complain after the fact, it unquestionably won't be a problem.

I mean, Tanya declares confidently in her head. Weiss the sensible man agreed. The reason I listen to my subordinates' opinions is that I want a third party's point of view. Then I make a careful decision based on that information.

If there aren't any issues, then this is a juncture that demands bold action.

"Good, then we'll move out like faithful dogs. Let's accomplish mission the General Staff gave us."

Being a member of society, being part of an organization—work—is like that. But there are good people supporting me. It's probably rare to get to devote yourself to work with such proud, professional colleagues.

The functional beauty of an organization that unites to fulfill an objective… It's not an expression I like, but I suppose if we're paying our respects to the classics, "The invisible hand of God is a pretty apt description. Now then, Major Weiss, go find Lieutenant Grantz. As soon as Lieutenant Serebryakov gets back, we'll draw up our plan."

The man known as Colonel Mikel slowly moved the cigarette in his mouth closer to the lighter. It wasn't as if he was smoking a particularly good brand.

It was the same old ration of "grunt tobacco." Still, tobacco was tobacco, and he was free to smoke it... As long as Mikel was afforded that, he had no complaints. The modest freedom to fill his lungs with cheap cigarette smoke was heaven compared to the gulag.

As he exhaled the purple fumes, Mikel was thinking about the strangeness of fate.

It had been a few months since he had been released from the concentration camp and his supposedly deleted military registration had been reinstated. The war with the Empire was changing Mikel's fate in ways he never expected.

They had taken his orb away, but then the army gave him a new model. He never thought he would fly again, but the sky returned to him.

He had ground down, had endured the cruelest of treatment, but the fatherland still needed him. It had to be a blessing from God.

To say he didn't have any beef with the Communist Party would have been a lie.

His friends collapsed on the ground in the bitter cold... Their frozen bodies that didn't make it to another dawn, their suffering faces... You couldn't tell him to forget them.

But more importantly...he was a Federation soldier. He had sworn loyalty to his motherland, so if he could fight for her, it wouldn't do to mix up his priorities.

Thus, he wholeheartedly welcomed the Communists' decision to re-form the mage units—as long as his friends would be given positions.

For that, he would suppress his antipathy toward the party members, even if they were more like the devil than the devil from the Bible himself.

But... He calmly observed his situation, nearly scoffing. *They must have summoned us because they're losing.* Defeat makes states act without regard for appearances. The status of the mages who were loyal to the previous regime was so low, they risked eradication if it wasn't for this very situation.

Which was why despite getting his enlistment reinstated...he never expected the circumstances behind his orders to be explained in detail. The orders the dear party gave him were part of a scheme that was much more well-thought-out than any "mere soldier" could ever imagine.

He couldn't possibly ask for an explanation of every little thing.

As long as they had their reasons and things had to stay confidential, everyone agreed that all they had to do was carry out the missions given to them. They didn't want to go back to the gulag.

Well, let's rephrase that.

They hesitated to voice their complaints openly. That foolish move would put not only themselves in danger but their friends and families as well.

There were good things and bad things about savoring his freedom with a cigarette. The officers next to him seemed rather relaxed as they smoked.

"Colonel, are you sure there's no mistake about the orders we were given?"

"Use 'Comrade.' You never know who might be listening."

"S-sorry, Comrade Colonel."

He nodded at his careless subordinate and wordlessly put a hand on his shoulder. He could understand their impatience.

Even an order to stand by could make people who had spent time in a concentration camp antsy because it meant their future was unclear.

What meaningless cruelty must those sadistic camp guards have inflicted for the sake of bullying them?! Those who had been in the gulag were rendered extremely sensitive to the feelings created by an uncertain future.

Though they had been released, reenlisted, and formed as one of the rare mage units on active duty in the Federation Army, they couldn't relax for a moment.

The battalion was, in the eyes of the Communists, a battalion-size gang of potential traitors.

As before, they were under surveillance, and it wouldn't be strange for them to be purged on a whim at any time.

But more recently, that had started to change.

The improvement in their treatment had them wondering what happened; in his unit, they speculated that it had to do with the worsening war situation on the main lines. Then they weren't even sent to the main lines but to the north. And after that, they were ordered to stand by.

Mikel himself had done an awful lot of investigating, but he had no idea what was going on. In other words, it must have been the will of someone so high up that underlings like him would never be involved. But he just didn't know why.

The fatherland was in crisis, so it was strange that they hadn't been allocated to the main lines.

At first, he wondered if they weren't trusted. But in that case, the political officer attached to them was bizarre. The one keeping an eye on them was a very different breed from the ones they'd had before—from the Central group.

Was it possible that he'd been sent not as added surveillance but to send them off somewhere else? That was the sort of rumor Battalion Commander Mikel had to shut down day after day.

Everyone thought this day would be like the others.

"…If we can just show them what we're good for… Ah, I guess I'm going in circles…"

The idea that war was a way out, would lead to the future, was the worst. Using your fatherland's struggles as a way to achieve personal success was deplorable.

But when he thought of the families still in the camp…he felt like he had to perform at least well enough that they would be freed. He wanted to give his men's children and their families a normal life.

I want to preserve the future. As far as Mikel was concerned, that was the duty of an adult. That was logic that even war couldn't undermine.

Which was why he did believe this: *We need them to think highly of us.*

When one of the officers beneath him rushed into the smoking room to inform him that the esteemed commissar from Central had asked for him, it was no wonder he hoped it was a chance.

The commissar met him as soon as he set foot in the command facilities, as if he had been waiting for him, and his face was unusually tense.

The mere sight of him without his shady smile was enough to elicit some very natural astonishment from him.

Chapter **IV**

"Comrade soldier, I've been waiting for you. Oh…" Before getting into details, he offered him a chair.

As in, *Please take a seat.*

Mikel had thought the political commissar was practically of another race of people who couldn't be upset by anything. But now, looking visibly nervous, he was obsequiously offering Mikel a chair?

A member of the Commissariat for Internal Affairs? Acting this way toward a man who was his enemy in the class struggle?

"Would you like some tea, Comrade Colonel?"

His mind was blank.

Tea……tea, tea?

"Oh, right. You don't have to be tense; there's just something I'd like you to hear. True, I'm a party official and you're a career soldier with *many years of experience*, but aren't we comrades fighting together against our fatherland's enemy now? Comrade Colonel, I should think we could have tea together…"

The offer made it hard to tell him how strange this seemed.

These political officers, thought Mikel with a wry smile. *There's got to be a better way they can make conversation. They're great at bullying their enemies, but when it comes to winning over allies, they've got nothing?* Apparently, he had a critical flaw that was difficult to cover up.

"I would be happy to join you, Comrade Political Commissar. But I thought perhaps…there was something you wanted to talk to me about?"

"Oh, you knew, Comrade Colonel?"

It would have been easy to spit, *How could I not?!* Even without the flowery words, he could see right away. After all, the man's normal expression of something like suppressed condescension had taken on a brownnosing hue.

…As someone who had lived under the heels of others all this time, Mikel had to notice it, even if he didn't want to.

"There's no greater happiness for a soldier than to be of use to his comrades and his party. Whatever is it, Comrade Political Commissar?"

What empty nonsense it was to work for a party you didn't believe in. It made him want to lament, *Oh Lord.* Surely even the Lord, although he might wince, would forgive him some tricks necessary for survival.

Then was this the Lord's protection and forgiveness? The political commissar began to speak as if a dam had broken.

"Very well, Comrade Colonel...allow me to consult with you. We've actually just received special orders from Moskva. They're instructions of the highest priority from the Central Committee."

"Special orders from Moskva?! Comrade Political Commissar, I haven't been notified..." He protested because he was the battalion commander, after all. Of course, he knew how little Moskva trusted them. It made him sick. But if they were going to be entrusted with such an important mission, he would want to be preparing far in advance.

"My apologies, but it was top secret, and I only just found out about it myself."

"Top secret?"

"Yes, an escort is needed, Comrade, and you and your own comrades have been ordered to provide it. According to Moskva, it's a civilian ship from the Commonwealth and...you're to coordinate its defense with the Commonwealth marine mages on board."

A civilian ship from the Commonwealth. *Wasn't the party cursing them as despicable pawns of bourgeois imperialism just a few years ago?*

A civilian ship from there *is visiting a northern naval base? And Moskva is telling us to protect it?* It didn't seem at all likely.

No. The absurd truth hit him.

"You're saying Moskva has special orders for us?"

"Comrade Colonel, it's a mission of utmost importance. I'm sure the party and the fatherland have significant expectations of us... Let's rise to meet them together."

The political commissar's creepy smile as he held out his hand irritated Mikel.

Moskva, the party members—none of them was paying any attention to us a few months ago. And now I'm supposed to be comrades with this guy with the chilly smile? What a dramatic twist of fate. It's surreal. Cliché, in fact.

And what other words are there to describe it? Whoever said, "Truth is stranger than fiction," hit it right on the nose.

"Of course...but... We're really just escorting a civilian ship?"

Still, what's the deal with escorting a civilian vessel? What the heck are they telling us to protect?

Chapter **IV**

Mikel had been doing his utmost to collect information since his release. But there was no way the newspapers published by the party contained truth and the news as is. Reading between the lines to figure out what hadn't been written was no easy task.

"If it's not confidential, I'd like you to tell me: It seems slightly excessive to me. Are its passengers or cargo that valuable?"

We've been stationed up in the relatively quiet north despite the main lines turning into a stalemate.

I thought the only reason Central would send a detestable political commissar here was to get rid of him...but apparently I was wrong.

He was suddenly very curious about what was being entrusted to them.

"It must be quite some cargo..."

"Yes, well, it is valuable without a doubt. But compared to the actual target of your services, its load probably isn't as important."

What's that supposed to mean? Mikel wondered, but the political commissar continued right on talking.

"We want you to treat this defensive mission the same way you would a mission in airspace over the capital. Keep a sharp watch."

"I understand that we're escorting a civilian boat, but I just don't get it. For starters, even if you tell us to protect a ship, I can only wonder what we should actually do. In that case..." *I have to tell him that we simply can't do what we can't do.* Mikel continued, "We have no maritime navigation training, and on top of that, our unit has no anti-submarine doctrine. I don't really think we'll be a useful convoy escort."

"Oh, but Moskva isn't asking you to perform a maritime or convoy escort."

The response confused him. As far as Mikel knew, ships sailed through water. If they were being told to escort the ship, the only possibilities he could come up with were flying above the convoy or sailing alongside it.

He wasn't even familiar with the navy in the first place.

"Comrade Political Commissar, you're being too vague. I realize I'm not well versed in matters pertaining to the sea, but I'd appreciate it if you'd explain. Aren't we going to be guarding the transport ship?"

"You are correct, Comrade Colonel."

I don't understand the context of this at all. Mikel was about to cock his head when the commissar's next words confused him even further.

"But it's not a convoy. What we'll be protecting is a single, huge transport ship of Commonwealth nationality."

"Huh?" The question slipped out at that news. *We're providing this powerful of a guarding force to* one *boat?*

"It's sailing alone? That's awfully reckless. I've heard imperial subs are lurking around… What a dangerous thing to do."

"Ha-ha-ha. You're right. Under normal circumstances, I'm sure that would be true; however, Comrade Colonel. This ship *must* sail alone. Contrary to what one might think, that's probably the safest option."

What? Just as Mikel was about to cock his head in confusion, the commissar continued hesitantly.

"It got attacked by a powerful imperial aerial mage unit and still managed to break through—the RMS *Queen of Anjou*, code name: Queen of the Sea. It's currently the largest ocean liner in the world."

"The RMS *Queen of Anjou*? That's a name I don't know."

Although I suppose I should have heard of it if it's the biggest ship in the world.

"…It's new, only made its maiden voyage a couple of years ago. It may not be very well known in the Federation."

"A few years ago?"

"Either way, well, er. It would be great if you could not worry about that."

Oh. It was then that Mikel scoffed at himself internally for being so stupid. Of course the political commissar would have a hard time saying that.

Its maiden voyage a few years ago!

That was when we were in the gulag learning how far we could go before our humanity would break. He was forced to recall how they were unable to get any information about the outside world.

A slightly awkward silence hung in the air. But this wasn't all bad news for Colonel Mikel. At the same time, he knew for sure that a favorable wind was now blowing.

"I've overcome that unfortunate misunderstanding and am grateful that the party has a place for us now."

Mikel was desperate. If this went well, it could lead to a promotion. It seemed like a chance. But the chance didn't come free. If he failed this special mission from Moskva, he, and even his family, wouldn't get off easily.

On the other hand, if he could pull it off... If he could pull it off, maybe he would be allowed to take back what he missed so dearly. Though they were being treated better, his family was still in the camp.

If he could provide a normal life for them with this...

"Not to rush, but I'd like to hear the details of the mission. Please tell me."

"I'd expect nothing less from you, Comrade Colonel. Your response is encouraging."

Mikel wasn't thrilled about the prospect of getting worked so hard by this political commissar smiling at his luck. But Mikel knew from experience not to make enemies for no reason.

He gave the commissar a vague smile and figured he wouldn't be tainted to his core just for shaking hands. If he didn't shake hands with the devil and drink vodka together with him, he'd never last until the Lord's return.

"It's damaged...but can still sail. That's how it made it to our navy base. However," he continued in a voice suppressing his disgust, "the effects of the imperial strike cannot be ignored. The attacks targeted the deck and the engine, so the damage is profound. Our comrades at the base are working as fast as they can to fix it, but they say it will definitely take a few days."

"I have a question. Will the RMS *Queen of Anjou* be carrying things we need in the future?"

"Yes, that's right."

Perhaps the rumor that the so-called West Side was sending us military gear, industrial parts, and a ton of medical supplies in support of the fierce fight on the main lines was true.

Surprisingly, maybe it's best not to discount those tiny whispers.

"For that reason, we must provide complete protection. That is the special mission for you, Comrade, and your comrades from the party executives."

"It's an exceedingly great honor to bear the party's expectations. But, Comrade Political Commissar, what does 'complete protection' mean?"

It was unusual to specify a single ship and send in a mage battalion. Anyone would guess there was a catch. As for Mikel, he understood that they needed to protect the RMS *Queen of Anjou* that the West Side was sending over.

But he didn't understand the particular repetition and emphasis on *complete*. In a way…that was a reasonable question for him to have as a soldier.

To the political commissar, the need for perfection was clear as day. But though he was deeply sorry, he didn't explain any more.

"It's the heart of our maritime supply line. Comrade Colonel, no matter what happens, we want you to defend it to the last."

That was all the political commissar could say, in his position. In that sense, his answer could qualify as conscientious.

That said, as a member of the Commissariat for Internal Affairs, he knew.

…He knew what Comrade Loria would do to anyone who failed.

He knew the Commissariat for Internal Affairs didn't hesitate to turn a present-tense person into a past-tense person.

And knew how incredibly cutthroat the key figures were during wartime.

That's why the job had to be done perfectly.

"In other words, pull no punches. Do whatever it takes. Send it back to the Commonwealth without letting it get another scratch?"

"Exactly, Comrade Colonel. Moskva, the Commissariat for Internal Affairs, and Comrade General Secretary Josef are all hoping that our wonderful foreign friends have a peaceful trip home."

Though the true meaning of the political commissar's ghastly, repetitive exhortations didn't get through to Colonel Mikel…they were enough to give him a sense of crisis and make him realize how important the mission was.

In a way, you could say the two of them agreed on something for the first time.

"I see. I understand Moskva's wishes very well now."

Once the political commissar said that much, what other choice did Mikel have, in the Federation, than to accept?

In the party, there was nothing higher priority than the wishes of Moskva and Comrade General Secretary Josef. At least he hadn't been told to die, so he probably wasn't allowed to complain.

And so.

On that day.

Colonel Mikel stood in front of his battalion and barked, "Comrades, it's as you've heard. Our role is to be guard dogs. Stick close to the ship until it makes it safely home!"

""""Yes, sir!""""

>>> **THE SAME DAY, IN WATERS NEAR FEDERATION TERRITORY, IMPERIAL ARMY SUBMARINE UNIT DISPATCHED TO THE NORTHERN SEA, FLAGSHIP U-152** <<<

"Colonel von Degurechaff, I realize it's not my place to say this, but... are you serious?"

Lieutenant Colonel Tanya von Degurechaff is surprised to be asked such a question so suddenly.

Crammed inside the cramped U-152 is a mage unit—that is, three companies' worth of personnel. She thought they would hate being smashed together in the small space, but they consented so easily she hadn't been paying enough attention.

She assumed the submarine crew would be cooperative.

"I'm having trouble understanding the intent of your question, Captain von Schraft. What do you mean?"

There's nothing more obnoxious than having your resolve questioned over and over.

To Lieutenant Colonel Tanya von Degurechaff, a decision is a decision. Once she makes up her mind, even if a terrible god stands in her way, she'll blast her way through if she has to.

No. After a moment's reflection, she gracefully corrects her mistake. *If a terrible god stands in my way, I'll be delighted to blast it to bits.*

"You're really going to attack the naval base?"

"That's what I've been saying this whole time."

It's fine for Captain von Schraft to question my sanity. I respect his free will.

Tanya could argue loudly that he misunderstands her, but she has no intention of interfering with the thoughts and beliefs of a naval officer of the same rank as her.

That's what it means to be liberal.

But. Tanya acknowledges there is one point that her duty necessitates she argue. Things that should be said must be said.

"With all due respect, Captain, it's the Supreme High Command and the General Staff's wishes. I don't believe we're at liberty to have an opinion."

"You make a good point. I can't argue with that. But..." He smiles wryly and moves out from in front of the periscope. Then he casually pushes a wooden box into the space. *Oh, fine sailors of U-152, when this war is over, you should pivot into the service industry.*

He must have realized the periscope was impossible for a child to look through. That's just the sort of thing I'd expect from the navy; they appreciate people with their heads screwed on.

"Take a look at this, Colonel."

"...All right."

The superior lens is telescopic. The Empire's optics technology maintains its praiseworthy reliability even in open water in the Northern Sea.

That said, it's still just a periscope.

"Can you see? No offense, but I'm guessing you can't."

Of course, U-152's periscope is properly maintained and fully functional. There's just a fundamental limit to what it can do. In reality, visibility is awful and all she can see is a haze.

"You're correct. But it's not just because I had to stand on tiptoe to look?" she asks as she steps down from the irritating box with as straight a face as she can manage. She's not about to undervalue a specialist's knowledge and make a decision without getting the opinion of Captain von Schraft or someone on his crew. "I guess I'm hoping maybe a submariner with plenty of experience might have a different way of looking at things..."

"Sorry, but I must disappoint you."

"...So then?"

"Well, we have confirmation that the princess of the sea is at the base. It's just that we know nothing else." How disagreeable of him. He's just shrugging and saying, *Guess they shook us.*

And yet how natural and open. Or perhaps we should say it suits him. Even if the Imperial Navy is a straitlaced bunch. Or maybe all submarine units are like this?

Chapter **IV**

For better or worse, submariners aren't generally bound by convention.

Well, if they can do their jobs, that's fine. If they follow the bare minimum of rules, then an outsider doesn't really have the right to complain.

"And we don't know where the enemy is. We submariners like to watch for our chance and then attack. Frankly, we prefer to be cautious."

"...What you say certainly makes sense. But the intel we received from the air fleet has proven far more useful than what we got from the joint intelligence agency of the Army and Navy Commands. You could say that now is our chance—we should take the initiative and strike."

"I can't deny that, but they're probably keeping a close watch."

"They probably haven't even dreamed that mages would sneak over there on a submarine. Sneak attacks are a classic method, but that's because they're so useful."

Even Pearl Harbor[5] was, logically speaking, a huge gamble that never should have worked. Or think of the submarine operations to enter Scapa Flow.[6]

To be fair, the British bomber units who, back when the Luftwaffe[7] was alive and kicking, broke through the Nazi air screen and harassment-bombed Berlin had commendable skill and bravery.

And I'm not averse to acknowledging the bravery of the Communists.

But...they're making a structural error. The Red Square International Airport Incident is a fine example. We learned this when we attacked Moskva: They're great at conspiracies, but they're not always perfect when it comes to the serious stuff. For another instance, there's the case of Inchon, when the strategic transportation hub that had to be resolutely defended...was not defended.

"We'll take the enemy by surprise. It's an old trick, but that's how

---

[5] **Pearl Harbor**   "Let's cross the entire ocean and attack the U.S. Pacific Fleet at their base!" is easy to say, but actually doing it is nuts.

[6] **Scapa Flow**   Scapa Flow is a natural harbor and was a base for the Royal Navy. It was into that well-protected harbor that the German Navy's U-47, commanded by Günther Prien, penetrated during World War II. It got past the lookouts and sank the battleship *Royal Oak* that was anchored there. Captain Prien's greatest enemy wasn't the Royal Navy's warning screen, however, but his own boat's torpedoes. He fired seven at the anchored ship, but five of them malfunctioned... He was furious and said it was like having a "dummy rifle."

[7] **Luftwaffe**   The German air force during World War II.

you know it works. Going at them with a traditional method wouldn't be so bad, would it?" Tanya adds that the best way is the tried-and-true way. "Of course, I don't mean to look down on the proper, orthodox methods."

"I'm sure you don't. Doing things the orthodox way is best, *if it's possible*."

Everything he's saying makes sense, but Tanya has to inquire about something. "May I ask you something straight?"

Captain von Schraft signals with his eyes for her to continue, and Tanya throws him a fairly insolent question.

Thirty knots may be incredibly fast, but if the exit point is known, even a novice at naval operations like Tanya can come up with any number of plans. Why weren't the submarine units or the navy acting?

"If you know the ship is in the port, can't you just ambush them with the subs here? You've identified which port it's in, right?"

"Of course we considered that. We considered an ambush, and a wolf-pack attack, and also a mine operation where we planted a field along its projected course…"

"This is just the opinion of an amateur, but none of those methods sounds so bad."

Those are the orthodox methods. They take full advantage of submarine-specific properties. The imperial submarines led by U-152 should be able to do those things.

"Yes, *if they were possible*, they wouldn't be bad."

"If they were possible?"

There are an awful lot of overtones going on here. We're talking about the basic options when conducting a commerce raid operation.

They're completely normal ways to use submarines. Frankly, she can't shake the question of why they would be impossible.

Weren't submarines originally designed specifically to do those things?

"Is there…some problem? If you don't mind, I'd like to hear about it."

"Of course. Well, first, the plan of using submarines to build a mine screen…went up in smoke when a unit that nearly sank put up a fierce protest."

"What in the world happened?"

One, sure, but the entire unit nearly sank?

Did they build a minefield to defend against submarines? *No...they shouldn't have enough forces to build a minefield capable of blocking all submarines from sailing the Northern Sea.* So she says, puzzled, "As far as the briefing I read, the Federation isn't very good at fighting with mines. What I heard at home is that they're sticking pretty close to their coasts."

"Yes, that's all correct, Colonel."

Captain von Schraft puts on a smile that has a hint of irony about it. Still, he's not sneering at her information. *So then, what's the issue with waging mine warfare?*

"As far as I know, we're the only power attempting mine warfare in the Northern Sea. And that right there is the issue."

When Tanya seeks an explanation with her eyes, the submariner scoffs as he shares his woes. "The sensors of the new magnetic mines have a critical defect. In these high latitudes, and in this area rich with mineral resources, the magnetism is particularly powerful, you see. We can't expect these garbage triggers to work properly at these levels."

"You mean they don't go off?"

"The opposite! It's terrible!" he says, and though he's smiling, a tense, weary emotion comes through. Why would this submarine captain who boasts he fears nothing look so stressed?

What happened? She can't help but be curious. "If they go off, that's better than if they didn't, right? Even if they go off early, that's less of a problem than if they fail completely, no?"

"If they weren't exploding at times that they really, really shouldn't be, maybe."

...Hmm. She feels like she's heard this somewhere before. When she thinks about it, she recalls that the friendly subs trying to take out the Entente Alliance fleet were troubled by torpedoes that exploded too soon.

"You mean they're exploding before the enemy ships are anywhere near them?"

"*Nein, nein, nein!* Nothing so charming as that. The triggers are overly sensitive... Shockingly enough, they react to the submarines!"

"Huh? To the subs...?"

"Yes. They were nearly sunk by the mines they laid themselves. We never should have tried fighting with mines."

For a moment, she doesn't understand what Captain von Schraft has just said.

She doubts her ears, and her jaw drops slightly.

They wouldn't be able to perform a sneak attack like that.

"...Huh?!"

"It's incredible—the damn things will even respond to the U-152's magnetic signature. It seriously makes me wonder if agents from Commonwealth Intelligence have infiltrated our underwater explosives development department."

Magnetic mines work by reacting to magnetic signatures. In theory, submarines also have magnetic signatures.

But doesn't that mean they have safety mechanisms to keep them from exploding? How can you even lay them if your own boat causes a reaction?

"And on top of that, the torpedo fuses are rotten."

"You'll have to excuse my ignorance, but they haven't fixed that yet?" Tanya asks, utterly astonished. She had seen a torpedo shot by a submarine on an operation in this same Northern Sea explode too early, but she feels like that was ages ago.

Regarding mechanical problems, Tanya's impression has been that imperial manufactured goods are reliable. That it's possible even now for the Empire with its national strength to keep pumping out high-precision industrial products.

But the Empire's marine weapons like torpedoes and mines keep having shameful failures?

"Mm, we've made progress since before. Things have gotten better."

This is what true shock feels like.

Did the definition of *better* change from "improved" to "worsened" when I wasn't looking?

"B-better...?" She nearly says, *This is?* but swallows the words because they would be too rude. Still, this is too much. The submarine units are the most active part of the Imperial Navy. Yet the primary arms we're giving them are defective?

"Things really have gotten much better. Believe me."

"I-in...what way specifically?"

"It's an important military secret, but all right, I'll explain it to you. The contact fuses are so-so. At least, if you make a direct hit, they'll explode more than half the time. Well, if the angle of incidence is shallow, it's like shooting the same old dummy rifle, but..."

Tanya gapes at him and shouts, incredulous, "...W-wait a sec! You're saying that a direct hit only explodes half the time?!"

Misfires happen, of course.

She knows that for a fact.

Even the shells the artillery fires are sometimes duds. Some torpedoes misfire; that she...can understand. But to Tanya, the fact that even a direct hit triggers only half the time is utterly absurd.

And Captain von Schraft continues in a self-deprecating tone, as if he wanted to see that reaction from her. "Hmm? We love the contact fuses compared to the others."

"Sorry, but could there possibly be something worse?"

"There is—this. There's a problem with the depth-keeping mechanism, so we can't aim torpedoes for direct hits on ships with shallow drafts. Specifically, ones like destroyers and so on."

The grave revelation that the submarines don't have a way to combat destroyers... Even though submarines are so vulnerable themselves.

They can't even torpedo their natural enemy, those escort ships that scatter mines everywhere...?

"So that leaves us with our dear magnetic triggers as our hope...but due to the high latitude, we keep having issues with them. In the Northern Sea, if our only option is magnetic triggers, we have a better chance of survival if we stay quiet and dodge the depth charges."

"...You'll have to excuse me, Captain von Schraft. There are no words to describe the circumstances the submarine units are in. I'm impressed you've been able to carry on fighting..."

"Thank you, Colonel von Degurechaff. It's understanding, not pity, for which there is no substitute. Even so, may I vent about one thing?"

Tanya nods yes, and the captain begins speaking in an even voice.

"The most hopeless thing of all is that..."

Suddenly, she realizes...

Everyone on the bridge seems to be resisting some urge.

"The navy's Weapons Division stubbornly claims that the issues are all operational errors. They're convinced their torpedoes are perfect." He snaps on the U-152 bridge how ridiculous it is. "As proof, they keep guaranteeing us that they worked *in the lab*. That's their response to them not working in battle."

"...I'm completely dumbfounded. I can't believe you have to fight a war with weapons you're not even sure will work or not. You're being jerked around by the developers' egos—you have my sympathy. Please let me observe when you load the developers into your torpedo tubes."

"Sorry, but that bit of fun is restricted. It'll be a party for submariners only; I hope you understand."

"Ha-ha-ha. No, that makes sense. It was a presumptuous request. I'd appreciate it if you could even just tell me how it goes."

"You can count on me for that, at least. I could even print up a leaflet and send it over."

The delight of blowing fools away... It's a forbidden thrill. Yes, I see how outsiders shouldn't be poking their noses in.

In that case... Tanya makes the appropriate gear switch and brings the conversation back to reality. "Anyhow, I understand your situation now. It's no wonder submarine attacks go so poorly."

I had no business talking about orthodox methods. *No*, Tanya corrects herself. The joint intelligence agency's plan was for the submarines to deal the final blow via torpedo.

In other words, the information about the defects either hasn't gotten to them, or they didn't find it important.

It's stupid, but the Imperial Navy, which has expanded so rapidly, is awful at troubleshooting. It's become a wholly useless organization. Time to make some cuts.

But making that report comes after dealing with this.

"As things stand, all we can do is observe, or maybe fire torpedoes if we're lucky. I want to support you in the base raid, but...as frustrating as it is to say, we can't."

"It's a huge help for you to even carry us this far."

"U-152 is a submarine, you know? Not a transport ship."

"No," the duty officer on the bridge grumbled. "As long as the eels can't be counted on, U-152 is a transport ship that sneaks around the sea. Much to our regret, though we were built to sink transport ships, we ended up becoming one under the water at some point."

How true, she wants to sympathize.

But there's nothing more useless than blaming them for problems they didn't cause.

Tanya knows that the people on the ground are frequently exhausted by the top making systematically impossible demands. Though in theory, encouraging people is fine organizational management.

You morons who discount the power of words, you scum who sling abuse! Whether it's the teeming swarm of Being X's allies or just a bunch of idiots, it can all just rot.

"No, no, you're a fine attack sub. You're going to unleash us, so I think you can consider us something like aerial torpedoes."

Aircraft carriers don't attack, themselves, either. They're just platforms from which to launch the planes on board. But are there any soldiers who underestimate an aircraft carrier as a transport ship? Not if they have normal intelligence.

"Ha-ha-ha, a torpedo that soars through the sky?"

"Yeah, and you can use the word *unleash* just like for torpedoes."

Sensing the improving atmosphere aboard the sub, Tanya allows her lips to slowly curl into a bewitching smile. A ballistic missile platform is also a fearsome ship.

Calling it a part of mutually assured destruction is plenty correct. Although at this point in time in this world axis, the idea is still an armchair theory.

"...Don't you think that's something?"

The crew members who replied, "Sure is," probably think it's just a cute story. But even a cute story can inspire people to be ambitious once more.

I introduced words to General von Zettour as an inexpensive weapon, but...if they can be used to support allies, as well? Logos! How powerful.

Perhaps it's because she's thinking those things?

"That's fine. Then quit sulking about a transport mission and concentrate on preparing to launch our aerial torpedoes."

Hearing how smoothly Captain von Schraft says it, Tanya realizes something with a start. *Was this whole conversation just a skit for the crew?!*

Really? she does wonder, but the next thing he says convinces her. Speaking in a casual tone, the captain of the sub seizes the hearts of his crew.

"Anyone with a free hand, I have something else for you to do. Even if we're shooting into the air, a torpedo attack is a torpedo attack. We need to add to our sunk tonnage. The treasury's got a bottle for anyone who comes up with a way to threaten the brutes at Fleet Command."

Amid the cheers on the bridge, Tanya discreetly removes her cap and waves it at the captain. *Wow.*

"I finally understand why Submarine Command, despite being strangely cooperative in sending out boats, starts talking circles around me right before the attack."

"Ha-ha-ha! Sorry, Colonel von Degurechaff. I'll apologize on behalf of all our officers for using you, an outsider, to further our own purposes. The torpedo troubles are really eating away at morale, both for us and for all the other submarine units."

She can't argue with morale problems.

And it's true that the torpedoes are defective. Tanya knows the pain of being handed faulty weapons, so she understands and can even sympathize.

The Elinium Type 95 is ridiculously flawed. It's a toss-up which is worse: that or a mine that explodes right near a submarine the moment it gets laid.

Who could fight a war under such conditions? It would drive you nuts.

"I understand painfully well. I'm not going to hold a grudge over getting used or anything like that. If I get a chance, I'll report to the core General Staff members about the torpedo issues."

"We'd appreciate that so much. Thank you."

Surely exchanging textbook salutes is enough, then. Inside the cramped submarine, on the crowded bridge, there's no reason to annoy everyone with prolonged motions.

All that is left is hashing out the administrative details.

"So what are you actually planning to do, Colonel von Degurechaff? That ship is enormous. Honestly, I think it will be very hard to sink. If we succeed," he says, continuing in a lighter tone, "do you think we could have half the tonnage?" But his eyes show his concern for us. "Can you tell me how this is going to work?"

"Basically, we'll be taking a classic approach. We'll distract the enemy with a feint, and in that opening, the task force will go about blowing it up." Tanya gives a brief explanation of the plan. "Therefore, most sneak attacks are distractions with a task force delivering the main blow. Well, even if we fail to destroy the enemy ship, we'll have achieved a distraction. We'll be counting on you to recover us."

"What a bold plan. Understood. We'll get it done."

>>> **OCTOBER 8, UNIFIED YEAR 1926, DAYBREAK, FEDERATION TERRITORY, NAVAL BASE** <<<

For First Lieutenant Serebryakov, the sight reminded her for a moment of the Rhine front.

No matter how much I try to bury the memories of those days, the smell of gun smoke brings them back. I'll never be able to play in the mud like a child again. Mud recalls irritating yet nostalgic memories.

How could I ever forget the days I spent holed up in the trenches?

"Oh God, forgive our enemies."

The one who began singing next to me was my superior officer, feared by our enemies as a monster. It makes sense that even allies are quietly calling her Rusted Silver instead of White Silver.

Still, I know Tanya von Degurechaff better than anyone in the 203rd Aerial Mage Battalion. In fact, I've served under her since before she earned the *von* in her name in the war college.

She's the officer who let me live while the guys I joined up with, Harald and Kurst, became so much ground beef.

That eminent figure, that person, that senior member of the forces…

She doesn't seem to believe in God. Yet she was praising Him on the battlefield…? The moment I think, *Don't give away our position…*, I remember her clenching her orb on the Rhine front and praying just like this. She doesn't talk big at all; in fact, she's modest. Reality is far too unreal.

She's crazy. There's something strange about her.

"Oh God, forgive our enemies."

The enemy mages scattered every which way.

Two companies of Federation aerial mages were being toyed with by a single opponent. Her own company didn't even have time to jump in.

"It's not that the enemy is stupid, just…"

That's what it's like to murmur a mixture of surprise, admiration, and astonishment in spite of yourself.

Despite the sneak attack—I suppose—the Federation had responded with surprising speed.

Though they came with a force of two companies from a different direction to cause confusion, troops were scrambling to meet us immediately. I'd heard the Federation Army's rear was completely relaxed, but apparently not.

We should have anticipated it, but there were Commonwealth escorts with them. Well, no, that much was according to expectations. There was only one problem: Their coordination was actually not too shabby.

It was a regiment of Commonwealth mages plus the same number of Federation mages. I couldn't deny that I was shocked that the two countries managed to coordinate just as they had said. I thought they would be sloppier, but I underestimated them.

…Our battalion even managed a direct attack on Moskva. Yes, we were the veteran 203rd Aerial Mage Battalion, and yet… I nearly despaired at the tenacity with which the Federation aerial mages and wall of ground forces devoted themselves to keeping us from breaking through. We were all prepared to be subdued and wiped out.

But a single soldier's fierce fighting turned the tables.

"Those poor ignorant lambs."

The motions of loading a mana shot, protected by a special sealing formula, into her rifle… She wasn't even using a formula bullet but a shot formed from her own magical energy.

I knew how powerful that would be.

The colonel cackled—no, she giggled, smiling like a child. It was positively surreal to see her eyeing the enemy with her tender gaze and licking her lips.

She snickered, but what was so funny? She was terrifying.

I guess it's a perfect distraction.

"I'll have a romp with them. It shall be most amusing."

No, maybe it's better to call it a steamrollering.

Despite calling it a distraction, each one of Colonel von Degurechaff's shots was undoubtedly ripping through the enemy mage's defensive shells as if they were delicate candy sculptures.

Chapter **IV**

The enemy units bunched up, dumbfounded, in spite of themselves, and we kept firing without a moment's rest, but...mages' defensive shells are practically the definition of strong. It's hard to imagine anything with enough juice to break them that easily.

I had heard from the colonel. I had seen her rage on the Rhine front. But it was now that I had more experience myself that I understood what an outlier that power was.

So this is the full power of the Type 95?

When I heard there was only one person in the whole army who could use it, I thought it was an awful lie, but no.

...Isn't it too much for a person to handle?

"Amusing, most amusing."

She laughed as she fired the intense barrage of formulas. Contrary to her lighthearted tone, Colonel von Degurechaff's formulas were full of crafty tricks. When I took a closer look, I saw there were optical sniping formulas and guided formulas deceptively modified to be harder to detect.

If you only dodged the optical lines of fire, you'd be riddled with holes.

But surprisingly, the Federation mages realized that.

"Colonel Mikel to all units! Break! Break! Get outta here as fast as you can! We can't take this one! Don't even try!"

She had no idea how he figured it out, but the enemy commander at the head of his group shrieked over the open channel that everyone should dodge. At the same time, he handled the situation brilliantly himself. He bent his flight path so hard and lost so much momentum in the process, he nearly fell out of the sky.

Then the Commonwealth commander roared evasion orders, too. Both instructions resulted in clear changes in their units' movements.

Emergency evasion was strictly prohibited in the manual. The Federation had been forced to do it not once but repeatedly, and now the Commonwealth mages, too. Their formations began to come apart.

Anyone could see the airspace was exceedingly dangerous; the closely packed units were performing highly mobile erratic evasive maneuvers, and who knew where they were dodging next.

When seen from above, their desperate movements to escape the God of Death's scythe just looked like clumsy struggling. They were so sluggish. They weren't going fast enough. They got too late a start to dodge the approaching blade.

"I shall sing praises of the Lord."

Rapturously.

Practically joyously, Colonel von Degurechaff began singing in a high and somehow pure-sounding voice. With a merry smile, she seemed to delight in it. It was a smile without a hint of reproach. A truly charming, out of place smile, pretty as a picture.

If you didn't know her, the battalion commander...it was a cheerful smile like you'd find in a painting.

But lurking behind that smile was an absolute will to fight.

"We're going to play with the Empire's archenemy. What fun!"

What she formed was a manifestation formula, pouring in vastly more mana than ever before. Making up the unbelievably dense four-layer formula was extraordinarily thick magical energy.

Most people would be shocked.

However, I knew—that Colonel von Degurechaff didn't actually have a huge amount of mana. She had only a little more than average.

It was entirely possible that I had more. If you lined up a select group of mages like their battalion by mana amount, it would be faster to count from the bottom to find the colonel.

But even questioning the significance of that was absurd.

"Our archenemy shall dye the earth with their blood."

With a gleeful shout, she fired *that thing*.

Having increased its density as she managed its size, she unleashed it.

That very moment, it scattered.

A red, red something spattered the earth in huge quantities.

"The game is to dry that up—enjoy!"

Dripping red liquid. Pink things that used to be humans, flying everywhere. And opposite that scene was a beaming little girl. It was so surreal, it made more sense for me to suppose I had gone insane.

No, maybe I really did go insane.

While I was thinking this and that, I was keeping my hands busy making optical sniping formulas to put holes in the enemies who fell through the cracks of my commander's attacks. The enemy mage named Mikel, who had shouted evasion orders earlier, was still moving.

So I needed to aim for the enemy commander. *I was baptized on the Rhine, too*, I recalled.

The conditioned reflexes I had soaked up, optimizing myself for combat... Now that I was used to it, it was rare I didn't know what to do.

"Ohhh, praise be to the Lord."

The sight of my superior officer nodding with satisfaction and beginning a confession of her faith was horrific. I didn't get even a glimmer of madness from her beautiful, innocent eyes. They were the eyes of a stubborn servant of logic, full of pure reason.

But that's what was so horrific: those eyes stuck on that doll-like face.

Still, it was the superior officer I knew by now, and the mages writhing on the ground were only enemy soldiers who needed to be finished off.

Even the Commonwealth marine mages, who fed us a taste of bitter defeat, ended up like this when we went hunting for them. The 203rd's reputation was alive and well.

The renown we built up in Norden, in Dacia, on the Rhine, in the southern continent would continue to compound glories.

"The promised land shall open."

The demoralized enemy mages were trying to split up, but it was too late. The battalion's follow-up attacks found their marks.

I was casting optical sniping formulas unconsciously. In that soundless void, the enemies went down so easily. Only a few—including, irritatingly, the commander—were still doing fine.

That said, they probably didn't have the energy to resist anymore.

This was supposed to be a distraction, but it turned into a massacre.

It was so silent, as if to not interrupt the prayer.

"Now sing, now sing."

Never mind that this was a battlefield... Even though it was a battlefield... On this hushed battlefield...

"I shall praise the will of God."

Our superior had a huge sneer on her face.

That means, I thought, all of a sudden.

"Grantz, if it goes well, that's great, but... If we fail to destroy the ship, I don't think she'll stop at kicking our butts in this state of malevolence," I grumbled over the wireless without thinking.

I was answered by a man's voice, trembling to its core.

Of course, it was Grantz.

"05 to my cohort painting such a horrific picture of the future. Gimme a break. I'm so, so scared, I'm practically shaking."

"Huh? You're all ready?"

Lieutenant Grantz nodded. "Yeah. This'll be no problem. I mean, the colonel gave us such an incredible distraction. I won't complain if any numbskulls who get that kind of support and still fail get sent to the firing squad. Okay, I guess it's about that time. Let's sync our watches: three, two, one, boom." He didn't even have to say, "*Watch this!*"

From the port came the thundering of…a massive explosion.

"See?" I heard his voice in the background and was sure he was wearing a proud grin.

Now, then, I thought. *I'm sure the U-152 crew will share some canned food with us, at least. If things go well, I can get us a bottle and playing cards. If we're lucky, there will even be dessert?*

All right. That got her fired up.

A tasty meal, something sweet, and wine. Rather than worry about the tough stuff, let's have some fun for now.

 OCTOBER 8, UNIFIED YEAR 1926, EVENING, MOSKVA, THE COMMISSARIAT FOR INTERNAL AFFAIRS

In Moskva, the newly built Commissariat for Internal Affairs building had long since turned into a nightless fortress. With the strict blackout, light wasn't pouring out, per se, but still, if you walked by, you would be able to see the officials coming and going inside.

Anyone had to concede that the staff of the Commissariat for Internal Affairs was extraordinarily diligent in keeping up their war efforts compared to most of the Federation's public servants.

To be frank, they were, in a way, the steel-clad vanguard of Communism.

Their efficiency, their self-sacrifice, and their unflagging spirit made them indomitable workers.

Of course, the majority of them were normal humans. But that didn't diminish their drive to work.

And the source of their diligence was…simple fear.

"Comrade Loria! The inspection failed to find any misappropriation, corruption, or improper conduct! Neither were there any reactionary remarks made regarding the inspection itself!"

A Commissariat for Internal Affairs official, wearing an immaculate uniform, read the report. He seemed about to continue when the dull thud of a fist slamming down on the table interrupted him.

He froze as a glare rolled to fix on him, and the room's occupant snapped, "I'm fairly certain I ordered you to expose improper conduct. Let's be clear. You really didn't find anything?"

"N-no, Comrade, we didn't."

Hearing that quivering reply, Loria's expression was sternness incarnate.

Then he pronounced the man's sentence.

"That's fine. Comrade guards, take this fool away. Sabotage during wartime is a crime against the nation."

"Yes, sir!"

"P-please wait! This must be some mistake!"

The man protested as the guards grabbed his arms and began to drag him away, but Loria flatly denied him.

"There's no mistake at all. Your case was a dummy conducted as part of an internal audit of our staff. We had the object of your inspection perform the corrupt act, and we have record of the inspector taking the bribe."

"Wh-wha—?!"

"If you had just reported that…things would have been different, but you accepted the bribe without telling us. That's enough," spat Loria.

He didn't have time for a single pointless action when time was passing moment by moment.

"I'm sure a single punishment will be a better lesson for these idiots than a lecture. Next!"

"Er, Comrade Loria…"

Loria turned a gaze of merciless intensity on his hesitating subordinate. Even with that questioning look, the response was slow in coming.

"What? Let's have it. Hurry up!"'

"It's bad news…about the Queen of the Sea…"

Sensing he wasn't getting anywhere, Loria asked directly. And his expression tensed at the nervously delivered information.

There was probably no way to stop that twinge of emotional fluctuation.

The fact that something had happened to the ship entrusted to them by their precious—yes, in a way precious—"bullet shield" made Loria seethe with rage.

It wasn't clear what the John Bulls were up to, but he and they had come to an agreement. After all their reluctance, he had persuaded them. He had ordered dozens of Federation officials slowing him down to be shot; either that or he threatened and buttered them up to secure them as allies. All of that, and yet...

The supporting sea route that they needed in order to continue the war, a symbol of their joint struggle, had only just been opened.

Though casualties had been taken into account, they were hopeless if they couldn't defend the one boat he ordered them to stake their honor on protecting.

He was sure he provided the necessary units, fighting force, and discretion to get it done.

But they still couldn't do it?

"Those incompetent bastards. What were they doing? Do you have a detailed report?"

If they don't have an excellent reason, I'm going to make the ones responsible regret surviving the mission for as long as they live, Loria swore in his head as he requested the report.

The silver lining for the official who had been asked was that he actually did have the papers with him. If he had blundered by not bringing them...God only knows what his fate would have been.

After all, the word *forbearance* had been missing from Loria's dictionary for ages.

"Here it is, Comrade Loria... I don't know how they found out, but apparently they sent in a Named mage..."

"...What's that?"

The inept political officer continued making justifications for the report.

But I told them. Apparently, this guy is stuck in the old way of thinking, where mages aren't worth paying attention to. Perhaps he was trying to shift the blame? The report went on and on about how unfortunate their position had been.

Chapter **IV**

It was a surprise that the man thought he could get away with making excuses like that.

But... Loria was conscious of a stirring in his emotions as he wrestled his irritation down.

Aside from this one garbage political officer, everyone was putting in a splendid effort.

"Comrade Loria?"

"So there aren't any mistakes in this report, hmm?"

Everyone here was endeavoring to their utmost ability, working without wasting any time, and giving their all. For Loria, it was the first time in a while that his eyes popped wide open in admiration of their magnificent professional awareness.

Perhaps because he was reading it after dealing with those other inepts? It was even refreshing.

"N-no, sir. It's the first report, but we did a rough confirmation of the damages!"

"That can be investigated later."

They're fighting my fairy, that little imp who attacked Moskva. Teaming up with the Commonwealth and then standing our ground and suffering casualties...is not a bad excuse.

No, more importantly.

"The issue is the enemy who attacked. You're sure it was...the unit that laid its grubby hands on Moskva? The 203rd Aerial Mage Battalion?"

"O-of course! As you say, Comrade Commissar, that is the conclusion the inspection unit on its tracks reached! They guarantee their identification 100 percent."

"Very good. When the documents arrive, make delivering them to me highest priority."

"Yes, sir! Right away!"

"You're free to let others take over any other ongoing mission you may have. In any case, I want to know where this unit is."

"I-I'll get to work on it immediately!"

What wonderful news.

We found her. A few losses are piddling trivialities in the face of my genuine love. I'm even moved to pay my hardworking men a bonus like a capitalist. I should probably arrange some extra rations for them.

Although I'm not pleased that we had one fool who misunderstood his role to the last.

"Also, Comrade, take these orders."

"Sir?"

"It's orders to execute the incompetent idiot who slandered our hard-fighting comrades. Yes, don't blame the men on the ground. I'd like to send Colonel Mikel a gift, actually. Arrange for the highest-quality drink and cigarettes to be delivered to him."

"Shall we poison him?"

What?! He glared at the man, nearly dizzy with confusion. *What the hell is this guy talking about?*

"...Comrade, were you not listening to what I said? A gift, I want to send him a gift. Just try and lay a thoughtless hand on Colonel Mikel and his troops—you'll get a comprehensive lesson about what happens when you make me mad."

"Y-yes, sir!"

That was as much as Loria could stomach. He was aware that the Commissariat for Internal Affairs was a gang of useless sadists. He recognized it, and he was taking measures to improve it.

But this was how things stood.

Just incorrigible.

He just wanted to sink deep into his exceedingly pure thoughts...but instead he had to endure the faces of these dolts? He truly struggled to understand why.

To repeat, it was unbearable.

The others had gathered that he was angry by the time he waved them off. "All right, everybody out." The moment he said it, they all ran away like fleeing rabbits.

That was so funny that it eased his frustration somewhat.

Which was why he gazed at a photo he pulled out of his desk with a smile.

"Ahhh, my ever so lovely, lovely...little fairy. You're a bit too naughty, but... Well, I'll just be happy we know where you are."

You like playing hide-and-seek, don't you?

"To appear like this just as I was forgetting you, you're quite—quite the tactician! It makes my heart race!"

You like to tease, don't you?

"I'd nearly forgotten my passions, and now you've got me all riled up. Oh, you, you little… This is…"

It's just unbearable.

Swallowing that last comment, Loria thought, entranced, of his beloved fairy.

He did have a mind to blame the troops on the scene for failing to catch her, but his relief that they'd found her was stronger.

He didn't really think a unit of that caliber could shoot his fairy out of the sky.

"On the contrary, they did a great job locating her. Yes, Colonel Mikel, was it? He…truly did a fine job. Considering what he was up against, I can only say he did a fantastic job surviving and bringing the intel back to us. I need him to work hard for me."

How about a game of tag? I'll be It and catch that girl.

"Ahhh, I can't wait. I really, truly can't wait."

Let's play.

"Yes, I need Comrade Colonel Mikel to do his best… So I'll give him and his troops the best support possible and deploy the best reinforcements. Someone who'll make a favorable impression on the Commonwealth would be good."

I'll send her lots of friends.

That lovely jokester fairy. Surely the privilege to have her was his alone, so he was so excited to trap her. He was looking forward to it so much that before he knew it…

"Well, this is no good. Now I'm all hot and bothered, and at my age."

What a bad girl. It just builds up; it's too much—how am I supposed to help it? What a troublemaker she is. To think I'm this excited to push her down.

Of all the—?! It's too soon!

──────────── Someone shouting in the General Staff Office ────────────

Of all the medical facilities in the Federation, the navy base ones were the most advanced, since they kept in touch with the West Side. At least, you could call them proper hospitals. They were staffed with a full complement of trained medical professionals.

And it went without saying that they paid attention to not only numbers but quality, too. As far as medicines, they were far and away the most well-stocked thanks to the drugs carried over from the West Side.

At least, unlike the exceedingly gruesome intensity of the frontline treatment environment, this place was incomparably blessed. It was a real hospital with pristine sheets, the sharp smell of disinfecting alcohol, and a properly cleaned linoleum floor.

The medical officers on the forward-most line, who were reported to be running low on medicine, had given up even dreaming about facilities like these.

But no matter how well-equipped the facilities were…

"Hey, hey, help me out! Please, I need a cardiac stimulant! Hurry!"

"Cut it out…Thomas! Jackson is already asleep!"

"Colonel Drake! You can't be serious! Please don't talk crazy! Jackson! Hey, Jackson! Stay with us! You're going home, aren't you?!"

Wartime hospitals were…hospitals.

Seeing one of his subordinate officers shouting, unable to accept the death of a lifeless young mage…he was already used to this.

What a rotten thing to get used to, lamented Lieutenant Colonel Drake internally; some part of his parched heart wanted a stiff drink as he stepped into the room.

"Hey! Examine him again!" Thomas lashed out at the Federation medic.

Chapter V

"B-but…"

Drake understood Thomas's feelings to a painful degree.

Mage units were proud to have bonds as close as a family's. No, their relationships were thicker than blood. How many officers could remain calm when losing a friend who accompanied them through thick and thin, who broke bread with them?

"Don't die here!"

And on top of that, he recalled that Second Lieutenant Jackson was First Lieutenant Thomas's junior by a year. *They were friends since the academy*—he had to put it in past tense. It was a terrible shame to Drake as well.

"Lieutenant Thomas!"

"Colonel, there must be—there must be some mistake!"

That said, this could go on only so long.

"You have lots of other fellow soldiers who need treatment. Keep it down, Lieutenant Thomas!"

"But!"

He wouldn't call it a tantrum.

He could understand losing composure to the point of rejecting reason.

…It's pretty hard to get used to…this.

If he hadn't been forced to witness so many of his subordinates' deaths that he'd become almost immune, how wonderful that would have been.

It was a horrible job and a horrible position to be in. But casualties were inevitable in war. As long as they were inevitable, officers needed to accept them as such and do what needed to be done.

"Cool it!"

He popped Thomas one and took advantage of his shock to drag him out of the room as if he was kicking out a nuisance. *Luckily*, it should probably be said? Some of the idiot's friends who were worried about him picked him up.

Alcohol and time were the only things he could prescribe to fix that issue. Tonight, there was nothing to do but drink like fish. *I'll give them time to share memories of the deceased and have a good manly cry.*

Drake winced a bit when he realized how much he had been drinking since the start of the war. He was always drinking in the worst way, never to enjoy it; he might as well have been drinking rubbing alcohol. At this rate, he felt like he was going to forget how to savor a good drink.

But. He returned his consciousness to reality and bowed. "I'm sorry my officer got in your way. Please examine the other injured."

"No, it was…"

"No matter how we paint it, it's true that he caused trouble. Please allow me to apologize."

Drake had told his mages in no uncertain terms that they were to treat the Federation medical officers and staff with respect.

Their allies were pouring finite medical resources into them.

Bowing your head and thanking the personnel who worked so hard for you and then turning around and heaping abuse on them was wrong. Which was why Drake didn't hesitate. He bowed deeply to the young medic Thomas had been bothering.

That was his job as the responsible party.

"Please don't trouble yourself. Surely it's only natural to have feelings about the loss of your subordinate." From off to one side came a gentle soprano voice.

Considering it was a hospital, military or no, there were still enough female personnel that it wasn't rare. Not to mention that men and women had been serving together in mage units and rear divisions for quite a while now.

The woman who had spoken was perhaps in her early twenties? With a somewhat tender look at him, she walked over. But in the uniform of a line officer…? Drake hadn't seen her before. When he checked her rank, things felt even stranger.

Despite having drilled the ranks of the Federation forces into his brain, he didn't recognize this armband.

Strangest of all, the moment the medic saw her coming over, he gave a parting salute and rushed off to work.

Drake knew from experience what that meant.

It was like rats escaping a ship. When trouble arrived, nimble marine mages scattered in the same way.

"Excuse me, you are?"

"I'm Liliya Ivanova Tanechka, one of the humble gofers others might call a political officer. I'm a low-ranking political commissar as well as a first lieutenant in the Federation Army. Please call me Liliya."

A mild demeanor and polite way of speaking.

But what she was saying was very important. *I never thought the day would come that we'd have anything to do with political officers or commissars or whatever.*

"*Humble* is one I'll have to look up in my Federation language dictionary later. I'm Lieutenant Colonel Drake of the Commonwealth's First Expeditionary Marine Mage Force."

"It's a pleasure to meet you, Colonel Drake."

She didn't seem at all like a mere first lieutenant, but whatever. He had orders from the fellows at home to treat political commissars not as military but as civil servants.

While he didn't have direct experience, he'd heard more than enough rumors.

The one about them being a pain in the arse was proven by the medic who'd skittered away like a rabbit earlier. *I'd really like to avoid trouble...*

"Now then, I must perform my unpleasant duty."

"Duty?"

"Oh, I suppose it's a misleading way to put it."

Drake braced himself, but the woman straightened up and then bowed.

"As a party member, I extend our sympathy and condolences for your sacrifice and contribution. As an individual, I'm very sorry for your loss."

"I appreciate you saying that. With your sentiments and condolences, I feel I'll be able to show my face to his family...despite being a good-for-nothing commander. Thank you."

Then he slowly told her.

They weren't the only ones to face that horrifying imperial mage unit, the Devil of the Rhine and her gang. The Federation Army had sacrificed many as well.

"It's late in coming, but please accept the gratitude and respect of one Commonwealth officer for your country's sacrifice and for fighting alongside us."

"It's an honor. Certainly, that's the best farewell gift for my fallen comrades."

Her words contained more sincerity and integrity than mere lip service.

That's what made him hesitate.

"…This probably isn't the sort of thing an outsider should say, but…"

"Please, anything. The Commissariat for Internal Affairs said to hear out any opinions our allies have."

Perhaps he was careless because he was given permission?

Although the home country had told him to be careful…Drake let his request slip.

"Then one thing. I hope you won't blame your officers too much."

"You mean you're putting in a good word for our comrade the colonel?"

"I don't mean to interfere in domestic affairs, but…"

"I'm eager to hear what you have to say."

"Colonel Mikel and the others from your nation did their very best in the fight."

Colonel Mikel and his men had faced the Devil of the Rhine with them. Drake found himself arguing how bravely they had fought.

Frankly, he was afraid he was crossing some line in Federation culture by saying that. He was so worried he had made trouble for the men already detained that his face tensed up before he could stop it.

"The party has a philosophy of rewards and punishment. But this is war. Sadly, even doing your best doesn't guarantee success." She smiled at him. "Please put your mind at ease. I don't know if it will do anything, but I'll write a note saying our comrades' best efforts were thought of highly by an external party."

"To be perfectly frank, I would really appreciate that…but are you sure it's all right?"

"All right?"

"Officer Liliya, I don't presume to know your position in your country, but is it all right at this juncture to leave a written record that you approve of an outsider's opinion?"

"Hee-hee-hee. Seems like your concern for me has taken a strange turn."

She laughed peacefully in her gentle soprano.

She didn't seem worried about herself one bit.

"I'll be fine," she declared with no hesitation. "Just because you did your job well doesn't necessarily mean results will follow. Unfortunately, that goes for my country, too."

In the bright blue eyes looking at him, unwavering, was her firm will.

"But using that as an excuse to punish someone isn't how Communism works. You could say that defending against that is our job."

"...Huh?"

"Oh, have you been reading imperial propaganda?" She winced and asked him not to believe it. "Unfortunately, I must say, I know much is said about the Federation and our mother party. But the truth is what you see here." She pointed at herself and then pointed at Drake with a smile. "We're humans, too. Do you think you could see us as your neighbors—as we are, without discrimination?"

"I misjudged you. I do feel as though I've met a friendly neighbor."

He bobbed his head and was about to reach out when he finally remembered where he was. *If I kiss her hand, I'll probably get walloped.*

He hadn't been this impressed since meeting blue bloods back home. But this was the Federation. Honestly, it was hard for him to imagine that any old families remained...

Which was why he proceeded to ask her a question—he felt he was in the presence of someone quite unexpected. "By the way, do you mind? Perhaps it's rude to say, but you seem awfully young, Officer Liliya."

"Do I look inexperienced? I did just graduate from the academy..."

"Ah, how tactless. I shouldn't have brought up the topic of age with a woman. How awful of me. I'm terribly ashamed."

As he apologized, he winced inwardly that he was missing his opportunity to learn about her background.

If she was from an old family, then whether it was the Federation's Red Army Academy or the political academy, they probably would have refused her entry based on her status.

It wasn't as if there were no red nobles, but the name Liliya Ivanova Tanechka didn't ring a bell. He had never even heard of the Tanechka family.

"Apparently, a man can grow coarse in the company of rowdy marine mages without even realizing. I must be crazy, asking a woman her age." He bowed again, repeating how incredibly embarrassed he was, and looked to see how she was reacting... A wry smile.

Not irritation or confusion? Sheesh, no more probing that will only end in disgrace. Just as he was thinking how to pull as much information out of her as possible, he noticed a first lieutenant approaching.

It was Lieutenant Mary Sue.

Though she counted as Commonwealth personnel, she was actually in an Entente Alliance voluntary unit sent over from the Unified States.

They had been literally obliterated. A company of them had been attached to the RMS *Queen of Anjou* on a direct support mission, and the result of their second encounter with the Devil of the Rhine left the majority of them incapacitated. There were only four left.

The ones who barely survived, like Mary Sue, were just enough to form a platoon. It was utterly tragic.

"Excuse me, Colonel. About the burial..."

"Sorry, I'm a bit busy right now. Let's talk later, Lieutenant Sue."

Though he had allowed her to debate him on this topic a few times... he didn't want to get into it in front of a third party.

Drake sent Political Officer Liliya an apologetic glance.

"Umm, I don't mind. Go ahead."

"Are you sure it's all right?"

How annoying, he couldn't help but think. It would have been fine if Lieutenant Sue had just taken a hint and withdrawn, but...

"I'm not so heartless that I don't have respect for the sacrifices of people with the same aim as me. Hello, may I have your name?"

Once she bowed and set a polite introduction in motion, Drake couldn't find an excuse to stop them.

"I'm First Lieutenant Mary Sue. I'm part of a voluntary mage battalion from the Unified States."

"Well! So you're not working in the rear, huh?"

The commissar expressed her surprise at meeting another woman serving on the front lines. Unable to come up with a reason to shoo her away, Drake was falling behind.

He couldn't even find a chance to interrupt their conversation.

"Oh, I'm sorry. I'm Liliya Ivanova Tanechka. If you like, why don't we be friends?"

Though she held out her hand warmly, she was passionately engaged in her work. *Yes, part of the political commissars' job is negotiating between Commonwealth units and the Federation.*

"But work comes first, right? Uh, let me know if I can ever be of any help."

Faced with that smile that seemed to say, *Feel free to talk to me anytime!* Drake couldn't very well pull the plug.

"Er, is that all right, Colonel Drake?"

"Sure, that's fine."

How much more at ease would he have felt if he could have rejected her suggestion right then? Of course, if Sue was going to hesitantly confirm with him, she could have thought about their position from the start. As Drake looked on, feeling ashamed about being unable to stop two people of delicate positions from interacting at this delicate juncture...the conversation was picking up, if nothing else.

It was too late to regret not being more forceful and driving her off from the get-go.

"So...about the location for the burial..."

As he thought, Lieutenant Sue brought up the location where they would bury their dead. To tell the truth, it was a topic Drake was rather fed up with.

"I've already consulted with the Federation to get space here. It should have already been allotted. Was there something wrong with it?"

"...You want to bury them here?"

This again? Drake thought as he nodded. "That's right."

"If it was temporary...I would understand. But Colonel Drake, to bury our dead in a foreign country would be—"

"Lieutenant, I don't really want to say this, but it's regulation. As a rule, we bury our war dead in the land where they died. You should know that's standard practice for the Commonwealth, right? We can't be causing trouble for other countries during a war."

She had noticed the difference in values a long time ago.

Commonwealth soldiers were buried where they so bravely fell. And the official regulation stipulated that if possible, a memorial should be built on the land where they died.

Nothing more than that was permitted.

"If necessary, we can send personal articles to the rear. But generally speaking, our heroes sleep in the land where they fall."

"With all due respect, what about their fatherland? What about let-ting them go home to rest?"

In response, it should be said?

Lieutenant Sue was desperate in her persistence on this point. And it was something she had in common with the other former Entente Alliance soldiers: They had a deep-seated desire to be buried in their hometowns.

If that was how they viewed life and death in the Entente Alliance, Drake wanted to respect that as much as possible, but thinking what a headache this was, he had to point out something. "You guys need to remember that you're enlisted in the Commonwealth Army. This isn't the sort of thing I want to say, but…I can't have you forgetting whose forces you belong to."

"But…our eternal resting place has to be our home."

"I get it, but you're being too sentimental."

The Federation was preparing a memorial. And the regulations stipu-lated burial where the soldiers died. If, under those circumstances, they refused the Federation's memorial and said they were taking their dead home, it could spark a political dispute.

Why would the Commonwealth, who usually buried its dead abroad, take their corpses home? Who knew what the international aftermath of such a thing would be?

Considering the delicate nature of the cooperation between the Com-monwealth and the Federation…there was a lot of pressure on Drake, as a commander.

There was no way he could accept her plea.

Every time he received one of these insistent petitions, he could only turn it down.

"But—"

"Sorry, there's nothing I can say."

"…"

Just as an unpleasant silence was about to fall…

"Excuse me, Colonel Drake. May I say something?"

A gentle soprano voice dispelled the awkwardness.

"Sure, Officer Liliya, if you have an opinion, then by all means."

"Isn't it only natural to have feelings about your fatherland, about your hometown?"

Chapter **V**

"Of course."

"Then I should think it's only human to wish for home as your final resting place."

Drake was about to say that she was right, and his eyes widened.

"If you like, I can arrange for a cenotaph as a temporary resting place. And then once the Entente Alliance is freed, they could go home."

"...That would be much appreciated."

If the Federation was offering...

That certainly justified it.

At least, it didn't cross the line set by the home country. *Well, no, Habergram will probably throw a fit.*

But he was already prepared for that, since they failed to protect the RMS *Queen of Anjou*.

Perhaps being the one responsible was a tough gig, but...he had no reason to feel ashamed for humbling himself to benefit his subordinates.

"Okay, is that it? I should probably be going. Officer Liliya, please let me know if my troops give you too much trouble."

As Drake saluted and took his leave, his head was already filling up with procedures and requirements. If temporary interment could be arranged, then all he needed was authorization from home.

I can probably get it through if I push as not Commonwealth military but as a voluntary army from the Unified States. No, I will *get this through.*

Seeing Colonel Drake fairly stomp off like that, I felt like I had made a mistake. I kept bringing up the same thing over and over again.

I nearly gave up when I saw how he was suppressing his irritation at my request.

...I don't think I said anything wrong.

But I do understand that my request made trouble for him.

Then I remembered what happened and hurried to thank the person who threw me a lifeline.

"Um, Officer Liliya?"

"Can I call you Mary?"

"Of course."

She's Colonel Drake's counterpart on the Federation side and a political officer.

"Thanks. Please call me Liliya, too. You don't need to use the title. If possible, I'd like us to be friends." Then she added, "Oh, and I've heard about you—about the people resisting even though the Entente Alliance was occupied by the Empire. It's an honor to meet you."

She seemed so kind, I had to go and ask, "You don't have a grudge against us?"

"A grudge...? Why would I?"

Liliya looked perplexed. Really, I shouldn't have asked. But my mouth did it all on its own. "We're the ones who started the whole war. The ones who caused the problem. Or—oh yeah—I heard people call our fatherland 'the bankrupt relative.'"

I borderline self-deprecatingly murmured the truth.

Everyone fighting the Empire whispered it. *We could have avoided this meaningless war if only the Entente Alliance hadn't been so careless.*

Sadly—I sighed a little in my head—*I'm already used to being talked about behind my back.*

"...Well, I can't deny that it was the Entente Alliance's cross-border operation that set things in motion. History will probably speak of it as the event that triggered this huge war."

Which was why when Liliya nodded her understanding, I braced myself like usual. I was sure she'd criticize us, reproach us, say it was our fault.

"You gave them an excuse, there's no doubt about that. But that's all."

"...That's all?"

I didn't understand, because I couldn't believe that was true. But when she smiled and said yes, I was so in awe, I couldn't even look straight at her.

"Enemies approaching the border get driven back. So, well...when it comes to your Entente Alliance Army..."

"Yes, I know. We crossed the border, so it was our fault. It's okay."

Liliya nodded slightly and replied, "But what the Empire did after that went beyond merely protecting its border. It should have been a small border conflict, but the Empire began a major mobilization. Don't you find that strange?"

"Wait, but from the military's perspective, isn't mobilization a natural response? I mean, look at the scale of this war. I can understand why they would call for a general mobilization."

"Yes, perhaps it was—if the Empire was envisioning a war on this scale from the very beginning."

"...?"

I didn't even have time to ask what she meant before she gave me an explanation.

"Don't take this the wrong way, but if the Empire just wanted to deal a blow to the Entente Alliance—this might sound strange, but...there was no reason to mobilize their entire army."

When I gasped, Liliya gave me a little nod. What she said next completely shocked me.

"And on top of that, they carried out this large-scale mobilization and advanced north. But then what happened when the Republic hit the western industrial district on the Empire's flank? As the whole world knows, the Empire reacted with surprising flexibility to stop them—despite the fact that the main imperial forces were all deployed up north."

"That's..."

"An army can't free itself from its initial plan."

She made the statement quietly but with so much conviction. It was something that every soldier knew.

You couldn't move an army on a whim. Even with advance prep and careful arrangements, the army was a prisoner of uncertainty.

So then why was the Empire able to hold the western front despite the unforeseen attack?

"If they hadn't been prepared for it, there would have been no way... When I heard this in Moskva, it made sense to me. The Empire was using the Entente Alliance from the start."

I never thought of that. But now that she mentioned it...I was able to accept it as a new viewpoint.

Still, there was something that made me think, *But...* If what Liliya was saying was true... I gulped and asked, hardly thinking, "You mean our government was tricked?"

"I don't know. But from what I heard, there's a possibility that intentional provocation was involved."

"So the Empire made them believe it wouldn't respond to a cross-border operation?"

"It's all just a guess."

Yes, it's all just a guess. At that point, I tried to keep a cool head. There was no way to know what the Entente Alliance government had been thinking at the time.

It was all speculation.

It was just a hypothesis with no proof, mixed with the hope that it was true. But could it be that my father and all my friends had to die for *that*?

"Yeah, you might be right, Liliya. Or you might be wrong. But it's important to look at things from different perspectives."

"Yes, it's good to have lots of points of view."

"Thanks. Regardless of whether I believe it or not...you're the first person who hasn't treated me like a troublemaker."

What was even more important was that...I hadn't been rejected. Of course, everyone welcomed us warmly. But the tone of their comments put us on edge: *Do they think of us as a nuisance?*

It was something I hadn't felt at Grandma's house...this malice.

As the war escalated and the number of casualties increased, I had started to feel it in the Commonwealth.

If I said I didn't expect to sense the same thing in the Federation, I'd be lying.

"You didn't do anything wrong, so if any of my Federation comrades says something... No, if anyone says something, let me know. That's part of what I'm here for."

"Thanks. I think you're the first person I can talk to."

"What? Mary, what about Colonel Drake? He seems like a good guy. I'm sure he would at least listen to you."

"Yes, but...he's a Commonwealth soldier to the core. I mean, he is considerate. But I think he'd be lying if he said that he doesn't think this a mess the Entente Alliance made."

I imagine both of us felt it—that wall between us due to our disparate loyalties.

Colonel Drake was fighting for his fatherland, and I was fighting for mine. When two people are fighting for different fatherlands, there is bound to be some disconnect. It's sad but true.

Chapter V

"…I guess I never did this before."

"Never did what?"

"I don't think I ever talked about this sort of thing to someone from a different country."

Until I met Liliya, I could only share my worries with the other members of the voluntary army… And now, most of my fellow soldiers had fallen.

It's the duty of those who remain to free the fatherland my father and those men and women believed in. But… I wiped away the tears that were about to fall and smiled. "Ah, I guess I'm relieved to find that this kind of conversation isn't impossible."

"I wish you great fortune in life, Mary. There will be hard times, but there will be good things, too. Life is long."

"It's weird, huh? But yeah, I guess that's one way to put it."

"That it is, my friend."

She beamed a rosy smile at me.

It was a wonderful smile.

"Oh, I like that—that phrase."

Her smile was so bright, I could hardly look at her I felt so overwhelmed.

"Then, once again, it was nice to meet you, Mary."

I took the hand she offered.

It was warm and kind.

That's why I could smile, too.

"Yeah, same here. Thanks, Liliya. My friend."

Nice to meet you, my friend.

》》》 OCTOBER 16, UNIFIED YEAR 1926, THE NORTHEASTERN PART OF THE **《《《**
EASTERN FRONT, THE SALAMANDER KAMPFGRUPPE GARRISON

The mood of the commander of the Salamander Kampfgruppe in the east, Lieutenant Colonel Tanya von Degurechaff, is plummeting like the pressure in a hurricane.

Partly because she's still on a research and investigation mission to test Kampfgruppe operations—they've been assigned to a part of the front line far removed from the main fighting area.

While the main forces gather in the southeast and prepare for a major operation, the Salamanders have been told to get some experience surviving the winter in the northeast, which is considerate. You could say that a flank patrol mission that can double as training is a thoughtful arrangement.

But if you can be thoughtful about that, then... The hand she's been dealt has Tanya mournful to the last and at her wit's end.

"...Wars shouldn't be dragged out. We're going to use up all our precious veterans. Do they really think this ragtag crew is going to be able to hold the front?"

The units she's received are even greener than expected.

"The majority are new recruits, not career soldiers. It's too much for the scarce veterans we do have to handle... Agh, what a headache."

Having said that much, she realizes she's talking rather irresponsibly, but she can't lie about how she feels. She really is despairing at the cards in her hand.

Lieutenant Colonel Uger from the Service Corps was telling the truth when he said the core personnel would be veterans. He did indeed get us veterans.

If you have a reliable former classmate from the war college on your side, things get a lot easier.

Still, even Uger is...just a single staff officer. He's not in a position to orchestrate everything. It was good that he secured us some veterans... It's just too bad he couldn't have seen to the quality of the new recruits as well.

Tanya overestimated the amount of training they would have, and she can't regret it enough.

Though they're training in parallel with position prep—mainly the village in which they're garrisoned for winter—it's impossible to expect good results.

They don't just need proper battlefield conduct drilled into them—they don't even have a solid grasp of the most basic education a soldier needs on the front line.

It's like tossing a new sales team member onto the front lines when they don't even know about the company's products yet. Setting aside the fact that you're trying to fill employee openings, it's bound to cause confusion.

Chapter V

Furthermore, the newbies aren't even the only problem. The officers we've been allotted are also far from ideal.

We requisitioned part of a building that must have been a Federation Communist Party facility for HQ. When I had my reliable officers war against the new officers, albeit on a map, the results were dreadful.

No, some of them deserve praise. It's just that there are a lot more inepts.

Even if I evaluated with the most indirect phrasing and was as optimistic and hopeful as I could be, they still aren't skilled enough for me to be able to trust them as officers.

And those are my subordinates.

Sitting with Major Weiss commenting on the newbies' performances in the HQ common room, it ends up about 10 percent praise and 90 percent criticism.

"Captain Ahrens was the best of the lot. As the commander of an armored unit, he knows his stuff. His naïveté when it came to using artillery and mage units is acceptable because it's not his area of expertise."

"Yes, he'll be no problem. I heard it was Colonel von Lergen who got him for us... If only they were all that good."

Luckily, I suppose? Captain Elmer Ahrens, recommended by an acquaintance, is a decent officer. Once he's trained, he'll be plenty good.

But he's the best one.

Having to feel relieved that at least one of them is even usable is a horrifying state of affairs.

"That Captain Rolf Meybert in the artillery should just be shot."

"Colonel..."

"I know; we don't need to go over it again. Still...I can't believe I have an inept worker manning the artillery. Who knows how much ammo he'll use up? This is the east, you know!"

The Imperial Army's artillery doctrine has specialized in and been optimized for trench warfare. Armies always carry their past battles with them. Apparently, in order to optimize for a new battlefield, you have to pay the terrifying lesson fee of experience.

Having your head filled with the assumptions of old battlefields during training with the theorists...might still fly in the west. *But...*

Tanya vents in a thoroughly fed-up voice. "Throw away the experience you got on the Rhine front! The supply lines we're premised on are too different."

"Yes, Colonel... Our supplies are vulnerable, aren't they...?"

"It's worse than that, Major Weiss. I'm sure you're painfully aware, too. I can't have anyone wasting shells. Our supply could be cut off tomorrow for all we know!"

The eastern front's supply runs through the mud. Horses are the primary means of transportation. Trucks can just barely be used to supplement, but the road isn't paved.

The conditions are just too different from the western lines, where we were abundantly supplied with shells via light rail. Supplies are not a given here. To put it in extremes, we can't even trust that the communication lines will stay up.

"Major Weiss, do you remember the nonsense Meybert said the *third* time you severed their supply lines during the map exercise?"

"You mean, 'The ammo stockpile we started with was unrealistically small, which is hampering the artillery's performance'?"

Weiss wrung the words out in disgust. He and Captain Meybert had been repeating the same scenario for educational purposes.

And yet. Tanya spits. "That idiot Meybert just doesn't learn. No, he just says, 'That's weird.' Thanks to which he's going to be a bad influence on the other numbskulls."

"Captain Lienhart Thon and Lieutenant Klaus Tospan will be fine. Those two are infantry, so they can handle any trouble on their own."

Was he trying to distract us? Or trying to find some point in their defense?

Tanya can understand that he's attempting a roundabout topic change. Even so, she's of the opinion that there are some problems to point out. "Thon and Tospan are both blockheads. They think they can handle things, but they're newbies who might as well not even know how to change a diaper."

Weiss, silently wincing, probably doesn't have any response to that. But he is starting to look worried.

Ah, I do somewhat regret that. Tanya realizes then that she was getting too emotional.

"I wanted to ask about the replacement company sent for the aerial mage battalion." Tanya steers the conversation back toward administrative matters and asks Weiss's opinion.

"It's a full twelve mages led by First Lieutenant Theobald Wüstemann, all new."

"That's what I heard. So give me your frank opinion of both the commander and the unit."

"They're on the better side of both ability and quality."

Oh? His remark surprises Tanya. The replacements Weiss received from the home country had been abysmally lacking in mobility skills. "So better than expected? Fill me in."

"Yes, I think Personnel must have been somewhat selective when choosing them for us. They're doing just fine in terms of eagerness and book learning."

Tanya urges him to continue, and he sighs.

"On the other hand, as mages, they have a critical dearth of experience."

"So that's what's wrong with them."

The truth we can only lament...

Regardless of how high quality they are, these newbies haven't been given any time to gain experience. Inevitably, then, they don't have enough.

"Exactly, ma'am. It's not just the commander; all the replacements have this problem... I think we should put them in a company together."

You can't get a unit to cooperate well if the members' levels of training are all over the place. I'll have to be aware of their very different capabilities and try to find an appropriate use for them.

"That's probably all we can do." Tanya sighs her lament. "So the 203rd Aerial Mage Battalion temporarily becomes a battalion plus a reserve company..."

"It's unfortunate, but let's have Lieutenant Grantz put the newbies through the mill as planned."

"Can we make something of them? I get that they lack experience, but the last I saw, it seemed like they couldn't even perform basic maneuvers."

No matter how good a teacher Grantz is...

The experience problem will still require time.

…One day is twenty-four hours.

And for reasons of physical strength as well as other military duties, it's impossible to train for twenty-four hours straight.

The worst part is that these mages we've been allocated might as well have failed the flying course. They wouldn't have made it through the skill-training curriculum Tanya knows. These newbies are so lacking in competence that if this was before the war started, she would have sent them back to redo basic.

Which is why she has to repeat her question.

"Major Weiss, I'm not doubting your opinion. Still, don't you think inferior ability is different from a lack of experience?"

"You make a good point, but this time it's really not an individual-level issue. I checked with Lieutenant Wüstemann, and…if anyone, it's the instructors in rear forcing them through absurdly accelerated training who are at fault. I was surprised. These guys have less than a hundred hours in the air. We're talking two digits."

Tanya nearly yelps a reflexive *What?* Two digits of flying time…?

"You're saying they're so green they haven't even logged a hundred hours yet?"

"According to Lieutenant Wüstemann and the other newbies, if you hit a hundred hours, you're sent straight to the front lines."

"That's an awful excuse, but I understand… We have no choice here. Let's just be grateful we got replacements. I heard that since this huge war broke out, the army has drafted every able-bodied person, but I didn't know we were wasting them with such shabby training."

In a total war, the types of new soldiers a commander will get can be broadly divided into three categories.

The first is simply people who have recently reached conscription age. To make it sound nice, it's a human resource that renews every year. They're a mix of wheat and chaff.

The second is draft-exempt people who volunteer.

Tanya has a hard time understanding this, but some people, despite being exempt from the draft, volunteer for frontline service. By the way, many of these people are essentially the wheat you want. The only catch is that it's hard to get your hands on them.

Chapter V

When committing to a doctrine of total war, the state squeezes out every available iota of its human resources. The majority of those still exempt, then, are a tiny number of experts in science and technology or medicine, and so on. When they volunteer, the research institutes in the rear throw them into the mix without complaint.

Still, I heard that even if some researchers and doctors volunteer for frontline duty, the General Staff rejects their request directly. How I envy them. I genuinely want to trade places with them, but since it's impossible, I'll leave it at that.

So the final group consists of the people who are caught by the expansion of the draft. It must mean that the army needs the people who used to be exempted for age, health, or fitness reasons.

From those three sources come replacement troops who have gone through accelerated training. We have no choice but to be happy if they are eager and intelligent; this is the reality of the Empire's human resources situation.

…Isn't it just horrific?

"Under the circumstances, it's great to have an armored unit in good condition. Luckily, there's nothing wrong with their gear or discipline. The commander, Captain Ahrens, and his troops are a good unit. I can't thank Colonel von Lergen enough for sending them to us."

"That's true, but…" Tanya winces. "Major Weiss, the problem is the infantry and artillery, who make up most of the Kampfgruppe's head count."

"…It's unclear whether they'll hold up in mobile warfare, huh?"

"Given a Kampfgruppe's duties, mobile defense will be hard to avoid. But…" She stands with a sigh and walks over to the window.

Outside, an infantry unit is building a trench.

"Now isn't the time to worry about mobile warfare. Apparently, the commanders have had the latest elastic defense theories beaten into their brains… Those guys at the infantry academy are idiots."

Remembering when she had the two commanders draw up the blueprint, Tanya sighs. They must have learned it at school. They proposed a defensive line plan in keeping with the meticulous defense theory the Empire is so proud of and elastic defense theory.

"Colonel, with all due respect…there's nothing actually wrong with elastic defense theory."

"No, that's true, Major Weiss. As long as you have *the right soldiers, the right gear, and the right supply system*, I can't deny that it's ideal."

Elastic defense is the tactic the Imperial Army devised during its experience in the trenches on the Rhine front. Though you drive the enemy off from the front line, the assumption is that you'll move as well.

In terms of pure logic, it's utterly correct.

For a limited number of soldiers to defend a wide area, moving around is the one option.

After all, if you hole up in one main defensive position, you'll get surrounded. In order to avoid that, you don't make the main defensive position where you engage in defensive combat. Instead, you construct spider holes and simple firing positions up ahead of the lines for warning and keeping enemies at bay. You can repulse them as soon as you discover them.

It's a clear theory, all fine and well.

If it has any issue, though, it's that since you're moving around, there's no way to construct a firm line.

"But it's uncertain whether this Kampfgruppe can even handle mobile warfare! You're telling a regiment-equivalent force of one aerial mage battalion, two infantry battalions, an artillery battalion, and an armored company…to defend an area that would take a division to cover?"

"Maybe they were half-joking?"

"Joking? When Thon and Tospan proposed constructing an advance line, their faces were dead serious."

Just remembering it drains her energy. She even asked them if they intended to take a division and defend the whole area.

But they only stared at her, puzzled.

"They just don't get it."

"They still think elastic defense is the right way to go about things?"

"They must. So we have to go check the line later. Their work might not be up to snuff."

Tanya has judged that their options right now are limited. Frankly, all they can do is convert their village into a stronghold.

She's accepted that they'll probably be surrounded, so they need to tighten defense in every direction.

Thus, being surrounded is now a given. She's not interested in the argument that they shouldn't get surrounded. There must be a limit to how much a small number of troops can cover.

No matter how sharp our watch is, there will have to be a hole somewhere that allows a sneak attack. If we can't accept the version of the future where we suddenly get surrounded, we'll be wiped out in the end.

"You know...even I think the idea of going under siege is ridiculous. It's extremely irritating that we have no other option. But it's because of that that we need to make sure our defenses are constructed securely."

"Yes, Colonel."

"And on that point, I'm concerned that the infantry commanders are being too lax. I would feel better if you would make sure they're doing a proper job, Major Weiss..."

"Understood, Colonel. May I borrow Lieutenant Serebryakov?"

"That's fine. Do a thorough inspection."

"Yes, ma'am."

Tanya bobs her head and says she's counting on him.

"That numbskull Thon still seems to be attached to elastic defense."

"...What can we expect? I can't deny that positional defense is vulnerable to envelopment and artillery barrages. It's probably difficult for Captain Thon to escape the main current of existing ideas."

Weiss's expression is a bit tense. He continues that he feels like he can sympathize in some ways. It's not a bad thing to look for the good points in your troops.

"But," Tanya snaps, "if you like advocating so much, maybe you should change careers and become a lawyer." She continues, "Listen, if we were in a situation where we could use elastic defense, he would be right. The problem is that he doesn't acknowledge that our reality is not the right environment for it. What can we do with subpar artillery and a pile of newbie infantry who can't handle mobile warfare besides positional defense? Ultimately," she adds bitterly, "we need to keep the troops where they can hear their commander's voice."

It's like managing part-timers at a shop.

If we had a shift leader we could trust, things might be different. By giving them some authority and having them use their discretion, the boss's—that is, the commander's—load would be lightened considerably.

But what if a very busy shop is allocated only inexperienced part-timers who can't be trusted to make their own calls? Then, just like a commander leading the charge, the shop owner would have to be at the register all day.

"If he doesn't even understand that much, he's incompetent, and on top of that, he's stubborn! I want to have him shot! It's really too bad that there's no rule allowing us to send inepts to the firing squad."

"Excuse me, may I say something? If you want to make such scathing judgments, maybe you should have tried to become an inspector."

"That's a great idea, Major Weiss. When we retire from active service, let's aim for legal circles together. Although I bet I'll end up meeting you in court."

It's actually not a bad idea. Tanya smiles from the bottom of her heart.

For a retired soldier, that'd be a pretty respectable job. At least, it would be safe and stable.

"Ha-ha-ha, that's terrifying. Well, before you get mad at me, I'd better get moving. I'll arrange the inspection and everything…"

"Good. Make it rigorous."

Weiss salutes and leaves the room, and as she sees him off, Tanya thinks over their situation again with a dissatisfied smile. It would be impossible to say they've been dealt good cards.

But they've already started the game. She's not allowed to quit just because she got a bad hand. She can only try as hard as she can.

So let's think about what's possible with the cards she has.

"Sheesh, this just isn't worth it. Should I apply to the General Staff for overtime pay? Mm, I guess I have to check the rules first to see if that allowance even applies to officers and commanders of combat units."

>>> OCTOBER 19, UNIFIED YEAR 1926, THE NORTHEASTERN PART OF THE <<<
EASTERN FRONT, THE SALAMANDER KAMPFGRUPPE GARRISON

Training, constructing the position, and more training.

What brings color to the Salamander Kampfgruppe's days of being stationed far from the main eastern front, in the northeast, are endless training and exercises. Undertaken with the aim of increasing cohesiveness and making sure everyone acquires basic skills, they ring out in the form of shouted officer and noncom orders.

At least no one participating in the exercises is slacking off. That they're all taking their training very seriously is...a silver lining. But even watching them do that, Tanya is terribly impatient.

The new recruits have plenty of drive but not those all-important skills to match. Not being able to rely on her subordinates for even the most natural things is eating away at her nerves.

The snail-paced improvements are already making Major Weiss and Tanya's plan to have the newbies retrained before winter really sets in seem hopeless.

Late at night in the building requisitioned as Kampfgruppe HQ, Tanya looks over the weather team's data and sighs, desperate for more time.

"...It'll be full-on winter in just a few weeks? All the prep we still need to do is going to severely limit the amount of time and resources we can put into training."

And on top of that, they're short on equipment for exercises. At home, they could have used an exercise range or other facilities. But where they are now is the front line, albeit removed from the main conflict area. It's great for getting the soldiers used to the atmosphere of a battlefield, but in terms of facilities, the disadvantage is inescapable.

Of course, they say one real battle is better than a hundred training sessions, but...I can say this from experience: The amount of blood shed on the battlefield is inversely proportional to the amount of sweat shed in training.

"Educate these guys with no foundation and have them ready for mobile battles by January? I think I could be more optimistic about teaching penguins to form ranks and march."

You can decrease losses even by just making sure the troops know how to dig trenches and use spider holes. It's also important to teach them how to distinguish friend from foe in a melee fight and when not to throw a hand grenade.

Panicked newbies often turn not only themselves but the soldiers next to them into casualties. It might benefit us more to put penguins on the patrol line than recruits who scatter in fear.

"…When I heard some countries give penguins honorary ranks, I thought that was in awfully bad taste, but perhaps it was an abstract protest that penguins or bears would be more useful than panicking rookies."

I had thought they were merely mascots, but it's important to gain a correct understanding of things. *Well, that's a discovery*, thinks Tanya as she drains her hot coffee and slowly stands up.

When she glances at her watch, she sees it's awfully close to the time she had planned. Soon she'll receive Major Weiss's scheduled report from his watch on the patrol line.

If there aren't any issues, I can probably turn in for the night. It might not be a bad idea to get a cup of water to wash my face before I go to bed.

Despite it being the front lines, as long as there are mages around, there is never any shortage of hot water, which I'm grateful for. Obviously, I can't unconditionally soak in a bath all day, but if I want hot water to wipe down with, all I have to do is heat it up with a formula.

"My eyes are so tired. It can't hurt to put a towel over them and rest for a while."

Even in the middle of a trench battle, mages benefit from a little bit of flexibility. Which makes me really feel how inestimably far a civilized lifestyle goes toward maintaining one's humanity.

Regular, civilized habits.

When you're experiencing the irregular series of abnormal phenomena that is war, keeping your own lifestyle disciplined is indispensable for achieving a daily rhythm.

Humanity is a stronghold of the mind secured by the routine of daily life.

"Oops, this is no good. I'm going to be late for Weiss's check-in."

I gotta hurry, she thinks, and just as she's striding toward the door…

There's a sudden knock on it. No, more like some kind of harried pounding.

Ohhh, good-bye.

Good-bye, my tranquil, wholesome, orderly evening.

Hello, shitty irregularity. Tanya braces herself.

"Come in!"

"Excuse me, Colonel. We've received an urgent report!"

It was her adjutant, First Lieutenant Serebryakov, who popped in looking tense. Something awful must have happened, exactly as Tanya had expected.

This is a fine hassle.

I don't know who the hell it is, but they've got an awful lot of nerve if they're disrupting my wholesome, civilized habits. I'm going to reeducate them with the order of justice and civilization.

"It's from Major Weiss on the patrol line."

Tanya urges her to read it, and in response to her glance, Visha nods and continues her report.

"It's the enemy! We've spotted the enemy."

"Where?"

"They appear to be coming from the enemy's sphere of influence. It looks like two brigades of Federation infantry. They're rapidly approaching Forward Patrol Line One."

It makes her want to click her tongue—*Tch.*

She was expecting this sort of attack.

As in, *We can't avoid being outnumbered.*

She knew early on that should the enemy attack, the power disparity between them would grow. Unlike the Imperial Army, which has to spread its forces along the sizable defensive lines, the Federation Army is free to concentrate its forces on a single point. It was less of a guess and more like a sure thing.

Still, though, two brigades? If they're coming out for a scuffle, that's practically the definition of *excessive.*

If they had been hanging around during the day, repelling them with an aerial attack would have been possible, but…at night, the accuracy of anti-surface attacks is awful. A melee on the ground, and in the dark at that, pretty much cancels out the aerial mage battalion's strengths.

"These damned Communists. They want to start a fight over this backcountry? They're too strong. Have the forward patrol guards retreat. At this rate, they'll be swallowed up by the wave of enemy infantry."

"Major Weiss has already ordered the retreat on his own discretion."

Great. Tanya nods at Serebryakov's report. Weiss took the risk of making his own call and made the right one.

Later, we may be reprimanded for this decision, but when there's no time to lose, what you need is decisiveness. A subordinate who can resolutely make the appropriate call on their own is invaluable.

"That's good. I approve. Please tell him I said it was a great decision."

"Yes, ma'am. I will."

"While you're at it, make sure we're ready for them to arrive. Let the commanders at every rank know to make sure their recruits don't accidentally shoot the patrol units."

"Understood. I'll do that right away."

"Oh, and Lieutenant Serebryakov, call all the officers. I intend to keep it short, but I want to drum our situation into their heads."

"Understood. I'll begin preparing for the arrival of the patrol units immediately. Orders will be given to prevent accidental friendly fire. At the same time, I'll summon the commanding officers from each branch of the Kampfgruppe." Lieutenant Serebryakov repeats back the orders with aligned heels and a salute. The moment Tanya nods that there are no misunderstandings, she dashes off.

Because she understands her job very well, Lieutenant Serebryakov is a trustworthy adjutant when it comes to her communication duties, too.

She'll be sure to take care of things.

"Well, I guess we're going to be busy. These guests have no manners. We've got to beat proper visit-paying procedure into them."

I've got to pay them back for obstructing my sound sleep.

And so Tanya rushes to Kampfgruppe HQ, ready to fight.

While she was gone, the work to update enemy movements on the map had continued without a hitch. Tanya smiles upon seeing that the data from Major Weiss and the others out on recon is properly reflected.

Though it's nighttime, Major Weiss, who even has experience with reconnaissance on the Rhine front's no-man's-land, makes reasonable decisions on the whole.

Even if tonight's duty officer is the relatively inexperienced First Lieutenant Wüstemann, we're still lucky it's not First Lieutenant Grantz—I still have some concerns about him. This is really a silver-lining situation.

That said, Grantz is trustworthy if you give him clear instructions.

And he did educate the newbies up to the bare standards an officer should meet. Even the least experienced officers are first lieutenants. We should be able to expect more from them than second lieutenants fresh out of the academy.

So, having summoned the officers, Tanya is sure that things are going smoothly. Frankly, she doesn't think there is any reason something would go wrong.

Which is why when all the officers are woken up for the emergency summons and gathered, Tanya finds it strange to notice a familiar face is missing. It's only natural that Weiss isn't there, since he's out engaged in a reconnaissance mission.

The one glued to the enemy army sending them info about their movements doesn't need to be at the briefing.

But Tanya furrows her brow and asks Captain Thon's subordinate, "Lieutenant Tospan, where's Captain Thon?"

"He's working at infantry command. He said it's something necessary for keeping the units in line."

Certainly, since he's the commander of a mostly newbie-filled infantry, I can understand why Captain Thon might not be able to come.

But really, if someone was going to be left behind, it should have been Tospan.

It makes sense to be anxious about all the new recruits. But if he's underestimating the risk of all the commanders not being on the same page, he's not qualified to be a line commander.

"I'm pretty sure I told him to come immediately. Tell him to get over here as soon as he's done."

"Understood."

What a total headache, Tanya laments, but she realizes she can't really blame Tospan for it and switches gears. "All right, Lieutenant Serebryakov, you can begin the briefing."

"Yes, ma'am! Then I'll go ahead and explain our situation."

She's good at explaining things efficiently.

In this, my adjutant, Serebryakov, has a great understanding of my intentions. She gives such a capable explanation with the map—including how much power we can expect from the enemy, the route they are advancing along, and everything else we know about them so far—that I could even see recommending her for the staff officer track.

Sadly, she hasn't graduated the regular course at the academy.

I feel like they should lower the hurdle so graduating from the academy isn't a prerequisite. When I get a chance, I should talk to General von Zettour about it.

That said, although it's a contradiction, I would also feel like a fool for letting such a talented adjutant go.

Ah yes, a manager encounters this fundamental conflict of interest when trying to both look at the big picture of human capital optimization from above and be considerate with human resources on the ground.

It's nice to have excellent personnel on the track that will allow them to become even more excellent. But it's tricky, since they can't build up the requisite experience when they're taken out to study.

Oh, Tanya realizes. *I also have to consider whether the Imperial Army can afford to be leisurely training up frontline officers at the war college.*

"The enemies we're seeing don't appear to be the same Federation Army that we're fighting on the main lines. They're probably someone new. The ciphers we've intercepted aren't the same code we usually see, either."

"I have a question. Does that mean we could end up clashing with units from the existing enemy plus these new forces?"

"Yes, Captain Meybert. You are correct."

"…Will we have enough shells?"

Weiss and I have been pointing this out to Captain Meybert forever, and here he is bringing it up as if he just remembered it.

Even this guy tends to be viewed as a veteran compared to the other officers we've received. In other words, the front lines really can't let go of officers who would make good staff officers.

It's a never-ending dilemma.

We're desperate for outstanding high-level staffers, but we need the lower-level officers—that is, the source to be cultivated into such positions—on the front lines with top priority. Which side to put weight on is an unsolvable conundrum.

That said. Tanya switches gears.

"That is all. The enemy vanguard will arrive in about two hours. Let's get moving."

The moment my adjutant finishes the explanation, all the officers heave a huge sigh. They'd been dragged out of their sleep rotation and the first thing their groggy eyes see is the news that two brigades are headed their way to attack.

That's one way to wake up.

And while Tanya's still watching, they begin to say whatever is on their minds.

"This makes me really glad we built that patrol line. But wow, two brigades?"

"Right. That's overwhelming compared to what we've got, Lieutenant Tospan."

They all grumble about how the coffee their orderlies brought them tastes like mud.

Tanya nods at Tospan's comments but pushes her lips out in amusement when he mentions the power gap. She's beginning to accept that they will always be overwhelmed by the matériel power of the Federation Army.

No, she just knows that she has to accept it.

"Shit, again?"

"It's the same as always with these Federation guys, but they send such a huge number of troops to such a small fight! Is the rumor that their soldiers grow on trees true?!"

Lieutenant Grantz and Captain Ahrens, who have experience with the eastern front, should both be all right. They may be griping, but bold smiles are on their faces.

It's hard to use aerial attacks in a night skirmish…but we have a fair amount of people who have fought at night before. The fact that there are experienced officers in both the mages and armored units with experience puts Tanya slightly more at ease.

"But these guys aren't impossible. We should be happy we don't have to get into a *fistfight* with two brigades!"

"You said it, Captain Ahrens. Well, they may not be sitting ducks, but if we haven't confirmed any enemy aerial mages, we'll take them out one way or another!"

"Whoa, there, Lieutenant Grantz. Let's see what the brave armored unit can do. An armored unit conducting a large-scale counterattack—a massacre—is a sight to behold. We'll perform defensive support and then nail the counterattack."

Tanya is relieved to see that Captain Ahrens seems to understand his job very well. Fortunately, the leader of the armored unit knows what his mission is; she would expect nothing less from someone with experience in the east.

Armored unit commanders frequently hate defense support because it invites attrition. It's practically their instinct. They're always hoping to concentrate and wait as reserves until the decisive point of the counterattack.

But Ahrens doesn't seem to actively despise defense support. *Well, I appreciate the offer*, thinks Tanya.

At this point, it seems like there are only infantry approaching their lines.

"Message from Major Weiss. He'd like to take a battalion and conduct a delaying attack on the enemy infantry."

"…I'll allow it. Tell him to slow them down and thin them out. But also that limiting our losses is top priority. Make sure to tell him I can't have him running the mage battalion into the ground for no reason."

"I'll be sure to tell him, ma'am."

And her vice commander Weiss is another soldier who knows how to bully the enemy. In war, you've got to hit your enemy in their weak points first.

Anti-surface attacks by mage units are usually markedly less effective at night, but…veterans know what they're doing. The enemy infantry may not have many weak points, but Weiss will be able to hit them from the sky. His skills and achievements are worth believing in.

I don't think foot soldiers under attack by this dead-serious soldier will be able to break through our position's perimeter.

As long as our infantry holds out, I'm convinced we won't need the armored unit. It's important to save the shells for the moment we really need them.

Just as she is about to settle on her proposal, planning to get it through Meybert's head that they need to save shells, Tanya realizes something.

"By the way, Lieutenant Tospan, what is Captain Thon doing?"

It's been a long time since the meeting started. Even an idiot would know that he should have shown up by now.

"Ma'am, he's, uh…advising the troops."

That's what he said last time.

But… Tanya points out the window at the muddle of foot soldiers and says, "And yet they're still so sluggish. What is that? They look lost, like they don't even know what they're supposed to be doing."

They aren't moving like infantry who need to get to their positions and prepare for an enemy attack.

Perhaps they haven't been given proper directions? As far as she can tell from the window, some have been assembled and are just standing there holding their gear.

The sight must have been a shock even for Lieutenant Serebryakov and the others who walk over to the window with flashlights.

The partially built defensive lines, the limited manpower. And the newbies with hopelessly little experience.

If this is the state they're in, I can understand why infantry commander Captain Thon didn't show up at the commander's meeting, but…something is weird.

There should have at least been some word. And even before that… Tanya can't hide her irritation and turns a sharp glare on Tospan.

If this is how they turn out when Thon is in command, he should be discharged.

"You laid the phone lines, right, Lieutenant Tospan? Call up Captain Thon's command. I want a report on their status."

"About that…"

"Lieutenant Tospan, that wasn't a request. It was an order. Call up Captain Thon's command. I'm pretty sure I had you set up the phone lines, yes?"

"A-actually, Colonel…"

"What is it? I'm running out of patience!" Tanya urges him with her eyes to continue—and then doubts her ears when she hears what he has to say.

"…Captain Thon is out scouting."

"Huh?" The question is out of her mouth before she realizes; the news is so unexpected. *The infantry commander is out—during an enemy attack, of all times—scouting?*

Away from his unit?!

"Now?! Why did he leave his post?!"

"It was an independent decision. He said officers should be up on the front lines patrolling like Major Weiss…"

If we were going to do elastic defense, sure, that's another measure we could take. Getting a handle on the enemy's situation and then driving them back with mobile warfare would be one option.

"But," Tanya must add, "with their force so much larger than ours, we can't be entertaining plans like that. Does he not realize that?!"

"H-he went on officer reconnaissance to confirm how much larger! There's nothing wrong with corroborating Major Weiss's report with observations from different sources! Won't acquiring relevant intel allow us to deal with them more effectively?"

"That's enough—shut up!" Tanya spits, at the mercy of her seething emotions. "Tospan, you numbskull, do you really believe what Captain Thon said was the best course of action? It's incredibly inept!" This nonsense is more than enough to warrant her rage.

If she can't send a few bullets into whatever numbskull passed this guy in the officer aptitude eval, she won't be able to stand it.

No, acknowledging his command authority was a mistake. I should have attached a blocking unit so any inept workers could have been executed immediately. But it's too late for regrets now.

In that case… Tanya makes up her mind. Now is the time to pour all her energy into damage control.

"Lieutenant Grantz!"

"Yes, ma'am!"

Luckily, Grantz, who has relatively extensive defensive line experience, happens to be free.

It's not as if she envisioned this day would come, but she drummed him full of trench-war and defensive-combat experience on the Rhine front.

He won't crack from a few shells and an infantry attack by night.

"I'm lending you Wüstemann's company. Take Lieutenant Tospan with you. Then take over that bottomless idiot Thon's command! You can do the infantry fight like we did on the Rhine! Defend, don't fall back, repel them!"

"Yes, ma'am!"

Grantz, who responds with a prompt salute, has the minimum

knowledge a soldier needs. Orders, acknowledgment, and resolute action with no complaints.

Meanwhile... Tanya turns back to Lieutenant Tospan with a warped expression.

"...Is Captain Thon going to be suspended?!"

"Of course he is!"

"Please wait! Captain Thon is a good commander! Even if you're a lieutenant colonel, do you have the right to do that...?"

This numbskull is spouting nonsense during the precious and very busy time we're prepping for combat. How come he doesn't understand the glaring fact that this benefits the enemy?

"Lieutenant Tospan! I did not give Captain Thon permission to leave his post! Why is an officer leaving his post before construction on the perimeter is even finished?! That one huge problem itself warrants him being stripped of his command!"

"He was only acting on his own discretion! Captain Thon has that authority!"

This idiot.

"I ordered him to defend this position! Actions that don't align with the intention of the one giving the orders don't count as acting on your discretion! That's just defying orders! And I'm here at the same position as him in the first place!"

"Don't you think he must have judged that there wasn't a moment to spare to ask you? It's essentially the same thing as when Major Weiss had the forward patrol line retreat."

"Lieutenant Tospan, are you serious?!"

"If I wasn't, I wouldn't say this sort of thing to you, Colonel!"

This bastard.

"You're telling me to treat withdrawing the forward patrol line as the enemy approaches like nonchalantly strolling away from your position?! You expect those situations to stress me out equally?! If you can convince a court-martial of that, then let's hear you try!"

"Wha—? Now you're just being unreasonable!"

I've about had it with this piece of shit. As Tanya's hand reaches unconsciously for her pistol, she threatens him, unable to suppress the murderous intent in her voice. "I don't want any more crap from you while you're commanding in combat. I don't have time for this. If you insist on continuing..."

She didn't even have to say, *You had better prepare yourself for what comes next.*

Tospan turns white as a sheet, and there's even fear in his eyes as he looks at her. Well, the moment the numbskull goes silent, she announces it as a done deal. "Consider Captain Thon missing in action! We can't acknowledge the command of an officer who is MIA! When he gets back, tell him to present himself at the Kampfgruppe command!"

Who's going to go there while we're in combat? Even if he does, I won't let him bother us until the fight is over. I'll just say I was busy and had technical difficulties.

On top of that, Tanya realizes she needs to explain and give them the full rundown.

Setting aside Captain Ahrens, it seems like a good idea to not give the rest of the newbies any excuses.

"It seems like there are still some dummies out there who don't get it. I guess I have no choice but to explain."

"Huh?"

"Officers, here's what's going on. Listen, it's a simple matter. We're going to be surrounded, but the enemy is only capable of surrounding us by spreading themselves very thin."

The advantage of a defensive perimeter is that it doesn't have to stand up to all the enemy forces head-on. And the most wonderful part about it is that officers and noncommissioned officers can keep tabs on their subordinates in close coordination.

When keeping newbies disciplined, it's important to have the person leading them right nearby. And during a night battle, that importance jumps.

I can't imagine the Federation Army is much more blessed on this point than the Imperial Army. Ultimately, it's only two brigades of infantry. If it's a night attack with no artillery or aerial support, we can take care of it.

She declares it out of not arrogance or exaggeration but experience on the Rhine.

"So the enemy's first attack can't last very long. We'll watch for them to start running out of breath and then send in the armored unit."

Chapter **V**

We may be treating the symptoms, but our plan is perfect.

It's the standard method of defense that has been established in the east. If you hole up at one point, you can only defend that point, but if you can't build a series of defense lines, all you can do is protect yourself.

"We'll break down their attack by launching into the holes where they can't take much more. It's simple. The important thing with these defensive lines is for us to not crumble first. Keep a tight hold on the reins so the newbies defend their positions."

We have to accept that we're being surrounded.

Then all we have to do to complete our positional defense is make it through the enemy's first attack and succeed in countering.

"Therefore, Captain Ahrens, your unit is the only one that is all reserves. We don't even need defense support. Until further orders, stay inside the line and save your punch for later."

Stop them, hold out, drive them back.

We're merely repeating the classic siege battle pattern used across all places and time periods. Tactics are regressing to an awfully primitive level in the east.

It's a terrible shame to Tanya that they can't put the creativity of civilization and intelligence on display. But she doesn't have leeway to be picky on this muddy battlefield. There's no need to fight with stones like in World War IV. We should be happy we get to do battle with firearms.

"Any questions?"

"Excuse me, Colonel. For the counterattack, wouldn't Major Weiss's 203rd Aerial Mage Battalion have more impact?"

"And by that you mean?"

Lieutenant Tospan follows his disgrace with a suggestion. He must be awfully sure about it. Captain Ahrens confidently gives his own opinion without hesitating.

"Please give the armored unit defense support orders as well. Our unit is here to work with the infantry. Please let us help defend."

"No. The armored unit is best saved for a decisive juncture."

Tanya's logic for flatly refusing is the idea of concentrated armored forces.

Essentially, it won't do to split up their impact. The classic theory for employing armored forces is that they should be saved for a single decisive strike.

"Hold on. The theory of concentrated armored forces assumes that the defensive lines are in good condition. Without the armored unit, won't the lines suffer too many casualties?"

That's certainly an ironic twist.

I'm using the logic that the commander of an armored unit would use, and Captain Ahrens uses the kind of logic that someone who is the commander of not-armored forces like Tanya would use...

"The lessons we've learned in the east urge us to use armored units as supporting defense. Surely you know that, Colonel."

As Ahrens asserts, in the east, defending lines without armored forces carries too high a price. The lines frequently collapse before the counterattack. That's how fragile lines of infantry are without reinforcement.

"That's a good point, but our circumstances are different this time."

"Circumstances, ma'am?"

"Captain Ahrens, we're a Kampfgruppe. I'd like you to keep that in mind. Listen," Tanya continues. "We have artillery, infantry, and mages building our defensive lines. This is the golden combo that protected our lines on the Rhine."

In some ways, the Salamander Kampfgruppe has advantages over other units. Its mages with experience on the Rhine have been through intense trench defense battles. And they've built a defense perimeter, albeit a simple one, around the village where they're garrisoned.

"So barring something completely unexpected, our lines will not break. We probably don't need to worry." She glances at the subordinates she trained, and they seem to have understood.

It's a bit too slick, but Lieutenant Grantz offers a witty rejoinder. "You can count on us, Colonel. We have the shovels for which we were so famous on the Rhine front. Leave the welcome of our Federation guests up to us. We'll be sure to show them the finest hospitality." He thumps his chest as he proclaims his willingness with a confident expression. Compared to many of the guys here, he's young, but he has more military and combat experience than his age would indicate.

Even Grantz is now a seasoned veteran.

"As you can see, he's a bit of a brownnoser, but even Lieutenant Grantz is an elite soldier who earned the Iron Cross on the Rhine. You can trust him with the lines, Captain Ahrens. Oh," Tanya adds. "I should also point out that the 203rd Aerial Mage Battalion is borderline low on members. Lieutenants Wüstemann and Grantz are supporting the infantry. If I give the rest to Major Weiss, that's only two companies."

"…We're also just an armored company."

"Have you forgotten how numbers work in other branches? A mage company is twelve people. That's twenty-four in total. There's no way that many could hold a forward position for very long."

Even if they can keep dealing damage, an aerial mage battalion has very different qualities from an infantry unit. To reach for something similar, they're probably closer to the air force. Even if fighter planes and attack helicopters can blow away enemy ground forces, they can't take over that location.

That's a job for infantry supported by the armored forces. On battlefields of any time or place, the right number of infantry with armored support are critical for that last task.

"You mean, in order to counterattack, you need enough people to hold the position?"

"That is correct. A mage battalion packs a punch, but armored forces are the appropriate troops to counterattack and fortify our foothold. Luckily, it doesn't seem like the enemy has armored units. So in this positional battle, we'll fight infantry with infantry and mages with artillery. Well…" To put them at ease, she adds, "Of course, if it looks like we're getting overwhelmed, I'll send in the reserves early. But I want to keep the armored company as the ace up our sleeve. Questions?"

"No, Colonel, none. I understand our mission. I'm sorry to have taken up your time."

"It's fine. I always welcome a pertinent question."

On the contrary, I should encourage the officers to ask questions. What's important is having the moderate attitude of an expert. You should always ask if you don't know something.

Of course, that means meeting the minimal requirements to be an expert.

Naturally, Tanya has no intention of valuing inept workers who barely understand the area of their supposed expertise.

Time is finite.

"Any other questions? All right. Very well, gentlemen, time to get to work. All units to your positions on the double. Get going on your defensive battle orders."

Along with Captain Ahrens's fearless salute and Lieutenant Grantz's usual salute, Lieutenants Wüstemann and Tospan rush to salute as well.

And then when Lieutenant Serebryakov gives her textbook-perfect salute as usual, Tanya responds with a salute of her own.

Now then, time for work.

No, this is a culture war to enlighten our uninvited nighttime guests as to what proper manners entail, whether via shells and bullets or bayonets and shovels.

And is that the artillery getting things started?

Tanya, the personification of atheism, is so tempted to believe the truth that artillery is God that it's difficult to deny.

"Colonel, incoming from Major Weiss. He says observed fire should be possible now."

Lieutenant Serebryakov is in touch with Major Weiss via the wireless, and this message is truly good news that should be praised as such.

Wonderful, she nearly murmurs.

Tanya is about to smile in spite of herself when she controls her facial muscles and picks up the direct line to Captain Meybert and asks him pointedly, "…We got a message from Major Weiss that they can spot for the artillery. There's no mistake?"

"No mistake, ma'am. His patrol team took the long-range wireless set and observation instruments with them when they left."

This guy is crazy about his specialty, so he'll be fine.

How wonderful.

No, even better is Major Weiss himself. What a guy.

That was such a smart thing to do. This is what makes old hands like Weiss so dependable in a crisis. *That said…* Tanya doesn't forget to draw the line at hoping for too much and overestimating their ability. Though Weiss and the troops *are* veterans.

"We can't expect the impact observation to be very accurate in the dark!"

Whether anti-surface attacks or observations, the veil of night obstructs your view. The golden duo of artillery and spotters is no exception.

"Please let us do it. These aren't the same conditions, but we were trained for night artillery battles on the Rhine." Captain Meybert is full of confidence.

It's not the sort of claim an officer who talks big out of ignorance would make. At the very least, the unyielding craftsman temperament he has when it comes to his work can be trusted as reliable skill in this case.

So Tanya makes up her mind to let them do it.

"Okay, fire once you get the request from Major Weiss."

The artillery is the true ruler of the battlefield. Or perhaps it's the only god—a real one—you should believe in. *Either way*, Tanya adds another prayer. "But one thing, Captain Meybert: Make sure you stick to your ammunition allotment. Unfortunately, we need to be frugal with our shells."

"So we can't just go all out?"

Even Tanya thinks how great it would be if they could. It felt so invigorating on the Rhine front when the artillery opened up on penetrating infantry units!

If it were possible, I would definitely want to do it. But, exceedingly unfortunate as it is, the Imperial Army's shell situation won't allow it.

A person can't give what they haven't got.

"It's dark. It wouldn't be worth it to go all out."

"So we can't? But we…?" he asks feebly, but the answer doesn't change.

"Sorry, but I want to prioritize the Kampfgruppe's ability to continue fighting. If given the choice between a Kampfgruppe whose artillery can do its job and a Kampfgruppe whose artillery has run out of ammo, I'm compelled to choose the former."

"…Understood."

And Captain Meybert proves through his actions that he's an artilleryman who can do his job with care.

Almost as soon as she hangs up, the first shot is fired for observation.

The report roars in the night.

How pleasant even a single *bang* can be!

The moment the shell hits the ground, Major Weiss and his unit must be sending detailed observation data to the Fire Direction Center.

This is gonna be great, thinks Tanya, and the moment she is waiting for arrives almost immediately.

Readied gun points all roaring at once create the best music for a battlefield. *Ahhh*, she nearly sighs in awe of the splendid thunder!

How reassuring this is.

"...The artillery is doing a good job."

"Captain Meybert is an outstanding soldier."

"Lieutenant Serebryakov, he's just obsessed with his field. If I loosen the reins, he'll fire every last shell. And then he's the type who'll say, *I did a good job, so give me more ammo please* with a straight face."

"Oh, ha-ha-ha-ha."

That said... Tanya does acknowledge that he's doing a good job.

The shots sound at extremely regular intervals. It must be due to a tremendously high level of discipline. No signs of bad maintenance or breakdowns, either.

"...I may have underestimated him. He may be obsessed with his field, but within that field, he knows what he's doing, without a doubt."

In any case... Tanya gives her spirited approval to the artillery's vigorous barrage.

Major Weiss is spotting, and there are no enemy mages in the air to obstruct him. The fact that she doesn't even detect any speaks to the imperial air supremacy.

Of course, the Federation Army has launched this night attack probably because they realize they're at a disadvantage in the sky. Theoretically, it was smart to attack at night when the fighter planes can't do anything.

The only problem is... Tanya grins, laughing at the Federation's mistake.

The 203rd Aerial Mage Battalion is capable of all-weather combat...to a limited extent. Technically, I should add that it's everyone besides First Lieutenant Wüstemann and his company.

The only aerial mage unit capable of long-distance flights at night, my baby the 203rd Aerial Mage Battalion...probably isn't who the Federation side was expecting.

"Sorry to interrupt your fun, Colonel. It seems like the Federation Army's advance unit is approaching. They must have been attracted by the sound of the guns."

Chapter V

"I see, so Lieutenant Grantz and the infantry are engaged with the vanguard?"

Yeah. Tanya goes so far as to extend her empathy to the poor Federation soldiers.

Usually it's extremely difficult to get a handle on the enemy's location during night combat. But we, the Salamander Kampfgruppe, are doing something to expose our position: the artillery fire. The Federation advance unit must be grinning right now, thinking to themselves that we've revealed our main camp's position by firing blind.

But that's a fantasy. It's fleeting, futile, wishful thinking.

Those poor soldiers compelled to jump into our defensive lines, which have long been prepared for the welcome party—I pity them so much I don't quite know what to do.

"Would you like me to confirm?"

"I don't want to bother officers in combat any more than necessary. I'll leave it up to him. I don't think Lieutenant Grantz is such a numbskull that he can't command some defense."

"Understood— Hmm? Colonel, it's Lieutenant Grantz himself on the phone."

Serebryakov holds out the receiver, and Tanya takes it. "What?" She can't believe it, but then her subordinate's voice reaches her ear.

Rather than giving a report of some disaster, he sounds confused. "Colonel von Degurechaff, this is Lieutenant Grantz."

"Is something wrong?"

"It's a bit strange. The enemy infantry's attacks are sporadic. It seems like their aim is to keep us pinned down on this line as a distraction."

"So you're saying two brigades aren't putting much pressure on you?"

The artillery may be doing a good job, but defensive combat is still intense. *Yes.* Tanya's belief on that point is firm.

After all, it's only the defensive position of a single Kampfgruppe. The only way to stop two brigades with a regiment's worth of troops is to make good use of your position and put up an out-and-out resistance. Hence having Grantz and Wüstemann commanding the infantry.

…So if they aren't feeling the pressure?

"To be honest, ma'am, the enemy attacks are too scattered. The infantry attacks hardly seem coordinated at all."

"Thanks for your thoughts. I'll take them into consideration. Report in immediately if anything changes."

"Understood."

After setting down the receiver, Tanya heads for the long-range wireless machine. She calls Weiss, who is currently in flight.

Out of the slight fear for what if, she asks, "...Major Weiss, any more enemies coming?"

"Not that I know of."

"Lieutenant Grantz is reporting that the enemy infantry's attacks are sporadic. If it's a feint, we should see more coming or a mage unit. I just want you to check."

"Right away."

The wireless disconnects with a *bzzt*, and Tanya resumes thinking. It's actually fairly difficult to understand why the attacks would be sporadic.

And because she can't read the enemy's intention, it seems even stranger.

"Sporadic attacks... Could it be search and attack? No, our location should be somewhat clear from the artillery barrage..."

Then what if the enemy advance unit was purely recon-in-force?

"...Are they trying to find a weak unit along the defensive line?"

Hmm, Tanya thinks again. Just like in a trench battle, a reckless charge would result in a marked increase in casualties. Poking the line a bit first to see how it reacts isn't a bad approach if you can allow for a certain amount of tactical losses as necessary costs.

Basically, that would make it an ultimate form of search and attack where they send in a sacrificial unit... Given how rich the Federation is in human resources, it could employ such a method. But I can't be sure.

"Lieutenant Serebryakov, do me a favor and get me some coffee. Brew it a bit strong. I want to clear my head."

"Understood, ma'am. Right away."

With a thank-you, Tanya reabsorbs herself in her thoughts.

The periodic sound of gunfire is proof that the artillerists are following her directions and limiting their use of ammunition. But Tanya suddenly senses something is off.

Even the shots that should be continuing around the edges of the perimeter seem to have grown sparse. Does that mean they've shifted to hand-to-hand combat?

No. Tanya immediately rejects that possibility. Though the enemy charged, there hasn't been any report of the lines being broken. And besides, there aren't any of the shouts you would expect from a close-quarters fight.

"…I guess waiting is hard."

"Ahhh, sorry to keep you waiting, Colonel."

The one who responds to her quiet utterance is Serebryakov, who has returned.

I didn't mean to imply she was bringing the coffee too slowly…

A wonderfully fragrant cup of coffee is handed to her with a smile.

Though the aroma is somewhat weaker than it was in the beginning, the coffee—again from Lieutenant Colonel Uger—is not half-bad.

After all, it's proper coffee. She gets to drink proper coffee on the front lines. She can't thank him enough, to the point where she finds herself thinking, *I should probably send something sweet to the rear again…*

"Oh, good coffee requires a bit of a wait. Thanks."

"You're welcome. Please enjoy."

"Sheesh, this must be proof that the fight is going in our favor. I mean, the commander and her adjutant are chatting over coffee."

She ventures to speak in a relaxed tone, bursting with confidence and loud enough for the others to hear. It's important for the commander to appear composed in a crisis.

Of course, the fact that she would also like to be allowed to enjoy her coffee is another big part of it. She brings the little cup to her mouth and then gives a small nod, *Yes.*

As requested, it's black as the devil, hot as hell, and pure as an angel. No, I don't know whether angels are pure or not, and seeing as Being X exists, maybe they're extinct.

Regardless, as the image would imply, this coffee is remarkably free of impurities. To rid your thoughts of noise, you have to have this clear a sense of your work.

Now then, I need to consider the different pieces of this situation.

First, the information from Grantz's report.

They aren't feeling much pressure from the enemy?

The possibility that Grantz is a numbskull and misunderstanding something, while slight, does exist. But he *is* a veteran. He's a mage who's been through plenty of nasty fights and survived. I don't think he would get confused about the force of the enemy. Then the other possibility is that he's become numb to fear and simply can't sense the pressure?

"No, he's not so valiant as that."

I wouldn't go so far as to call him sensitive, but Grantz, like Tanya, is essentially a good person who doesn't approve of war. He's the sort of guy who I'd be able to work well with as government officials or in some other job if the world weren't what it is.

Then I suppose that makes his observation correct?

Which means... Is the enemy attacking with something less than two brigades? But the one out observing who made that report is Weiss. Would he miscount the number of enemies?

No, that definitely can't be it.

"Nnngh. This really is weird. I can only imagine our premise is wrong."

One of these pieces must be off.

Tanya suppresses her agony so her subordinates don't notice.

Maybe the enemy is gathering to take advantage of a weak point in our defensive line? Or are they going to tweak and launch an all-out attack once they get an idea of what our lines are like?

Just as she's about to groan, *I don't know...*

The infantry phone rings.

At this point, Tanya braces herself for the worst possible news. Feigning nonchalance, she picks up with a hand that is nearly trembling and hears...

"This is Lieutenant Grantz. The enemy attack is petering out."

What an unexpectedly calm voice.

"The sparseness of the shots isn't because you're in hand-to-hand combat?"

"No, as of right now, we haven't allowed them to storm us."

"You're sure?"

It's such good news, it's a bit hard to believe.

"I'm in contact with all the defense points. None of them has been penetrated."

"There's no damage to the phone lines?"

"No, they're fine, too. All the cables are currently functioning normally. I'm in contact with every post."

Grantz's voice is filled with conviction and confidence. He's not lying or confused.

Tanya leaves him with an "Okay, got it" and puts down the receiver.

I should probably believe my troops' observations.

"I need to get to the bottom of this…"

Then I have no choice but to play my last card.

"Lieutenant Serebryakov!"

"Yes, ma'am. Officer reconnaissance?"

This is the very definition of a *ready reply*.

My adjutant manages to even pick up on my intention—I could give her a bonus.

"You're not like that numbskull Captain Thon, right? I'm counting on you."

"Yes, ma'am. I'll get going right away."

She's so dependable. Tanya smiles; the trust she has in her adjutant is genuine.

Which is why while she waits for a follow-up report, she can even let her subordinates see that she's leisurely enjoying the coffee Serebryakov prepared for her before she left.

I want to know. I want to figure out what's going on. She doesn't let them see these urges.

She needs to radiate a commander's calm.

Like she has nothing to worry about.

As a commander who puts her troops at ease, she enjoys her coffee and reacts to the outcome. In other words, once you're the commander of a Kampfgruppe, your job starts to be more like a management position.

Well, once you're a high-ranking officer, you already have more opportunities to stay behind at the combat direction center. Personally, Tanya welcomes that—with open arms.

But she does feel just a tad anxious about not seeing the enemy movements with her own eyes. The benefits to making calls on-site are greater than you might think.

What is going on? she worries. This is such a difficult proposition, but she doesn't have enough time to think.

"Colonel, these aren't brigades. They're the shells of brigades."

"What? It's a night attack by two brigades? What do you mean, shells?"

"I confirmed how they're operating and realized that the Federation soldiers are new recruits as well. So it seems like they're concentrating their forces within reach of the commanders' voices."

"...So they're operating in tight ranks?"

"Yes, Colonel. I think we can suppose that the artillery's observed fire wiped out the main enemy force."

Tanya finds herself cracking up. That's how important and refreshing Serebryakov's report is when she returns from her reconnaissance.

"I see, I see. That's terrific. Thanks, Lieutenant Serebryakov. That's some great news."

"I'm happy to have been the bearer of good news to the colonel I love and respect."

"I haven't gotten news this good since Dacia. Sorry, Lieutenant, but I'd like to have you go straight into an aerial search."

"Yes, ma'am, I'll continue my observation mission!"

"No, that won't be necessary. I'm changing up your mission. Major Weiss and the others I'm going to order to patrol the forward patrol line as they have been, but I want you to take control of the zone."

The moment the words exit her mouth, Tanya realizes she's beginning to shift them into a pursuit battle—putting a controller in the air without worrying about her being shot down.

More than anything, she's sure they're going to trample them.

How wonderful.

"Me, ma'am?"

"At the moment, you're the right person for the job. Controlling a pursuit battle will be good experience."

"Yes, ma'am. I'll do my best."

When the wireless cuts off, Tanya puts down the receiver and calmly accepts her error. "...What a surprise. Captain Meybert accomplished the most? I admit my mistake. I'll have to apologize to him later."

The artillery must have done a perfect job.

Even taking Weiss's spotting into consideration, the artillery is more capable than I thought.

This point is something to reflect on as an area to improve when commanding units outside your field as the leader of a Kampfgruppe. I should probably let the General Staff know. Interesting—it's so difficult to understand the other branches. But I can't deny that I misread Meybert. So I should apologize.

Still…

"It can all be done at the party to celebrate our victory."

So Tanya picks up a receiver she hasn't grabbed even once since the combat began. It's obvious where it leads.

It was the armored forces, no doubt waiting on the edge of their seats— *Now? Now?*

"Captain Ahrens!"

"Yes, ma'am. Is it our turn?"

His question is brimming with ambition. It's undeniable that his attempt to hold back the *Please let us go* on the tip of his tongue is failing. He must really want to fight. In fact, he wants it too badly. And that's what makes him the best one to send crashing into the enemy at this moment.

"Most of the enemies were blown away in Captain Meybert's barrage. The rest are pretty much the dregs still following their original attack orders."

"So you're ordering us to obliterate the rest of them?"

"Exactly. Do your thing."

The armored forces, one part of the elaborate apparatus of violence that is the Imperial Army, must be used at the perfect time.

And the time to truly unleash their driving force is right now.

"Leave it to me."

"Lieutenant Serebryakov is up observing. Let her guide you."

"I appreciate the support! I'll begin the counterattack immediately. We'll take observation support from Lieutenant Serebryakov and commence our armored charge!" Ahrens is so eager he repeats back the orders as if he can't sit still.

"Good," Tanya says, and not a moment later, she replaces the receiver.

Having boarded his tank, Captain Ahrens is no doubt shouting *Panzer vor!* about now.

He's the epitome of restless energy, but…you can also say he's reliable at times like this.

I'm sure the counterattack will succeed.

The Federation Army is already falling apart, so I don't think they'll be able to handle the impact of our tanks. *And when that happens,* she murmurs in her head as she brings her cup of coffee to her lips, *the enemy infantry's will to fight will pop like a balloon and scatter to the four winds.*

If I send in the right amount of infantry just as the sharp thrust of the armored unit pries them open, our victory is a sure thing. And I'm certain Weiss's group out on the patrol line they built will take care of mopping up any remaining enemies.

We already demonstrated this in Dacia and other battles in the east, but showing again how vulnerable ground troops are with no air support by using a one-sided anti-surface attack against them wouldn't be bad.

No, it wouldn't be bad at all, thinks Tanya just as she's tilting her coffee cup, but then she realizes something.

"…Crap. That was stupid," she mutters.

The suggestion that she had failed to take something into account gathers the attention of everyone at HQ.

"Colonel?"

"I should have had Lieutenant Serebryakov make me another cup of coffee before sending her out. As it is, I can't ask for any more until the fight is over." In response to the inquiries from worried faces, Tanya upends her empty mug to express her failure.

"Ha-ha-ha-ha-ha-ha! You're about the only one who has her do odd jobs like that, Colonel!"

The personnel can't hold back their laughter, but Tanya resolutely states her case. "Still, though. We've been together since the Rhine front, and the coffee she makes is the best. It's always better to get someone talented to do the job, right?"

"If you were a stern-faced soldier, that'd be a declaration of love, Colonel!"

"Hmm...I'd be reluctant to marry for coffee. I'd still like to enjoy being a member of the free class of singles."

Tanya currently has no plans to enter into a social contract and abandon her freedom. Besides, having to choose between being mentally homosexual or physically homosexual must be an awfully rare dilemma. This is one of those things it's better not to overthink.

Thus, Tanya adheres to the old saying about passing over things you can't figure out in silence and stops that train of thought.

But apparently, everyone reads her silence and wry smile as composure.

"Brilliant, Colonel. No one is nervous anymore."

"Oh, Lieutenant Grantz, are you free now?"

Grantz has shown up, but thankfully he seems fairly relaxed.

"I'm on my way to get supplies before going out for the pursuit battle. I figured I would pop in here while I was at it and see if you had any instructions."

"Right now, Captain Ahrens's armored unit is counterattacking. Eventually it'll be the infantry's turn. Then again, maybe the artillery will finish things off before you get a chance."

"I doubt the enemy will be foolish enough to bunch up again. But wow, Captain Meybert's barrage was magnificent."

"Lieutenant Serebryakov said the same thing. He really did a fine job this time; I'll have to apologize."

As their conversation proceeds at a steady clip, Tanya raises her estimation of Lieutenant Grantz up a notch. He demonstrated sound ability as an infantry commander today.

Grantz has thorough communication habits and is capable of making timely analyses of a situation. The results of his observations should be deemed admirable. Even a subordinate who was so useless I nearly gave up on him at one point has developed into such a fine soldier. It makes me feel like I must be a pretty talented teacher.

At the same time, on the subject of subordinates she's given up on, Tanya suddenly realizes there haven't been any follow-up reports.

"By the way, I remembered, since we were talking about infantry: Where the hell is Captain Thon? No matter how numbskulled he is, you'd think he'd hear the guns from this big, huge fight."

"It certainly is strange."

"Lieutenant Grantz, do you know something?'

"Huh?"

Grantz looks blankly at her, but Tanya continues questioning him as if to say, *Hey, c'mon now.*

In a sense, who aside from Grantz would know? He was in command of the perimeter.

"I mean, no one saw him?"

"…Now that you mention it, I haven't heard from him. But, Colonel, I haven't heard anything about him, either."

"Check with Lieutenant Tospan. I want to figure out where he went."

"Understood. Shall I put together a search party if necessary?"

For a second, Tanya almost tells him to do just that, but she rethinks it. They're still in combat. Taking even part of her precious fighting force out of the game at a time like this would be as good as marking herself utterly inept.

Dividing one's forces would undoubtedly lead to defeat. They would probably fall into the dark bottom of a ravine like Communists taking their first step toward Communism.

"No need. And I want you here just in case. Prep for the enemy's counter or an attack from another unit they scrape together."

"Yes, ma'am. So I should participate in the counterattack?"

"Yes, that's right. I'm thinking of leaving command up to Lieutenant Tospan and sending you in. For crying out loud, where is Captain Thon off screwing around?"

"I'm curious, too. He seems a bit headstrong, but I don't really think he's the type to abandon his duties."

"We'll probably learn once we've cleaned up the battlefield."

Has he ended up a corpse? Or maybe a prisoner? In the worst-case scenario—if he fled in the face of the enemy—I'll find him and execute him by firing squad.

In any case, I don't need a numbskull like that in my Kampf-gruppe. Lieutenant Tospan is difficult to tolerate, but Captain Thon is impossible.

"…Do you really think that's how it'll turn out?"

"Well, let's quit speculating. Captain Meybert flipped our expectations on their heads, after all."

"Understood. Then I'll be going."

Grantz gives a proper salute before he leaves, but even he used to be a useless youngster. As far as Tanya knows, humans can grow.

The problem is that that growth is only a possibility.

Even Weiss, Tanya remembers, committed the error of evading infantry "anti–air fire" in the war with Dacia.

I can't deny that humans also make mistakes. Even Tanya isn't averse to admitting she's made her share.

Puff up my chest and say all my actions are beyond reproach?

I don't want to be such a fool.

But that's precisely why…

All I can prescribe for dolts who can't admit their mistakes and correct them is a bullet. Allowing dolts like that to remain in an organization will ultimately eat away at it.

"Captain Ahrens's unit has succeeded in breaking through and begun cleanup. He's requesting infantry support."

"Okay, got it."

Meditations and contemplations end here.

I've got no choice.

What a scarce resource, as always: the time for careful thought! A Kampfgruppe commander is forever desperate for it and endlessly lamenting its scarcity.

"The pursuit battle is going smoothly, then? Actually, quicker than we thought?"

She glances at her watch and the map and sees that Ahrens's unit broke through sooner than expected.

She had heard he was good. But his skill in commanding that instrument of violence that is an armored unit despite the darkness reaches truly praiseworthy excellence.

And when she catches herself thinking that he must have led from the head of the formation, she can't hold back her wry smile.

An officer who leads the pack, executing their duties properly…

An officer charging out front isn't always a good officer. But one who knows when they need to be out there and doesn't let that moment slip past…

That officer is worth a fortune.

Which is why, as a higher-ranking officer, Tanya can't lose a diligent lower-ranking officer like Captain Ahrens.

"Send a message for me. *I expect great things out of you, but I want to celebrate the victory together. Whatever you do, don't be unreasonable.* Make sure he gets that."

"Yes, ma'am."

A signaler takes down my message and sends it to Captain Ahrens over the wireless. Ahrens really does show promise. Ordering him to do too much and losing him would be a terrible shame.

It's interesting how in a single battle, the outcome of a person's actions clearly indicates whether they should be killed or survive to be exploited.

"And get the infantry moving on the double. A company with Lieutenant Grantz commanding, and have Lieutenant Wüstemann's mage unit go with them."

"Understood. Right away, ma'am!"

We'll flood the gap the armored unit opened with infantry. Infantry is the branch of the armed forces that is like water. Where there's a hole, it will soak right in.

Thus.

Or perhaps it would be better to say *as a matter of course…*

By the time the sun rises, the Salamander Kampfgruppe stands on the battleground as the victor. As if our reign will last forever.

And on top of that, the fighter planes Fleet Command dispatched to support us have been strafing the ground one after the other, improving the results of the pursuit battle even more. They may be fighting fierce air battles where entire forces are lost over the main lines, but here in the northeast, imperial air superiority is unwavering.

Faced with the imperial fleet and its all-encompassing control of the sky, the Federation is silent. They recognize the hopeless power disparity.

And so, by the time the sun is setting once more, the imperial troops have complete control of the field.

It's a victory.

Though it was a small battle, this regiment overcame two brigades with furious effort.

And who did it? The provisional Salamander Kampfgruppe, which had only just been formed. This proves without a doubt the flexibility of

Kampfgruppe formation and operation for the General Staff, too. Well, they won't not appreciate us, regardless.

In Tanya's mind, *they won't not appreciate us* means their evaluations of us won't decrease and we won't be overworked.

But Tanya is confident that she's a good, sensible person.

She understands very well that taking on such an unusual attitude when you've won is strange. In most cases, victory is socially recognized as a result to be celebrated.

We've repelled a large number of enemies while incurring few casualties.

Tanya is accommodating enough to understand that her troops would want to celebrate.

In one room of the building where the Kampfgruppe HQ is located...

Chairs and tables are arranged in what seems to have been a dining room at some point. Here, Tanya bows her head to the key players of the victory.

"Nice work, troops."

Prefacing with a comment that the offerings are nothing special, she brings out bottles from her personal stash (which every officer should have hidden away somewhere). These are the drinks she's been keeping to thank her men with, and she pours for them herself. Finally, she lifts her coffee cup and makes a toast.

"To our victory!"

""""To victory!"""""

Now, then. Tanya sets about doing what she needs to get done before the officers get drunk. "First, Captain Meybert, I want to express my respect for your work. I misjudged you a bit. I hope you'll accept my apology."

An officer's apology to a subordinate is the moment they reveal that their view was wrong. It's not an easy thing to do. But it's better than being seen as a fool who can't recognize their mistakes.

"No, it's thanks to the proper observation that we got results. We owe much of our success to Major Weiss's skill."

"But the first shot was so close! Your unit does good work, Captain Meybert. You're so skilled I'm not even sure you need spotters."

"What? No, we were only able to perform so well because you were there. You flew at night, and we even asked you to spot for us! Any run-of-the-mill artillery officer would be able to get results with your support. Having eyes in the sky makes all the difference."

Listening to Weiss and Meybert's exchange, it's clear they're both professionals who know their jobs well and respect each other.

Boy. Tanya cracks a smile. *I've got a ways to go.*

For better or worse, she's been judging people with the temperaments of craftsmen by the standards of average folks.

They need to be evaluated on their specialized skills. Obsessed with artillery? No, he's a specialist. This is a man who knows how to use the artillery. He has a thorough knowledge of it. That is Captain Meybert. If that's the case, then it's Tanya the staff officer's job to understand how to best use his skills.

Evaluating officers based on prejudices is a grave error.

From now on, I'll have to get over my anger at people obsessed with their specialties and my past traumas related to them so I can learn to assess these craftsmen in more appropriate ways.

"Very good. Major Weiss, you should sincerely accept Captain Meybert's compliments. You did an excellent job, too. Thank you for patrolling. And…" Tanya turns her praise on the equally talented armor commander. "You too, Captain Ahrens. About that last charge in the counterattack, it was magnificent how you maintained unit discipline despite the fact that the operation took place before daybreak. And that's all I can say."

"Thank you, Colonel. I don't know if it makes me lucky or unlucky, but I seem to have gotten used to the east's famous night raids. It feels like I'm back home, or something like it."

"Me too. Man, I'm not sure how I feel about getting used to having my sleep disrupted, though. I wish they would at least let me sleep at night like the kid I am."

When she mumbles how tired she is and bites back a yawn, her subordinates smile awkwardly. Well, it's no wonder she gets laughed at.

That said, it's a physiological demand. As long as my body wants sleep, there's nothing I can do about it. Even Tanya must throw in the towel. Sleeps affects adults and children differently. My great need for sleep is just another facet of my personal situation.

But before she gives in to her sleepiness, Tanya remembers one more thing she must say. "Now then, I'll be honest. Lieutenant Tospan, I'm disappointed. Regardless of any directions Captain Thon gave you, failing to report actions that go against my orders is a problem."

"...Yes, ma'am."

There are way too many people who misunderstand this, which is frustrating. The only people allowed to take actions not in the manual to cope with situations not in the manual are people who have mastered the manual itself.

If someone who doesn't have a good handle on the basics just does whatever they want, we're only going to have problems.

An officer's permission to act on their own authority is the same. Frankly, it's discretionary power for officers with *intelligence*. It is absolutely not a justification for numbskulls to act like the idiots they are.

"Given your record thus far, I've judged that you don't deserve the word *insubordination* yet. There won't be a next time."

You never know what kind of ways people who don't know the standards will deviate when they tweak the manual, whether it's customer service or following military procedures.

Although Tanya hasn't explicitly explained this to Tospan, she has found one use for this stupid parrot who can only faithfully repeat what Captain Thon said.

First Lieutenant Tospan's only function is to spit back out whatever he's told.

In other words, regardless of what an officer like Tanya orders him, his only function is to stubbornly say whatever his direct superior tells him to... There are ways to use an automaton who doesn't inquire any further than necessary, right?

It's just like shogi pieces. A pawn may not be a critical piece, but it has its uses.

"Lieutenant Tospan only lacks experience. After growing from this battle, I'm sure he'll endeavor to redeem his name in future actions."

"Major Weiss, aren't you going a bit too easy on him? Anyhow, what I said stands. Don't betray my expectations again."

"Yes, ma'am. I'll do what I can."

"Very good. I hope you'll learn well from this."

If Tospan can just learn who his real boss is, that'll be plenty. If he can do that much, I should be able to find a use for him.

The Empire is running out of human resources. We may belong to the General Staff, but that doesn't free us from having to deal with inferior quality resources.

We have to learn how to come to terms with our situation and make what we have work for us.

"Oh, speaking of a lack of experience, Lieutenant Wüstemann. I'm expecting a lot of growth out of you and your mage company. But today I'll be content that you put up a good fight."

In that sense, Wüstemann and the others who were sent to replace the ten we lost are not horrible substitutes.

On the other hand, as a good pacifist, Tanya von Degurechaff is forced to grieve. War wastes so much human capital.

"But seriously, combat where the goal is attrition feels so wasteful. I want to hurry up and get this over with."

The other officers smile and agree with their superior. It's only natural, since war is a risk surely no one welcomes.

For some reason, the world always thinks soldiers are pro-war, but that couldn't be further from the truth.

The fundamental truth is that soldiers detest war. And the officers serving in combat units on the forward-most line wish for peace like the most dedicated of specialists.

And a pacifist as passionate as I am must be a rarity, Tanya thinks as she reflects on herself. I'm opposed to the barbarous concept of war from the bottom of my heart.

I grip this gun and this orb solely due to my contract with the Reich.

"All right, troops, nice work. It may be difficult to relax and celebrate while the tension is still fresh, but...I want to allow each unit their celebratory toast."

From the bottom of my heart, I can pledge my soul and proclaim my wish.

Even in our exceedingly harsh reality, where the god we should pray to is nowhere to be found and an evil called Being X or whatever runs amok...

...It's important to have hopes and dreams.

Chapter V

"Okay, then once again: To victory! And to *the hope that this war ends soon*! Cheers!"

"""Cheers!"""

>>>> OCTOBER 20, UNIFIED YEAR 1926, THE NORTHEASTERN PART OF THE <<<<
EASTERN FRONT, THE SALAMANDER KAMPFGRUPPE GARRISON

It's so simple to say to "make toasts to victory."

*But...*when Tanya's eyes open in the bed in the house where she's rooming, she grins wryly as she gets up.

Minors are prohibited from drinking and smoking. There aren't any exceptions for that, even in the military. About all you can do is suck on some candy.

More importantly, this immature body cannot resist the sleepiness and stay up at night. Of course, this meant that Tanya went to bed at a healthy hour last night as per usual.

But there was another reason she left early. When their superior is hanging around, the troops probably feel like they can't let their hair down. There's no reason to keep up that tense boss-and-subordinate relationship even off duty.

Tanya was considerate enough to allow them to partake in their post-combat drinks in peace. As a result, she has woken up fairly early, but it's a refreshing wakefulness.

That said, everyone else was probably up late drinking. Having slowly slipped out of bed so as not to wake her adjutant and orderly, Tanya reaches for the water jug herself.

No, she half reaches for it.

The moment her hand touches the ceramic...she suddenly notices an unusual chill.

"Hmm?"

Wondering if she has a cold, she puts on her cold-weather high-altitude flying coat, immediately feeling better.

Perhaps the temperature has simply dropped. Even for early morning, this cold is awfully intense. It's cold even for fall. Almost as chilly as when I'm flying.

Am I coming down with something after all?

Should I have the kitchen in HQ prepare me something warm to drink just in case?

With that in mind, Tanya steps outside the house to go see the officers on duty. That's when she realizes.

It's strange. Tanya stops in her tracks, assailed by an intense feeling that something is wrong. Something has changed. Something has appeared that shouldn't be here.

It's…the color.

The color…the color of the world is wrong.

Everything is different from yesterday. With a sigh, she looks up at the sky, which is completely overcast and irritatingly *white*.

White. She freezes in spite of herself at the brutal color.

She recoils, but as her leg tries to take a step back, she forces it to stay still through her willpower. In front of her dance pale, delicate sparkles.

They're fantastically beautiful. Perhaps if things were different, she could have written a poem about them.

But now all they are to her is a mass of fear.

She glares as if she can melt them with the heat of her gaze, but alas, she is forced to realize she cannot win.

Her clenched fist speaks for her.

If she could scream, she would.

She would abandon herself to her emotions and release the *You're kidding me* stuck in her throat.

She's been keeping a close watch on the weather forecasts.

Yes, even though the weather team guaranteed them two more weeks, she's been requesting the meteorologic maps and going over them every day without fail.

But despite that, despite all that, it's snowing?

It's such a splendidly malicious present. It means the magnificent and most dreadful eastern winter is upon us. Everything will be covered in snow, which will turn to slush and eventually transform the terrain into muddy swampland.

It's the worst season. When armies are forced to give up on the whole concept of *movement* and can only writhe in place.

Tanya glares up at the sky and murmurs, "But if the heavens stand in our way, then we'll win against the heavens. We must."

How many more nights will the Imperial Army officers be able to sleep without shivering?

It's easy to deceive herself. *This snow is unseasonably early.*

She can also cling to the fair weather forecast. *Tomorrow it will clear up.*

But it's meaningless.

If she can't accept reality and face the terrible situation, all that road leads to is a dead end. She would scatter her bones on this rotten land after becoming a frozen corpse.

That's an exceedingly unpleasant conclusion.

Anything—anything but that awful fate.

"…I have to survive. I have to survive and go home. I do and my men do, too. I don't have any surplus personnel to hand over to that fucker General Winter or whoever."

So Tanya sets off once more for HQ. She's in such a hurry, she begins to jog and then eventually run. She calls out to the duty officers.

I suppose this is the usual.

"How are we doing on winter prep?!"

When Tanya comes flying through the door, her question is impatient.

"As far as cold-weather gear, we have high-altitude operation uniforms for the mage battalion, but… Colonel, I'm sorry to say that we don't have enough for the entire Kampfgruppe…"

"I…really don't think we have enough gear for the entire Kampf-gruppe."

Despite the party last night, Major Weiss and First Lieutenant Serebryakov, who are on duty, give clear answers.

"Hmph. Lieutenant!"

"Yes, ma'am."

"Question the prisoners. Find someone who worked in acquiring clothing. Preferably someone from near this area. I want to ask them about winter and get their opinion."

"Are you sure?"

It makes sense for Serebryakov to be concerned and ask that question. It's definitely a possibility that such questions could reveal to the prisoners that we're hurrying to prepare for winter.

Chapter V

But Tanya is able to make her declaration with confidence. "It's more important to get through the winter than worry about giving the prisoners information they don't need to know."

The difference between a field army having countermeasures for the cold or not is a fatal one.

"The air fleet owes us a favor. Let's have them deliver some warm clothes to us from home."

"I'll authorize that. Major Weiss, if necessary, use funds from the Kampfgruppe treasury. You can also use General Staff classified funds."

"...Are you sure?"

"Of course." Tanya doubles down. "What do you think those classified funds are for? Should I have used them to buy a ticket to my class reunion?"

"Ha-ha-ha! Like to buy your dress."

"For real. We can have a ball on this pure-white dance floor."

It's as good as if General Winter had invited me to a ball—shells with a chance of plasma splatter as we whirl through the sky above this snow-white field.

How wonderful it would be to scream, *Eat shit!* and leave.

"Excuse the question, Colonel, but do you know how to dance?"

In response to Serebryakov's tangential question, Tanya smiles. "I'm an amateur, and I can't hide it unless I'm dressed up. So I don't mind if I leave the dancing to the people who know what they're doing. But no one knows how, probably," Tanya adds in annoyance.

For better or worse, the Imperial Army is specialized for interior lines strategy with the assumption of national defense.

The winter envisioned by the army mainly deployed around the Empire is not extremely cold, with the exception of Norden.

"Anyhow, wake up the officers. I don't care if they're hung over from their toasts."

"Freezing snow will be just the thing to wake them up from their dreams of victory."

"I think it might be too effective..."

"While you're at it, have the other officers discuss cold-weather countermeasures in their units. Tell them to maintain at least minimum field operation capability."

And so, standing before the gathered officers, Tanya swallows her sighs and broaches the topic with her usual frankness.

"Now then, officers of the 203rd Aerial Mage Battalion. Let's hear your views on winter battles—if you have experience, that is."

"That's a good point... We do have a problem when it comes to winter battles."

Tanya nods at Weiss's remarks. Sadly, there isn't a winter expert among even the seasoned vets present here.

"That's true. Setting aside our old hands, even the ones from the Eastern Army Group have hardly any winter battle experience."

"I beg your pardon, but since the Eastern Army Group had the Federation as a potential enemy for ages, you should have an idea, shouldn't you, Major Weiss?" Apparently, Lieutenant Grantz is a smart-ass.

Well, when you're young and inexperienced, that's how it goes, I suppose. The horrifying thing is that the person saying this is one of the relatively experienced members of our Kampfgruppe.

Tanya and Weiss, who both sigh, must be worried about the same thing. This is the pain of the commander. Or of management jobs, you could say.

"I'm sorry to say, Lieutenant, that the winter I know is the Reich's."

Tanya nods that that's correct.

"In other words, our defense plan mostly involved guarding our borders. It doesn't take real snowfall into consideration. Even if it did, it would have depended on your location."

"Oh, really?"

"Hey, Grantz, how much did you learn about winter camping in the academy?"

Weiss goes back and forth with Grantz to convince him. That said, Tanya smiles wryly. It's no wonder he wouldn't know how much Grantz knew about winter.

The accelerated course had long been the norm at the Imperial Army academy.

If it's not something a soldier is likely to use immediately, the academy leaves off at encouraging self-study. The know-how for winter battles is surely one of the most undervalued subjects. For better or worse, the Empire was focused on protecting its own land... Expeditions were hardly worth the mental space.

"If we hadn't spent a winter in Norden, then we wouldn't have any experience at all."

"Norden?"

Grantz's blank face reminds Tanya—although he has the presence of an old hand, Grantz joined them midway.

He went through the academy after her and must have been on the wartime early graduation schedule.

"Oh, right, you were part of the group that came in on the Rhine. So you didn't see any action in Norden, huh?"

"Nope." Grantz shakes his head. For him, the Rhine was the location of his first training in the field. Though he's flown over the Northern Sea, it's undeniable that his experience is unbalanced.

"Then I guess we should have the people who were in Norden around the start of the war handle the prep work."

"That makes sense. We should leave it to the people with experience."

I guess this is all we can do, thinks Tanya as she decides to leave it up to Weiss. "Major Weiss, sorry, but I want you to get the cold-weather gear even if you have to use up all the confidential funding. I'll give you Lieutenants Grantz and Wüstemann as support."

And she can educate some subordinates at the same time—two birds with one stone.

"Yes, ma'am! I'll try ordering as if they're for the aerial mage units."

"However you prefer. Oh, I want all of you to check if any of your subordinates have experience with winter battles or areas known for their extreme temperatures. If anyone knows some tricks, I want to make use of them. Make sure the other units do the same." Then she adds, "Also, Lieutenant Serebryakov, I ordered you to survey the prisoners...but I'm not sure how well that will go. Their resources and experience are fundamentally different from ours. We'll just have to be creative and do our best with what we can."

"Understood. I'll go get started on the survey right away."

When he glanced outside, it looked like fall.

Though it was late autumn, the scenery was still colorful. Not a bad season for puffing on a cigar and gently exhaling—*poof.*

"...Wish I could take Berun's weather over to the front lines," Zettour murmured unconsciously.

A clear autumn sky.

Alas. He turned his gaze back to inside the room where Operations staff, having gone pale in their faces, were shouting in a panic.

The cause was a single word.

Snow.

Snow was white and merciless.

On that day at the General Staff Office, the officers were so upset with the whiteness of their bread that they dunked it into their coffee.

White plains.

Oh, how fantastic, how lovely! As long as it's not where our army has to be deployed!

Which was why Zettour and his friend beside him were forced to listen to the screams of the mid-career officers.

"Snow?! It's snowing?!"

"Call the weather team!"

Furious, the staffers clutched briefcases; agitated, they shouted out changes to the timetables and marching plans.

The collapse of the weather estimates had a huge impact on the ground forces.

The General Staff had planned for a safety margin and anticipated winter that was earlier than anything they had set in previous years, so having an even more unusually early arrival of winter really pulled the rug out from under them.

"I thought we would have trouble avoiding a winter battle, but... Rudersdorf, we didn't anticipate this, did we?"

"It came out of nowhere."

Rudersdorf—his friend, his accomplice, or simply the man in charge of this room—sounded irritated.

Chapter V

That spoke to the mental state of the Imperial Army General Staff, which was in an uproar like a kicked hornet's nest over the single word *snow*.

"They don't even have the necessary equipment. Can you expedite shipments of winter supplies?"

"We're rushing to make the arrangements. Supplies should begin getting to the frontline troops within the next few days...but only to troops within reach of the rails."

Shoving his cigar into the ashtray, Zettour looked up at the ceiling with a tired face; he knew how important it was to prepare for winter. Which was why he had prepared for the worst and arranged for the manufacture of winter gear. He had the production lines working at full tilt. But he didn't think he would have to deliver the items to the front lines this instant.

At this critical instant...

What they could send to the front were fuel and shells—essentials for the offensive. That and the horses and fodder Zettour and everyone in the Service Corps had arranged in a frenzy of preparation.

The schedule for the domestic railroad network was already timed down to the week, defying their limited transport capabilities in order to just barely serve up enough of everything necessary for a major offensive.

Now that had to be revised to get winter gear to the front lines while also preserving the supply of essential consumables like shells and food?

Frankly, the gravity of the situation was clear as the point officers of the Railroad Department under Zettour in the Service Corps hurled every curse they could think of at the heavens and then clung to the timetable.

But the Railroad Department actually had things relatively easy.

Those in charge of Operations had, up until yesterday, been given "a few weeks," but that time had dropped to zero with no warning.

The Operations officers' debate grew only more hostile.

"The central observatory kept telling us it was going to be a mild autumn..."

"It's not a mistake or a fluke?!"

The reply to that wishful thinking was undeniable proof that reality was always heartless.

"The guys at the observatory have thrown in the towel. We have to just assume the coming of winter is an established fact at this point."

There were grumbles, sighs, and a few moments of silence during which cigarettes were plunged into ashtrays. Everyone was gnashing their teeth in frustration and obvious impatience. A suffocatingly grave stillness filled the room.

"...Shit. We're out of time. Have the troops evacuate."

That one comment caused the room to explode like so much lighter fluid.

"The lines are already under as much strain as they can take due to our offensive! We must reorganize now!"

"Don't be stupid! Are you seriously saying we should pull out?"

"We need to secure depth. We could compromise with a partial offensive and a partial reorganization..."

All those speaking were staff officers, the backbone of the Empire.

These men were military specialists, thoroughly trained with intelligence optimized to carry out their duties. And the Reich's staffers, without a doubt, had no equals. Those men in pursuit of a single clear conclusion were forced to disagree.

Of course, it went without saying that matters of operations and strategy should be debated among people with diverse viewpoints.

"This is no joke! Are you serious? Are you planning on telling the frontline troops to just play in the slush?"

"Then are you saying they should stand by shivering until the snow falls? Why don't you think of how we can best use the short time we have left?!"

And since both the argument to attack and the argument to protect had their theoretical grounds, the debate grew ever more emotional and the tone more distressed.

"Are you saying we should gamble our vulnerable supply lines on something as unreliable as the weather?"

"It's a reasonable calculation!"

"How?!"

The logistics supporting the troops deployed on the vast eastern front were shockingly fragile. It wasn't only the Service Corps who were forced to understand that but everyone in Operations as well, even if they didn't want to.

The sporadic raids on the supply lines...

Chapter V

The attrition of personnel, the burden of transporting shells and other goods—it was like a hemorrhage that wouldn't stop. Expanding the lines any farther would be a serious burden on their already overworked supply network.

That alone could be fatal...so with the added issue of unpredictable weather, the decision to stay put was utterly sound.

"If we act now, we can still advance! If we put an end to this before the transportation conditions worsen, there will be no obstacle to wintering sooner."

But at the same time...*it was still possible to advance if they acted now.*

"Are you saying we should advance?! You're saying to go forward without proper winter gear when we're not even sure we can guarantee supply lines will stay open?! How do you expect our army to survive?!"

"If we don't attack fully here, time won't be on our side! Remember what happened with the Commonwealth and the Unified States! Strike while the iron is hot! What other choice do we have?"

The faction advocating action had a point. Time was not on the side of the Empire, their Reich.

Their national power was dwindling, and their working population was suffering serious losses. The last-ditch measure of having women work in the factories was now normal. There was also a serious commodity shortage. Even with a rationing system in place, the Empire was critically low on resources.

"So your plan is to run the whole army into the ground over this hopeless gamble?! If we don't retreat, our army will disintegrate!"

"We can't pull out now! Do you have any idea how close we are?!"

"If we act now—if we act now, we can advance! How do you know we'll be able to break through the reinforced enemy next year?! We can't miss this chance!"

The nation was weakening, as if it were being slowly tortured. Though the Imperial Army still boasted strength, it was impossible to say the prolonged conflict wasn't taking its toll.

So a few officers had to point out that harsh reality in particular.

"The army is already disintegrating in the east!"

"We run the risk of wearing the troops down completely! Don't underestimate the cost of delaying our move!"

"You're saying to destroy our troops on a suicidal charge because some cowards are prisoners of fear? *That* is out of the question!"

Next to the table where the debate between mainly mid-career officers was heating up, at the desk positioned in the back of the room, the two generals letting their tobacco silently smolder exhaled their smoke along with a sigh.

Even the way they silently stubbed out their cigars resembled each other. Lieutenant General von Zettour and Lieutenant General von Rudersdorf.

But one of them was scoffing, fed up with their subordinates' shameful behavior, while the other was so disinterested he wasn't even listening.

Well, it was the natural outcome. Both generals had braced themselves the moment they heard the word *snow*.

As the deputy chief of the Service Corps, General von Zettour had already given his answer. Thus, urging his subordinates to debate was simply a form of harsh brain training.

The same went for General von Rudersdorf. As the one in charge of Operations, he knew they needed to switch gears to consider realistic measures.

It was because they understood the factor of time that they both gave their conclusions immediately.

Faced with the results of then tossing their conclusions to the mid-ranking officers, knowing it would do no good, Zettour had to admit he regretted it.

"We've got a hundred schools of thought here."

After much debate, their arguments had devolved into mere opinions. And what made his head hurt was that the ones involved didn't even seem to notice.

"When do you suppose they'll realize that even if our answer isn't the right one, it's a waste of time to debate?"

"Hmph, it's because Personnel is always picking these guys who think they are clever enough to be staff officers. We've reached a stalemate. Evacuating the troops is our only choice. Anyone unsure about such a crucial point is a second-rate officer."

"Isn't that just the irritating truth."

Sheesh. This was what it means to want to lament. *They're a select group, and yet the Imperial Army General Staff is full of these guys who think they're so smart. Unbelievable...* Both generals disapproved.

But..., it had to be added.

To be fair, both General von Zettour and General von Rudersdorf were notorious for having the highest minimal expectations in the General Staff.

The two ravens of the Imperial Army boasting the greatest intellects...

Hardly taking any notice of the average staff officers, the two had already comprehended what the arrival of winter meant and begun their grieving.

"Winter came too early. Since we couldn't predict it, we'll have to put up with the accusations of incompetence and cope with the situation."

"Yes," Zettour agreed and then asked about something that worried him. "But after reorganizing the lines, are we going to mount another offensive?"

There was only one problem.

What they needed to discuss now was what to do after winter. On that point, Zettour and Rudersdorf didn't agree completely.

"...What other means does the Empire have? We need a way to end this war. With the front so hotly contested, the chances of settling things via leisurely negotiation are slim."

"If necessary, we could put together a plan to wait it out."

Zettour said that was what total war theory was for. The attritional containment theory he and his division had been proposing assumed that major losses were inevitable but was otherwise quite solid.

A powerful munitions manufacturing network and self-sufficient economic behavior had emerged in the Empire.

So Zettour was sure of it. "We still have the freedom to act. There's no need for us to limit our own choices. We don't have to discard the option of a long war of attrition."

"Logically, that's valid. So I can't deny it, Zettour." There was something sorrowful about General von Rudersdorf's expression as he let his cigar smolder. "I understand, but...," he continued. "I know you do, too. The Empire is just barely keeping itself afloat. And that's only possible because of the discipline of our total war doctrine."

"Allow me to correct your misunderstanding, General von Rudersdorf. There are no obstacles to maintaining the minimum. At least not at present."

"That only holds true for military supplies, right?"

"I can't deny that. We've nearly reached the limit of what we can do to prop up declining food production. We've seen a rapid increase in shell production, but...the poor quality makes me despair." Zettour nodded and acknowledged the truth his counterpart raised.

The main workforce producing the Empire's agricultural yield was missing a huge chunk of its manpower, and the other critical issue was that the army had requisitioned all the horses they normally used for plowing.

It was none other than the Service Corps that had rounded up the horses they were using to transport supplies, so Zettour was painfully aware of the heavy blow they had dealt to domestic agriculture.

To be frank, the effects were worse than he had expected. In a way, it was their own mistake that they were stuck eating turnip after turnip.

"Expecting a long war is different from hoping for a long war. We think we should leverage our strengths to attempt a breakthrough on the operational level."

"And I'm not denying that, Rudersdorf. But you understand, too, don't you? It's too big of a gamble."

"Curse my incompetence. I hate that I have to gamble for the outcome of this major event in the Empire's history," he muttered.

Compared to the usual vigor in his voice, he sounded so weak. *If you were going to give me such a trembling reply, you should have just consulted with me from the start...*

"...Hmm. Well, come and talk to me if need be. But we have to start by preparing for General Winter."

"Agh, that pain-in-the-neck General Winter."

The timing was completely off.

They couldn't hope for an offensive according to the army's plan. So for the time being, the eastern front would enter what could kindly be called a lull. To put it unkindly...they would be giving the Federation time to reorganize. It was immensely frustrating, but there wasn't anything they could do to combat forces of nature.

Not being able to make any predictions about the operation after the winter was exasperating. And on top of that, there was no telling what kind of attrition they would suffer during the winter.

Having to formulate a strategy under such opaque circumstances was…completely unheard of. How could they plan for the future when they didn't even know what they would have on hand?

Still… There General von Zettour revised one of his opinions. *There are infinite variables. But if we can define even one of them, it's not a bad idea to nail it down.*

"At this point, I'm going to get that proposal in front of Supreme High Command no matter what it takes."

He was talking about the "autonomy" plan he had hit upon due to a suggestion from Colonel von Degurechaff.

He'd worked Colonel von Lergen to the point of exhaustion, but after the political maneuvering using Lergen's contacts, combined with accepting the huge risk and fortune involved, he was beginning to see results.

It was tangible—Zettour could sense that there was something to it.

"The autonomy plan? I agree that it seems efficient, but—"

"Climax rhetoric, Rudersdorf! Listen…" He made his point as simply as if he was explaining a universal truth. "Rather than having an enemy country next door, it's better to have a country that is not friendly with our enemy next door."

"That's for sure."

"And a neutral country would be even better."

"Of course. That makes sense."

"In that case," Zettour finishes as if he's proposing an evil scheme, "the best for the Reich would be a friendly country that has interests aligned with ours."

"Are you planning on becoming a midwife or something? That's terribly commendable…" His friend smiled, and Zettour smiled back.

He wasn't looking in a mirror, but he was sure of it…

My— Our faces must look so wicked. That thought suddenly flitted across his mind. *But so what?*

"If necessary, I'm not opposed. I've even prepared a place for the blessed event to occur. I'll probably choose the godparents. Plans for the baptism are already set. Then if the government only recognizes it, our burden should lighten a little."

"You mean the newborn baby will work for our side like a full-grown adult?" Rudersdorf scoffed as if he found the prospect ridiculous, but Zettour handily knocked him down a peg.

"Listen, friend. Even a little girl has been useful in this war. I'm sure infants and toddlers have their uses. *At the very least, they can shield us from bullets.*"

"That's the *worst argument I've ever heard.*"

"Without a doubt. It's absolutely despicable, and I'm aware of that. That being said," Zettour continued, "I'm a fairly evil member of this organization despite my virtuous nature, and as such, I'll carry out my duty as I must. All I'm permitted—no, all we as General Staff officers are permitted is devotion to our duties."

They had pledged their swords to the fatherland, the Reich. On that day, the day they were commissioned, they swore to protect it from anyone who would do the country or the imperial family harm.

So if the fatherland deems it necessary...

Why don't we, as General Staff officers, become as evil as it takes?

General von Zettour had even begun radiating an air of grim determination, so for a moment, he was taken aback by his sworn friend's hearty laughter.

"Ha-ha-ha-ha-ha-ha-ha-ha!"

"Did I say something wrong?"

"No, in theory, you're quite right. But you seem to have one amusing misunderstanding, so I couldn't help myself."

"A misunderstanding?"

"What are our dear General Staff's staff officers famous for?"

The cheery smile on his friend's face was also a dry one. But rarely had he heard something that made so much sense.

"Well, it's definitely not their great personalities."

"Let's be frank. Shouldn't we make ourselves known far and wide as eccentric, formidable, and cunning?"

"Ha-ha-ha-ha-ha! Yes, you're right, of course." *Oh, we're already here?* "Every one of us looks sensible, but we must all be unreasonable. All we have to do is use brute force to do what must be done."

The lid was open from the beginning.

So hell will beget hell by our hands?

Shit.

It's all too easy to accept this future he's painted.

I may not like it as a good individual, but
I promote it as an evil member of an organization.

Lieutenant General Hans von Zettour

The Imperial and Federation Armies were focused on weathering the winter, leaving the front lines relatively quiet; meanwhile, those in the rear had long been plotting with an eye toward what would happen after winter ended.

Unlike the skirmishes on the front lines, these were plots where the boundaries between friend and foe weren't so clear.

But it should probably be said...

Unlike the conventional battles where they suffered crushing defeats at the hands of the Imperial Army, the Communist Party had far more know-how when it came to conspiracies and scheming.

The party executives may have been reluctant, but they still admitted that the Imperial Army was an unsurpassable instrument of violence, precise beyond belief. But at the same time, the party members chuckled to themselves.

The Empire knows how to make a machine for violence. And they know how to use it. Though it was shameful, the party executives had to accept that.

And yet, the party elites could declare with confidence that it was all the Empire could do.

War is only an extension of politics. And on that point, the Communist Party presidium was sure the Empire was making a fatal mistake.

"It's the Imperial Army driving the war. Apparently, the military has begun to dominate politics in the Empire," it was murmured, and how cleverly, at the party meeting. This was the presidium's collective impression. *The military is only a means to political ends.*

Even faced with receding front lines, the party executives were still calm enough to boast. After all, they were sure that the Imperial Army was a bunch of idiots who acted on a purely military perspective.

Chapter **VI**

Military might is but a single factor. Power, control, and government are necessarily a fusion of violence and politics.

"The politicians have fallen silent, and the bourgeoisie have begun fighting the war for their own aims. I see they can build a formidable army, yes. But while they may know how to defeat enemies, they don't seem to know how to make allies."

Why should the Communist Party be afraid of an enemy whose army treats war as an extension of military matters and completely lacks political perspective?

Surely history will bring an inevitable victory to the party and the fatherland, as well as Communism.

That was their rock-solid conviction.

So then…

"To meeting new friends!"

"To the military cooperation of our two glorious nations!"

Candid toasts rang out at the Commonwealth Embassy in Moskva.

Waiters served caviar and vodka, an orchestra invited for the occasion gracefully performed both countries' anthems, and well-dressed visitors talked among themselves in whatever way they preferred. It was an elegant social space, no less luxurious than before the war. The only thing signaling that this wasn't peacetime was the presence of impeccably outfitted honor guards and soldiers proudly sporting their dress uniforms.

But that was appropriate for the nature of the occasion. This was a banquet to celebrate the establishment of their wartime pact to expand cooperation and prohibit any separate peace agreements with the Empire. The diplomats calmly chatted over colorful glasses of deceit and hypocrisy filled with their shared interests.

"…They don't have any allies. Does the Imperial Army mean to fight against the entire world to the last corpse?"

"It's absurd, but I think they're halfway serious. They give plenty of thought to winding up their punches, at least. After that… Well, you know."

The men suppressed their guffaws.

"You're exactly right. They still can't escape the idea that *everything* can be solved through military might."

"Ha-ha-ha. Well, I'm relieved if that's how the Federation sees things, too. Let's hit that powerful Empire with the truth—that they aren't strong enough to take on the whole world."

It was an exchange that blended empty words with each side's requests. But when it came to directness, the Federation was capable of speaking without affectation.

"Yes, let's. And we'd appreciate it ever so much, then, if you would establish a second front. As friends, we need to help each other out," the man added—expressing, albeit as sarcastic inquiry, *Where are your ground forces?* This was the Federation's explicit expression of their wish for the Commonwealth to carry more of the burden.

Yet they wouldn't be able to call themselves diplomats if that little bit of sarcasm made them flinch.

"I'll make sure to tell the key players back in Londinium." Even a child could be sent on an errand. What government funds asked of diplomats involved much more wordplay. "But even at home, we're currently fighting a major air battle. We would love to be able to defend our fatherland and also help out our brothers-in-arms, but there are so many tricky issues involved…" The Commonwealth diplomat who nodded in heartfelt sympathy added dramatically that they were having problems.

"Issues?"

"Yes." He casually showered the Federation diplomat in snark. "We can't neglect air cover for the convoy supporting the Federation, either. Why, just the other day, one of our ships that wasn't safely under our air defense umbrella suffered terrible damages in an attack *at one of your naval bases*. Considering that, things are a bit difficult…"

After implying with that jab that helping out the Federation was causing its own problems, he feigned nonchalance and called to a waiter in a deliberately sunny voice.

We don't have a grudge against you! was what he implied…but he could interact with such ease now precisely because the Federation owed them one.

But the Federation diplomat wasn't a child who would get flustered and run out of words to say. Beneath his smiling mask, he heaved a conspicuous sigh, prepared to retort. "Well, we're holding down the ground lines as the sole representatives of all the allied countries, you know. It's a terrible shame we don't have enough hands."

Chapter VI

"So I guess that goes for both of us. We're in a very similar situation…" But in response to that biting reply, the Commonwealth diplomat gravely nodded. His brief comment took the end of the Federation diplomat's words and transformed their meaning. "Not only did we lure the formidable Imperial Air Fleet to the west and protect our homeland, we're also operating a support convoy for an ally country—fighting deadly battles all the while against patrolling imperial submarines, at that. The burdens on us are just so big, you see…"

"I understand those difficult circumstances, but don't forget that we're taking on the imperial ground forces almost entirely on our own."

"Of course, it's precisely with our ally nation's hard work in mind that we launched the support convoy. We're risking a crisis in homeland air defense in order to have escorts flying along the route! Our soldiers are bending over backward. My heart aches for them, but if it will save our ally…"

"My! I was just thinking the same thing. It must be because we're luring the enemy's main forces away from our ally."

"Ha-ha-ha." They both laughed, inwardly cursing, and shook hands. It was a peaceful, diplomatic exchange.

Though they attempted to conceal it with flowery language, what the men from both countries really felt was this: *Your country should be stepping up to take more of the brunt.*

And their frank assessment of each other was: *We can't trust that these guys mean well.* Yet, they found a common interest in the fight against the Empire.

So as experts in politics and diplomacy, they could be sure that despite the vast differences between the Commonwealth and the Federation and their deep-seated distrust of each other, circumstances could arise that would allow them to cooperate on this one thing, the fight against the Empire. That was how sure they were that the Empire knew nothing about politics.

If a leader who paid even a little attention to the diplomatic and political situation had been at the Empire's helm, it would never have been besieged from all sides like this.

If the Empire had taken advantage of the Commonwealth's and Federation's traditional discord, would the two countries have even managed to create a superficial alliance against a common enemy? Actually, if it hadn't gone ahead with the Northern Expansion Doctrine, the Republic never would have had to enter the fight, and the whole war could have been avoided in the first place.

In other words, the Empire was digging its own grave.

After observing, hypothesizing, and verifying, the party executives, who were specialists in politics and conspiracy, were able to believe it wholeheartedly as a logical conclusion: *The Imperial Army is only capable of comprehending war from a military point of view.*

Of course, victory would be costly.

Still, with General Winter's support, the land of Mother Federation would stop the Empire. Then time would solve things.

Their firm belief was that due to the Empire's mistakes, victory was certain.

Until Loria, head of the Commissariat for Internal Affairs, called an emergency meeting of the presidium, that is.

"Comrade, you said there's an emergency?"

"Yes, Comrade General Secretary. Something has occurred that needs to be handled immediately."

"And that is?"

"…The Imperial Army has…"

It was rare for Loria, and out of character, to trail off. And he had never let his eyes glance around the room like that before.

"The Imperial Army has joined forces." Getting a look that asked, *With?* he hesitantly spoke again. "Yes, with…them."

"Comrade, who did the Imperial Army join forces with?"

A direct question from the General Secretary himself. A query from the very top was enough to make a man tremble, yet an officer of Loria's caliber failed to reply.

That alone was a sign of bad news.

Someone perceptive may have noticed—that the head of the Commissariat for Internal Affairs, Loria, that devil in human's clothing, was terrified.

"They've shown signs of joining forces with the separatists… A provisional government has been established in their occupied territory, and they've begun the process of transitioning to a civilian administration."

He seemed to have braced himself, and the next words came. The moment everyone heard them, they had trouble comprehending what the small man before their eyes was saying.

"Listen, comrades. The Imperial Army is...in the process of forming an alliance with the separatists. Yes, the nationalists and the Empire have joined hands."

His report lacked energy, which was rare for Loria. He didn't even try to hide his despair but relayed the news in a shaking voice.

A curtain of silence had nearly fallen on the room when, finally, a few people's brains belatedly began to understand what the report meant.

The trash calling for separation from the Federation and the invading Imperial Army were both simple obstacles to the party. Luckily, the plan was to have them kill each other.

After all, the violent machine of the Imperial Army, incapable of compromise, and the nationalists who had no intention of bowing to anyone were sure to get along horribly. In fact, Loria and the rest of the Communist Party executives expected it to be excellent PR.

...The Imperial Army as tyrant and the Federation Army as liberator was to be a great attack in the propaganda war.

And they thought it would be perfect precisely because of the people's wavering faith in the party.

They needed to convince the masses they were on the theoretically correct side. The plan was to sell them the dream, but the damn Empire turned out to be surprisingly unsporting.

"We should probably assume that the Imperial Army's—the Empire's—policy has done a one-eighty. I'm repeating myself, but this report is nearly a sure thing. It seems the Imperial Army and the separatists are building very close relations."

But the idea was supposed to be that the more the Imperial Army rampaged on its "war of suppression" or whatever against the partisan activity, the more the separatists would hate the Empire and cling to the Federation.

Instead they were joining forces?

Not even just that but transitioning to civilian rule?

"As head of the Commissariat for Internal Affairs, I must warn you. The Imperial Army is coming to destroy our ethnic policy."

This would overturn their very foundation.

No, worse than that.

Several people stood up, seemingly without thinking. They stared at Loria with eyes wide open, and the moment he nodded at them to say, *It's true*, they all began to shout.

"...They're helping the separatists transition to their own administration?!"

Shocked screams echoed throughout the room.

"Of all the—!"

"It can't be!"

"Are you sure there's no mistake?!"

Though bewildered, the ones who all shouted denials were the veteran party leaders. Even the ones who had fought through the hard times were distraught.

Wow, their exclamations have no individuality and intelligence, thought Loria with a wince. *Do extreme situations somehow limit the verbal abilities of humans?*

On the other hand, he did understand. It was no wonder. With a heavy expression, he turned to the General Secretary and held out the latest report. "Comrade General Secretary, please take a look at this."

The report had several pages. It was so dangerous, it couldn't be copied. The Federation *would be in trouble if it couldn't get the Imperial Army to be cruel invaders*.

No, it wasn't even a hypothetical at this point.

If this was true, then their multiethnic state was being undermined in the present tense.

The only way to maintain support for the Communist Party was to fight tolerance with tolerance.

If they were to be more permissive about nationalism than ever before, that might be one way to encourage resistance against the Empire.

But once the presidium reached that idea in their contemplations, they had to reject it. It would be an utter nightmare.

"The situation is dire."

"So there's no mistake, Comrade Loria?"

"No, Comrade General Secretary. The data in the report has been screened very carefully."

The most that would be allowed in their multiethnic state was affirmative action. Generosity on par with the Empire's, featuring unconditional praise of nationalism, would be tantamount to the destruction of the Federation. Or maybe the party would even collapse and Communism's cause would be undermined.

"…Hmm. Are you sure you can trust the source?"

"It's based on reports from our undercover agent and political officers. We did our best to verify and guarantee its accuracy." *Am I keeping my voice even superficially calm?* It was hard even for Loria. "The data from both sides matched. All the reports strongly suggest that the Empire and the separatists have formed a political alliance." So he stated it firmly. "There is no room for doubt."

All the indications the Commissariat for Internal Affairs was able to acquire pointed to the truth that the two supposedly hostile countries were now beginning to work together.

The shock at that moment was such that even Loria could hardly believe the conclusion. But there were too many signs that this was reality to ignore it. The greatest proof was the emergency rescue request that had come in from a partisan unit like a scream.

They should have been swimming in a sea of the people, but the staggering news was that they were being wiped out.

The results of the follow-up investigation were even more distressing.

The ones on the ground with the mission to wipe out the partisans weren't from the Imperial Army but a peacekeeping unit. And when they looked into it further, it was the local peacekeeping unit with support from the Imperial Army!

At that point, it became apparent that there was an alliance. They had to acknowledge it.

"There is a dramatic change taking place within the Imperial Army."

The pure violence machine had sprouted a bud of political context comprehension. And it was growing at a terrifying rate.

The roots were surely too deep, so it was too late to nip it.

The Empire was learning to see from the viewpoint of politics. The hard-core military state was building on its past experiences. That was more of a threat than if the violence machine had received fifty reinforcement divisions.

Failing to notice early signs of these qualitative changes was a serious mistake. So Loria had to accept the reproachful looks from the now pale-faced participants in the meeting.

"...But the change is too fast. We thought we knew the Imperial Army, but perhaps the extreme circumstances of war have enabled a rapid transformation?"

Riding in his car through the streets of Moskva, Loria thought to himself.

At its root, the crisis before us is the impossibility of our nation's structure to maintain its legitimacy.

No matter how much they went on about the "evil invaders" from the Empire...if the nationalists happily defected to the Imperial Army's side, the Federation would be a laughingstock, howling in vain. He could easily envision the worst-case scenario. A journalist from a third nation would surely be the trigger.

They would figure out of their own accord that the nationalists were siding with the Empire and write an article. Even just denying that one article would require a massive amount of work.

"Most pressingly...*our image abroad is horrible.*"

The gazes directed toward the Communist Federation from the governments on the West Side were terribly cold. Publicly, they proclaimed that they were companions in a joint struggle, but he was sure that inside, they didn't feel even the faintest flicker of friendship.

We joined hands only reluctantly in order to combat our immensely powerful enemy, the Empire.

Even the Communist Party had that one point in common with the West Siders. Suppressing their antipathy, they had pretended to join up with a capitalist nation they didn't trust.

In a nutshell, the two powers were connected only by shared interests. The two sides were shaking hands against a devil they were desperate to ruin.

"They probably hope that we and the Empire will take each other out. If I were in their place, I would happily do the same thing. Shit. I had to put up with those annoying nightmares, and this is what I get?"

Son of a bitch. Loria heard his own voice arguing back in his head.

Facing its powerful neighbor, the Empire, would be a catastrophic crisis for the Federation no matter when it happened.

Comrade General Secretary's decision to start the war as a preventative measure was valid.

But from a national defense perspective, we should have done whatever it took to avoid this nightmare: a confrontation with the Empire, reining in the center of the continent after toppling neighboring countries with its martial power.

"We were prepared to bear the brunt."

The problem is that those multidirectional warmongers really are good at war, if nothing else.

Their army, which should have far outnumbered the Imperial Army, was crushed by the counterattack in the blink of an eye. The more Loria investigated, the more he was forced to realize that these neighbors were too dangerous.

"…And we are left without allies…*for now.*"

In a crisis, you want lots of friends. Unfortunately, in the classroom of international society, the Federation was the poor, lonely child ostracized by the others.

Be that as it may, we can't mistake our situation.

Surely, it wasn't inconceivable to gain friendship if they worked for it. In other words, friendship was attainable. The search for new friends was not a lost cause.

"Let's have the wonderful friend we call public opinion work for us. Isn't democracy simply marvelous?"

Even if he appealed to the emotions of this logical government devoted to raison d'état, all he would get out of it would be lip service.

But… Loria smiled a genuine smile as if he had located his enemy's weakness.

"So far, throwing in idealists seems to be going well… Even if we can't fool the diplomats, we can get the soldiers and the amateurs. It's too great."

There were countless people with bad impressions of the Federation, but surely they would begin to hesitate when they noticed the disparity between that image and the soldiers and party members from the Federation they actually met.

That psychological gap was the key to the Federation's propaganda strategy.

The more intelligent and sincere a person was, the more likely they were to interpret their situation as *I was prejudiced*, without any extra help.

"Yes, employing idealists as political officers is so useful."

Idealists got respect not for their ability but for their personality. Once they gained some experience, they were perfect.

But an idealist made a great story even if all they did was die holding their position. Just showing them carrying out their duty could have an effect.

"The people of the Federation are so inspiring, heroic, and devoted. Let's make idealists into martyrs by the dozen. We'll make them saints of the Communist mythology."

Everyone likes heroes.

Everyone loves honest people.

Everyone respects sincere warriors.

Walking Federation PR machines devoted to their ideals, so noble and good. Lately, there was no end to Loria's love for idealists.

They were the secret weapon that would secure the West Side's wonderful public opinion as a friend for the Federation.

If the Empire is going to team up with Federation separatists, then we'll firmly join hands with the West Side.

"It might be fun to see which friend is stronger. Oh, how interesting."

This was war—a competition for swindlers to see how well they could manipulate people by concealing their dirty intentions with empty fluff.

Let's speak of ideals. We'll praise the public-facing attitudes. And then we'll compete—to see who gains more popular support. Let's have a clash of trivial appearances and facades.

Everyone loves beautiful things. I'll give you illusions if you want them so badly.

I'll hand out dreams.

"Ha-ha-ha, does that make me Daddy-Long-Legs, then?"

Kind, gentle Daddy Loria probably. Quite the buffoon, no?

"Or maybe Santa Claus. Ha-ha-ha, this is delightful. Either one seems fun. I guess I'll be delivering hope, dreams, and beautiful fantasies."

Idealists deliver illusions and mirages.

Since I'm the one managing them, does that make me chief of the post office? No, no, I should be a bit more elaborate and call myself the Santa Claus of Hope.

Chapter VI

Ohhh. There Loria had second thoughts.

"No, attractive men and women are more popular. They would probably be easier to use."

It was clear that to hand out beautiful dreams, it would be best for beloved, beautiful people to drive propaganda.

Considering his own appearance objectively, he reorganized his plan.

I should definitely not be public facing. Loria laughed at himself. He had no intention of getting so foolishly carried away by the urge to be the center of attention that he couldn't make that judgment.

"To think the day would come that my screening process for political commissars would be searching for idealism with an emphasis on looks... Life sure is unpredictable."

That's what makes it interesting, though. Every day is full of new discoveries... Is this what they call rejuvenation?

But he wasn't averse to admitting that not everything about it was good.

He couldn't help but get turned on.

On that point, he found an awful lot to regret about his personal tastes, and it was hard not to get discouraged.

For example, take the communications officer he dispatched to the Commonwealth Army, Liliya Ivanova Tanechka. *What a tragic waste. Ten years earlier, I would have wanted to make her unclouded eyes glaze over, make her breath ragged...*

"Why does everyone have to ripen beyond my tastes...?"

Sadly, by the time he met her, it was too late.

"They say love is once in a lifetime, but I guess you can't take these sayings from the Far East lightly. Each meeting should be dear to your heart."

Loria had also been taught not to cry over spilled milk.

Which was why, with renewed determination, Loria smiled.

"Wait for me, my fairy. I'll catch you; I'm sure of it."

This time, this time I won't let her go. Standing by while this supreme flower wilts would be the greatest folly in all of history—I can't do it.

Beautiful things must be appreciated while they are beautiful.

I have no doubt that that is my most important duty.

When Lieutenant Colonel Tanya von Degurechaff receives the message, she is so impressed she bursts out laughing.

What a splendidly devious move the General Staff has come up with.

Honestly, the approach itself is classic. Even cliché. But it's also rare to have a plan that so precisely grasps the enemy's weakness and takes advantage of one's own strength.

To the Federation, this will surely be a more terrifying attack than a million-bullet volley.

"Gentlemen, a notice from the General Staff. Remember this: Apparently, we're going to liberate the minorities suppressed by the Federation."

In response to her good news, the officers are silent and tense, seemingly confused.

"We're going to *liberate* them?" First Lieutenant Serebryakov sounds as if she can't quite believe it.

"As a means to some end?" First Lieutenant Grantz, for his part, can't seem to hide his skepticism. That's the typical attitude of an experienced soldier toward any public-facing statement that seems impossible to make.

I suppose you could call it being respectful while keeping your distance?

Major Weiss is the only one maintaining a wise silence... The others are nodding in agreement.

Sheesh. Tanya feels compelled to despair.

These guys know combat, but they don't know anything about politics. This is precisely the problem with them.

No matter how much you win, it's meaningless unless you can use that victory politically. That's the absolute truth, but these guys have a tendency to forget it completely.

No—to be fair, the intense combat on the eastern front doesn't give them much time to remember.

That's not uncommon in war, though.

"As Lieutenant Grantz says, perhaps it's a propaganda effort? No one would actually believe it. But they might pretend to."

Chapter **VI**

"That's a very interesting opinion, Captain Ahrens, but what's the basis for it?"

"The people here. I'm sure if we started losing, they would raise the flag of the enemy," the captain spits.

That's probably the general view on the front lines. I have no doubt that anyone who has served in the east would agree right away. Objectively speaking, it's a rule of thumb that is hard to deny.

Everyone is forced to be aware of the reality that many kiss the hand they wish to cut off.

Two different types of nations make the most suitable example.

"You mean how every house has both the Federation and imperial flags?"

"Yes, you know about that, right, Colonel?"

"Taking the side of the victor, even superficially, is simply the wisdom necessary to survive for these people caught in a war. Blaming them is a waste of effort."

I get why Captain Ahrens is angry. But Tanya thinks it's like going about your sales approach in the wrong way.

Like being upset that skis won't sell in the desert.

"Theoretically, the General Staff's proposal makes sense. Eliminating some enemies with words alone can't be a bad deal."

"That's for sure. But getting called a liberator puts me on edge."

"I feel the same way. Sorry, Colonel…"

While some imperial soldiers apparently take the title of liberator seriously at first… It's hard to call someone a friend if you're not sure they'll stay your friend once the rain starts falling.

They've probably seen the imperial flag abandoned in tough times.

Captain Ahrens and Major Weiss, having seen that happen, must realize immediately that they aren't being welcomed as liberators.

"It's not that I don't understand, Major Weiss. But the higher-ups have defined us as liberators. And they have a great idea to go along with it."

"…I hope for once it's actually a good idea."

"Put your mind at ease, Major. I guarantee this one."

You may go in calling yourselves liberators, but unless you can sell that idea to the people, the plan will fall apart sooner or later. But if the higher-ups make practical use of politics, you'll be in a different strategic universe from mere wishful thinking.

We have instructions from Lieutenant General von Zettour. The text from the General Staff proclaiming us liberators has clear meanings between the lines.

You can read it as "divide and conquer." As gears in the machine, we have to get moving.

Thus, Tanya declares in a stern voice, "Setting aside whether you agree with it or not, here's your notice. This applies to officers at every level, no exceptions. From now on, 'accidents' involving civilians in our jurisdiction must be dealt with more properly."

These many citizens simply want to preserve their normal lives. The reason they want to turn on us is…most often misconduct by occupying units. Those horrible mistakes only feed the guerrillas and benefit the enemy.

"Considering there might be some damn numbskulls who don't understand, a test. Major Weiss, you get it, right?"

"Yes, of course! You mean you want us to treat issues the same as we would if we were garrisoned in the home country?"

Well. Tanya smiles. *I don't need to worry about Weiss.*

"What?! It's not orders to cover up carelessness?"

But she got some dramatic reactions from the idiots who apparently still didn't understand… It's so perfectly in line with her expectations that Tanya's concerned.

First Lieutenant Tospan gapes at her as he blurts out unbelievable nonsense.

The instructor who passed him in the academy should probably be culled. How did they even manage to get him through? I'd love to ask someone.

"Lieutenant Tospan, Major Weiss has stated my intentions correctly. A soldier's misconduct will be treated as the officer's misconduct. This is an occupation. Learn the art of administering occupied territory… Even if it's a mask, we're expected to act as liberators."

"But how will we prevent espionage?"

The idiots are warbling again. I really can't handle the ones who are not only incompetent but don't even realize it. Perhaps, as the old saying goes, industrious idiots should be shot.

"You'll figure it out."

"Huh?!"

"Deception, disguise, information warfare. It's what you officers are here for, right? Or can't you do any work unless you're holed up in no-man's-land?" Enduring a headache, Tanya flatly rejects Tospan's objection.

Still, internally, she feels gloomy. The reason is simple: She has been forcibly reminded once again that the commander of the majority of her forces, the infantry, is inept.

As long as the numbskull captain who was supposed to be commanding, Thon, is MIA, she has no choice but to leave the troops up to Tospan, but...can he really command them?

For better or worse, he's the type to follow directions; she knows that much. So she was convinced that if she gave clear orders, things would work out.

I thought he would do what he was told as a matter of course... But then Tanya realizes the truth.

If someone is too stupid to understand the orders, how do you command them? She never imagined there would be such a moron among the officer ranks. This is the definition of *frightening*.

The thought that pops into her head is to get rid of him.

On the other hand, even this guy is a precious human resource. Wouldn't it be more productive to find a use for him? But considering the lost opportunity cost, maybe my only choice is to shoot him.

"...Colonel, I understand what you're trying to say, but..."

"But you think there's a limit on how courteous we can be to the unpredictable masses?"

"Please consider the stress on the men. Can we really expect them to smile and act like they would at home when they're worried they could be shot at any moment?"

Her thoughts had nearly started circling, but now they snap back to reality. The question was asked with a sober expression, and she nods her understanding.

"Captain Meybert, that's a good point, but..." She smiles. "That issue will be *cleared up momentarily*."

"I beg your pardon, Colonel."

"Yes?"

"Could you please define *momentarily* for me?"

I suppose it's an artillerist's instinct to request concrete numbers.

The attitude of removing any traces of confusion or doubt regarding your superior's remarks is…actually one I approve of.

"That's a good question, Captain Meybert."

It's infinitely better than subordinates who interpret things however they see fit. She's even more thankful, after Tospan's idiocy, that she can trust Meybert not to do anything stupid. Tanya gives him a clear response.

"More specifically, 'right away.'"

"Huh?"

"Seeing is believing. Well, I guess in this case, it's 'hearing.' That's the end of this debate. Anyone who is free, come with me."

From every single blankly staring officer issues the simple question, lacking so much as a hint of creativity or individuality.

""""Where?"""""

"Isn't it obvious?" Tanya smiles. She points to the living room they're using as a dining hall. "Let's turn on the radio. General von Zettour will be giving a delightful address at noon sharp. Oh," she adds. "We can have lunch, too. Do you guys have time?"

>>> THE SAME DAY, IMPERIAL OCCUPIED TERRITORY IN THE EAST <<<

"This is Lieutenant General Hans von Zettour speaking on behalf of the Imperial Army."

Distrust, suspicion, curiosity, or disinterest?

Most of the listeners were a crowd who had been told only that this address was an "important announcement." But that was enough to get them to stop and listen.

It was no wonder. A lieutenant general from the Imperial Army, impressive in his type I dress uniform, was up on a dais surrounded by nationalist group leaders.

"Dear listeners, I have something to tell you: We are fighting together against a common enemy—that is, the red menace."

So Zettour made his topic clear from the start. *We, the Empire and the nationalists, are not enemies.*

This prefatory remark made his position clear and plainly indicated where his speech would go.

Still, that much had been said numerous times in imperial occupied territory as part of their pacification efforts.

With such lukewarm remarks, he would never gain their trust. Which was why he carefully packaged the poison in pretty, empty words.

"What the Empire wishes is clear. All we want is peace and stability for our fatherland."

People prioritized who was talking over what was being said. That was why Zettour made his appearance alongside the nationalist leaders.

To show people the sight of them standing together.

He inhaled, as if catching his breath, in order to create a pause. The moment he saw his words had sunk in, Zettour continued.

"The Empire does not wish for war. We—*I* do not wish for war. And yet the sad reality is that war continues. So I—*we* wish for hope. The Empire wishes for hope." And he looked to the men behind him, as if talking to friends, as he continued, *"Just like you*, I am a person who wishes for peace and calm."

The men nodded—slight motions, but they did nod.

And that was enough to serve as the trigger.

He was sure that the distance between the audience and him had shrunk.

"Peace! Peace! Peace! If not for the red menace, would any of us have taken up arms?" *I'll reach out to them like I'm discussing the truth with friends.* "Truly, that is the fundamental reason we were forced to arm ourselves until today. For ages, nations have required border guards to protect their own from approaching evils."

I'll make this so lovely and sincere sounding that I even fool myself.

"We simply follow our proud, noble forerunners in this endeavor. We'll continue fighting the threat of the red menace for as long as need be."

So though he knew it was the work of the devil, he lit a fire of hope for the people who wanted to secede from the Federation.

In the east, they needed depth. They didn't have the leisure of being picky about how it was achieved. If Zettour wanted to go about it with clean hands, his only choice was to pray to God. Launching another counterattack would take time, so he had to dissemble for the sake of the Reich.

"But we have only taken up our swords to protect ourselves."

Easy now. A breath and a moment of silence to make sure his words were reaching all his listeners. When the time seemed right, he began to say the words he had so carefully calculated.

"Of course, we want to run to the aid of our fatherland in crisis. But once peace is restored, all we wish is to lay down our arms and return home. I myself am a resident of the Reich who, like Cincinnatus, only wants to go home to his farm and till the soil of the *Heimat.*"

Dreams are pointless.

The soldier Hans von Zettour is smart enough to understand that he would probably never be permitted such stability—such peaceful, satisfying days.

Yet I'll be that contemptible man who encourages those impossible dreams despite understanding their absurdity.

"And so I declare in the name of the Reich that we do not demand land; our earnest, heartfelt desire is to coexist with independent peoples who have their own land and sovereignty."

The Federation was a multiethnic state where many peoples were gathered under Communism. But how many of them joined the Federation of their own volition?

How many were staying with the Federation because they wanted to?

The various peoples had tasted enough of the truth under this harsh rule—the truth behind the grand propaganda—to make them sick.

The reaction when they woke from the dream and realized the ideals they had been shown were beautiful illusions was extremely intense. Having been caught up in the great social experiment, the candid wish of these people was to escape the faded yoke of Communism.

So Zettour was able to speak with a kind of conviction.

"We have no intention of annexing the occupied territories. I understand the powerful love we all have for our homes."

There was nothing false about this principle.

"...Who doesn't have feelings about their fatherland?"

If there's a crisis, I'll go running. I've been prepared for that ever since I was commissioned.

"Who doesn't have feelings about their hometown?"

Zettour knew it wasn't for him to hope for a peaceful future when this was all over. He was an adult whose efforts in this war had resulted in piles of young corpses.

Win or lose, he could only do his duty.

"Our home countries, our land, our hometowns…"

But he refused to regret it. He swore to defend the Empire, the Reich, the country he loved, to the bitter end. And to that end, he would fight, pouring the youths of the country into a war of attrition, that absurd waste of human life, and he would win.

What a fucked-up job.

To protect our country, we put the children we should be defending through a meat grinder.

How incredibly absurd. Children paying the price because the adults don't have a plan! It shouldn't be allowed. If there's such a thing as purgatory, we'll never find out. I'm sure we've reserved our seats on the express to hell.

"The people behind us, the future of our children, the stability of our nations—all this is on our shoulders."

So Zettour raised his sonorous voice and appealed to the audience's emotions.

Everyone wished.

They wished for their hometowns to be peaceful. They wished for the people to be at peace. And ultimately, they wished for a peaceful future for their children.

"Just like Horatius on the bridge, we know we must stand our ground. Our future isn't so cheap that we would simply give it away to the red menace."

So they wished.

"Today, as of this moment, I, as representative of the Imperial Army, declare the military district to be under civilian authority. I hope the future of the Reich and our good neighbors will be a bright one."

Even Horatius didn't defend the bridge alone. He had reliable friends standing with him. They must have known what their fate would be.

"My good neighbors, I have a favor to ask of you. The difficulties ahead are the same for both of us, so I urge you to please, for the children's future, stand on the bridge alongside us. Friends!" he called to them. In front of their leaders, he acted as if he was one of them. "Please let us fight…for the future…"

I'll trail off, overcome with emotion, and give them a good manly cry. With tears in his eyes, Zettour straightened up and looked around.

The venue was full of passionate stares focused on him. Until now, the audience had been silent, but here came a moan that couldn't be put into words.

He had their emotions where he wanted them.

Looking around the room, he gathered as many eyes on him as possible, breathed deeply to steady himself, and traded his Logos for that ticket to hell.

I'll go ahead and despise myself. Oh, Hans von Zettour, you've become an honest liar in the interests of your country.

"I cannot give you orders. And I can't even really make a request and feel good about it. So as one of your neighbors, I suppose all that is left is to bow my head and hope."

But that's why I'm begging.

For the fatherland's future.

"I beg you, as a good neighbor. I hope that as fellow warriors standing shoulder to shoulder on the bridge, and as brothers who will share the bread of peace together one fateful day, you will allow us to walk with you."

Do these people I'm egging on know what's in store?

Maybe they think they do. But without having seen all the corpses of children or having heard the now all-too-familiar wails of the bereaved, it may not even be possible to understand.

As a good individual, I grieve so much: Is this all really necessary?

As an evil member of an organization, I accept it: yes.

We must hold the defensive lines until road conditions stabilize. That's what the General Staff decided. Regardless of my own opinion, the orders came down.

It was possible to object and counter until the decision was made, but…once a major policy was decided, there was no longer any room for debate. The only thing to do was carry it out with all one's might.

I've got to execute, thought Zettour self-deprecatingly.

With this ineptitude, I couldn't find any other way. Lieutenant General Hans von Zettour, feeling deeply alone, could only snap bitterly.

So hell begets hell. Fuck me.

(The Saga of Tanya the Evil, Volume 5: Abyssus Abyssum Invocat, fin)

Appendixes

Mapped Outline of History

Mapped Outline of History

❶

❷

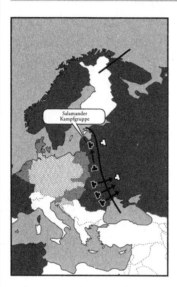

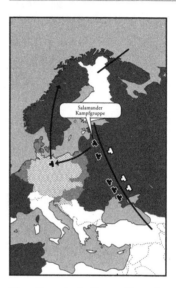

Both armies fighting on the eastern front continue their operations while beginning to think about how to make it through the winter.

The Imperial Army General Staff begins reorganizing in preparation for a major operation.

Meanwhile, the Salamander Kampfgruppe is sent to the east to be combat tested.

The General Staff considers the Salamander Kampfgruppe to have accomplished the mission it was formed for and orders it to return to the capital.

After a very short break, the core unit, the 203rd Aerial Mage Battalion, is sent on a mission over the Northern Sea.

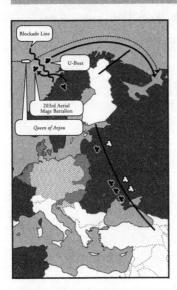

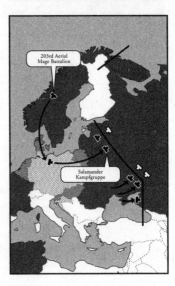

Off the coast of Norden, the 203rd Aerial Mage Battalion engages in a series of commerce raiding operations. Though they get results, they also suffer heavy casualties and lose 25 percent of their members.

The Salamander Kampfgruppe is re-formed, and with the 203rd Aerial Mage Battalion at its core, it is sent east once again. They set about building and securing positions to protect a wide area.

The Empire changes the system of government in occupied territory. They initiate the Good Neighbor Friendship Policy to transition from military to civilian administration.

Mapped Outline of History

General Commentary

The Imperial Army has been able to maintain superiority or parity on all fronts.

On the other hand, exhaustion from the prolonged fighting is beginning to surface, so planners are looking for a way to end the war as soon as possible.

Rough Sketches of the
Computation Orb Revealed

Computation orbs are
the result of applying
scientific observation
and analysis to the
legendary phenomena
brought about by orbs
and scepters commonly
known as miracles—
that is, magic—and
coming up with a
practical way to man-
ifest them. It's a tool
that optimizes the
interference that a
mage's mana has on
the world to make
practical use possible.

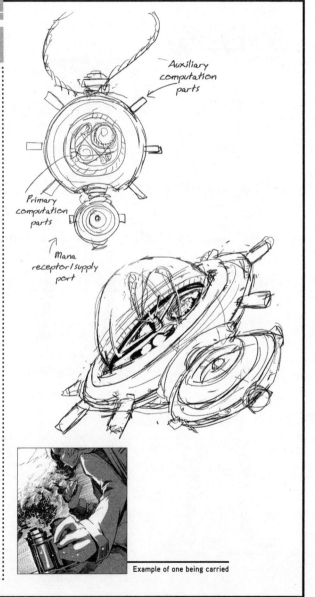

Auxiliary
computation
parts

Primary
computation
parts

Mana
receptor/supply
port

Example of one being carried

Appendix

Rough Sketches of Tanya Degurechaff Revealed

The early version of Degu I took when I had my first meeting with the editor. (Rejected proposal)

Flattery mode

PROFILE

Prominent nose

COMMENT FROM
ILLUSTRATOR SHINOTSUKI

Young girl, blond hair, blue eyes, white skin. But she has an office worker in his thirties living inside her, so I kept her hair simple and bunched in the back. The ends are curly and frizzy, probably because she doesn't take very good care of it, but if she looked after it better, she'd have nice, soft hair. At first, I gave her the orthodox long blond hair, but then I felt like it wasn't really suitable for a muddy war atmosphere, so I ditched it. Carlo requested that her eyes look like "dead fish eyes." I'm careful not to make them look too full of life.

Short and blond

Hair that gets in the way is fixed back

Sort of frizzy from lack of care

Uniform is too big

HAPPY

HE'S DEAD!

YES!

COMMENT FROM CARLO

When I first saw her, I screamed, "What the heck?! This is great!" There was only one major problem. Degu paid for her officer's uniform out of pocket. In other words, it was tailor-made. I tried to think of some excuse to have her wear the baggy government-issue one, but after agonizing over it, I thought discerning people would get mad at me, so this version became a mere vision. I'm glad she can see the light of day here.

Afterword

To everyone who picked up Volume 5, I'm sorry to have kept you waiting. To the heroes who bought all of the volumes through 5 at once, nice to meet you. I'm Carlo Zen.

This came out later than planned, but I would appreciate it if you would believe me when I say, "I wasn't slacking off! I was doing my best!" …There's going to be a manga and a TV anime!

By the powers of a great many people combined, plans for a manga (Chika Tojo's doing it!) and anime are in the works.

Back in 2013 when I said how brave Enterbrain is, I never dreamed all this would happen.

So you're a hero of heroes, huh, Enterbrain…?

No, maybe I should have foreseen it to some extent. Every time I had a meeting with them, I did sense this pretty heroic aura.

Yes, it was…a peaceful holiday afternoon. When I lumbered out to an event—a meeting—what I saw before me was a café where sophisticated people drink tea.

It was a cheerful meeting. After having the "Do a bit more xx; make it xx" (censored) conversation, we discussed the manga, the anime, my new book, and whatnot.

If you're not going to call that heroic, then what will you?

And so, though I can't quite believe it, there are manga and anime projects starting up…I think? I'm reflecting on how lucky I am to have the support of so many people.

And now I must extend my thanks once again to everyone who has helped me out.

A warm thank-you to Tsubakiya Design for the design, Tokyo Shuppan Service Center for the proofreading, my editor Fujita, and to the illustrator who always does such wonderful illustrations, Shinotsuki.

And of course, my gratitude goes out to you, the readers supporting me. I hope to see you again next time.

January 2016 Carlo Zen